The Lore of Shapinsay

By
KRISTA HOLLE

Edited by Stephanie Hacker

Cover design by Reese Dante,
http://www.reesedante.come

ISBN: 0985002514
ISBN 13: 9780985002510

To Mike,

for loving my little selkie novel even before reading the first word.

I

THE BIRTH
~1848~

*"When angels fell, some fell on the land, some on the sea.
The former are the faeries and the latter were often said
to be the seals."*

The men of the village were bumptious idiots. This is what I concluded. They could not see that their greedy nature soured my trade as well as the delicate taste of my eggs.

"It's a fair trade," I insisted. I turned the basket so Mr. Westness could more clearly see the voluptuous basket of blue and brown eggs I collected that very morn. Other crofters gathered under the shadow of the stony pub to haggle over their weekly increase.

"Nae, lassie," Mr. Westness grumbled, scratching his wiry blonde beard. "I'd not settle for less than eighteen."

I eyed the pail of salty oysters and licked my lips, already imagining the rich stew I'd simmer that evening. "Only three more," I said, shifting my weight and fiercely meeting Mr. Westness's stiff gaze.

"Ye are not the sweet female ye pretend to be," he consented with a darkened brow as he thrust over his heavy pail. "Others may see a fair rose, but I see a stinging nettle."

"Even roses have thorns," I bit back as I received the pail. "If my nit-wit brother Blair were here, you would have settled for a simple dozen. Humph, last week your herring swam rebelliously in my stomach. Even your own wee-pee-pants knows better than to let them sit in the sun too long. What is he now…five?"

"He'd be seven, but small in stature," Mr. Westness growled.

I gave a prim smile and turned away. The older men resented my inability to mold myself into a meek and silent girl. I was resentful too. Ma and Da had been resting under the moor since I was thirteen, stolen too early from the rattle.

At once a heart piercing wail silenced the rowdy arguing of crofters. We looked at one another as a plank door several houses down clattered open. Mr. Trulloch, a mason shipped in for the construction of the Balfour Castle, swept past us with a small woolen bundle in his arms. His eyes grew at his unexpected audience before narrowing defiantly. My annoyance with the unfair trade melted away when the gentle cry of a newborn bairn tickled my ears. My friend Astrid had given birth!

"Nearly a week late," I cried. "The bairn will never be on time again!"

"Well, let's see what ye got there," another mason roared as he punched Mr. Trulloch on the shoulder.

Thorfinn Trulloch ignored us both and pulled the wee bundle closer to his chest.

I took a few paces after him, confused by his aloofness and break in tradition. "Is it a boy or a girl?" The child's grandfather seemed to twitch at the question before trudging between two narrow buildings. Straight ahead was the fishy smelling harbor filled with dilapidated boats and a tired grey pier. "Mr. Trulloch?"

The wailing inside Astrid's house intensified. Mrs. Thompson popped her head out of the bakery at the same time as a dozen other shoppers ascended into the street to investigate the noise. Men tugged at cocked bonnets and looked around nervously while women gossiped without shame. I glared at the growing mob furtively peeking at Astrid's door. "Where is the show?" I shouted. "This is private woman's business!" No one paid me any mind, and I stomped my foot in frustration.

"Fetch the trowlie doctor," someone hissed.

"What evil has the faery folk performed this time?" another asked.

"Faeries?" I cried. "Have ye all gone mad? Do ye not see the heather repelling the rascals above the door?"

"The faeries have left a mark on the child," a pudgy woman exclaimed excitedly as she tugged on my sleeve. "Why else would Thorfinn be too ashamed to show us his own grandchild?"

"It's her own mither's fault for allowing that wretched yellow dog near Astrid," a milkmaid told her. "Those beasts are bad luck to women ripe with child."

Something was terribly amiss, and I felt ill from all the talk. I took in a laden breath. The salty air was deadlocked with jinxes, rumor, and grief. I couldn't take it anymore. "What is wrong with the bairn?" I cried pushing through the crowd and stalking after Thorfinn. "Thorfinn!" He broke through the other side of the alley and whited out under a glaring sun.

An earthy woman with ruddy skin slipped discreetly out of Astrid's house. I rushed to intercept the knowledgeable looking stranger. "Are you the Mainland midwife?" I asked, queasily taking in the tankard of blood smeared conspicuously across her apron.

The woman scrutinized my flat stomach. "Aye," she said. She wearily pushed aside damp strands of hair. "Are you in need o' my services? You can't be more than a few months along."

"Nae," I blurted affronted. "Astrid, my friend, that's her newborn—"

"I'd be forgettin' what you've see here," she interrupted. Her sparse brows drew in tightly as she absently gazed towards the smithy. "Dis the blackest of magick."

"What's wrong with the wee bairn? It's practically my niece... or nephew."

The midwife frowned at my small wagon full of staples. "Take your wares home and bar your door, lassie. All will be well here soon enough." She dismissed me with an exasperated wave of the hand.

"Bar my door?" I recited after her. "Why should I? I've enough charms in place to confound even the faeries. My dim brother can hardly find his way in."

She turned suddenly on me, forcing me to stumble to avoid touching her repugnant apron. "You are not young enough to be so naive. Do you not know that evil creeps from these waters at night?"

Sharks? Orca? Finfolk? I hadn't an inkling of what she was talking about. "Of course—I know all about it." I crossed my arms under my breasts, offended by her assumption at my ignorance. Blair and I were isolated at the north end of the island, but I'd never been accused of being simple minded before. The words used to describe me were usually: stubborn, derisive, even independent to a fault, but never dim.

"Good, take caution!" she said shoving past me and bustling towards the ferry. I hardly noticed the midwife anymore. I was timidly staring at my friend's house.

Childbirth is a messy business—a private business. I turned to leave, but a pitiful wail pierced my heart. After hesitating for what seemed an eternity, my feet slowly and awkwardly began to shuffle down the sandy lane to my friend's small two story dwelling. It was still new with bright white mortar gleaming between the stones. At the door, I took a few gulps of tainted air before pushing the rough planks aside.

"Astrid?" I called, peering through the smoky room. The bulky wood table was filled with soiled platters and the picked remains of a goose. "Astrid?" A muffled sob broke from the adjoining room then wheeled into a low agonizing cry. A desperate cry. A hopeless cry. Oh Odin, the sound of one's soul being severed. My heart clenched queasily inside my chest, and I leaned heavily against the chilled wall for support. Something *was* terribly wrong with my friend...or her baby. I motivated my feet forward and swung the door open on a squeaky hinge.

My blood froze when I saw Astrid already on her feet, half dressed and meagerly wrestling against her neighbor Biorn, a burly carpenter with disturbing pale blue eyes.

"Kait!" Astrid wailed with the dark hunted eyes of a doe. She seemed to find new life and began thrashing wildly. With tiny, tender feet, she stomped on Biorn's booted foot and then kicked him rightly in the shin.

"Let her go!" I demanded taking a few bold paces. "You'd man handle a woman?"

"Go home, Kait," her mother ordered from the foot of the bed. I hardly noticed the stout woman before. "There'll be no birthday feast prepared this day."

"What's happened?" I asked filling with dread once more. "The villagers are flapping their lips like bees' wings."

"Stay out of this," Biorn replied gruffly as he twisted Astrid's tiny wrists together. "There are things here ye know nothing about."

"They took him away!" Astrid wailed. "Pleeease, Kait, you could get him back!" Her face was blanched into a bloodless yellow that hovered above her weightless shift like a ghost.

"Haud your wheest!" her mother scolded. "You are always speaking when there should be silence!"

"I—I dinnae understand," I stuttered, tearing my eyes away from the disheveled bed soiled with Astrid's gruesome afterbirth. It was a source of fearful bad luck. "Your Da has him. I saw him a few moments ago just down the way. Probably showing him off."

"No!" my friend sobbed, crumbling into herself and trembling. "My—bairn—is—gone!"

"It's no bairn," Astrid's mother spat. Her face was red and shiny from exerting her will over her weakened daughter, "but an animal with selkie paws—webbed and all."

I felt the blood drain from my face. "An animal?" I repeated. "It—it can't be."

"It gives you no right to take him away!" Astrid moaned. "I—love—him!"

"It's for the best," Biorn added. Astrid screamed and fought once again to free herself from the carpenter's coarse hands.

"The father..."

"He'd be no sailor," her mother answered. She gave a sardonic sounding laugh as she swept her hand over her eyes. "Wodden, shield us all from this evil. The loin of an animal has stained my pure daughter!"

My mind grappled to fit the pieces together. Astrid told everyone that the child's father was a bonnie sailor from Port of Ness. He was said to have had honey sideburns that garnished the most admirable of chins. It was a brief and scandalous affair. The young man was docked one moment and gone the next. The cargo ship, Golden Chance, weighted as enough evidence to suit everyone.

"I'm certain your Da will be back with your wee one soon," I offered. "After the shock wears off." My stomach turned uneasily.

"It's not likely," Biorn said. "Thorfinn aims to drown the creature in the sea."

"But that'll be murder!" I cried.

"It's not a sin," her mother insisted. "The creature was not even human." Her eyes were less certain than her cruel words.

"It's a hulking lie!" Astrid shrieked. "I saw him well enough—a handsome lad to be certain."

"Aye, as did I," her mother proclaimed with a shudder in her voice. "Eyes too dark, with skin pale and translucent like an onion's. And those paws..."

I escaped outdoors and broke through the crowd still shamelessly speculating over the exact nature of Astrid's bairn. Shielding my eyes against the glaring sky, I scanned the workers' houses pressed together in a row of tight, uniform shoulders. Thorfinn had not yet returned.

Racing towards the bay, I tripped over a loose pile of creels and nets tossed carelessly at the base of the stone levee. Cursing, I unsnagged my foot and scrambled over the crumbling wall. Halfway down the ancient stone pier, I spotted Thorfinn. The woolen blanket that had been so sweet and plump before, fluttered like an empty wrapper at his side.

"Thorfinn, what have ye done?" I screeched as my gaze darted over choppy grey waters. Wispy white strands of cloud raced to join the midnight blue horizon. A storm was brewing far away. "Tell me ye haven't done this bad thing." The wide open currents of wind whipped my straw colored hair into a rat's nest around my face and eyes. I clawed it impatiently away.

"It's not your business," Thorfinn groaned.

"It was your daughter's bairn!" I cried, stumbling onto the pier. "Your own blood!"

"He wasn't one of us," he said. His tired form slowly brushed past me.

My mind scrambled to think. How long had the infant been in the water? Two minutes, maybe three? I rushed down the remainder of the pier and frantically searched for any sign of it—a bubble, a foot, a movement. Oh Odin, the wind was stirring the water and making it cloudy! To think of the wee creature down there!

I hiked up the hem of my dress and climbed down the sharp, barnacle encrusted rocks. Unlike the other villagers I could swim, but here? Oh, damn Thorfinn to Hel! Beneath the seemingly playful surface, powerful roosts tugged and pulled in streaming highways that led to certain death. I sunk my face beneath the surface and searched until my eyes became sore. Five minutes. Gasping, I tried a different spot. Six minutes. A small grey fish swam under a long piece of spar. Seven minutes. I razed my knee on a rock while sprawling for a new position. Oh, bloody, bloody, he was nowhere to be seen. Gasping and dripping wet, I curled on a rock and cried over the baby's watery grave.

2

ATTENTION CAPTURED

When I returned, the crowd had thinned, but talk of the dead bairn had spread like wildfire. Half a dozen women remained to cluck and crow over the disturbing matter like a harem of white hens. Their matronly kertches bobbed up and down in their hair like rooster's comb. The square shaped cloth was a symbol for the married—and the matronly. I scowled miserably at the cruel display of gossiping women.

"The seal men haven't set foot or flipper upon Shapinsay in these many years," Mary Crawford was saying. She was a blathering bessie with an affinity for bad news, but she was also the first to know things. I paused by my wagon to listen.

"Malarkey," Finna snipped. "The selkies were stretched out on the rocks near Ness of York just days ago. There'll be a rookery there soon enough."

"But those were selkies, just plain ordinary selkies," Mary said with a knowledgeable air. "The selkie men are a tad more clever. They're not dumb cods waitin' around to be hooked or netted."

"Just ye wait," Vaila said, a pretty new grandmother with flame colored hair. "Thorfinn has started something awful here. They'll find the bairn, and then there'll be an awful price to pay."

"It would have been better to have disposed of it on land—perhaps down the felkyo's well," Mary said.

"Ha, if the old witch can't eat the bairn, she can drink it."

"Hush, ye hairy old crones," I snapped, unhappy to be joining their circle. "It's Astrid's bairn we speak of. It is half of her."

"Why is your hair all wet?" Harriet asked with a frown. She was the boot maker's wife and thought herself superior for the fine black boots she wore.

"Never you mind," I said with a scowl, squeezing the water from my hair.

"The good half was spoiled," Finna replied, picking up where I'd left off. She was another crofter with rodent eyes who'd come to trade her cabbage and turnips. I liked her less than the others for the way she smacked her lips.

"None of the women will be safe to go anywhere near the water without a man to protect her," Mary said looking quite pleased.

"Not practical and insulting," I said. "It is plain that we live on an island. We can't spit without hitting water."

"Don't ye know the vile temper of the males?"

"But the selkie folk are harmless," I protested. "Aren't they?"

"Nae, Kait," Mary said, overly appalled at my ignorance. "When the males get an itching, the water will not hold them back. The sea dogs will prowl through the village at night looking for bonnie young lassies to steal or ruin."

"This is true?" I asked surprised. The women's gossip usually led down different trails such as Tomasin Cleary's new scandalously young wife, or the secret trysts of Bess Gorie and young Ortak in the Kirkman cemetery. I had never before heard them discuss the selkies that shared the island with us. They were scenery taken for granted, like the eastern stone bluffs and the wide-open spaces above miles of rolling green. Such as it was, I never felt unsafe swimming near the seals. They were harmless rascals.

The males were renowned for being mischievous not dangerous. On one occasion, Mr. Ratchford, a village fisherman, woke to find his new fishing boat missing. It was found two days later hazardously perched on a skerry on the north side of the island. An unpleasant prank, aye, but no one got hurt. Only Mr. Ratchford raved for days about the devilish ways of the selkie men.

The selkie women on the other hand were thought to make fine brides—or trophies if one considered that she needed to be captured off guard. They were well known for their supernatural beauty and meek ways, but no one ever heard of a successful capture. This however didn't stop the men from loudly illusioning such a feat around the pub tables. The men outnumbered the women on the island three to one and were enraptured by the subject.

"Aye," Auor answered an expert weaver who was suspicious of all men, especially feral ones who lived under the sea. "I've seen their foot prints curiously circling my smokehouse, sniffing it out I'd say. And just last week, their prints were all around Hallbera's house. See, she is just coming of age. They can smell her ripening with their dog noses. Astrid was only their latest conquest."

I anxiously tugged at a snarled strand of hair blowing around my shoulder. "But why do they not settle for their own women?"

"Have ye not been listening?" Auor scolded. "They do not look fer love, but come to make us miserable, see? They do it with their quiet acts of revenge."

"Precisely," Mary agreed. "It's why we dinnae hunt selkies anymore. The males will pull you under the sea at his pleasure. It's best not to provoke them."

Mr. Berry waddled by with a wheelbarrow full of wood shavings. His rounded cheeks puffed up into a red appley smile. "What are you wenches blathering on about?"

"Go on down the way," Auor shrieked. "Do you wish me to spread your pretty blonde curls all over the road?"

"Aich," the boat maker complained. "You'd not be touching my haul. It's fer Frank."

"How will I know one?" I asked dropping my voice. "They look so human. Even Ola Gorie's eyes are dark enough to pierce."

Finna simpered and smacked her lips while the others laughed. "There'll be no mistaking."

"Bar your door securely tonight," Auor cautioned. "You'll have little power against the enchantment of a selkie man."

"They can do magick?" I asked.

"Aye." Her eyes grew large as if she were seeing me for the first time. "Ye are young and bonnie—an irresistible bait to their kind."

Were the older women having sport trying to frighten me? I couldn't be certain—I wasn't a goose like them. "Then I'll go and see Mr. Lennie. He'll surely have a charm that will protect me, perhaps a bone or a ring of sutherland."

"That ol' trowlie doctor won't help you," Finna said shaking her head fervently. "Their beauty is their magick. There's no fighting that."

I studied her weathered face a moment to gauge her sincerity. "Truly?"

"You are an ignorant lassie. Don't ye know that their skin is as white as cream? Hardly ever is it touched by wind and sky. And their eyes are said to be as black as the patches between the stars. And don't expect to see an old selkie airing a weathered and wrinkled skin. The sea keeps them forever young."

"It's true," Vaila added, twisting a ringlet of red hair. "The sea holds its own magick. Have you ever seen a wrinkled fish?"

"Or a fish with grey hair?" Finna cackled before sucking on her teeth.

Auor glared at the others. "Heed our warning, Kait, and lock yourself up this night. This kithy wind will pass o'er soon enough."

As the women gazed smugly at me, I felt suddenly like the victim of a horrid goose joke. Were the sheep dangerous? Were the fish? "Have any of ye actually ever *seen* a selkie man or woman?" I challenged.

The women were quiet a moment before Mary piped up. "My cousin startled one o' the females rounding the tip of Papa Westray in his fishing boat. He got an eyeful of white skin right before she dove. Made his wife Lucy crapping mad."

"Disgusting," Auror murmured.

"They've no sense of decency," Finna added.

I smirked at all the excitement over timid, prank playing creatures. It was clear the women knew no more than I did. I tossed my hair over my shoulder. "I'd not be afraid of a lily skinned man this day or any. They're nothing but weak little lambs, afraid of their own shadow."

~Selkie~

I heard the burd wailing long before he gasped at the sea. The others heard too. The creature penetrated our heads with such obnoxious piercing that we squirmed within our skins and rubbed our ears against the golden floor of the ocean. But the sound drew us—our curiosity outweighing the pain.

The others seemed to know right away. The sound of hunger they called it—the sound of something new. To me, it was the grating sound of a land louper—one of those who prefer swimming the land. What it was and why it was wailing was not important to me. It was enough to know it was one of *them*.

A giant hush swept over the ocean when the burd was unexpectedly dropped into the water. I shouldn't have been surprised. It was an act typical of the land loupers—sacrifice the weak for selfish gain. They'd forever brutally murdered our burds for their tender skins and oil. This was no different, and my rage towards all land loupers grew. *They* were the ones that instigated war, over and over again.

The wee arms and legs flapped like an awkward gull lifting into the sky. But it didn't fly, sinking instead as it gulped at the brine as if it were hungry for salt not air.

One of the females sensed it was in trouble and nudged the fat belly with her nose, but there was no saving it. It was a dumb creature that didn't know it should hold its breath. After a few cruel moments, the wee creature stopped moving and a feathery halo of sandy brown hair swayed around its tiny head.

We all moved in for a closer look and saw the webbed hands and feet. It was one of our own—a male. He was a bonnie little burd with stormy eyes, like an aggravated sea, and translucent skin. When the female closest to the turbulent waters of The String saw the hollow emptiness in the wee face, she thrashed her head to and fro and blew a mournful bubble. The males searched the wide glassy eyes of the others in pursuit of the sire. No one came forth, and I wondered at the sport of playing with a human girl.

It was then I noticed the killer peering through the ripples of grey water in search of her spoil. Had the creature accidentally slipped from her fingers, or had she grown tired of its wails? I hunched my shoulders and postured to fight, but the predator did not dive to claim her victim. Neither did she see the burd wedged between the rocks or the other selkies circling the pier. She was blind and deaf like all loupers.

The others grew ill of the scene and thrust themselves into the rapid currents while I held back to study the female. She was slight, even for one of *them.* This I could see even through the loathsome cloth that hugged her wee diddies and drowned the rest of her willowy frame. Her eyes were too round, mirroring the clearest parts of the blue sea. Of this I could forgive, but she was marred—the sun spotting her nose and cheeks with tiny brown grains that ran together into baked tawny patches. Her thick mane of hair was typical of a louper—bleached to a golden hue and utterly uncombed by the sea.

I thrust myself backwards when she dipped her face in the water searching. My lips curled over my teeth in warning, but she didn't notice me hiding among the kelp.

I decided I would enjoy snapping her frail neck.

After she left, my keen ears zeroed in on her quick but deliberate voice, my furor growing with each jilting word. I spiraled in frustration when she scoffed the greatness of the selkie men—men so great the sea could not claim nor tame. She was a dumb girl who knew nothing about my kind. How easily she had killed our kind, but then she would die easily too. Justice required no less.

When the others hauled out on smooth, flat rocks to warm; I swam north towards the place called Galt Ness, following the mocking voice that seeded like a parasite in my mind. By now, I had learned that the other loupers called her Kait. It was a name fit for a murderer, and it fit her smug face.

I broke the surface of the water and watched a wave curl and thin out across packed sand just shy of her toes. She seemed to be contemplating the blue firth and the powerful sea beyond. My heart pounded loudly in my ears as her eyes danced over me. When her gaze changed direction, I gave a loud satisfied huff. My dark coat was too well camouflaged among the cloud umber and the dusky rocks that lurked beneath.

Her brow wrinkled in displeasure, and I could almost read her thoughts. To her, the water was a barrier, even the walls of a prison. She couldn't have been more wrong. The ocean was a universe she knew nothing about, and her ignorance pleased me.

Curiously, I watched her pull her dress up over her head and shrug it into the damp rocks below. I wasn't surprised to see that she was wearing even more clothing underneath. I had heard of the many ways loupers sought to dress themselves. I cocked with curiosity when she held her arms open to the wind that relentlessly pounded the barren island. Her thin shift twisted and turned around her narrow hips while wiry sea grass snapped warnings at her feet. She seemed to be thinking about...swimming. *Go ahead and swim louper.*

I pleasantly mused at how vulnerable she seemed next to the water. In the surf she would have a hulking disadvantage, with no power to save her own scrawny neck. I'd seen humans thrash and choke just trying to keep their faces above the surface. I'd even seen one drown. *Swim louper.*

All at once she startled me by bursting head on into the wind before splashing up to her bony knees. When the water tugged and churned at her waist, she dove under the scalloping white caps. I sucked in my surprise then closed my nostrils to dive, eager to witness her failure.

The loupers preferred their clumsy boats over the delicate, fluid skin of water. In fact, they seemed to avoid getting wet at all costs. Mystified, I watched the awkward strokes of the girl as she pulled at the water with cleaved fingers. Finally, her face resurfaced with a ragged gasp. I laughed at her weakness. The girl had only held her breath for a few seconds, proving her ineptness at surviving in the sea.

I ruffled my coat and quickly plowed towards her, imagining the tiny silver bubbles that would escape her rounded lips when I pulled her down to her own watery grave. Vengeance was sweet. Faster and faster I thrust my tail, spiraling weightlessly into the cold depths below her.

Briefly, I lost sight of her when I sped through a wall of quivering green kelp. When I entered the shallow water near the shore, I resurfaced to see the louper bungling towards the rocky beach. Her shift was no longer airy and white but sticking to chilled pink skin like a repugnant paste. She gasped over her knees before turning to look directly at me through dripping tendrils of wet hair. Her hair had turned dark in the water as did her eyes. I was careless; she had heard me laugh.

For the briefest of moments, we looked at each other. What did she see when she saw me—a dumb animal? A man cloaked in a skin? It was a deception; I was neither of those things. With satisfaction, I realized her face was filled with fear. She clutched her dress to her chest and raced barefooted through the grass. *Run and hide, Kait—I'll still find you.*

3

A SENSE O' JUSTICE

I barely looked up when Blair came in rubbing his thigh. "Owwww," he groaned, pausing above our large stone table waiting for me to ask him about *his* day.

"Obviously you've been out to pasture all day if ye haven't heard," I said with a lazy peruse over his dirty trousers. "Ye smell like sheep. Soon I'll be shearing you."

"The ram with the broken horn tried to take me down," he complained as he collapsed into a driftwood chair across from me. His boyish face was shaved smooth again. Rough—smooth—rough—smooth—Blair was a fickle man. "I'd eat him for sup if I dinnae need him to breed so badly."

"Astrid gave birth to her bairn," I said in a bruised voice.

Blair's woodsy brown eyes flickered up. "The bairn did not survive?"

I stared at my stubby fingernails, torn and scraped from crawling across the rocks. "Nae, he was born as strong as the northern sweevy. It was his grandfather that led him by the neck to his untimely death." The memory of Thorfinn returning from the pier with that wee blanket still in tow, assaulted a raw place in my heart again and again. I wiped a tear from my eye. I didn't have the courage to face Astrid after that. She'd know the moment she saw her father.

I then told Blair all the awful events of the morn, finishing with the suspicious appearance of a single selkie out in the firth.

"You don't believe the selkie was the infant's father, do you?"

"Aye, I do believe it. The selkies prefer the eastern side of the isle. When's the last time you saw one frolicking out back?"

Blair picked his teeth a moment. "Your imagination is getting the best of you. No one has seen the selkie folk in years."

"Does this matter? They're private creatures who are very much alive and well in the firth. They aren't seen until they want to be seen."

"Did you make eye contact with the sea dog?"

"What does this matter?"

"Truly you've been sheltered," Blair said with a smirk. "It's the only way to tell the sea folk apart from the ordinary selkies."

I sniffed. "Eye contact—aye."

"Then ye most definitely captured the attention of one of the selkie folk," Blair said amusedly. He pushed a blonde curl behind his ear. "Probably a hulking man lookin' for an obedient wife. He'll be very disappointed to find you."

"It's not funny," I grumbled. "The creature charged me."

Blair shrugged, serious once again. "He was probably just claiming his territory. The sea dogs don't like sharing their water, but they're harmless enough."

"The women in the village don't believe the selkies are so innocent," I countered. "Pull you under the waves in an instant they say."

"What would *I* be doing outside my boat?" Blair said with a loud laugh.

"Absolutely nothing," I said. "*I* on the other hand might be swimming."

Blair smirked. "Then you're not afraid to go in the water?"

"Serious?" I snorted. I scraped out of my chair to stir the oyster stew sweetly steaming over the peat fire. "I'd not be afraid this day or any." I paused to taste the hot, savory base. "I love the sea more than anything. Neither selkie folk, sharks, or sea monsters will keep me out."

Blair lifted a tankard to his lips and gulped deeply. When his face re-emerged, he was smiling mischievously. "Just to be certain, perhaps we should keep the fire burning tonight. That big male might be lurking about. They're afraid of fire, see?"

"That may be," I responded with my chin held high. "But ye can't scare me so easily. I may even sleep under the stars tonight."

~Selkie~

The tide was low, so the others glided effortlessly over the fisherman's hidden trink into the safety of the Ness of Boray Inlet. The nets that were cleverly hidden by the land loupers were blinking lanterns to the keen eyes of the selkie folk. When the others buoyantly rested, I retreated back to the island they called Shapinsay—the place where I had last seen *her*.

The moon was high in the sky, filtering just enough light into the water that I could swiftly maneuver around the unexpected skerries and coral reefs. As the dark silhouette of the island grew, so did my rage. She still lived and breathed somewhere up over the hill, while death shimmied and churned in the waters all around me. The injustice haunted me.

I felt momentarily incapacitated when the sandy bottom brushed up under my belly. Here I couldn't be swift and strong, but susceptible to the whims of the loupers. I'd dwell on her territory only long enough. I didn't belong here anymore than she belonged in the sea. After patiently searching for human noises, my streamline body hauled further up the sandy beach where my skin was wiggled loose. As I stood, it slid away from my body as fluidly as running water. Instinctively, I pinned the mantle protectively to my chest. Without it, I was simply a soul.

I meandered through a thin strip of wetland in search of a hiding place, passing over one dense area of foliage after another. Nothing was secure enough. After a short walk, I found a little stone wall that seemed to hold the moorland in. I carefully removed one of the larger stones at the base of the wall and substituted my most precious possession. When I was satisfied that my skin was completely hidden, I brushed my hands together and peered through the darkness.

The scent of the girl was all around—skin and salt, feather and grit, all permeated by the surrounding fragrance of heather. Before she had been diluted by the brine, but now I received her into my nostrils with full force. The scent made me heady, and I shook myself to focus on the task at hand—avenge the selkie folk. A wee light at the crest of the hill beckoned me forward.

Her stone house was nae bigger than a cave, and I smirked at her meagerness. With satisfaction, I tromped through the leafy garden growing vile smelling roots beneath the surface. At a tiny square window, I stopped and peered in. Inside the hearth, something orange and hot erratically twisted and turned like the dancing faery folk. It had neither substance nor shape, but still it lived and breathed. I shuddered at the strange magick. The word *fire* came to mind. Where had I heard the word—the elders? Through the dirty glass, I could make out the girl sleeping in the fire's glow. A dark smiled tugged at my lips.

The door opened silently as a cool gust of salty air blew in. When the air settled, I captured the virile scent of a young male mixed with sheep. Losh! How had I not noticed her mate's scent before? My eyes darted to the adjoining room looming like a darkened whale's mouth. I took several slow breaths and advanced upon the girl. A second sleeping louper was of no consequence to me.

The girl, Kait, was curled on her side, her flimsy white shift twisted around her like an upturned cloud. Her hair was golden once again, but now wound into a plait that snaked into the darkened folds of the blanket beneath her. I paused to watch her chest rise up and down with the consolation of a deep sleep. Here she almost seemed innocent—even defenseless. I shook off the lie. Silently as a shadow, I crouched beside her, studying the strange pale lashes that swept across her ridiculously spotted cheeks.

My finger swept impulsively across her cheek before sliding to her neck. Her warmth surprised me. She felt as soft and warm as a selkie burd basking in the sun. But here there was no sun, only the heat of a heartless killer. I secured her face within my capable hands... and hesitated. Something bothered me, and it was a moment before I realized what it was. A memory. The memory of a frail girl bravely swimming in water that was much too cold for her. I closed my eyes and took a deep breath, but the image of her clung like a fisherman's tricky net. No matter how much I tried, I couldn't shake it. Why should she swim?

Out in the distance, the gentle bleating of a lamb captured my attention, and to Kait's salvation, an idea was slowly born.

4

REVENGE

Blair returned shortly after breakfast with a small woolen bundle cradled in his arms. At first I thought he had sheared a sheep.

"Did you lose track of the season?" I joked as I dipped a rooster into a pot of boiling water. The bird was large enough that we'd eat cock-a-leekie for days, but first he needed to be plucked.

"I see nothing funny here," he mumbled. His brows were pulled tautly together, his face uncharacteristically ashen.

"You're lookin' a wee bit wabbit," I said concerned. "Aren't you well?"

Blair set the small bundle down on the bink, and the scaly feet I'd been holding dropped with a scalding splash. "Not this day!" I cried. "Not this day!"

On the stone table was a small lamb with creamy white curls. Its neck had been bent at such a peculiar and unnatural angle, it was clear that it had been broken.

"I found the newbie lying beside one of the older ewes," he said, fingering the lamb's tiny ear. "The ol' girl was nudging it with her nose."

"How, Blair?"

He shook his head bewildered. "There are no natural predators on Shapinsay. Someone intentionally killed it."

My hand flew to my mouth horrified. "The selkie man... he—he must have done it—the father of Astrid's poor bairn! You saw his prints prancing all over the croft as well as I did."

"Don't conclude things ye know nothing about," Blair warned.

"But there were no pampooties at all! Who walks around with naked feet but the sea folk?"

"Maybe they're mine," Blair said grumpily. "I could have been sleepwalking. It seems I have a matching set of toes as well."

I stared at my brother a moment, considering this possibility. "Well, did you sleepwalk last night?"

"Dunno," he said with an impassive shrug that made me want to scream.

"Come," I ordered, pulling on his hand. "I'm gonna test your rotten feet."

Blair humored me outdoors where the sky had melted into a heavy wool blanket of seamless grey. A familiar wind fluttered the bent and tender leaves of my vegetables.

Blair placed his foot inside the sandy loam, completely drowning out the more narrow print beneath.

"I knew it," I shrieked. "A water dog was prowling around the croft last night. Just look at all the damage. First he tromped all through the cabbage, and then the potatoes, and then the onions, and then the beans." I pointed to each place of offense. "He wants us to starve!"

"Why would a selkie man want that?" Blair asked. "Whoever it was, was probably just passing through, see?"

"Why would anyone hurt a helpless little lamb?" I fumed.

Blair raked his fingers through his hair appraising the evidence. "Kait, you're not going into the village today. I'm going to ask around and see if anyone saw anything."

"One minute!" I declared for the millionth time. "You were born one bloody minute before me, and now you believe you are my ruler?"

"When Da took his last breath, *I* became patriarch of this home," Blair said sternly. "You will do as I say."

"You're not my ruler," I said primly, ignoring his ferocious stare. "I've got more eggs to trade, but more importantly, I need to speak with Astrid. She knows things about the selkie folk."

Blair squared his jaw with a rapid shake of his curls. "You're not going."

The footprints and murdered lamb frightened him more than he would admit—but not me. I flung my hair off my shoulder and marched outside to retrieve my wagon from the byre. When I pulled it into the sunlight, Blair was leaning against the stones with his arms folded obstinately across his broad chest. "You're not going."

"Humph." I tossed my hair and began to set out towards the dusty road, pulling my wagon over the many bumps and pits. A cloud of dust rose in my wake.

Before I reached the first scraggy brush, Blair marched towards me and clamped a hold of my wrist. His grip was hot and painful. "It's not safe," he growled, dragging me back towards our small thatched house. "I'd find out who did this first!"

"Let go of me, ye big oaf," I shrieked, while frantically prying at Blair's powerful fingers.

With a grunt, Blair tossed me over his shoulder and muscled me towards the door. "I'm older and stronger than ye, see?"

"Da would paddle you o'er his knee fer this!" I cried, swinging and kicking with all my might. Before we broke the threshold, I struck out with a tight fist and inadvertently knuckled his left eye.

"Owwww!" Blair wailed before dropping me on the hard stone floor.

"You are a flea bitten arse," I groaned, rubbing my throbbing hip.

Blair nursed his eye beneath a cupped hand. "Damn, Kait. I said you're not going."

I stormed past him and began furiously pumping the quern. The grain inside crunched and crumbled into a weightless powder that floated all around. I'd not try breaking free again. The guilt from fighting made me think of Ma and Da.

We had days to cool down. An unsightly black bruise appeared on my hip, but Blair's eye puffed into a monstrous shade of violet. I apologized for making him ugly, but Blair became sullen and refused to apologize for bruising me in a place that couldn't be seen. Frankly, the injustice turned my mood pissy, and I bided my time near the croft resentfully.

For days I brooded over the mysterious footprints and the slaughter of our innocent lamb. The death reeked of revenge, but Blair seemed unconvinced that the selkie was responsible. *He* hadn't seen the creature's wicked black eyes and his curling black lips. As time passed, I felt increasingly desperate to speak with Astrid. What did the bairn's father look like? Was the man her lover or a lecher from The Deep? There were many things I was desperate to know about the selkies, but the questions were not to be born. Blair hovered like a mother hen.

"We are almost out of barley," I grumbled on the third day of my confinement. I pushed gravied hare around on my trencher, certain that Blair was keeping me prisoner just for the spite of it. "It's been calm here. I'd wager that the selkie man has moved on."

"You don't know it was a selkie," Blair said. He slowly wiped his mouth on a napkin. "But it might be safe to go into the village for a bit o' bartering, if I go with you."

"Will you be holding my hand too?" I asked with a forced smile.

Later as the sun peaked behind the clouds, we passed two shepherds loudly complaining to one another in the shadow of the newly constructed parish. "It was only yesterday morn when my ewe birthed, and today I find the little lamb's neck snapped in two."

"What is this I hear?" Blair growled, storming the small circle.

Again? I froze in my tracks, paralyzed by the news.

Egbill Treb scratched his shaggy red beard. "Where have you been, Blair? The entire village is in a dither."

Blair's gaze moved grimly over the full street. In the shadows of empty shops, friends and neighbors quietly talked to one another, while looking nervously about. Only the children played war like it was any other day. "I lost a lamb three days ago—same thing."

"Then ye were the first. John here lost two lambs just yesterday. There is a scoundrel walking these streets. The constable was ferried in from the Mainland just yesterday to question the newcomers."

"Five new chair makers were shipped in from Ireland," John explained. "Our own chairs aren't good enough fer the fine tables at Balfour Castle."

"Chair makers don't kill lambs!" I cried, joining the group of ignorant men. "The scoundrel lives in the water!"

"Haud your wheest," Blair ordered. "You know nothing of the sort. It could have been ruffians from a neighboring isle."

"The selkie folk are angry for what we did to their own kind. Ask Thorfinn Trulloch. He'd know all about it, he will."

Egbill and John exchanged meaningful looks.

"Well it would be the truth," I cried. "The selkies are not as gentle as the ignorant men assume. First I was charged by the brute, and now all the lambs are dead."

Egbill dropped his eyes, fingering the coins in his pocket. "I'd spar with ye, Kait, but there's been other news. Have you not heard?"

"I've been held prisoner," I said flicking an annoyed glance towards my brother. "What happened?"

"Astrid's body was pulled from the voe three days ago."

John shook his head sadly. "Thorfinn's been inconsolable."

An awful pain exploded inside my chest and stole my breath. "Astrid drowned? The same day as...." I couldn't finish. Tears sprang from my eyes and spilled down my cheeks. Oh Odin, where was the justice? First Astrid's sweet bairn was ripped from her bosom and then Astrid herself. My mind swarmed with questions, the grief only worsened by the terrible unknown. Had the wicked selkie come back for her, or did Astrid kill herself?

"I'm sorry," Egbill said. "I know she was your friend."

My only friend. The pain constricted my breath further. She had lived on Shapinsay only a short time before we met at the New Year's bonfire. We bonded immediately and saw each other as much as we could. As a unified front we teased Blair and opposed the village geese. And when there was nothing else to do, we sat together and prattled on while darning socks or kneading dough. If she had been romantically involved with one of the sinister creatures, she hadn't confessed it. But then who would confess to such a culpable thing?

I gave a few ragged gasps and leaned into Blair. He felt as solid as a stone wall and was quick to support me at the waist. "She killed herself from the grief?" My brother seemed to pull the question from my mind. I was grateful, but there were dozens more just like it.

"My wife's been blathering on with her own theory," Egbill said as he lowered the rim of his hat. "She's been in a tizzy fer days."

"What did Miriam say?" I choked out through a blurry haze of tears.

The shepherds exchanged worried looks. "She says that a selkie man dragged her under the sea."

Poor, poor Astrid. Did she cry out for help, or was there a muffling silence from under the monster's paw? The image of Astrid's last moments was too horrible to bear. I broke from the men with a sob and swept towards the pub. My skirt tangled between my knees in my haste to get stoatin. "Oh, bloody,

bloody, *he* did it. The devil himself left footprints through my garden."

Blair caught me by the shoulder and held me firmly. "It's not proper for you to go in there," he hissed. "Only men are allowed."

"How'd I know what's proper?" I bit back. "I dinnae have a mither, sister, aunt, or even a friend!"

Blair lowered his face near mine as he caught me securely by the shoulders. "Nae, but ye will always have me."

5

DIS POWERFUL MAGICK

My furor cooled, but I could not stop remembering Kait—the one who would swim. I wondered if I had made a grave mistake in letting her live. When the others divided into the northern sea to hunt, I circled Shapinsay to further ponder her fate. The human girl intrigued me, haunted me, and a question bore itself under my skin. Why did she kill the burd?

Could she not see that the burd was as much human as it was selkie? Did she despise our kind so much? I'd never been so close to a land louper as I had been with Kait. I touched her skin and felt the warm columns of heat pulsate through her pale throat. My heart raced when I traced the soft skin that folded around ten perfectly formed fingers—hands that looked just like mine. Was her form really so different than my own spirit? The similarities between us disturbed me. Why did she have to kill the burd?

I blew out a string of silvery bubbles and dove to the deepest depths of the bay where the water ran cool and pressed heavily against my ears. Here it was dark and beautiful and nearly silent—and I didn't have to think of the girl.

I distracted myself by scratching against rough stones and by coursing over ridges and trenches that flaunted shadowy blues, purples, and greens. Playfully I submerged myself in a forest of dense green kelp, musing over the sluggishness of the skiff that sailed ignorantly above. I turned and twisted inside the playful green arms before bouncing from my hiding place. Everywhere my tail touched, glittery clouds sprang. A curtain of tiny stars sluggishly rolled into currents so blue...so blue... they challenged even the girl's eyes. This thought frustrated me, and I hoisted myself towards the surface.

A drizzly rain pelted my face when I hauled out on a smooth, flat stone. Just over the hillock, the voice of Kait and her mate carried. If I strained hard enough I could hear her deliberate yet lilting voice from halfway across the island—it was etched in my memory like a scar.

"Kait, it's not healthy fer ye to ignore the attentions of so many. Magnum is a good man. He'd provide well for you."

"Why'd ye tell him I was in the byre? The hens do not tattle and make so much noise as you."

There was a long pause. "Kait, the constant sounds that come from your mouth drown out even the greatest sweevy— even a hurricane."

"You are an imbecile, and his beard hid last night's sup."

"He came all this way just to give you a pin. It's a family heirloom. It belonged to the cloak of a Viking."

"It is a pauper's pin compared to Ma's."

"He intends to marry you."

"He can intend all he wishes. I don't like him. He's a bampot like all the others and only wishes for a wife so she can tell him when it's raining."

"I gave him permission to court you. It's time to grow up, lassie."

"Blair, ye are one minute older than me, and if you think I'm going to sit idle while that ancient man ogles me from across a table, you are more fool than he."

This conversation I did not understand at all. What did it mean to marry, and what was a wife? Why was Kait's mate trying to tempt her with a pin? New questions. I was furious with myself for caring. I hated Kait, but I needed to find answers.

When it became dark, I wiggled out of my coat and hid it once more in the stone wall. A windswept rain immediately soaked my skin and trickled its way through to my scalp. I wiped a stream of water from my face and looked longingly at the secret place that held my skin. *Nae, nae, nae, let it be. I'm not that cold.* With a growl of frustration, I resolved to keep it safely hidden, far from the reaches of soiled louper hands.

I circled the stone house with more curiosity than before. The same strange light was glowing from the windows—firelight. I had learned from the elders that the fire lived and breathed as much as ocean, but was fragile and greedy. I was warned to never touch it.

I sloshed through the mud past the hen coop to investigate the strange looking tools resting against the byre. At once I captured another whiff of Kait's mate. With my nose held to the wet sky, I stretched my neck to fully take it in. It was strangely familiar, filled with the complexities of Kait and something else too—wind, moor, oil, and peat. It was then I realized he was too closely linked with Kait. He was not her mate but a member of her own pod—a brother or perhaps a father. This was why he'd gone unnoticed the first time I'd come. It irritated me that this revelation should matter. I began to turn away, but then cursed myself when I reached for the grimy handle of her door instead.

~Kait~

A hand slid over my mouth and stifled my scream before I was even fully awake. When my eyes sprung open, I was ready to be filled with the image of a most ghastly villain, but instead it was forewarned magick that filled my eyes, and I was filled with awe. A man in the lightest sense of the word, loomed over me with eyes so wide and feral, I thought he might howl to the moon. His words came out rough and breathy. "If you make a sound, I'll snap your scrawny neck."

The sensible fear one should first feel when they are first assaulted, oozed reluctantly into me, and my eyes strained towards the darkened bedroom. *Wake up, Blair.*

"He sleeps like the dead," the selkie hissed as if he read my mind.

Oh, bloody, bloody, the fire had done no good at all. I silently cursed my ignorance and Blair's lame advice. The man above me was pearly white and as naked as the day he was born. Even in the blushing light of a dying fire, I could see the smooth skin of his chest and the tiny folds at his tight stomach as he curled over me. It was instantly clear why the women in the village laughed when I asked how I might recognize a selkie man. He would wear a lein and trousers no more than a fish.

The selkie man slipped his hand from my mouth then sniffed his palm.

"What?" I squeaked.

His dark eyes turned on me with such wildness and intensity; I believed his promise to break my neck. I pressed my lips together too frightened to move, but also mesmerized by the extraordinary sight of him—a wildebeest about to be eaten by a majestic lion. I was frightened—wasn't I?

"Were you dreaming of swimmin' in the sea?" he asked in a low and scratchy voice. It seemed the first sentence he'd uttered all day.

"Ye ask about my dreams?" I said stupidly. My eyes moved slowly over his beautiful face. He was not the porcelain doll that the women depicted, but more exciting with dark, haunting eyes that were as troubled as a cutter caught in an unexpected squall. Neither had I expected the wavy hair that hung like an American aborigine between us. His presence was dark, mysterious, and oh, so wild.

"Even your ears aren't so weak."

Oh Odin, he's asking about my dreams. My mind swam to moments ago when I had been happily safe and dreaming of...I struggled to remember...Magnum—the horrid, middle-aged farmer who lost his first wife by working her fingers to the bone. "My dream was not so pleasant as swimmin' in the sea."

The selkie's eyes grew. I couldn't tell if he was appalled or surprised by my answer. I wondered what difference it made. Dreams were only nonsense.

I struggled to sit up, and the selkie made no attempt to stop me. "Are you going to ravage me?" I rasped over a dry throat and tongue. I hiked my blanket fearfully over my naked shoulders as a shield. Is this what happened to Astrid right before she was dragged to her death? Would Blair wake tomorrow and wonder what happened to me, or would he assume I'd gone into town? I imagined how I'd look when they found me washed up on the beach all wrinkly and bloated with sea. My mind felt clouded, even uncertain about the horrors of such a death. Aich, I was speculating my own death! It was *him. He* was doing something to me.

The selkie studied me a moment, and I thought his lip twitched with a hint of amusement. "Do ye wish to be ravaged?"

I gave a dry, nervous swallow and turned on my ankles, prepared to run if necessary. I suddenly felt very fast. "If you try, I'll make more noise than you ever heard, then Blair will wake up and smash your head in. You're not as large or as tall as him." I glanced anxiously towards the darkened doorway, and the stranger followed my gaze. *Wake up, Blair!*

"The male?"

"My brother is very protective o'er me," I said staunchly.

The selkie looked back towards the bedroom before suddenly turning with a cat-like hiss. "Go ahead and scream," he threatened. His black gaze cut through a haunting veil of dark hair. "But I'm quicker than I seem. You'd be dead afore your brother wakens, and I'd be gone."

Gone? I winced at his words, but he crouched motionlessly as a crane with no attempt to carry through on his threat. "What do you want?" I squeaked. I didn't want him to leave.

Unashamed of his nakedness, the selkie man rocked back on his heels. He seemed to be near my own age—nineteen, perhaps twenty? I wasn't afraid to look at a man. I'd accidentally seen Blair huddled over the sae-bink when he bathed, but this man was magnificent in every way with no semblance to my brother. I absorbed the tight, yet narrow planes of a body he didn't bother to hide. Every part of him was as enticing as the next with hard sculpted ridges that gently tapered into a tiny waist. He *was* magick. I bit my lip in a concerted effort not to reach out and touch the smooth satiny skin.

Golden bands of firelight danced off the selkie's pale face as he scrutinized me. Did he guess my internal struggle? I felt my cheeks burn and spread to my ears. "I've not decided what I'm to do with you yet. Why did you murder the burd?"

A selkie pup? My mind swam with even more confusion. "I'd not do such a thing," I gushed defensively.

The stranger narrowed his eyes in loathing. "How easily lies spew from your lips."

"Nae," I cried. "I never even approach the rookeries. The town council forbids it."

"You didn't drop the burd in the water? I saw you standing on the pier." He lifted my braid then dropped it as if it were coated in filth.

"What?" *The pier.* It was then that the ghastly memory of Astrid's son returned to me. A lad I never got to see. At once I realized I was being blamed for his murder—the murder of a half selkie bairn. "I—I was searching for a bairn—my friend's child. It was the child's own grandfather who killed him." I desperately needed the selkie man to believe me. I could be a thief, a bint, even a murderer to anyone else, just not him. I bit my lip again. *Had I completely lost my head?*

"This is true?" he asked. His eyes flickered towards the glowing embers with uncertainty.

"Aye, is this why you're here? You believe I hurt your wee one—the fruit o' your loins?"

His brow bunched up in anger. "The burd was not mine, but does this matter?"

"Any death is tragic," I blurted, strangely relieved. "I swear o'er my ma and da's graves that I didn't do it."

He turned over the fringed edge of my blanket to examine it. "How can I believe the words of a louper?"

"A louper?"

The selkie snorted with disgust. "How can I believe *you?*"

"It's easy," I said with a wide gaze, taking in every line and angle of his face. I realized his eyes seemed sleepy even when he was wide awake. I wanted to laugh out loud at his preposterous and unparalleled beauty. "You trust me."

The selkie snorted again before rising and moving towards the door. I began to panic.

"Were you the one who killed my friend?" I blurted. *Please let it not be him. Please let it not be him.* I braced myself for his answer, not wanting to despise the only selkie man I'd ever meet—I wasn't even certain I could. He entered our home uninvited and then threatened my life. Why should my head be filled with flowery thoughts of him? If Blair were awake, he'd club his head and then light our table with his magnificent oil.

The selkie's face clouded with confusion or perhaps irony. "You'd accuse *me* of murder?"

"Did you drown my friend?" I asked more forcefully. I rose to my feet, bunching the tartan blanket around my middle. "Near a week ago. She had long brown hair and a wee mole on the arch o' her cheek."

The selkie glared at me.

A tear trickled down my cheek, distraught at his refusal to answer. "Her name cannot be spoken," I continued, "but she was so fond of puppies and riddles."

"Nae," he grumbled at last. "That is not my way. I prefer to drown women with sun strangled hair like yours."

My heart froze. "You'd kill me for havin' blonde hair?"

The selkie smirked. "Aye, wan reason is as good as another."

I stared at him a moment, debating whether he was torturing me with strange selkie humor. "But you killed our lamb, did ye not? Was it because it had white curls instead o' black?"

His brow knotted at my question. "I am only a dumb animal without the wits for such a thing."

"You have the wits," I insisted. "Why do you try to distract me from your crime?"

"Crime?" he scoffed. "Why do you question my honor when you don't even know me?" He reached for the door's handle.

"Don't go," I begged, spontaneously reaching for him. My fingers slipped through his dark hair, and the selkie froze as if I had sapped all of his strength.

"You'd have me stay?" he asked in a soft, bewildered voice.

I bit the swollen place I had chewed inside my lip. "Or I could go with you." Was dying a bad thing? I felt confused, uncertain. The thought of his pale body twined around mine as we both slipped under the sea was intoxicating. It was juvenile, illogical, even impulsive, but I did not care. I only wanted to be with the selkie man, and death seemed only a small price for the pleasure of his brief company.

"Ye wish to die?" he asked with a small growl.

Die? I *was* losing my head. The magick the village women spoke of was miniscule compared to the overpowering allure of a real flesh and blood selkie man. Still I clamored to think of something that would keep him with me. "Sometimes I dream of diving to the bottom of the ocean." The confession was true, but it sounded breathless and desperate.

The selkie man turned to face me with more of the same curiosity. "Do you not know that you are a land louper? The sea is no place for you."

"When I crest the hillock out back, all I see is blue for miles. It is my home too, only my view is different." I glanced towards the bedroom where Blair continued to heavily sleep. "You truly are not afraid of my brother?"

"I am not afraid of anything," he quietly boasted. His eyes dropped to the thin fabric draped around my shoulder. As he reached out to touch it, my heart began a savage assault inside my chest.

"It's cloth woven from a loom," I managed with a dry swallow. "The weave o' my dress is much finer. Have you never seen cloth before?"

"Not close," he mumbled, moving the cloth between his fingers. His fingers felt cool and ticklish against my skin. I didn't have the strength to do the proper thing and smack his hand.

"That's my Bride's Cog spinning wheel," I said, pointing to the opposite corner where turned spindles housed the finest spoked wheel on the island. "I spin wool yarn with it. My loom is being borrowed by Mary Crawford."

The selkie stared flatly at me before shaking a strand of hair out of his eyes like a horse shakes a fly. "When you dreamt you were diving, what did you see?"

I bit my lip to hold back the grin. "I dream of exploring the coral reef, upside down, with my toes high above me."

"Being upside down. This is what you dream of?"

"Nae, I dream of being weightless—light as o' feather and exploring the sea like a kittiwake explores the sky. Is it as beautiful as they say?"

His dark, exquisite eyes moved meticulously over my face, and like a thief, craftily robbed me of my breath. "Aye, but the beauty changes with the currents."

For a few moments, there was only the amplified sound of my breath raggedly pulling in and out. A flush of heat spread to my cheeks as I realized my foolishness. "Since you're not going to kill me, maybe you could tell me your name."

The selkie propped leisurely against the door and scratched his lean chest. "What make you certain I'm not going to kill you? I've not yet decided."

"Why should you?" I answered nervously, taking in the great abundance of white skin. "You seem more likely to take a nap. Your name?"

"Name?" He frowned with annoyance. "I'm a selkie."

I felt the stymied expression on my face. "You don't have a name?"

He stared at me as if I were an imbecile.

My eyes moved thoughtfully over his somber face. "You look like an Eamon."

"Would you put a hat on my head too?" he asked gruffly.

In the next room, we both heard Blair yawn and then shuffle out of bed.

"I shouldn't be here. You distracted me," Eamon snarled, and then he was gone.

6

A CHANGE IN CURRENT

A completely irrational happiness swept over me, and I spun loftily around on my toes with a girlish giggle. I had encountered a selkie man and lived to tell the tale!

"Hmmm, dancing," Blair mumbled sleepily as he staggered to the fire. He scratched his bum then rearranged the cinders with a long iron poker. "I heard voices. Who were you blathering on with?"

I laughed loudly then rushed to a dark patch of window to peer out. "I almost think I was dreaming," I admitted. "Perhaps you should pinch me."

"How about a hot poker," Blair mumbled with his face leaning over the fire. "That'll be certain to wake you."

"A selkie man was standing right here," I mused retracing the path around the door. I giggled again. "Either that or he was a very naughty streaker from the Mainland."

"Ouch," Blair nursed his singed finger in his mouth while his eyes burned attentively into me. "What is this rubbish you speak of? Did you *dream* someone was here or not?"

I twirled around again with my shift hiked scandalously above my knees. "I wasn't dreaming. He was truly here, just moments ago threatenin' to kill me."

Blair lunged towards the door and swung it open. A gust of heavy wind billowed in and bent the flames.

"He couldn't have gone far," I said peering around his shoulder. "I could try and call him back."

Blair closed the door and leaned heavily against it. "This is a bloomin' problem," he said, hanging his head against the door. He struck it once for good measure.

"Why is it bad?" I asked, my mood dampening. "He didn't try and hurt me. He wasn't even very large."

"What was he doing here?" Blair asked as his eyes flew down my flimsy shift in alarm. "Did he touch you?"

"We were just visiting. Ye said yourself that the selkies are harmless."

Blair studied me with a frown. "He put an enchantment on you. You've lost your wits every bit as much as Tipper Gray. We'll go and see Mr. Lennie after the sun rises. He'll be certain to have a cure."

"That ol' witch? Blair, you are too cruel. There's nothing wrong with me. I'm healthy as a horse."

"You're floating around like a plucked feather and dancing too. You're enchanted, see?"

My mind raced to understand what Blair was telling me. Enchanted? Of course I wasn't enchanted. I felt far too good. I smiled at the memory of Eamon and the way his cool fingers slid across my mouth and latched behind my jaw. I'd kiss those fingers given another chance—his full lips too. "The selkie didn't mean me any real harm. He was more curious than anything. Also there was the matter of the drowned bairn, but it's been all cleared."

Blair slumped into a straw backed chair and shook his head. "Revenge—aich. The demon means to come back fer you. He'll drag you under the sea first chance. From the looks of you, you'll be leading *him* to the water."

"I'm not afraid o' the sea."

"Then you're a fool. The sea keeps fools."

I peeked out the window and caught sight of my own plain reflection. "He didn't try to hurt me," I repeated less enthusiastically.

"He'll be back. He's the one causing all the mischief."

"But you said that the selkie folk were gentle—"

"I know what I said," Blair growled. "It's the sort of thing the men say to comfort our women. We know the legends as well as anyone else. Have ye forgotten what happened to Astrid so quickly?"

"You would speak her name?"

Blair let out a heavy breath. "There is something I need to discuss with you."

I slumped into a chair across from him. "You sound very formal. Shall I put on Mither's brooch?"

"It's not a joke. The sheep are nae longer profitable, and I'm thinking of making a go at whiskey."

I shrugged my arms across my chest, feeling suddenly cold. "You're speakin' gibberish."

"Sloan's father made me an offer I can't refuse. I'd be his apprentice on the Mainland, and one day when he's had his fill, I'll take over the business. Did you know that there are women over there that do nothing more productive than curl ostrich feathers all day? They garnish the most comical hats."

"You can't do this," I cried. "Sloane is only trying to trick you into to marrying her."

"Sloane has a line of suitors all with more jingle in their pocket than me," Blair retorted quickly. "I'd be lucky to have her. Besides, the pickings are slim here on Shapinsay, and I don't intend to remain a bachelor forever."

"Then bring the remora here," I blurted. "I'd sleep by the fire every night and give you newlyweds all the privacy you can stand."

"I've decided," Blair said. "Mr. Yorston and I shook hands."

I stared at my barmy brother. "Then go on you pig headed numpty. But I won't be going with you. I'd suffocate in a large town sooner than the sea."

"I've just decided. You'll come with me or marry Magnum. It's no longer safe for you to stay here alone. Tonight has convinced me of it." Blair studied me anxiously. "Think, Kait, whiskey will always fetch a fair price. In Kirkwall there is a pub on every street. We'll be well to do, and ye won't have to labor o'er the hens anymore. If ye like, I could buy you a blue dress."

"Is that supposed to entice me?" I asked with a glare. "I like my hens and I hate blue."

"Then marry Magnum. He's offered to take you in. He's got a soft spot for blondes."

"Offered to take me in? Have I been up for bid?" I shrieked. "Like a basket or a chair?"

"It's not like that," Blair said. "It was just talk."

"I hate Magnum."

Blair leaned forward over the bink. "He's a good man with a steady increase. Everyone likes him."

I scraped out of my chair. "We'll talk more tomorrow, when there's not so much ale in your belly. Apparently your head is swimming up your arse."

In the morn, Blair stiffly told me he was taking the ferry into Kirkwall, and I politely told him not to come back. After he left, I brightened considerably and set to un-cooping the hens and scouring the croft for selkie footprints. A nightful of steady rainfall left the ground soft and impressionable, and I was delighted to find a perfect pair of prints circling the area around the well pump. I followed the narrow prints to the hen coop and then to the byre. Eamon seemed to spend a great deal of time here, because the grubbing hoe and spade were out of place, and a bale of straw had been dissected by one tool or the other. After that, the prints ducked under the washing line and disappeared out over the moor.

With nothing but Eamon on my mind, I quickly completed my morning chores: washing and hanging last week's clothes and scrubbing the flagstone floor. Once satisfied that the house was clean enough to receive visitors, I set to peeling potatoes. When the stovies were roasting under glowing red coals, I skipped off towards the beach. I was disappointed that there were no more footprints. The rain had swept the sand clean.

Looking out over the voe, I felt exhilarated, reckless, and even flirtatious. I peeled off my dress and let it fall carelessly into the sand, then pointed myself towards Dronsday Island—a small island too insignificant to be noticed by anyone but selkies and kittiwakes.

I took off running and fell exhilarated from the weight of the water around my knees. The first few strokes were cold and jolting, but I pulled at the water and pummeled through the oncoming waves. By the time I entered the firth, my heart pounded loud complaint inside my chest. As the water grew deeper, my strokes grew less confident, and I began to fatigue. Every so often, I reclined on my back to catch my breath. All around me the blue water rocked and churned, pulling me first one way and then another. I watched the billowy clouds stretch and mold into sea animals—first a smiling osprey in a bonnet and then a tiny selkie pup.

I marveled over my shoulder at the great distance behind me. I'd traveled farther than ever before. The shadows of massive rocks inched under me like slow mysterious whales. Determined to reach Dronsday, I relentlessly scooped at the water, one arm over the other like a tireless windmill. Finally, my toes brushed over the surface of a clammy rock, and I clamored and clawed for the pebbly beach beyond. Exhausted and trembling, I collapsed on the smooth, flat stone. A fulmar buzzed overhead and cocked his head at me. I gasped happily at my triumph. *I did it!*

After the sun warmed me, I wrung out the hem of my shift and tested my legs. Shakily, I made my way around the perimeter, pausing to explore a small cave tucked beneath a stony ledge. A band of brilliant light cut through the stony ceiling, penetrating the turquoise water below with glowing yellow bands. Happily I waded through the shallow lagoon, carefully peering through the clear water for partins or other pinchers that might grab hold of my toes.

When I returned to the beach, I gaped at a set of meandering footprints that drew near the cave before turning and disappearing into the water. The second toe was just longer than the first with the tiniest of gaps between them. They were identical to the narrow prints roguishly circling the croft. An unaccountable joy surged inside me—I had once again drawn the selkie man's attention.

"Eamon, are you here?" I cried. My eyes moved swiftly over the water then retraced the isolated beach. "Eamon!" I ran down the beach, but there was only smooth rain dimpled sand. Disheartened, I climbed up a lichen covered rock to wait for his return.

Hour after hour, I stared across the firth, kicking up sand in the same tedious path. My sandy shift dried, and my hair blossomed into a blonde tangled mass. Every so often, a cargo ship or fishing doree joined me in the bay, but never hide nor hair of selkie folk. As the blinding sun moved across the sky, my frustration grew, fueled by the unshakable feeling that he was purposely hiding from me—perhaps even watching. When the tide dragged the sea up to my feet, I kicked at the water and decided to swim home.

I dove into the frigid water with another gasp and kicked furiously towards the open firth. Almost immediately, I realized that the currents had dangerously changed, tugging and pulling with an unseen power towards the open sea. The harder I fought against the water, the more determined the roosts held me captive, carrying me easily like driftwood in a northerly direction. Coughing and spluttering, I returned to the desolate island to wait for a retreating tide.

Uninterested in the same stagnant scenery, I walked to the north side of the isle and separated smooth rocks into piles of white, tan, black, and brown. After this mundane task was completed, I traipsed through the rough sea grass to get a better view of the island from above.

I paused to rest at the summit, and peered through a creviced boulder, catching my breath at the absurd and magnificent sight below. Half dozen selkie men and women were serenely basking on the rocks below in nothing but their birthday suits. Beside each was a velvety grey skin. They were oddly quiet, each enthralled in their own silent experience and seemingly unaware of the other. Like great sleeping cats, they unabashedly sprawled and stretched, completely oblivious to their own nakedness.

I cringed at the visual assault of women whose bodies were painfully ripe and beautiful like clusters of exotic grapes. Each was lovelier than the next, with glassy hair that shone like the surface of a loch. Next, I surrendered to the visual allure of the men. Like the women, their bodies were slender and white, but hard and sculpted, seeming as cold and stony as the rocks they laid on. One was on his belly with his face hidden under a mane of scattered hair, but the other two lifted their faces reverently towards a rose and amber sky.

I hesitantly stepped out from behind the boulder. *Courage, Kait—courage! The selkies are timid creatures.* "I'd be looking for someone. Dinnae be afraid."

The women's doll-like eyes sprang open as they squeaked their surprise. At once they snatched their pretty little skins and dove below the ruffled surface of water with tiny splashes.

The one whose face had been hidden, looked up. "Oh," I gasped, surprised and flustered to see Eamon's black brooding eyes cutting into me. He didn't seem happy to have been discovered.

The other two males looked at one another and laughed robustly, while three little selkie heads peeked out of the water to watch from a safe distance.

"Why should we be afraid o' you?" one of the older males asked. His large obsidian eyes moved condescendingly over my shift. "Do you have a harpoon hidden beneath that rag?"

I glanced down at my thin underclothes humiliated. "Aren't you afraid I'll steal your skin?" My gaze flickered back to Eamon.

"Come fer my skin and see what happens," the largest threatened. He postured his shoulders aggressively with an eerie smile.

"We don't speak of other's skins," Eamon warned in a raspy, unused voice. He rolled over, innocently exposing every plane and valley of his taut body. He seemed angrier than the others, but sweeter, more delicate too. An angry angel.

"I—I dinnae mean any harm," I blurted, the strange inconsistency blinking out of my mind. "Please, Eamon, I'd speak with you alone."

The two older men looked at one another with puzzled expressions.

"She means me," Eamon growled, brushing his hands contemptuously together. "The name is not of my choosing."

The older ones looked at him in surprise before erupting in boisterous laughter.

"Come, John," the largest joked as he nudged his friend. "Let's find *Frayah* and *Auor.* They'll be missing us."

Stupid, stupid me. I kicked at the sand, angry with myself for embarrassing Eamon. Already, I was making the wrong impression. I only wanted him to see me as I saw him—wonderful—beautiful—mesmerizing.

The aggressive male surged into the sea with a powerful sprint, but the other stopped at a rock barrier to address me.

His black eyes were startling bright and full of jokes. "If ye were wise, lassie, you'd stay away from this young wan." He gave a brilliant white smile. "He's not yet tame." He adjusted his coat then gracefully dove beneath a wave. A moment later, a little grey tail flapped at the surface of the water over fifty yards away.

"So ye really do not use names?"

"I thought I was clear on that," Eamon said as his eyes moved sleepily over my face.

I looked off towards the jagged rocks where the selkie men had disappeared. A new wave crashed and filled the air with salty spray. I shook my head incredulously. "Then how in creation do you address one another?"

"The selkie speak with a look or a nudge. If that doesn't work, we bite or use a swift rock to the head." Eamon's dark brows pulled together. "You take an interest in the selkie folk?"

My cheeks warmed under his intense gaze. I wanted to smell his long, exotic hair, kiss his animal mouth, and measure his wee waist with my bare arms. I took a deep breath to slow my erratic and indecent thoughts. "Are the selkies not the best secret of Shapinsay?"

His eyes grew wide then narrowed just as quickly. "It's a clumsy secret," he said with a look of annoyance. "I saw you swim off. What happened?"

I gave a coy smile. "The tidal currents are too strong for me, but I'm glad. I hoped I'd see you again. Are you terribly offended by the name I've picked for you?"

Eamon shrugged as he brushed a patch of sand off his chest. "I don't know," he said gruffly. "Why must everyone and everything have a label?"

"Obviously it's convenient."

"What does the word...Eamon mean?"

I twisted a strand of hair around my finger. "Hmmm, I believe it means protector...aye, that's right."

"Protector? This is how you see me?" He folded his brow dubiously.

"I—ugh—nae. Names in our world are given in honor of someone else."

Eamon glanced off towards the rocks. "Tell me about the other Eamon who has claimed a place of honor inside your heart."

"I know of no other," I said with a dry swallow. "You would be the first if you wish."

Eamon furrowed his brows as he considered this.

"Your skin has magick in it," I said scrutinizing his coat mounded on a nearby rock. "It's what makes you a selkie." I wanted to inspect it up close, maybe even try it on, but I realized Eamon was following my gaze with alarm.

"You show too much interest in what's mine. Do you mean to take it from me?"

"No," I cried stunned. "Hide it if you wish. I won't look."

Eamon glared at me before sweeping up his skin and marching towards the water.

"Don't leave me all alone," I cried running behind him.

"Then scat yourself home to join your sheep reeking brother. He'll be wondering where you are."

"Have ye forgotten that I can't leave?"

Eamon turned with a look of disgust. "You've had little problem venturing this far."

"Are ye so strong that the tide has no significance to you?"

"Aye," he said proudly. "I am strong."

"Well, I'm not," I snapped with tears in my eyes. "If you care so little, why were you watching me?"

"Did ye not hear the warning o' the wise wan?" he asked in place of an answer.

"The one who smiles—I don't like him."

Eamon dropped his gaze. "Do not trust me."

"The older one talks condescendingly," I muttered.

"Everyone says I can't be trusted. Would it frighten you to know that I nearly killed you once."

I buried my toe in the sand, discomfited by his frankness. "My memory's not so short. I can see that ye don't want to kill me so badly."

Eamon shook his head. "Not yesterday, but five nights ago. You never even knew I was there. We're invisible when we want to be."

"You were in my home once before?" I asked astonished.

Eamon nodded with a grimace and flicked a pebble into the water.

I stood dazedly beside him, reflecting on my mortality, while the sun dipped lazily behind Rousay Island. Gold and amber light seemed to be folding into soft wooly blankets above the hills. "What made you decide not to kill me?"

Eamon looked me in the eyes and then shifted his focus to my hands, nervously twisting at my waist. "Your hands."

I looked at him strangely and flexed my fingers. "But why?"

"You don't have the hands of a killer," Eamon said with a frown. I watched in astonishment as he gingerly collected my sun baked hand in his. He looked over my short nails and then the calloused areas on my palms. It was not a romantic gesture, but the examination a doctor would give to his patient.

"They are not as soft as yours," I said, immobilized by his cool touch. He narrowed his eyes over a tiny white scar on my knuckle—a souvenir from Blair's fishhook. His own white fingers were smooth and flawless with opalescent moons crowning his short nails.

"Of course not," Eamon said, dropping my hand. He looked unhappy with himself, but I felt shaken from the separation. I studied his hand fidgeting at his side, longing for it to envelope my hand again—this time like a lover. Was it even possible for a selkie male to look at a human woman with sparks in his eye? I felt shy—uncertain. "I'll wait out the tide with you."

"Really?" The crippling fear that he'd suddenly run and dive was replaced with an inexorable joy. Happiness spread like a banner stupidly across my face. If pity was progress, I had made some.

"You swam again," Eamon said with a reluctant grin. He slumped in the sand and shrugged his lengthy hair behind an ear. I positioned myself as close as I dared, then pulled my knees nervously to my chest.

"Why does this surprise you? I don't swim as well as you, but I'm not afraid of the water."

Eamon gave a short, throaty laugh that reminded me of a seal's bark. "Then ye are not like the others."

"Nae," I agreed with a giggle. "There is no one like me."

"And you are not afraid of me."

I peered over at his sinewy form propped lazily on his elbows like an open breeze. A wonderful wave of white skin plummeted down his thighs and milky hips before rising to a tightly rippled stomach and chest. How could I be anything but completely and utterly beguiled? "You're not hiding a pistol or a dagger in there, are you?" I joked.

Eamon furrowed his brow. "I do not speak selkie to you. Why do you show off with foreign words?"

"I'm sorry," I said, quickly reviewing my error. "I was only speaking of weapons like a stick or a rock. I didn't mean to offend." I licked my lips and gazed anxiously at Eamon. He was obviously sensitive to our differences. If only he could see through *my* eyes—he'd see that except for a few critical boy, girl type differences, we were practically the same. "There's something I want to tell you before it's too late."

Eamon beamed a pebble into the water, tensing the vertical hollows in his jaw. He seemed uncomfortable, even nervous. I quietly sniffed at the absurdity. He was a mysterious and beautiful selkie man from The Deep, and I was a dingy little shadow in comparison. Damn. What would I have that could possibly entice him? A wicked mountain of twisty hair and the willowy body of a very young boy? Damn. Damn. Damn. I took a gulping breath and just blurted it out. "I'm not afraid o' you, but I'm terrified that I'll not see you again. Is that crazy?"

Eamon beamed pebbles into the waves as if he had gone stone cold deaf.

"Did you hear me?"

"I'd not be leaving just yet," he muttered with a glance. He gazed off towards Rousay with a rigid expression. "Tell me about the nets the humans use fer catching fish."

"Ye don't understand me," I spluttered. He didn't understand the magnitude of what I was telling him at all—the emergence of what I was feeling. What was a trite little heartbeat in my chest compared to my obsessive need to always be with Eamon? My breaths strained in and out, and I began to feel dizzy. *Clear the head, Kait. Clear the head. He's not even human. Aich, he's not even friendly. What does any of it matter?* "I'd see you again—every day if you'd let me."

Was it even possible? Could Eamon come and go as he pleased, or were there rules that forbade it? Would his skin shed at his command? Did Eamon have a selkie job or a family? Or a wife? Oh Odin, I felt ill that there was so much I didn't know.

Eamon held and captured me inside his dark, penetrating gaze. I felt helpless to move—every muscle waiting in deference to whatever whim would please him. My stomach flipped and then quivered nervously as his deep and brooding eyes took in every part of my face. He seemed to be trying to tell me something, but I felt lost and uncertain of the message. He had to feel *something* for me. "I'm here, Kait," he repeated more forcefully. "Now, tell me—about—the nets."

I smiled timidly, surprisingly reassured by the sound of my name on his lips. It was me that held his attention—me that drew and held his gaze. My breath waffled out slowly as a strange new feeling of gratitude washed over me.

Eamon captively listened while I stalled him with tedious information about creels, sprols, and other tools for baiting and catching fish. When the subject of fishing was exhausted, Eamon asked about the forked tools in our shed and then inquired about the purpose of trenching peat. The topics were neither engaging nor charming, but every moment was a sweet and precious jewel that strained inevitably through my fingers like a palmful of sand. For Eamon I would have been content discussing the fascinating points of soil all night. I never wanted the evening to end.

Slowly a giant gibbous moon rose in the sky, and the cool dark air descended like a damp blanket against our skin. Eamon frisked his arms briskly. He wasn't used to being uncovered at night, and my heart went out to him.

"Go on," I urged, motioning towards his skin gleaming over a moonlit rock like a silky black rug. "I know that you're cold too. I promise not to touch it."

Without protest, he collected his skin and swept it over his shoulders. The velvety mantle twitched then molded itself to Eamon's back and shoulders as if it were a living thing. I startled at the minuscule movements.

"It's alive," I gasped, eyeing the soft water tight hairs.

Eamon seemed relieved to have it next to him again and let out a slow rumbly breath. "Your eyes play tricks."

I gave a nervous laugh. "Nae, if I had blinked I would have missed it, but I saw it move just a hair. It's enchanted."

Eamon snugged the skin more firmly around his chest with a severe look of warning. "You'd blatantly look at it as if it were yours to wear?"

"So I can't look at it *or* speak o' it?" I asked incredulously. I averted my eyes towards a small crab scurrying towards the water.

"I don't like it." His black gaze locked on my face, waiting for me to make another mistake.

"You don't like a lot of things," I grumbled. As promised, I didn't touch the skin. Neither did Eamon offer a corner as I shivered beside him.

"In the sea, it's never cold," he offered instead.

"My fire keeps me warm enough," I snipped.

"Where is your fire now?"

After the moon crested high in the sky, the waves receded, exposing a wide silvery patch of pebbled beach. I stared with dread into the darkness, my muscles already aching from one swim across the firth. "I've never swam at night before. Perhaps we could wait till dawn."

Eamon stood silently beside me like an aboriginal warrior dressed for battle. Beside him, I felt exhilarated and a little bit frightened. "What is it about the water ye fear?" Long savage hair shadowed his face, but I could sense him watching me.

"Not the water—it's what's beneath. Tell me, Eamon. What's below the water?"

He touched my back and nudged me gently forward. "Nothing, Kait. Absolutely nothing."

I stepped into the frigid currents with a violent shiver. The wind picked up and assaulted my already prickled body through my flimsy shift. "It's cold!" I complained. I looked longingly back at Eamon wrapped in his toasty warm skin.

"Go on," he urged. "The water has not changed since the first time you crossed. I'll see that you reach Shapinsay whole."

"Will you come see me again?" My gaze flashed towards the water, unable to make a single move until I received a commitment from Eamon. He hadn't been friendly to me, but he *had* watched me so closely. What was he thinking when his sleepy eyes moved furtively over my face? I couldn't help but feeling I was a puzzle for Eamon to solve—a puzzle he'd only pretend not to care about.

"Go on," Eamon said more gruffly. "This giant rock will be the death of you, and the water's warmer than it looks."

"Promise me you'll come to see me," I cried, "or I won't leave."

Eamon kicked at the sand with a wince. "Aye," he growled. "Now go."

I let out a sigh and dove. The water thuggishly pushed and shoved, while inky water splashed in every direction. Repeatedly I blinked and gasped, straining to see the tentacles or tails of beasts that lurked below. Which island was Shapinsay? Dark, unfamiliar shapes loomed in every direction, and I was growing exhausted. *Oh Odin, where did Eamon disappear to?* Just as I decided on a new course, a warm and powerful body swelled up from beneath and gallantly nudged me in the right direction. Joy swelled inside me. He had been beside me the whole time.

7

MAGNUM

Kait plunged into the water with a little shriek and left me momentarily alone. For a few moments, I marveled at the gaping silence and the strange new sensation I could not name. Kait was like a cyclone that bent and warped everything she touched, and I felt shaken in her wake. I watched her sluggishly and awkwardly flail through the water. The determination of her swimming was fierce, and with this I could find no fault. I stepped into the water and plunged in after her, surprised by how easy it was to follow.

After too great a time, she stumbled exhausted into the sand and gulped at the air. I dropped my head to secretly watch her and was startled to see that the cold water had turned her skin dusky blue. When she had recovered enough to stand, she turned and wistfully gazed out over the starry water. "Thankee, E—Eamon," she called through chattering teeth. I surged like a champion inside, though I had done nothing special. *I'm here*, I wanted to shout. *I see you.*

With hunger and frustration, I watched her stagger up the beach towards her dwelling. The frail white cloth she had worn all evening, now clung to her narrow hips and thighs— enunciating perfectly the peaked, contracted skin beneath. A warm pleasant sensation rippled through me till it held like an exquisite knot in my belly. It was difficult to admit, but she *was* beautiful.

Still…she was a foreigner—a land louper. How had my thoughts strayed so far? Had I not smelled the extended sun on her skin and seen the flush of her burnt cheeks? She would swim, but she would never in a million years be a selkie.

My fur coat and flippers didn't matter to Kait. She'd mate us together. I'd seen the way she looked at me with vaulted blue eyes, cruelly designed to entice. Given the chance, she would tan my skin and imprison me on land. Time and time again, I saw her richly eyeing my coat as she designed to steal it. I was furious with myself for succumbing to such a simple lure as a human girl. I would not be her fool but remain strong and loyal.

I turned sharply towards the northern sea, closing my nostrils as I prepared for a deep dive. Deep within me, the most primeval need to fly, hunt, and thrash cried out. No one knew my traitorous thoughts, so I needed to prove to no one but myself that I was not weak.

~Kait~

When I stepped inside our little cottage, Blair sprang from his chair. The firehouse was glowing in warm yellow light and immediately blanketed me in much welcomed warmth.

"Kait, where in the devil have you been?" He took in my drenched shift then flicked his eyes away in embarrassment. "Odin, save us from her shenanigans," he moaned.

My words bent slowly around trembling lips as I hobbled towards the hearth. "I—w-w-was—swimming." Salt water rained from my body in dark grey streaks across the floor.

"You're blue!" Blair observed with a peek of horror. "Does this have anything to do with that evil selkie man?"

"Of course not," I lied. I wondered what it meant to have found him so quickly. A good omen, certainly. A small smile touched my lips and betrayed my secret as I reminisced over his tight narrow muscles, and the way his pitch eyes stormed my face for sense or meaning.

Blair became enraged. "The sea will be the death of you. Can't ye see this?" He threw a blanket over my shoulders.

I secured the blanket and wiggled out of my wet shift. "If you try and take me to Kirkwall, *that* will be the death o' me." I stepped over the sticky mound at my feet then searched for some place to hang my sopping clothes.

"You're too stubborn," he growled.

"And you are too bossy."

"I don't wish to argue further," he said with a heavy sigh. "But I'm responsible for ye till the day you marry."

"Then I'll get married," I promised with a nod to myself. I wrung my shift out over the sae-bink, wondering about the selkie legends—the matrimonial joining of human and beast. What would it mean to marry a selkie? Would our children have webbed hands and feet? I didn't care—they would most certainly have Eamon's dark and ceaselessly sleepy eyes. I only needed to dry Eamon out and get him accustomed to living in a house.

He did care for me, didn't he? I shuddered with fear at the possibility that I'd completely missed my mark. Maybe Eamon preferred a thick muscular female, touting flippers and a tail. I worried deeply. A life without Eamon seemed hopeless—a withering dying sort of thing that began every moment we separated.

Blair narrowed his eyes. "Your eyes have been opened to the many merits of Magnum?"

"Hmmmm," I said evasively. "But nae more talk o' Kirkwall. I can't stand it." I eyed him playfully. "And if I divined your future, what would I learn? Will you be getting married to the bonnie Sloane?"

Blair grinned. "It turns out that Sloane was not opposed to the idea, so I worked up the gumption to ask her father, and he wholeheartedly agreed. Turns out that he and Sloan had been scheming together."

"The whole apprenticeship thing was a scam?" I asked.

Blair kicked his feet on the table with a puffed chest. "I'd still make Scotland's finest whiskey. It was only a clever strategy to land Shapinsay's most handsome and eligible bachelor. We'll be passing the bride's cog before the summer solstice."

I grinned at my conceited brother. "Eligible, aye, but handsome? Perhaps Mr. Yorston meant to offer the apprenticeship to Erland Kelday. His golden curls and green eyes have the village geese all aflutter."

"There's nae mistakin'," Blair said sourly. "These golden locks are what Sloane dreams about at night. She can hardly keep her fingers out of them." He scowled at his drink a moment before licking foam off the rim.

"Sloane's wanted to get her hooks in you since we passed whiskey at Hogmanay," I admitted with a laugh. "I suppose everything's turning up roses."

Blair lifted his tankard with a wobble. "Slake your thirst, Kait. This is a night to celebrate."

"It seems you've already started celebrating. Will ye be stoatin on your weddin' day too?"

"I'm not the least bit drunk," he said with a wink. He took a deep gulp of ale then wiped the frothy bubbles from his mouth with the back of his hand.

"Not at all," I said with a laugh. I turned from the table and tossed a peat brick into the fire. Sparks blew into the room as the flames jumped higher.

"There's news from the village," Blair muffled behind another swig.

"Oh?"

"It seems our neighbor Tipper Gray was evicted from her croft and taken to Thieves' Holm."

"Is that not the fittin' place for a witch?"

"She never stole anything," Blair said with a frown. "Rummaging around in other people's byre is a different sort of crime. No one would deny she's guilty o' trespassing."

"But nae one knows what she's capable of," I protested, burrowing deeper into my blanket. "The ol' felkyo is as dark and mad as an Orcadian winter. She would have made off with Ma's wedding dress had I not stopped her."

"She never even touched it," Blair reminded. "She was just searching through the trunk. That's what she does—searches—all day long."

"This I know. She's searchin' fer black charms to work her spells: locks of hair, spiders, jewelry of the dead, and if she's lucky, the bones of a rat or a mouse. Who can say what horrible magick she would perform with something as splendid as Ma's dress?"

"Ye sound like ye know all about it."

"Aye, I've heard the women talk. I'd guess she searched the wrong house. Who'd she peeve this time—Queen Victoria?"

"Nae, a bit closer to home. She was found with her head poked up the Balfour's dirty flume."

"She was lookin' fer nests," I said with a yawn. "There's extra strength in the magick if the eggs are still inside."

"Either way, Eleanor Balfour found her herself. She's taken to bed ill from the encounter."

The rest of Blair's story blurred sleepily together. I knew the ending anyway. Tipper would be exiled for the rest of her life on an island reserved for thieves and murderers. I was too exhausted to care. That night I collapsed into bed, spinning with blissful thoughts of Eamon.

When I woke up the next morn, my head was still spinning. "Aich," I moaned, clutching my temples. Every fiber in my body ached as if I'd spent the previous day lifting gargantuan size boulders.

Blair swaggered in when he heard me stirring. His leine was untied and gaping over a sun browned chest. "You're burning up," he mumbled as he tested the heat of my forehead. "You're lookin' shilpit too—probably from pretending you have gills. Will ye not be fixing my bangers and eggs?"

I glared up at the tall blonde pathetically moping over me. He was freshly shaved because he was going to see Sloane again, but he had failed miserably at taming his curls. Flattened ringlets were stuck to the side of his head like wet feathers. "Of course, Blair," I said sweetly. "I dinnae realize that your noble fingers were broken. Shuck me out a couple of eggs, and then I'll show you what to do with 'em."

"Never mind," Blair grumbled as he stomped from our small bedroom. "I'll spare a copper fer a loaf of bread. There's less chance of getting my fingers bit off."

I didn't hear him leave, nor had I realized how tired I still was. When my eyes lifted again, it was more reluctantly. I had been dreaming that Eamon and I were frolicking in the open sea together—me as a mermaid, he as a man. We splashed on the surface then raced below black flying mantas. Flirtatiously we played and tickled one another in twisty gardens of dimpled yellow coral. When I wiggled away, he recaptured me under the bow of a barnacled ship with a sudden embrace that thrilled with newness. I looked nervously, expectantly, into his dark mischievous eyes, but instead of a kiss, Eamon's lips teasingly dove into my neck with a series of nibbles. I screamed in delight and feigned an escape through a strange coral bridge.

When Eamon didn't follow, a familiar fear began to pound in my chest. I swarmed all the places we had played, but he was nowhere to be found. Breaking through the surface, I continued to anxiously search. The wind hissed in my ears as I feverously scanned the empty whitecaps. *We belong together*, I thought over and over again. *This isn't right.* Fear turned to panic when I realized I had no idea how to find him again.

My heart was still thumping wildly in my chest when I realized Blair was talking to someone. After a few deciphering moments, I decided that Blair was the worst brother in the world. He brought Magnum home with him. Moments later they were both standing over my bed and staring down at me. Magnum nervously rotated his bonnet between his fingers while Blair rubbed the back of his neck. I wearily lifted my head before dropping it again into my downy pillow. There was no place to hide.

"Goanda boanda," Magnum said cheerfully. The old-fashioned greeting was meant to be playful, but it annoyed me. He was a thin man with bright blue eyes that shone beneath a prematurely weathered face. He wasn't altogether unpleasant to look at, but his beard was unkempt, and his nails were always too long and dirty.

"I'm not dressed," I protested, tucking the blanket up under my chin. "Out, both of you, now. It's not proper for you to be in here."

"Only a moment now," Magnum said with a smile that was partially obstructed beneath bristly grey wires. "I heard ye were sick. I brought you some hattit kit from the Mainland."

"You went all the way to Kirkwall to buy me sweeties?" My throat knotted above my queasy stomach. The gift felt as bad as a sapphire ring.

Magnum laughed. "Nae, Kait, I was delivering my haddock to McIvers, and I saw the hattit kit perched high in the window like a little yellow canary. It made me think of you." He presented me a brown package wrapped in string.

I eyed the wee parcel like it was a coiled snake preparing to strike. Magnum laughed again, thrusting it towards me. "Go on, then."

"It's been a long time since you've indulged in sweeties," Blair coaxed. "But Magnum here travels to the Mainland often."

"Thankee," I said miserably.

As soon as my fingers closed over the crinkly brown paper, Magnum added like a lightning bolt from the sky, "I only ask for one thing in return."

"Your gift comes with conditions?" I snipped before I could stop myself.

Blair frowned at me, but Magnum smiled back brightly. "Aye, but it's nothing bad. I wish for your company at the bonfire in four day's time—assuming you're better by then."

"She'll be better," Blair promised. "Nothing keeps Kait down long. Isn't that right, Kait?"

"This feels like a very long ailment," I said with a deliberate wobble to my voice.

"That's alright. If it would please you, we can just sit together. Mrs. Todd can chaperone. Her peppermint tea is renowned."

"Kait loves bonfires," Blair said, herding Magnum out the door. He dropped his voice just beyond the thick wall and added, "Ye and I have much to discuss. I'd rather it be sooner than later..." His voice trailed off. I struggled to hear, but both men had moved outside and were mucking it up like a pair of silly teenagers. After a few moments, my eyelids closed heavily and my thoughts grew distance.

Tiny rivulets of water were trickling down the square window panes when I woke again. The hagger seemed to have worked its way indoors because my hair was soaked to the scalp and the stuffy room was sodden with dense grey clouds. I groggily remembered a series of thunderclaps during the night. Had Eamon come again, or had the storm held him back? I bit my nails, worrying that I'd missed him, worse, that I had misinterpreted his dark, lingering looks.

The warnings from the village women haunted me, and I worried that Eamon was only using his magick to hurt me. If it was a trap of sorts, he had me completely hooked. Was he laughing at me? With a small comfort I remembered the promise

I had coerced out of him—the promise that he'd return. He would come wouldn't he?

For a very long time, I laid there trying to recreate the aching bones and the faintness from the day before. Anything to avoid seeing Magnum, but it was useless. I was cured.

I staggered into the next room and found Blair relaxing in the center of a billowing cloud of smoke. Propped importantly in his hand was a long black pipe. The grey smog insidiously creeping into every corner wasn't simply the result of Shapinsay's sinister weather. I stared stupidly at the spiraling, shifting smoke. "What malevolent faery jinxed ye last night?"

Blair casually waved towards the threshold. "The rib is still secreted away. See fer yourself. No faeries snuck unnoticed in *here* last night."

"Do ye mind explaining then, why you're smoking like a doused fire?"

"Not atall," Blair said primly. "Sloane likes the smell of pipes. It's a wedding gift."

"What did ye stuff down the bowl, a goat paddie?"

He clenched the stem between his teeth. "I see your feelin' better—the insults are fresh—not good, but fresh. Though you look like you've been dunked in the bay again. Ye didn't—"

"—No! I've been in bed all night." I touched my damp hair that was twisted like tangled seaweed around my shoulders. "My fever broke, so I suppose I'm better enough. The sheep—are they…"

"The sheep are skitterish but fine," Blair assured. "Your sea dog moved on."

Disappointment sank like a weight to the pit of my stomach before I realized the awful paradox. Eamon murdered our sweet lamb and terrorized the village. Why should I ache to have him back? Aich! What was wrong with me!? "Then there has been no more footprints in the garden?" I asked dejectedly.

"Nae, it will be time to harvest the potatoes soon. Little eyes are beginning to pop out of the ground. A fair winter's supply, I'd say."

My winter's supply. To manage all alone. I wondered where Eamon had disappeared to. Where did any of the selkies go? They hunted—aye, that was it. He'd taken to deeper waters to hunt.

"Kait, can you hear me?" Blair asked.

I looked up distractedly. "Hmmmm?"

Blair wrinkled his brow. "I'd have the truth about the other night. You've been acting strange. You haven't had any more encounters with *him* have you?"

"A glimpse of a selkie man or woman is a once in a lifetime experience," I told him glumly. *Oh Odin, I've seen Eamon twice now. What are my odds at a precious third time?*

Blair didn't look like he believed my story. "If he comes again, scream like a banshee, and get near to the fire as ye dare."

"Of course. Do I look like I want to die?"

"Ye were not so convinced of the danger the other night," he said as he blew smoke from the corner of his mouth.

"It was an enchantment as you said. But now the spell's worn off."

"And what's to prevent you from getting beguiled by the dog again?"

I bristled at the insult to Eamon. It was true that part of him was selkie, but he was also the most graceful and elegant of men. Why was it wrong for me to be attracted to him? I drew my nose to a flower for its buxom scent and lifted my ears eagerly to a tune that was jiggy. Eamon's allure was no different than those things. I didn't feel shame for loving a voice so gentle and stirring, it got lost in the wind, or losing myself in the wild, windy scent of his hair. Most of all, I could not regret the nervous exhilaration I felt when his exquisite black eyes moved serenely over my face.

"He's gone as you said," I answered grumpily. "What did ye mean by bringing Magnum here last night?"

Blair kicked his feet up on our ancient stone table. "Ye refuse to come with me to the Mainland, and I can't leave you here alone with a dangerous animal lurking about, so I have nae choice but to expedite your marriage."

My eyes grew in outrage. "My what?"

"Your marriage."

I kicked a pail full of onion peelings with an angry clatter, while Blair took another slow drag from his pipe. "I never said I would marry Magnum. He's not at all the sort o' man that catches my eye."

"What catches your eye these days—flippers and whiskers?"

I glared at him. "You're a smoking headbanger. One of these days, you'll trip over that leathery whip you call a tongue."

"Just 'cos you're jealous there's no need for names." He leaned back into his chair with a wicked gleam.

"What do you have that I'm jealous of?" I demanded.

"One minute," he replied smugly.

"You're not older," I growled. "We're the same age."

"Have it your way. That doesn't change the fact that the younger lads are not exactly lining up down the road. As sisters go, ye are not bad to look at, but your temper precedes you. Doesn't matter that the men outnumber the women. Most of the men just aren't brave enough to court ye. Ye intimidate them."

I tossed a snarled strand of salty hair over my shoulder. "I'm as gentle and sweet as a lamb to those who are kind to me. You should give it a try."

"I'd not be that interested in seeing that side of you," Blair said as he blew out a dense cloud of smoke. "You can show Magnum. He may be a little older, but he has the experience and confidence of a bull fighter. He'll be expecting you at the bonfire."

8

GONE

Da's old fishing doree was whole, but not completely sound. I stood in the cold drizzle and tested the hull with a sturdy kick. It felt spongy under the crumbly layer of barnacles, but it didn't matter, the water was standing between us. I was determined to paddle across the firth, on a piece of driftwood if necessary. If Eamon wouldn't come to me, I'd go to him.

The old block of wood was much heavier than it looked, and by the time I dragged it down the beach into the pelleted water, I was cold and saturated to the bone. Obstinately, I pulled my heavy skirt into the boat and heaved myself past the first rocks.

As I slid up on Drondsday Island, my arms were trembling. With a grunt, I fell into the wet packed sand, then scrambled to my feet when I imagined Eamon watching. Smoothing my skirt, I gazed up at the little white veins of marbleized light breaking through the grey. The rain had stopped, but my hair was hanging in damp mousy hanks around my shoulders. Also my clothes were dirty and wet. There was nothing for it, I realized with a grim sigh.

"Eamon!" I cried, lifting my skirt and kicking my way through the wet sand. A group of kittiwakes lifted off the rocks and shrieked into the sky. Feverishly, I scanned for footprints or other signs of disrupted sand. "Eamon! Please don't hide! It's Kait!" My voice drowned out in the wind.

Impatient to see Eamon, I crossed the tiny island and scaled down the western wall. My heart dropped when I found the same wonderful cave from before cold and empty. In my ignorance, I had assumed it to be a place selkies would congregate. The watery floor that had been so brilliant blue before had turned murky grey. The stony formations and ledges that covered the barren walls would be disappointing to even a selkie.

When I circled around to the inlet that had yielded the basking selkie folk before, my hopes crashed. The large, flat rocks were despairingly empty—every evidence of their blissful lounging, washed away with the storm. Visiting Dronsday had been a big fat waste of time.

I made my way to the water and despondently retraced the spot where Eamon had stretched like a feline beside his skin. In the small crevice of the boulder was a tiny white shell no bigger than the petal of a primrose. I examined the wee ridges and the glossy underside before placing it between my lips. The salt was savory and melted invitingly into my throat. With the sides of my tongue, I explored the powdery texture before impulsively swallowing it whole.

I froze when I realized what I did. Bloody Hel, what had I been thinking? I quickly reviewed my thoughts for some sort of rationality. There was none—only that I missed Eamon so much I thought my heart might break. The enchantment had worn off, hadn't it? It had been over two days since I'd seen Eamon. Was there a time limit on spells? Oh Odin, I was becoming as stark raving mad as Tipper Gray.

I thought about the old crone who always searched. Perhaps she had lost her own selkie man and was whittling her life away searching for a ghost. Is that what I was doing—searching for a ghost? I grasped a fistful of sand and pelted it across the boulders in frustration. Eamon had no intention of keeping his promise, and I felt utterly helpless to save myself.

*****

"One and half more days till the bonfire," Blair teased when I met him on the moor at dusk. He was trenching out the peat and flipping it out on the meadow to dry.

"Why does the bonfire interest you so much?" I asked grumpily.

"I love a good fiddle as much as the next man," he answered evasively. He peeked guiltily at me, then sunk his flat shovel into the moist ground; his curls hanging conspiringly over his eyes.

I felt too defeated to interrogate him. "When will ye and Sloane be visiting Odin's Stone?"

Blair leaned against his shovel, carelessly shrugging the hair out of his face. "The day I get married depends on you, now doesn't it?"

"Ye still expect me to yoke myself to Magnum?" I asked angrily.

"That was the agreement."

"I didn't agree to that!" I cried. "The selkie man has long moved on. There's no reason for you to hover like a mither hen. I can manage the herd myself, and the hens are shucking out more eggs all the time. Three or four trips to the village a week will bring in enough provisions for a wee lassie like me!"

"If you refuse Magnum's protection, we'll leave together in a fortnight," Blair answered sternly. "That'll give me enough time to sell the sheep and the remaining spools o' yarn."

I stared at him aghast. "You'd sell the sheep?"

"I can't very well marry Sloane a pauper, can I?"

"Blair, you are too cruel!" I kicked the shovel out from under his arm and stormed into the house.

I sulked in the gloom for a long time, purposefully avoiding any semblance of dinner for Blair's enormous stomach. When I heard him shuffle into the firehouse, I slammed the door between us. Almost immediately an orange glow seeped under the door. Blair had stupidly lit a lamp. He would burn away the last of our oil before we had a chance to purchase more. I was too angry to cry. The sheep were Blair's to sell, but surviving on the croft without them would be near impossible.

That night I feigned sleep. After Blair's breathing became deep and regular, I crept out of my bed and layed beside the warm fire, watching for any sign of Eamon with a sailor's vigil. Still he didn't come. Near dawn, I surrendered to a restless and unhappy sleep.

When I woke hours later, the croft windows were clouded over with dense white fog. Out on the moor, the sheep bleated with distress. I rushed to get Blair, but his bed was empty. He was already out on the moor shepherding those who had lost their way.

I slumped in a chair, considering my hideous options: marry a man twenty years my senior, or embrace the suffocating life of the Mainland. My heart ached as I thought of Eamon. There had to be more to *us* than just simple passings in the night. Had Eamon not searched *me* out that first wonderful night and then again at Dronsday Island? Surely his actions hinted at something deeper inside his own mysterious heart. Hope snapped and blossomed like a fore sail inside my chest. There had always been a third option—find and marry Eamon.

After raking my hair till it gleamed, I changed my dress for one that was patched and worn, but respectably clean, then wrapped one of Ma's fine shawls around my shoulders.

Following the summit of the hills, I came upon the plains of heather. When the terrain became rockier, I detoured around the salty ayres until I was heading straight towards the Bay of Linton.

When I crested the rugged cliff, I thrilled at the bustling scene below. The mist had cleared over the firth, and I could see for miles. Little grey selkie heads bobbed playfully in the frothy currents, while many more sprawled out on a pebbly shore. One mother barked a warning towards a little pale burd flopping towards the freedom of water. Behind them, a pair of lovers bumped noses. Further away, two massive males growled and butted heads over a waiting harem.

Obsessively, I searched for the one I loved. It annoyed me that I had never actually seen Eamon in his selkie form. The large grey males tended to be darker, some as black as coal with creamy colored specks or sand dollar patches that adorned powerful necks and shoulders. None seemed familiar or even cognizant of the skinny human frantically pacing above.

"Eamon!" I cried. The panicked shrill of my voice rang over the rookery below. Mothers rushed to protect their burds while others bellied towards the safety of water. I was making things worse! As the selkies scattered, I became increasingly desperate. "Eamon, it's me, Kait. You made a promise!"

One of the larger selkies hefted himself a few paces and became attentive of my commotion. He pointed his nose in the air and cocked his head. "Eamon, you see me! I know you do!" I laughed in delight. He was one of the solids with thick grey wrinkles cascading down his long neck.

I quickly searched for a route to the beach plunged tauntingly below. When no safe route could be discovered, I resolved to scale down the vertical cliff. I lifted my swirling skirt and balanced on the precipice. As I searched for sure footing, my foot slipped and dangled over open air. Grappling for something solid, I found a small lip that crumbled under the weight of my foot. Large rocks and crumbling debris jutted down the jagged wall while I hefted part of my weight onto solid ground.

Scrambling to my feet, I frantically searched for the solid grey selkie. He was urgently hefting himself towards the lapping water with the others. "Eamon!" I screamed. "Come back!"

"Kait, be a good lassie and come here now."

I turned in surprise and found Mr. Lennie, the faery doctor, nervously hovering paces from the edge of the cliff. He was bizarrely dressed in a tartan cloak that was secured below the neck with an ancient looking twig. His red cheeks looked to have been scrubbed with sand.

"Go on down the way," I said, feeling utterly captured. I backed away from him and felt my foot float over open air again.

Mr. Lennie's face blanched as I wobbled. "I've no need fer your medicine."

"I heard ye calling to someone," he said with one tenuous step. His eyes dropped to the vast space behind me. "Who were ye calling?"

I frantically searched over my shoulder at the beach below. The large selkie was gone. Eamon was gone. Tears stung my eyes as I sucked in a sob. "He—was—here—before."

"Come to me, Kait," the trowlie doctor urged. He took another cautious step with his cloak flapping at his sides. "Can't ye see that you're about to fall to your death?"

"Can't—ye—see—that—he's—gone?" I barked through a steady stream of tears.

"I never saw anyone," the little man said anxiously as his eyes darted over the side. He held out his hand to me. "Come and we'll talk about anything you wish. Do the selkies interest you?"

The selkies. My eyes dropped to my feet as if scales had been shed from my eyes. I was precariously balanced on the edge of a rocky cliff! One awkward move and I'd fall to my death! Long strands of hair whipped into my face as I absorbed this horrifying and nauseating fact.

"What did you do?" I gasped, backing away from the sharp drop.

"I turned the light on for you," he said.

"I'm sick of magick," I choked, dusting the dirt and gravel from my skirt.

"There's nae magick here," he said with an amused twinkle. "I just pointed out that you were about to fall." He studied me solemnly while he jingled coppers around in his pocket. "I'm afraid ye may be in need o' my services."

I shook my head furiously. "Nae, Blair and I have been very careful. There's been no sign of faeries around the croft."

"I've been doing this a long time, lassie. I'd recognize an enchantment anywhere. If not indoors, have you seen anything amiss in your coop or in the byre? The wee creatures don't mind sharing even the grungiest of spaces."

"There's been no sign."

"The goat rib I charmed for ye, is it still in place?"

"Aye, Blair assures me it's still there."

His gaze dropped to the blue firth rolling lazily behind us. A few selkie heads were cautiously bobbing offshore. "Kait," he said slowly. "Have you had any encounters with...shall we say... an unclothed man?"

I bit my lip a moment, following his gaze. "Aye, but I know what he is. Does it matter that he is not entirely human?"

Mr. Lennie grabbed my shoulder and pulled me further from the cliff as if I might be tempted to take a flying leap. "Does it not matter that you've been dangerously enchanted? You could have died."

"But I'm fine," I protested. "And it's not a real enchantment. It's the purest form of love I feel."

"You're wrong, Kait," he said. "It's an illusion like an illuminator's trick. You don't love him."

"Of course I love him," I said with a miserable laugh. "If it weren't for the cliffs we'd be together even now."

"Nae, you would not," he said. "The selkie folk stick to their own kind just as you and I should. There are only ordinary selkies in the Bay o' Linton."

"But, I saw him," I cried. "He looked up at me—our eyes definitely met."

"You saw just an ordinary selkie. There was no man beneath that grey coat. Their eyes can seem so human at times; they fool even the best o' us."

A fierce pain stabbed inside my chest and debilitated me. I lunged over my knees and took a few gasping breaths. I was desperately lonely for a man who would spend his existence doing one thing—evade me. I on the other hand would be cursed to always search for him.

"Ye said that ye can help me," I groaned from under a mound of tangled hair. "Form your ring of sutherland, or give me a tonic to drink, anything to keep me from feeling this bad."

"I can't help you," Mr. Lennie said gently as he patted my back. "The spells that the selkies cast are not the same as the mischievous pranks of the wee folk. They are more... enduring."

"Then what am I to do?" I gasped.

"Stay away from cliffs and the water," he advised. "The closer you are to the selkie folk, the more powerful their draw will be—especially now that they have their hooks in you. And tell your brother, so that he can supervise you better. You have no business so far from home."

"And what if I can't stay away from the sea?" I asked. "Death seems more certain than living now that he's gone."

Mr. Lennie led me a few more paces from the edge of the cliff. "I could never advise such a thing, but there are legends of those who have successfully captured selkie women. I suppose it wouldn't be much different for a man, though they are a tad more feisty."

"Steal his skin?" I whispered.

"Aye. He'd never leave you as long as you had it in your possession. You'd have to hide it in a devil o' a place—some place he'd never think to look. It would ease your pain I suppose, to have him near, even begrudgingly."

"How would I do it?"

Mr. Lennie took off his scally cap and scratched his scalp. "Ye lure him."

"How?"

"I don't know what attracts a selkie man—whiskers and herring? You could try using your feminine wiles, though I wouldn't know what good it would do. What attracted him to you the first time?"

I smiled sheepishly. "He came to kill me 'cos he thought I murdered a selkie pup."

Mr. Lennie gave a hearty laugh. "I'd not propose you kill anything. That'll not get you the sort of attention ye desire."

"He also seemed very interested in my swimming."

Mr. Lennie's white brows shot up in surprise. "You know how to swim?"

"Aye, since I was a peedie girl. Da threw me in the ayre when I first started to walk. Ma was furious when she found out, but she got used to the idea when she saw I wouldn't drown."

"And your brother?"

"Blair is as tense as a stray cat on the ferry."

"I think like your brother. Stay as far from the water as you can. You don't want to be pulled under by a roost, or worse a selkie demon."

9

MADNESS

The hours felt like days and the days like months. Time was my enemy from which I could find no reprieve. Would Eamon *ever* come? The hour of certainty was gone, and Eamon seemed as out of reach as the moon.

Was my swimming enticing enough to be used as bait as Mr. Lennie suggested? Even the moon was drawn to the stars. Could Eamon be drawn to a plain human once more? As I considered using myself as a lure and stealing his skin, the thought sickened me. It was his heart I wanted to capture, not his skin.

I woke coughing and reached for a smoky blanket. Ash had blown down the chimney and re-lit the room in a dingy orange glow. I rolled on my side and shivered as the howling winds intensified outside. The weather was unfit for man and beast alike—curse the rainfallers and windmakers. Drowsily, I watched the fiery shadows dance across the stone wall. One of the shapes slowly transformed into a long graceful selkie. The playful creature dove and arched its back before leaping in the air and morphing into the silhouette of a man—a man so straight and beautiful, he caused madness in women. When I looked again, the shadow man was gone.

When the sun began to warm the small window above, I quickly dressed and found myself wandering down an unfrequented stretch of beach with only a vague idea of where I might go. Everything was damp—the air, the sand, the moor. The howling winds from last night brought in huge amounts of rain that made the ground dark and spongy. I eyed the rocky ledge above. It was not nearly as steep as the cliffs at the Bay of Linton, but it would serve as a menace, should I lose my wits again. Would I be so weak as to lose my wits again? Oh, bloody Hel, why hadn't I avoided the cliffs like Mr. Lennie instructed?

I tried to shake my head clear of Eamon, but every thought willfully and joyfully raced back to him. Should I prepare grouse or hen? Which would Eamon prefer? Should I walk along Galt Ness or the Bay of Furrowen? Where would Eamon be? I spread fresh rushes over the cold stone floor in the hopes that it would be pleasing to Eamon's tender feet. While bathing, I feverishly scoured my body so I would smell sweet to Eamon. Was the enchantment intentional, or was it something Eamon had innocently left behind, like a trail of scented oil?

Where was he?

At the Bay of Furrowen, I lifted my arms to the skuther blowing stiffly off the water. Low streaming clouds raced to the east and lifted my hair into hundreds of ribbons. How splendid it would feel to be totally submerged under a wet slippery blanket that would slide and mold perfectly to my skin. A foamy wave lapped at my feet and seemed to bid me invitation.

With a demure nod and a stretch of my skirt, I folded into a deep curtsy. "I accept your distinguished invitation." I hurriedly removed my dress before diving into the water with a small girlish shriek.

The skerry from my memory was not far off the coast. It was a barren little rock always full of resting tern, but most importantly it was the sort of place that would be enticing to selkies.

The water tossed me like jellyfish, but I sunk my head into the brine and scooped fiercely at the waves. By the time I reached open water, I was gasping and just shy of the skerry. Unbelievably, my legs began to painfully cramp, and I reclined back to stretch my ankles. All at once my legs seized, and as if in a nightmare, I began to get pulled downward by the powerful sweeping draw of a roost. I tried to kick free, but it was a losing game of tug of war. The small grey bluffs from the north filled my eyes as salt water flowed into my nose and mouth. I coughed and gagged, but more water flowed in and then the world glazed over into a gauzy paradise that sparkled with energy and life. I was weightless and truly happy, then everything went dark.

"What do we have here?" a battered voice asked amusedly.

Another man chuckled. "A mermaid I'd venture to say."

I opened my eyes and peered blearily up at two windblown faces. It was Albert Kirkpatrick and his son Henry, both fishermen who spent the bulk of their time in the North Sea.

Albert had permanently squinty eyes from spending a lifetime staring across the water. His son, Henry, was still handsome and near my own age. Both wore grimy, knee length slickers that smelled of salt and fish.

"I suppose you're right," Albert said with a twitchy smile. "But this maid belongs to Blair Swanney."

"I'd not be one of Blair's sheep," I whispered coarsely. The sea had turned my throat raw and sandy. I struggled to sit up, but my foot was caught in a net.

Both men gave booming laughs.

"How'd I get here?" I asked with a shiver as the green hills of Shapinsay whizzed by. I was in a cutter, fifteen or more paces long with two billowing sails that propelled the boat in a south-easterly direction.

"We scooped you right out o' the water," Henry said, enthusiastically eyeing my sticky wet underclothing. Albert popped his son in the back of the head with a stern look.

My eyes shot dazedly around. "Where's my dress—oh, bloody Hel." Mortified, I dove on a heap of netting and balled it into my lap. What had I been thinking, swimming in the waters of Furrowen? The wicked currents fed right into The String. *Stupid— stupid me.* I'd let my fantasies run away with me again. Eamon was the one truly to blame, but I was simply incapable of any anger towards *him.*

"Take my slicker, lassie," Albert said, offering up his oiled jacket.

"Thankee," I said lunging into his warm sleeves. "What must you be thinking?"

"I'm thinking that you're the best thing we've caught all week," Albert said.

"I'd say," Henry agreed. "Last week we toted up a barnacle coated boot, though I suppose it's not much good without a match. We find the dandiest things in the water." His emerald eyes moved down my pale legs before I could tuck them under Alfred's slicker.

I glared at him. "Does your mither know ye ogle women's legs in their time o' need?"

"And what is it you'd be needing?" Henry asked with a wink. "I'd be sure to give it to ye."

"Does that invitation actually work on the hens in the village?" I asked tersely.

Henry mounted his foot confidently on a box of fish and flickered his tongue at me.

"Don't mind my son," Alfred said apologetically. "He's a lecherous numpty in need of a wife."

"A wife?" I gave a false sounding laugh. "I'd not be volunteering. You can let down the sails. I'd be jumping out here."

"And face the wrath of Blair?" Henry asked with arched brows. "Not a chance."

"I can't help wondering what you were doing in the water," Albert said as he coiled rope between his rough, weathered hands.

I stared up at him, feeling a sudden urge to cry. The skerry. Could Eamon be sprawled out there now? Maybe even waiting for me? I struggled to keep my voice even. "I was fishing just like you, only my boat sank."

"Alone?"

"What happened to your clothes?" Henry interrupted. His probing eyes searched for holes in his father's jacket.

"They were washed away in the currents, of course."

"And who would Eamon be?"

I froze, retracing the course of our conversation. "Who?" I asked.

Henry adjusted his narrow brimmed cap. "Eamon. Ye told us to throw ye back in, that Eamon would come for you."

"Nobody was on the horizon," Albert added with a frown. "You would've died."

Oh Odin, the madness was growing worse. Why couldn't I remember any of it? "I—I must have been dreaming," I answered. "My father use to say that the sea can play tricks on even the most seasoned sailors."

"Aye," Albert nodded in agreement. "The sea has powerful magick. I once saw my dead wife in the middle of a tempest. It took three strong men to keep me from plunging into the crushing swells. Even now I sometimes wonder..."

I smiled with gratitude towards him. Albert kindly changed the subject after that, complaining instead about the low coin he was certain to receive for his superior fish. When we rounded the Balfour's peninsula, the sail was lowered and the boom swung wide. We would soon be arriving at the busy pier.

✶✶✶✶✶

Blair arrived home shortly after I did, but not before receiving an earful from Albert and Henry. The pair stirred quite a commotion in the village after blathering on about my supposed maritime delusions and my scantily state of dress. The awful facts did nothing to quell Blair's worries about me, nor did they hasten his departure and my freedom.

"I can't leave you for a mere moment," Blair raged as he stomped about the room. "Did you think I wouldn't hear of the things that's been happening?"

"What nonsense did you hear?" I asked sweetly while rinsing blood from a meaty red stomach. I was preparing to stuff it with tasty morsels of minced lamb and beef. Haggis was Blair's favorite dish, and I meant to soften him with its hearty flavor.

"The tinker saw you out by the Bay o' Linton tight roping on the edge of a cliff, and today, Henry Kirkpatrick boasted to a pub full of men that he pulled Kait Swanney out of the firth all but naked. You should have heard the roar that caused."

"Nothing exciting about that," I said.

"Curse them all to Helheim," Blair cried as he slammed his fist against the wall. "Henry has quite a different opinion on the matter."

My face heated angrily. "Henry is nothing but a snotty clype with a face like a skelpit arse."

Blair shook out his bloody knuckles with a wince. "He also said you were mumbling incoherently about an invisible man. You're scaring me, Kait."

"The currents were a wee bit stronger than I anticipated, and then I swallowed a whole laundry basin of water. You know what salt water does to the head."

"You were purposely swimming outside the bay? I would have thought you had better wits about you. Even Da wouldn't have allowed it."

I rinsed my hands absently in the sae-bink with a shrug. "Nothing bad happened."

"Nothing bad?" Blair repeated. He ran a hand through his curls and stomped a few paces away. "Twice you almost died, and now the whole village is saying bad things about you."

"I dinnae care about what the villagers think," I said. "Only your opinion matters. Do *you* think I'm insane?"

Blair collapsed in a chair and buried his face in his hands. My heart sank at his silence. If Ma and Da were alive, it would not have mattered so much, but Blair was all I had left.

"What of Magnum?" Blair asked dropping his shield.

"What of him?" I asked as I dried my hands.

"He's to be your husband if he'll still have you."

I glared at my brother. "Perhaps some good came out of today after all."

"I'll talk to him," Blair muttered. "He's not unreasonable."

"No," I cried. "Magnum and I will talk first thing in the morn." As long as Blair thought Magnum and I were still getting married, there was peace between us. Blair was a simple man with a short memory, who could not remember that he was not apt to get his way.

10

THE BONFIRE

The next morning, Blair's sheets were empty. Where was my pig-headed brother? An uneasy feeling crept into every pore. "Not Magnum's!" I groaned. "Please not there!" My mind raced to place my brother some place reasonable, some place I could bear to live with. It was then I anxiously remembered that one of the ewes was preparing to birth. Aye, that was it. Blair would have wanted to greet the wee lamb and see that it was well.

I rushed to my trousseau chest and rummaged through a stack of linens before spotting the small Viking pin cradled in a short piece of lace. Around the perimeter of the pin, two tiny dragons coiled in a battle that would end in one eating the other.

It was a bonnie pin, one that would look fine on Ma's black wool dress, but I resolved to return it to Magnum right away. It was one thing for Blair to mistakenly believe I would wed; it was another for Magnum to believe the lie too.

I rushed outside with the shiny ornament in hand, in time to see Blair loping through the fog at the peak of the pebbly road. "What do ye think you are doing?" I cried. "Can't you hear the sheep carrying on by the wall? They don't have enough sense to drive themselves away."

Blair halted the merry tune he'd been whistling. "Aye, I heard them, but this was more important. I've spoken with Magnum, and he's willing to forgive you."

I halted rigidly, overcome with sudden illness. "What do you mean?"

Blair strolled by with a smug and lazy air. "I told you I'd make things right. The marriage is back on."

"You've been nothing but a spoiler these last days," I growled to his back. "I wanted to speak to him myself." Now it would be even harder to break the truth to Magnum. How would he react? Yell? Become pissy? I cringed inside to think he might cry. I wanted to kill Blair for his role in it all, but I had to continue with his game. As long as Blair had no knowledge of Eamon, I still had a chance at finding him.

"You can thank me later."

I marched after Blair. "What do I need forgivin' of—nearly drowning—huh? I explained to ye what happened. The brine poisoned my head. Invisible men—ha, I don't even believe in them." Marry Magnum? Never!

Blair faced me with a frown. "Magnum knows nothing about that. I'm not stupid enough to mention it myself."

I narrowed my eyes. "Then what in Hel's domain are you blathering on about?"

"Have ye forgotten that you climbed off the Kirkpatrick's cutter in nothing but your skivvies. This didn't sit so well with Magnum, but fortunately he believes ye lost your dress in the sea. I'd keep him far from Henry Kirkpatrick, though. He told Magnum that you were inviting him to look with your eyes."

"He what? I did no such thing!" I gave an angry shriek then marched back towards the house. "I'll pop his lights out when I see him again." Returning Magnum's pin would have to wait. I didn't have the stomach to face him suddenly when we were so very much engaged. Henry Kirkpatrick on the other hand...

"You behave yourself tonight," Blair warned. "Magnum will be expecting a lady."

I swung around puzzled. "Tonight?"

"Aye, ye promised Magnum you'd be at the bonfire."

"No," I shook my head furiously. "I'm too busy to attend. I got Da's boat afloat once again. She's more seaworthy than she looks."

"What would Da's boat have to do with the bonfire?"

I stared at my brother as if he were missing an obvious point. "I'd be going out to Linga Holm."

"To that wee isle by Stronsay?" Blair cried. "There's nothing there. Why, Kait? Why in the devil would ye go there?"

I twisted a long tendril of hair as I puzzled over his excitement. I would exhaustively search the barren shores for any signs of my beloved, but this could not be obvious to Blair. "I've not been there since I was a peedie girl. I wish to see if it's the same." I tried to sound like a sensible lassie who would never dream of swimming such a far distance.

"You're not going!" he hollered. "You're going to the bonfire, like ye promised Magnum. I've made things right for you, and he'll be expecting your delightful and charming company."

"But why must I go, Blair? The village will be swimming with fair lassies. Why must Magnum set his compass towards me?"

"It's a comfort to me," Blair answered. "I don't pretend to know what sparks Magnum's eye, but you haven't been acting yourself. I fear you've been bewitched by something dreadful. You insist it's not the work of that selkie man, but it *is* black magick. Perhaps it is the faeries or the work of a felkyo. Either way, Magnum will love you and watch after you when I'm gone."

I gave a quick laugh that was meant to comfort Blair, but it came out sounding maniacal. "I've never felt better," I spluttered. Secretly I wondered if swimming around Linga Holm would have any effect in capturing Eamon's attention. Pretending to drown might even work. If only I knew where his somber gaze was directed.

Blair frowned down at me, but I couldn't meet his gaze. "Would it be so bad to have someone provide for you when I cannot be there? A little love in exchange for a few meals."

I turned the cool pin over in my fingers as I considered the horrible thing he asked of me. Surviving on kelp and cockles was more appealing than marrying the very old Magnum. I shuddered to think of his lustful blue eyes leering over my body in a possessive husbandly sort of way. He would expect certain intimate things from me. Oh Odin, save me! The very thought made bile bubble up in my throat. Why could Blair not see that he was only postponing his own happy marriage? It was my job to protect *him*.

"I'll go to the bonfire," I said. I'd be Blair's pawn for only a little while and play his game. I'd pretend that I loved Magnum, but most of all, I'd pretend that Eamon did not exist—that I did not dream of him every moment. "It's still early yet. I'll be certain to be back in time."

"Ye don't understand," Blair said with a rough sigh as he shoved a hand in his dirty pocket. "I can't let you go. It's not safe fer you to go to Linga Holm."

My eyes grew wide—warlike. "I'm going," I insisted. "I'll not be wastin' a whole day snapping beans and sweeping floors that are already clean."

"What will you be wasting? There are chores to be done around the croft and the garden is beginning to look neglected. Ever since we found the animal's footprints in the garden, you've spent more time gazing out to sea than actually working."

"You're leaving me anyway, remember?" I cried. "Who will mind the weeds—the terns—the wind?"

"I'll sit on that cursed boat all day long if I have to," Blair threatened.

My eyes darted around like a captured animal. In a shot, I took off towards Da's beached boat. I hadn't made it to the wall before Blair tackled me into the grass, painfully razing my cheek. "Get off me you bloody berk," I screamed.

I punched and kicked with all my strength, but Blair held me tightly and murmured into my ear, "Keep the head. Keep the head. It will be alright."

When I couldn't break free, I surrendered limply beneath him.

"Kait, what's happening here?" Blair asked in a rough, unsteady voice. He was still pressing his full weight against me with his chin pinned tightly against my temple.

"Nothing," I grumbled. "Now get off. I'm done fighting." It was futile to war with someone nearly twice my size, even if I had twice as much spirit. When Blair eased off me, I gaped up in surprise at him. Tears were streaming down his boyish face.

*****

A mountainous blaze was already screaming towards the heavens when Blair and I arrived. The heather and peat had been drying for weeks and were spilling a sweet mossy smoke into the air.

"Fit like, Blair? Fit like, Kait?" the villagers cried as they milled happily by with cheeks that glowed from the warmth of their ale. Everyone was too happy to remember the incident from the Kirkpatrick's cutter. Casks were set strategically along the street for an easy drunk—a gift from the Balfours for the speedy progress of the castle.

In front of the tavern, a fiddler masterfully worked his bow. Jiggy tunes filled the air with a taut energy that spun festive dancers gaily around. Near the seamstress's shop, a circle of women clapped rowdily for drunken husbands. I laughed at the lively and comical steps of men who pranced and jiggled like they were thirty years younger.

Blair eyed me protectively with his hands thrust deep in his pockets. "I'd dance with ye if your feet are itching."

"That would be an atrocity to the Dronsay Fling," I said with a grin as I ducked into the shadows of the smithy. "I think I'll spare you and all Orcaidians alike."

Blair chuckled and wedged himself next to me. "Good, you'd only step on my toes."

I smoothed the extravagant folds of Ma's grey wool dress. It was the finest thing I owned, but made me feel like an imposter. I fidgeted again and touched the mass of braids coiled on my head. The prissy hair was at Blair's bidding and soothed my guilt for making him cry.

What if Eamon should come while I was away? Aich. My time would be better served if I were staged in front of my own predictable fire or conspicuously strolling along the rocky shore of Galt Ness. "Go on," I urged my brother, already planning to melt into the darkness as soon as I let Magnum down. "I dinnae need you to hold my hand." I guiltily fingered the round pin in my pocket, my stomach curdling with dread. My eejit brother was the one who had encouraged him. It was only right that *he* should be the one to spring the bad news.

"I'd not leave yet," he mumbled as his eyes shifted through the crowd. I groaned. Of course he wouldn't leave. Blair would see Magnum and I together first.

Auor squeezed between two drunken seamen. I inwardly groaned at the appearance of a village goose. The others would be close behind. "It seems that just about everyone is here." She shot me an appraising look then smiled at the frilly arrangement of my hair.

"I suppose," I mumbled.

The seamen swaggered into the street, gutturally singing an ol' Norse war song. *We are brave like Odin. Into Helheim we roam! We will fight the ship of nails. Fight Etin's dead! Though we breathe the ocean floor, we will rise once more!* One belched impressively and sloshed his ale over his breeches.

"Do ye not think *anyone* is missing?" she asked with a gleeful bounce.

"I suppose Magnum has not yet arrived," I answered listlessly. I pricked my palm as I squeezed the pin tighter.

"Hmmmm, I wonder where Magnum could be," she said more loudly.

Finna and Ingrid joined the circle with excited eyes. "Where could Magnum be?" they cried in unison. "Are you missing him?"

Ingrid pinched my waist painfully. "Patience, dear. He'll be along."

"I'm not impatient. I'd be speaking with him," I announced.

The women giggled. "Go on, slake your thirst, Kait. There's to be a celebration."

Celebration? Utter nonsense. I impatiently scanned the crowd for Magnum's annoyingly happy face. The sooner I set things straight, the sooner I could return home. "Blair, why isn't Magnum here yet? Is he trying to woo me or not? Blair? Blair?" I turned and found that he was gone.

My eyes swept over crowd in search of him. Dancers were beginning to orbit the enormous fire, but Blair was not among them, nor was there any sign that Sloane had come swinging her abundant hips and enticing my brother away.

All at once a great commotion was heard along the way—the arresting and debilitating sound of what couldn't possibly be clanging pots and pans. The uproar steadily grew before Mr. Drever's horse and cart broke through the shouting crowd carrying a half dozen numpty men foolishly carrying on with their mothers' stolen cookware. Oh Odin, it was a bachelor banging!

"Ooooooooooeeeeeeeeeee!" the men shouted. "One less stud on the market! Fair lasses bawl your eyes out or take your pick! Come and see!" A pair of middle-aged bachelors fell over with laughter before one lost his hat in the road.

I froze when I saw that in the center of the ruckus was a half-naked Magnum Muir grinning from ear to ear! His comrades had painted him with a sticky treacle mixture and coated his hairy chest with a barrel full of white feathers! My stomach rebelled against a thousand feverously gnawing rodents.

"Congratulations!" Auor piped. "You'll be glad to know that Magnum is off the spry. His days of winching the bonnie lassies is over!"

"Not this day," I groaned. I backed into the shadows to search out an escape, but Magnum had already spotted me.

"There's my bride!" he bellowed with a broad wave of the arm. Feathers caught in the wind and lifted over the mob.

I shook my head wildly and withdrew another step. "I didn't agree to marry Magnum!"

That's when I noticed the blonde idiot hop down from the wagon. "Blair!" I screamed.

Blair eyed me nervously then strode off towards the nearest cask. I ground my teeth together then started after him. His barmy plan would not work. I would not be pressured to marry Magnum, neither would I be part of an engagement celebration!

"It's alright to be a little nervous around him," Auor told me as she caught my arm. I looked at her while absorbing her repulsive message. "He has his fair share of looks to be certain, but don't fear. He'll know his way around the bed since you're not his first woman, see?" She crowed happily then elbowed Finna who was adjusting her kerch.

My gaze returned to Magnum, who gave a giant smile before pounding his chest like a great feathered ape. With confident strides, he closed the space between us before possessively twirling me around like a weightless doll. "Are you surprised?" he asked.

The world spun around, and I staggered against him. "Aye, much too surprised, but we must speak."

Magnum laughed. "Easy there, take my arm before you fall and soil that fancy dress."

"No," I cried as his drunken friends swarmed us. With dismay I realized that the fiddling and dancing had stopped so everyone could ogle Magnum and me—the newly engaged couple. "We must speak alone," I rasped, eyeing the immense crowd. I brushed a few sticky feathers off my bosom.

"She wishes to be alone with me!" Magnum cried. "Shall I trust her to behave like a lady?"

"You misunderstand," I wheezed.

The crowd cheered and tightened around us. I no longer felt the wind nor heard the roar of the fire. Sour bodies formed a fleshy wall around us, while my stomach continued to chew, chew away. "Magnum…" I struggled to breathe.

"Kiss her! Kiss her! Kiss her!" the bachelors chanted.

The awful clanging continued.

"Kiss her! Kiss her!"

Magnum imprisoned my face in his rough hands and stiffly forced his face upon mine. His lips were lost in the beard, and I became sickened by the coarse and filthy fur that enveloped my nose and mouth. At once I felt his chapped lips open and separate on mine. "Never do that," I gasped pushing Magnum away. I drowned my face in my sleeve, but it was too late to take the kiss back. The moistness was already there.

Magnum looked down on me, hurt and confused by my reaction. "I'd have words—" I started to say, but a woman screamed and everyone's eyes were ripped away. Like an angry hive, the crowd began to swarm and men began to shout. As the horde of people thinned, I saw what was causing the commotion.

Mr. Drever's cart was trembling under a roaring mass of rolling orange flames. In the center of the cart's bed, like a flaming crown of glory, was an overturned chair, charred and crumbling from the flame.

"It's one o' the chairs from the tavern!" a woman shrieked. "Someone torched a chair!"

"Wood is too precious for such waste," Ingrid cried with tears glistening in her eyes.

"Who did this?" Mr. Trulloch roared over the chaos. Flushed faces looked blankly at one another. No one had seen a thing.

"Wait here with the women," Magnum ordered. "The culprit could be hiding at the rear of the tavern." I stared at him, wondering if I was to obey like a child. Magnum paused to push a loose strand of hair behind my ear, before disappearing through the fray.

"The kiss distracted us all," Auor observed with probing blue eyes. There had been nothing right with the kiss, and everyone saw it. Bewildered, I frisked my arms against the cold then paced down the street.

A meager pail of water was splashed on the inferno, but the flames only hissed and rose higher. Several more buckets were added by scrambling farmers. The shouting grew as Mr. Drever struggled to release his terrified horse. At once the giant beast reared up on his back legs and snapped the leather harness restraining him. I gasped in surprise and stumbled out of the way, just as the horse galloped by into the darkness.

I collapsed against the silver smith's shop with my heart throbbing inside my throat. As I looked up, a cloaked figure moved around an enormous water barrel before slinking into an alley. I started to shout out, but a glimpse of a milky white hand kept me from making a single sound.

11

A MORTAL LURE

My days separated from Kait were not liberating. I wished to be free and strong, but with each new sunrise, her tentacles sank deeper into my heart, and I could not clear my mind of her. She'd poisoned me—aye, that was it—a sweet poison that beguiled and imprisoned the weak. I hated her and doubled my efforts to be free by taking dangerous chances. Coursing through the fishermen's nets made me feel exhilarated, but the others hated me for it. After that, I ventured into the northern sea and teased hungry orca with glimpses of my tail before narrowly escaping into more shallow waters.

When a tempest pushed the rest of the selkie folk into caves, I found the briefest distraction from Kait. With an eerie fascination, I watched a foreign ship being tossed to and fro in the most crushing of waves. Under the weight of a sweevy, the central mast snapped then toppled into the bow. An explosion filled the air as the massive boat lunged into the jagged rocks maliciously hiding below the spray. Instantly a gaping black hole ripped into the side of the hull and began gulping up massive amounts of sea.

The loupers that spilled into the sea didn't understand the simplest principles of staying afloat and flailed away the last of their strength before sinking like anchors to the silty sea floor.

They were nothing like Kait. She was still clumsy, but the strength of her stroke was not to be teased. I saw the freedom she felt as the currents concoursed obliquely across her body and strained through her tiny toes. That freedom belonged to me as well.

With the briefest surrender I allowed myself to remember the entangled snare of gold she refused to tame, and the lure of blue, blue eyes. When the loathsome white cloth slipped from her shoulder, my eyes grew with surprise—Kait was pale were the sun did not reach. The delicate collarbone that peeked out from under the heavy wet cloth was white and enticingly tender to the eye.

She wasn't this way all over. With annoyance, I blinked away memories of speckled cheeks that had been browned by the sun. Her lissome spirit was too well formed for such a marked flaw.

Kait was as wild as the sea itself and unlike any louper I had ever spied on. I began to wonder if Kait was not just the source of my weakness, but perhaps in some terrible way, the cure. Almost instinctively, I pointed my nose southeast back towards Shapinsay, compelled to see her just one more time.

Kait's house was too quiet, but hadn't I felt and heard the emptiness all the way from the tip of The Galt? I swung open the door and traipsed boldly inside. The room was dark and uninviting, the cold stone floors chilling me all the way through to the bone. *I am a hunter not a seeker. She does not control me.* I began to retreat outdoors, but a tender little feeling deep in my heart stopped me. I gave an agonized sigh.

Crouching before a hollowed out place, I investigated the place where the fire had dwelt. In place of flames were delicate layers of white flakes that turned to oily powder when I touched them. Immediately I looked around for a place to rinse my fingers. On the wide stone table was an earthen basin filled with stagnant water. I was surprised and satisfied when the grime rinsed away without any filthy residue, but I was baffled by the slippery and foreign texture of the water. With the utmost caution, I lifted the bowl to my nose. No salt. The water was bland and hinted of sandstone and other unpleasant minerals that dwelled beneath the ground. In alarm, I set the bowl aside.

After that, I circled the hard place on the floor where Kait slept, then moved on to the wooden shelves holding dozens of tinkering curiosities. I played with some large black pinchers, then a pair of matching spoons before inhaling deeply. The warm, sunny scent of her skin was everywhere.

My eyes cut through the darkness at all of Kait's things. She was a mystery that needed to be solved. Part of my drive to learn was stemmed from my need to free myself of her—another part was the hedonistic side that found pleasure in exploring her. Perhaps I would even seduce her—ravage her lovely spirit as other selkie men had done to docile females before me.

I pondered this thought uncomfortably before turning to the spinning wheel in which she had been so proud of. I gave it a hefty spin before pricking my finger on the briery spindle. Sucking the tang off my finger, my gaze danced inquisitively over her bowls, tankards, trenchers, turnspit, and a kettle. Beside the basin was a mortar and pestle with a pungent green herb left inside. For some items I remembered the uses, for others, I would ask the elders later. In the corner was a malodorous pot that I avoided with a wide girth.

In the smaller room were two weevily little beds concave from wear. I puzzled over the second bed before meandering to the corner where I inspected a broom, mop, and overturned pail. I proudly remembered that these were tools for cleaning. In the window, I fingered a yellow spray of flowers before turning my attention to a large trunk tucked between the beds. At the bottom, I found a lengthy cloak, dark and grey, like the lift before a violent storm. I slipped it on and felt immediately disturbed by the rough grating texture. I began to remove it, but then hesitated. It would provide much needed warmth against the cold night wind.

Outdoors I took new notice of the smoky plume billowing obnoxiously over the island. Only a tidal wave sized fire could make so much smoke. I shook my head in disgust and kicked at a rock, considering what I should do. Venturing further inland would be risky, and I had been warned against taking risks. Besides, Kait's voice was lost in the wind, and I was unsure of her direction. Aye, I would wait.

I threw open the byre doors, re-examined the strange tools there, then terrified the hens by beaming rocks on the roof of their domain. After trailing around the garden and uncovering a vegetable that peeled away in layers, I looked up at the plume again. I couldn't help but feel that the fire was the reason for Kait's absence. I thought about my skin secreted away in the wall, and then I thought about the enormous fire. I was not afraid.

The shadows hid me as I moved closer to the smoke and noise. I was startled by the close proximity of so many buildings, but then had to remind myself that the loupers were not irritated by the presence of each other. Around an empty boat-yard and down the street I stealthily moved, the sounds of festive music growing louder. As I crept closer to the fire, I pulled up my hood. Many loupers were in the throes of each other like a colony of crowded ants. I curled my lip in disgust. After tucking in the last pieces of hair, I strode boldly into their midst.

Almost at once I discovered the source of the music. In the glow of the fire, a magician was bent over a creepie with a look of deep concentration on his weathered face. Vigorously he sawed a cloved bow back and forth across his shoulder, creating short bird-like shrieks that melded gloriously together. It bothered me to admit, but the brisk melody was more lively and wonderful than anything from my own world and seemed to be the reason for all the dancing.

My attention turned to a group of women dancing with their skirts hiked up over their knees. Their faces were burnished from the heat and alight with mischief. One shrieked as she unpinned her hair, then staggered and fell into a heap of fabric. Another woman staggered happily to her rescue. "Vaila, you're giving it laldy this night!" Her speech was slurred, and I wondered about the reason for so much joy and clumsiness.

"I suppose Magnum has not yet arrived." I jolted at the strained, unhappy sound of Kait's voice.

Pushing my way through the dense crowd, I found Kait idling among a group of older women. Her hair had been swept out of her face to reveal eyes so dark and frightened; I thought

I had mistaken her. A new dress exposed a long white neck and teased at the wee diddies hidden below. I took a calming breath and wondered at the reason for the fear…and the dress. *I am a hunter not a seeker.* Impulsively, I took a giant step towards her.

The magician's bow halted when a pod of warriors rode rowdily down the street in a cart, banging and clattering all sorts of instruments that were normally kept by the hearth. I held my hands firmly over my ears at the piercing and painful disruption. At the head of the warriors was reined a great beast that snorted his contempt for the subjects he pulled. I postured to fight when the men stopped, but instead of an ensuing battle, the newcomers were greeted with slaps on the back and shouts of encouragement.

My confusion changed to anger when a nearly naked man strode forward to address Kait. *Magnum, the one Kait's been waitin' fer.* He was grinning arrogantly above a heavily feathered chest trailing tiny white feathers. The display was an insult and mockery to birds everywhere, but even I could see it was a louper ritual meant to entice females.

I balled my fists at my side, debating what I should do. At once Magnum picked Kait up and birled her roughly through the air before placing her firmly and possessively in his shadow. I shuddered with rage before storming into a darkened doorway and snatching a chair. With satisfaction, the dry grainy wood torched easily before I sent it hurdling into the louper's vacant cart.

Withdrawing into the shadows, I watched the hungry flames explode into thousands of glowing orange tongues that illuminated the darkest corners of the street. Undaunted by my fire, Magnum captured Kait's face in his large hands and gave her a kiss. My throat constricted painfully when I realized that

Kait was choosing her mate! Losh, I was an eejit! I turned away with a grunt, furious with myself for giving in to such a pathetic weakness—a bonnie human girl. My failure had been complete the moment my flippers pulled out of the sea.

My pain coupled when I realized the immense pain searing through my arm. A closer look revealed that the sleeve of my cloak had been charred away, exposing fiery red flesh. Now I understood the elder's warning. Seeped in anger and frustration, I loped away in search of healing water. I hated Kait for drawing me to her, but most of all, I hated her for kissing the furry man named Magnum.

12

REUNION

I stared after the cloaked figure with bated breath. Had I imagined the flash of pearly white skin, or were my eyes playing cruel tricks? My mind couldn't be trusted any longer, but neither could I risk ignoring what I'd seen.

When the men sprinted towards the pier with their pails, I hurled down the street after the one individual who wasn't interested in extinguishing the burning cart. At the head of the close, I hesitated for only an instant before breathlessly darting in.

It was so dark between the narrow walls, I couldn't see my feet. Not wanting to fall behind, I grappled forward and bumped into a broken crate, scratching my knee. "Bloody, bloody," I hissed, while rubbing the sore spot. It took a few moments for my eyes to adjust to the more concentrated darkness. The alley was filled with heaps of trash and leftover building supplies. The rank, chippy smell of mouse droppings permeated the moist air. With a shudder, I turned to leave, but someone snatched my arm, and I chirped in surprise. At once I was dragged behind a crate of empty milk bottles.

"Why are ye following me?" the man's hot breath rasped in my ear. He was dressed in a long black cloak, his sinister face hidden deep in the shadows. My blood froze like ice in my veins. The man was redolent of evildoings—probably a murderer. I was a childish, daydreaming fool. Why hadn't I listened to Magnum and stayed put?

"I'd go back to my friends, I thought ye were somebody else—" My breath was knocked out of me as the stranger slammed me against the hard stone wall.

"Lies," the stranger hissed. His hood fell away and folded up around long waves of savage hair. "Ye wish to steal my skin."

"Eamon," I gasped as pain radiated through my chest. My relief was so great, I didn't know if I should laugh or cry. I slumped against the wall, unable to take my eyes off him. "I scarcely believe that you are here. Do I dare blink?"

Eamon's dark eyes grew with confusion. "Kait?"

I felt a delirious grin spread across my face. "Who else would pursue an arsonist down a dark alley?" In the darkness his milky skin seemed to emit a pale silver glow like unfiltered moonlight. Eagerly I fed upon his exquisite face—angular and brooding with the smallest imperfection at the tip of his narrow nose.

"Go back to your mate," he said with a venomous glare, dropping his tight grip from my arm.

"Magnum is not my mate," I said suddenly alarmed. "He wishes to be, but I've not chosen him. I wouldn't even have come, but I was tricked by my bampot brother." Curse Blair and his destructive plans! He had no inkling about what made me happy. I kicked a lead pipe in proxy and bruised my toe.

"You'd have me believe your florid words not my own eyes," he snarled. "Ye kissed the furry beast."

"Nae! He kissed me. My stomach is still churning from the horrible experience." My eyes darted over his face pleading. Wishing him to read my mind and feel the frenzied desire I had for *him*. I finally found him or he found me, and I was crippled with fear that he'd bolt. Couldn't Eamon feel the powerful draw between us?

Eamon's eyes dropped to his arm, and I noticed for the first time that he was awkwardly cradling it.

"What is it?" I asked with a frown. Eamon refused to answer me, so I brazenly pulled back his baggy sleeve. Just on the inside of his creamy white forearm was a fiery red wound no bigger than my palm. "You've been burned!" I cried.

"It's still on fire," Eamon muttered, glaring at his injury. "Only I can't see the flames."

"It needs to be cooled with water," I said urgently. I took his hand and tugged on him, but Eamon stayed rigidly planted like a mountain of stone. His eyes were widely driven on the place where our fingers were twined together. "It's alright," I coaxed in a soothing voice. I gave his hand a gentle squeeze, marveling at how soft and buttery his skin was.

"The water *will* take the pain away."

Large, haunted eyes scrutinized my face before allowing me to pull him through a row of worker's apartments towards the harbor. Like a small child, he moped silently along. "Ye don't need to be jealous of Magnum," I told him. "It's absurd. He's old with a married daughter near my own age."

Eamon scoffed and batted aside his hood as if it were bothering him. "Jealous? Selkies hardly know the meaning of the word."

I smiled to myself, realizing that Eamon was indeed jealous. His expressions were candid as a toddler's and very different than his own gruff words. I locked this information into my heart with joy and caution. There was much Eamon would hide from me, but still I dared to hope.

As two links of a chain, we loped down the grassy bank into the gently lapping water. Eamon sunk his arm into the cool water with a quiet sigh, while I crouched nervously beside him. The gritty fish smelling brine soaked through the hem of Ma's fine dress, but I didn't care. I was with Eamon and for a moment everything was absolutely perfect. Above the shimmery black firth, a full moon hung like Odin's thumbnail. Somewhere near the castle a dog barked.

"It cools," Eamon observed as he hunched knee deep in water. A chilly breeze blew black strands of hair around his face.

I smiled at him and timidly adjusted his hair behind an ear. "The fire will die in an hour or two if the burn isn't too deep."

Eamon watched my movements cautiously, never taking his eyes off my fingers till they were safe in my lap once again. "It's not deep. I'd not be so easily hurt."

"I was worried when you didn't come back right away. Every day I've been at the water hoping..." I trailed off, embarrassed. How very, very stupid I sounded—and needy.

"Why should I come back?" Eamon muttered with a black glance. "What do you and I have to do with wan another?" He stepped out of the surf and kicked sand off his feet.

"But you did come back," I argued after him. "Why were you at the bonfire if not for me?"

He shrugged. "There was a celebration. I came to celebrate."

I felt my brows arch high, outraged at the lie. "Ye came to celebrate my fake betrothal?"

Eamon glared at me a moment. "What does that mean—betrothal?"

"It means...oh, bloody, what does it matter? Ye won't leave again, will you?" I gave a panicked glance towards the water as if he would dive any moment. The water looked so cold. It would feel like shards of shattered glass against my skin when I followed.

"Ye got me curious now."

"Engagement to Magnum is a terrible thing, but you're the one who sparks my eye."

Eamon gave a gruff sigh and turned away. "What would ye have me do, become a *land louper*?"

"Aye, live on land; you're hardly a fish," I cried. "Where's your skin, Eamon?" I hungrily searched the shoreline for it. The effect of Eamon's long absence was working its madness in me. The selkie skin *was* the key to my sanity—no my survival. I had to have it; I had to keep Eamon with me always. Oh, bloody Hel, it was nowhere in sight. He must have hidden it.

Eamon clutched my arm painfully. "What interest do you have in my skin? Have ye not learned to never speak o' it?"

"I'm sorry," I gasped, terrified by Eamon's response. "I won't mention it again."

"I'd be going," Eamon said as he dropped my arm. "I can't stand this peopled place. It reeks of all the bodies."

"Nae!" I cried, throwing my arms frantically around his tiny waist and pulling myself into the shadows of his cloak. "Take me with you." I felt my sanity slip away, but there was no mourning it.

Eamon eyes batted shut with concerted effort. The wind lifted a few fine strands of his silky hair and fluttered it against my open neck. I could feel in my bones that a part of him was drawn to me—a stubborn, willful part. From under his chin, I gave a few strained breaths and willed him to love me, to feel me in his arms. Through his cloak, his muscles were as rigid and guarded as a statue. Still my fingers moved and explored brazenly over the arch of his lower back.

"Where would I be taking you?" he murmured.

The words couldn't spill out of my mouth quickly enough. "Into a cave, under a rock, or into the turbulent sea. I don't care as long as we're together."

"You're mad," Eamon hissed.

"I know." I buried my face into his neck. Miraculously his arms slowly lifted and circled gingerly around my waist. Where our bodies touched, his magick pulsed and quivered, penetrating through me like hot alluring sunlight. Eamon felt incredible, warm and satiny, but not at all human. His fingertips began to move timidly up my back, tenderly searching my spine through Ma's finely woven cloth. Where the gentle pressure of his touch moved on, warm prints of heat hovered before melting into my skin—a shadow of his touch. At last his hand slid down my side and gently cupped my waist with a gentle squeeze. I was too absorbed in emotion to say a word.

He cared for me.

Quietly we held one another—selkie and girl. It made no sense, but I didn't care. I'd stay in this embrace forever.

Against my chest, I felt his heart pound. For reasons I couldn't understand, Eamon would fight an internal battle that revolved around me. But, I didn't dare ask him about it. I was too terrified that he'd take offense and disappear forever. Terrified he'd notice how tightly he held me back.

"Kait!" Blair called from a street away. We both turned towards the smoky orange haze hovering above the rooftops. A lone silhouette stepped out into the street and called again.

"It's Blair, my brother," I said, tugging on his hand. "We need to leave right now. From Ward Hill we'll see 'im coming."

"What does he want?" Eamon growled, rigidly holding his place.

"He's going to try and take me away since I refuse to marry Magnum, the man you saw kiss me."

"Marry?"

"I'd never do it," I said. "Neither will I go to the Mainland. His body may be stronger than mine, but not his will. I'd come back to you again and again if you'd let me."

"I don't understand." He swept a strand of hair off his lip and gave me a rough look. "What does it mean to marry?"

I paused a moment. "Selkies do not marry?"

Eamon snorted but did not answer. He was still uncertain.

I was an ignorant fool. A selkie would marry no more than a bear would sit for scones and tea. "In my world, we make the most solemn oaths to those we wish to mate with. It's a promise that we'll always be together. But I'd never, ever mate with Magnum. He's not of my choosing. If Blair loves him so much, he should marry him."

"Your brother rules you?"

"O' course not," I cried bitterly. I glared at my brother investigating the length of the pier before shimmying down into the damp water grasses. "I'm not marrying Magnum, and I'm not going anywhere."

"Ye should go to him," Eamon said, making no attempt to hide. "He's a member of your own pod."

"What does that supposed to—what? Nae!" I gasped, stung by the dismissal. "Are you trying to shoo me away like a fly?"

"Kait!" Blair cried again. His voice lifted in the wind. "Running away isn't going to solve anything!"

"Ye misunderstand me," Eamon growled as he scaled down the rocks to join me. He took a few quick, irregular breaths as if he were uncertain of what to say next. He was so scandalously close; his sweet breath warmed my chilly cheeks. The close proximity of his body was too beguiling, even painful. Aye, that was it; he was fulfilling his purpose and causing me pain.

"What is there to understand?" I asked miserably, eyeing the sculpted white chest gaping from the shadows. Like a cathedral, it was majestic and beautiful, too magnificent to be supporting such a lousy cloak. "If I leave, I'll never see you again. I can feel how much ye want to dive below the surf and disappear."

"It's where I belong, Kait. Ye and I..." He shuffled his feet uncertainly and looked away. "It can't be."

"What have ye done to me?" I demanded to know with tears in my eyes. "I don't *need* anybody, so why do I feel so lost without you?"

"I've done nothing." His eyes darted evasively out over the water—evidence that he definitely did *something*.

"Then why can I hardly breathe without your permission."

His penetrating eyes turned back suddenly. "Then breathe all ye wish. Ye have my consent."

I stared up at him a moment, wondering if I was to be mocked. "That's not the point. Why did you come here? Do I mean nothing to you, or do ye always travel in disguise amongst ignorant humans?"

"I was curious, nothing more."

A small anger flickered inside me. "What were ye curious about, Eamon? Are ye curious about our sheep, the potatoes in our garden, or maybe the tools in our shed?"

His face hardened. "You know what I was curious about. I won't say it aloud."

"Is this why you destroyed Mr. Drever's cart, 'cos you wondered about the color of my dress?" I was certain that Eamon must care for me. This is what he would not admit. This is what I *needed* to believe.

"The cart was worthless," Eamon spat. "And I did the shaggy beast a favor."

I stared at him a moment, struggling to comprehend his ranting. "The horse?"

Eamon shrugged.

I boldly clasped his hand securely in mine. His fingers were cool and slender—and limp. With a look of terror, Eamon watched me kiss his salty white palm. "Swear you'll come see me again. If you are curious about me, you can learn me all ye wish. We'll start with my outrageously naughty hair and work all the way down to my stubby toes."

"I'm meant to be on my todd," he answered with false confidence. He tugged the cloak away from his neck like it was constricting his breath.

"Then why did ye cast your magick on me?" I cried as another tear rolled from my eye. "Why did you have to do it if you wish to be a hermit?"

"I know of nae magick," he said, but the lie was all over his lovely face. He knew the power selkie men had over human women. He didn't care for me at all, but enjoyed the longing and the tears. How easily I dismissed the legends! Of course Eamon would lure me in and then feed off my pain—that's what *all* selkie men did.

"I almost died twice 'cos of you!" I cried. "On the cliffs o' Linton I almost plummeted to my death, and in the Bay of Furrowen I was netted out like an eejit fish in a skirt. You owe me this much. Swear you'll see me just one more time."

His eyes shifted down the length of me. "These words are true? Ye almost died?"

"I was searching fer you," I admitted. "I can't help myself. If you leave without the promise of returning, I'll still search for you."

Eamon was quiet for a long time. "Then I'll come back."

Hope swelled in my chest. *Oh Odin, let it be true.* "Can I trust you?"

Eamon's dark eyes moved slowly over my face. "Nae, but if you dinnae go back to your brother, he'll search fer you and find me. Frankly, I'm not in the mood fer killing."

It was the wrong answer, and I felt my madness leading me to a place I could endure. "My brother...that makes sense. It will be easier for me to get away if I play the good sister. If he believes I'm getting married, it will be easier for both of us. I could show you around the island. We'll have to avoid Magnum of course. He won't be forgivin' of his bride gallivanting around with the most bonnie o' men."

"Kait," Eamon said softly, interrupting my whirlwind of thought. He gave an agonizing sigh and kicked at the sand. "I can't make any promises."

I gazed up at him, unable to process the awful hint that he might not return. "I know ye'll be back—even on the morra at Galt Ness."

13

A SWEET DISCOVERY

I didn't know which was stronger, the cry of my skin or my desire to return to its comforting hold. With my heart flying out of my chest, I fled back to the wall, the place I'd hidden my skin and immediately snapped out the living, breathing part of me. Trembling, I wrapped myself securely in my mantle's velvety waves and folded over the rough wall to recover.

When the horizon streaked with the dewy colors of morning, I unsteadily rose and peered down at my feet. They were smeared with blood and dirtier than I'd ever seen them. In my haste to cross the island, my tender feet tore on dozens of sharp, jutting rocks. With disgust, I wiped them on the damp grass then fought to kick off bits of green. In one night, I had been severely burned, cut, and nearly frozen. Land was more inhospitable than I knew. How absurd that Kait would have me return again and again.

The coarse grass stung my ankles as I hurried towards the open water. My skin was already inching and binding itself into place. As I bellied through the shallow waves, I happily remembered the magician's music that jubilantly pranced like porpoises in my veins, and the way Kait's fire blanketed my wet skin in warmth. Was land all bad? Kait's domain was a wee droplet compared to the openness of the ocean, but her stones were smooth and sandy under my feet and her thick walls served to block out the island's battery of winds.

And then there was Kait herself. I closed my eyes to fully remember the way she looked at me—the way she devoured me with hungry eyes. I could see that she was not well, clearly besotted by The Lure, but I felt responsible for her—a protector as my name declared. I decided then that it was *her* weakness, not mine, that would drive me to Shapinsay once more.

~Kait~

Blair was ruggedly pacing a trench in front of the croft when I spotted him from the moor. Behind him the sun was gloriously lifting above the horizon, turning the lift into a bonnie shade of pink raspberries. "Your wayward sister has come home at last," I said with a grin.

"You've gone too far," Blair cried angrily. "Perhaps I shall lock you up."

I gave a little skip. "That would be a wee bit difficult since we have no locks."

Blair furrowed his brow, confused at my happiness. "Ye were gone all night. Where were you?"

"Where do you think I was?" I twisted a tendril of fallen hair dreamily. My hair had all but collapsed into a great mass of tangled sea grass.

"I'm afraid to speak it," Blair said with a growl, "fer fear of driving you into the sea."

"Can't a bride have any private time with her betrothed?"

"You were with Magnum?" Blair asked with surprise.

"Mmmmm, fer certain."

"But he was searching for you as well."

"As I was searching for him. It was only a matter of time before we found one another." My fingers danced across the hidden bruise Eamon pressed into my arm. "If you had searched the boatyard you would have found us, but then we both would've been embarrassed."

A smile lit across Blair's face. "You were with Magnum?"

"Brother, ye are slow this day. Would you like me to annunciate more slowly?"

He laughed and ran a smoky hand through his hair. "Nae, will you be seeing him again before the oaths. I mean fer it to happen in a fortnight."

A fortnight! My bampot brother was insane. "I do hope so," I said with a yawn. "I hope to see him later today."

"What changed your mind about him? Yesterday you were not convinced you wanted to marry."

"My eyes were opened to certain...qualities. Do you really want to hear the details?"

Blair laughed again. "Nae, not in this lifetime."

Sleeping was impossible. The sun glared through the window and ticked away the moments till I'd meet Eamon again.

Oh, bloody, I needed to sleep. I'd not meet Eamon again with dark bags under my eyes. I twisted back and forth in the sheets, trying to find the perfect position that would lull me into a deep and beautifying sleep, but it was no good. When my heart felt ready to explode, I threw off the covers, scrubbed my face clean, and raced successfully past an unsuspecting Blair.

At the rocky coast of Galt Ness, I nervously smoothed my hair and licked my lips while searching the empty waves. In the distance, a tiny skiff floated across the mossy silhouette of the Mainland. I couldn't see the thousands of people that lived there, but to me it was no different than Thieves' Holm—a place of imprisonment. I pulled up the hem of my dress and traipsed across the rocky ledge so I wouldn't have to look at it. Folding up on a large damp rock, I watched a pair dolphins with glossy grey backs stagger through the firth.

An hour went by and then two. The sun moved across the sky and brilliantly reflected off the water. My heart pounded with surprise when a fish jumped into the air. With a disparaging sigh, I climbed down the jagged steps to dip my feet into the splashing foam. Cold water rushed up my leg and drenched the hem of my skirt. A bonxie laughed from overhead. "I'm not afraid to get wet," I told the speckled bird. "Is that what you're thinking?" The bird laughed again and sailed to perch on a crusty white rock nearby.

With a determined nod, I hoisted my dress off over my head, but then froze when I spotted a little grey head duck below the water. I caught my breath as I wildly searched the water's surface. Was it a selkie or was my mind playing tricks? A moment later, a black nose sliced through the surface and bobbed a hundred paces away. "Is that you, Eamon?" I squinted at the little grey selkie, trying to imagine Eamon wrapped inside. Keen black eyes

blinked knowingly at me. They seemed to be saying, *I see you too.*
"What took you so long?" I cried, scrambling to the edge where
the water churned and splashed.

The selkie twitched his whiskers and disappeared again with
a twist and a dive. My heart thumped a symphony inside my
chest when I didn't see him right away. Was Eamon having more
laughs at my expense? The bonxie flew away and another wave
splashed and retreated. Frantically I searched the waves, my hair
drenching in the repeated blasts of salty spray.

"Don't leave, Eamon! Take me with you!"

At once a great wet body hauled out onto the rock beside
me. I startled in surprise and rebounded against a jagged stone
wall. Gently the selkie bellied around and nudged my ankle with
his shiny black nose. "Eamon," I said with a nervous laugh,
dropping beside him. Boldly I slid my hand down his silky grey
back and along the edge of his rubbery tail. I mused that Eamon
was much, much smaller than the solid grey selkie I had seen at
the Bay of Linton. Wreathed around his neck were scalloped
patches of creamy yellow. The ring reminded me of a golden
chain—the adornment worn by a king.

As my fingers moved cautiously to his fore flipper and the
claw imbedded there, the skin wrinkled and loosened before the
velvety folds bubbled up like a cozy morning blanket. With a
flash of white, the skin rolled to the side while Eamon, the
man, sprawled unabashedly naked beside me. He gave me a dark
glance then gracefully sat up and bunched his skin protectively
around him. I stared at him, too mesmerized to move.

Like a newly discovered pearl, his skin subtly shone with
a silvery iridescence. *A quiet rainbow,* I thought. I marveled that
I could have missed such an extraordinary thing before, then
realized it was the first time I had ever seen his skin without

the rosy reflection of a setting sun or the glow of a warm fire. He was completely unfiltered. Even his full lips seemed to glow like a silver moonbeam. Completely enchanted, I reached out to touch him.

"I kept my promise after all," Eamon said, following the flow of my outstretched fingers with wide, fixed eyes.

"You're so warm," I murmured as my fingers closed around his hard sinewy arm. Above the taut muscles, his skin was a soft and satiny like a newborn bairn. When I realized the boldness of my touch, I dropped my hand embarrassed. I bit my lip and forced my hands to sit idle in my lap as my eyes moved over his hair, not black as I had assumed but very dark brown with silken threads of sable.

"My skin keeps me warm, but it feels good to dry it in the sun." He arranged it on a high rock beside him, out of my reach.

For the first time all day, I felt relieved and relaxed. Even my thin shift was drying quickly under the warm high sun. What did it matter that I was dressed indecently? I seemed covered enough next to Eamon's stark whiteness.

"Why bother drying it?"

Eamon looked over at me, and for a guarded moment, I thought I had offended him by my interest. "For the briefest time, when I sink under the surf, I feel even more buoyant. It's a wonderful feeling to be so weightless."

"I love that feeling. Fer me it's like flying through a slow wet sky." My eyes returned to the water, but I felt Eamon watching me—no scrutinizing me. He could not understand why I should swim. I was beginning to understand that for Eamon, everything was black and white. There was no swim a little, love a little. He did things all the way, and it confounded him when others didn't follow suit.

"I want to ask you a question," he began slowly.

I smiled, pleased with his interest. It made me feel a little less one-sided—less pathetic. "Is that not why we're here? Ask me anything you want." My eyes drew criminally across his broad shoulders and down his narrow hips and thighs.

"Why are humans obsessed with fire?"

"Obsessed?" I gave a short laugh. "Is that how you see it?" I ran a finger playfully outside his fiery red burn. Eamon held as still as a salamander, closing his eyes lethargically to my touch.

"It's how we all see it," he said. "Loupers can't congregate together if there isn't fire present. I've seen this many times even though fire is dangerous." His eyes fluttered open at his own epiphany.

"I suppose we like the light and the warmth. Like your skin, it's a comfort to us."

Eamon nervously searched out his skin, still safely perched where he'd left it.

I awkwardly rolled a pebble under my fingers. "Aren't you supposed to try and seduce me?" I hadn't misunderstood the women. Eamon was clearly supposed to try and ruin my life. Was I too impatient or was Eamon not a typical selkie?

Eamon's black gaze snapped back.

"Do ye want me to seduce you?" Eamon asked in a bewildered voice. Incredibly, his eyes were round and worried like he didn't have the foggiest idea how to seduce a woman.

I felt my cheeks burn with embarrassment. "I was just wondering what your purpose in coming was. Did ye have pity on me?" The gods were finally pouring out their fortune on me, but I felt unworthy, even suspicious. I peeked over at his sumptuous, silver lips, imagining how they would feel parting and pulling on mine.

"Ye asked me to come," Eamon answered with a sidelong glance. "There is no more motive than that."

I twisted my hair around my finger until it snagged. "It's just that the selkie men in the legends ravage their innocent young victims before drowning them in the sea."

"We're back to this?" He sniffed and tossed a pebble. "Which part appeals to you?"

"Neither part, but if you're secretly plannin' on killing me, I'd like to at least get a kiss out of it." My heart raced at my own brazenness.

"Ye want me to kiss you?" Eamon asked with a look of alarm.

"No," I said with an impish smile. "You beguile me even now. *I* want to kiss *you*, if you can promise that nothing bad will happen."

"I can't promise anything," he said in a gruff voice. "I'm not to be trusted." His dark eyes dropped curiously to my own lips then softened.

My stomach twisted into a tight quivering vise. "I'll take my chances."

Eamon froze as I sunk my hands deep into his wild hair, his eyes paralyzed on mine. As our lips slowly and hypnotically melted together, a dangerous warmth aroused deep in my belly while my heart fluttered with pure joy. Eamon's fingers lifted hesitantly to my neck and then brushed gently against my cheeks. I shivered with pleasure and leaned into him. At first his lips moved cautiously, even placidly beneath mine, but as his enthusiasm grew, his kiss grew more powerful, more in control.

The heat slowly and dangerously rolled like ocean waves that refused to recede. Like a predator sensing weakness, Eamon secured my face in his strong hands and plunged his tongue, hot and foreign into my mouth. I kissed him exuberantly back, and after awhile, peeked up through my lashes, trying to memorize the burning black eyes and the silvery lips that passionately moved beneath mine. As I pulled away, Eamon objected with a soft growl.

"This is what ye shared with the man, Magnum?" he asked in a gruff voice. His smooth chest rhythmically rose and fell between us.

"No, not even close," I breathed. I stared transfixed at the shine on his sumptuous lips. Beneath my shift, my heart recklessly raced like a loose woman. Kissing Eamon was shameful and scandalous, and I would do it over and over again without regret. How could I make Eamon understand how much I loved him? How much my sanity depended on him?

"Your cheeks are flushed," Eamon observed with a relaxed smile that lit up his face like the sun. He awkwardly pushed a blonde straggler behind my ear. His fingers lingered behind my neck as if they were always meant to be there. "Aren't ye well?"

"It means I'm happy," I said with a broad grin. "Your cheeks are splotched pink too."

Eamon touched his cheek like it couldn't be true then gave me a bewildered look. "Then I must be happy too."

14

A MATTER O' TRUST

Selkies have no interest in time. We leisure our life away, playing and surviving, taking little notice of the sun's tireless pattern of rising and falling. When I became aware of how slowly the sun inched across the lift later that day, and how immovable the shadows had become, I became irritated with myself and took to racing a stocky male through the harbor under the eyes of a hundred hungry sailors.

When I returned to The Galt, I wasn't surprised to find Kait mounted like a figurehead on the rocks with her thin under dress twisting like a cyclone around her willowy body. It felt strange to realize she'd been waiting for no one but me—I *was* no one. I held my breath and dove deeply through the kelp, troubled by a relentless irking in the back of my mind. When I ascended back to the surface and saw her frenetically searching, I realized I'd been waiting for her too.

"There's someplace I want to take you," Kait said later after she'd kissed me. She playfully nudged the corner of my chin with her nose, like I had done before I shed. Her tangled mass of hair shifted over my bare shoulder, and I was instantly filled with her scent—sea, sky, feather, and something new—me. My kiss had inadvertently marked her, and I was surprised by how much this filled me with a sort of strength that had nothing to do with the sea.

I retrieved my pelt and dressed my shoulders like a cloak. Kait combed her fingers through her hair and pretended not to watch through strains of gold. She had not yet learned not to threaten my skin with her interest. "Where are ye taking me?" I asked stiffly, uncertain I wanted to leave the safe and predictable boundaries of sea. My mantle wiggled and shifted in between my shoulder blades in preparation for a dive.

"I dinnae mean to frighten you," she said nervously. "But, I mean to take you someplace safe you can go when your skin is...off."

"Your domain."

"No," Kait said quickly. "Blair wouldn't understand. He is mistrusting of the selkie folk and a firm believer in the old legends."

I searched her face for signs of treachery. Kait had lured me in even deeper with her frisky red lips, but still I wondered what she would do with me. It was not too late to fight, kill, or even retreat. Still, I didn't feel like doing any of those things. Kait left me feeling too blissfully wounded to care for the harpoon she had hidden. For now I'd follow her wherever she took me. "And ye are still foolish enough to trust *me*?"

Kait picked up her damp dress and held it to her chest with large searching eyes. "Aye, I have nae choice. Your will is my own—life or death, it all consoles me."

"Ye underestimate your own strength and will," I added. I had nae desire to discuss The Lure or any other selkie weapon. It wasn't just that it bothered me to think about those powerful things; they were not fer the muted ears of land loupers.

"I'd not be upset by what you've done," Kait said with a peculiar smile that made me feel a twinge of guilt. "You can keep the key you hold to my heart." She flung her hair over her shoulder and climbed up the wall with her toes splayed like an amphibian over the rocks. I watched her a moment. Who was luring the other? My mind relived the way her soft lips folded so domineeringly around mine and with a surrendering sigh, I leapt up after her.

We left the cascading tier of rocks and stretched out over the rolling green heath. Strange emotions stirred in my chest as I watched Kait swish along with long, purposeful strides that were neither graceful nor feminine. She was different from the other women—wild, lovely and more powerful than she knew. She snuck peeks at my bare spirit when she didn't think I was looking and often touched my arm or shoulder when she irritably spraffed about the crimes of her brother and the man named Magnum. She made me feel important.

We had just crossed over the small wall that divided Kait's territory when another stone house appeared. "There," Kait said excitedly. "It's empty as a washed up shell."

I looked warily at the domain, confused by the unfamiliar scent of a lone woman. "I dinnae understand. Who lives there?"

Sensing my hesitation, she took my hand and pulled me towards the door. "Nobody anymore. It once belonged to a felkyo."

"You'd bring me to a witch's house?" I asked, alarmed.

"No worries," Kait said as she thumbed the door's rusty lever. "She's been shipped off to Thieves' Holm."

I quietly padded inside the dark dwelling and looked dismally around at the felkyo's large amount of filth and clutter. Soiled clothing was strewn about the tables and chairs, while food encrusted trenchers reeked from an unused wash basin. A little grey mouse scurried into a crevice at the base of the wall. "I'll make a fire," Kait said with a sigh as she stepped over a greased boot. "Night still clings to these stone walls."

I batted the herbs drying from the ceiling and rained tiny leaves into my hair. I slowly circled the wee room. In the corner was a straw bed that reeked of mice and mildew. I glared at the vile sleeping container before hunching over a blackened figure etched in one of the stones. A closer inspection revealed the crude and troubling image of a single selkie. His long neck was arched high above his flippers as if he were barking fer help. Whoever had drawn the majestic being had imprisoned it on land *and* in stone. I smudged the awful omen into my hand. Losh, what was I doing here?

"I'm sorry about the clutter," Kait said, sweeping her hands together. Small flames were smoking heavily behind her and clouding the room with ash. "I'll fix it up, then it won't be so bad."

"Ye mean fer me to live here?" I asked incredulously. "Do I look like a filthy land lou— " Kait's eyes dropped to the black dust staining my palm. I cut myself off and glared out the filmy window. She wouldn't understand, and I didn't wish to hurt her.

"No," Kait said as she moved cautiously around a table like she might snag me with a net at any moment. I felt all my muscles tense into tight knots, still unwilling to flee from her. "When you come visit me, you could stay here. In two days time you won't recognize the place. What harm is there in visiting?" She took my black smudged fingers and held them to her pressed lips before peering into my empty palm. The selkie inside was gone.

Kait's blue eyes moved rapturously over my face as if I were great and important—as if I were her entire universe. "I love you, Eamon," she murmured as she pressed our interlaced fingers against her wee pillows—that soft, warm place she purposely treasured beneath her dress. I felt weak, confused, incapacitated. "I don't wish to be overly greedy, but I'd have you here as much as possible."

"Why are ye doing this?" I asked. "Ye slither like a serpent and snake me with your words."

"Because I always want to be with you," she said with a pale, frightened expression. "Do you deny feeling anything for me?"

My heart pounded at the agony of being pulled in two different directions. Kait was not contrite, but would *still* beguile me with wheedling words. "What are feelings if not the voices of the dead? They are as cold and meaningless as the stiffs thrown from the ships."

Kait looked confused a moment then laid her fingers on my arm with the touch of a butterfly. "No, your feelings are the compass of your heart. They tell you which way to go. When you are angry, do you not fight? When you are frightened, do you not flee? Your feelings are good. If you feel love for me then why not love me?" Hope filled eyes lifted to my face before she timidly slipped her arms around my waist. She seemed to sense my weakness—the part of me that longed for her.

I took a deep breath and boldly slid my hands down the coarse fibers of her dress and rested them at the small curve at her narrow waist. Kait fed me the confidence, even permission to touch her freely. She made me feel wonderfully reckless, even dangerous. A selkie who'd take what he wanted. Aye, I'd convince myself that I was the one in control.

Despite the cloth between us, Kait felt warm and luxurious beneath my fingers—like I was stealing a treasure from the loupers. "I know nothing of compasses, but I'm drawn to you," I admitted gruffly as my breath fluttered over her hair. "It's a weakness I can do nothing about."

"Loving someone is not a sin in my world, and I doubt it is in yours. Liking me is not bad."

I froze with the awful fear and betrayal. It was much worse than she knew, but I wouldn't say so.

"Eamon," she muttered as her red lips pressed against the open place on my chest. The warmth of her breath stirred against my raw skin and made me ache. "What is going on in your head? Your silence tortures me."

"Kait," I crowed, breaking free of her and grasping her tightly by the shoulders. "Ye make me feel as if I'm falling apart."

"It's supposed to be that way," she cried, suddenly flustered. Her eyes were large and uncertain. "I haven't been sane since ye first tried to kill me. Please don't leave, or I'll die of madness."

I dropped my hands and turned away from her pleading gaze. "I'm here right now," I muttered.

"But, I'd have ye promise—"

"I'm here *now*," I growled. I would dwell on Kait later when she wasn't needing me so exquisitely. I slumped inside a fraying chair and picked at a piece of untucked straw. "Tell me about the felkyo that lived here. I already feel the curse o' her presence. She marks the walls with evil messages."

Kait looked worriedly towards the drawing I destroyed. "It was only an innocent drawing not a spell. Tipper couldn't have known ye were coming."

"You've been here before?" I asked, practically falling out of the chair, feeling suddenly ensnared by four walls. What was I doing in a chair? What was I doing under a roof?

Kait planted herself hurriedly between me and the door. "Aye, a few times since she left, but it wasn't mine to clean. It'll be better next time ye see it—of this I swear."

I pulled my skin more tightly around my shoulders and surveyed the door behind her. Kait assumed I needed a tidy space, when I really just needed exalted blue sky above my head and salty sea air springing in my lungs. But I wouldn't break through her to get it.

"She isn't a real felkyo," Kait added urgently. "Most of the villagers were just afraid 'cos of how strange she acted. When her husband died, she was driven to madness."

I narrowed my eyes, disturbed by the lingering presence of the old woman. "Mad? What sort of dwelling have ye dragged me into?" Kait circled around me while I furtively followed her every move. Her sunny hair was twisted and tangled by the wind and riotously dangling above her waist. It didn't bother me as it should have, neither did I feel like leaving anymore.

"An available one," Kait cried. "Tipper's not that bad. She searches. That's all she does—all day long. I suppose that's why she never had time to clean." Kait tilted her head and a mass of hair swept unnoticed across her shoulders. "When she gets bored searching here, she searches the other houses on the island. At least the ones she can get away with. Weeks ago she searched the Balfour's manor and was caught. The next day the constable hauled her off to Thieves' Holm."

"Thieves' Holm—I think I know this woman. She has long grey hair—unattended by the sea or a comb, and she's withered like beached welk."

"Aye, but how do ye know her?"

I shuddered at the memory of the ghastly old woman. "She drives a hard look across the firth towards Shapinsay. At times she loses her wits and wails like a wounded animal. All the selkie folk know her. It's an unpleasant place to haul out 'cos o' the noise."

Kait's face wrinkled in pain, and I wondered about her compassion for a stranger. "She wails?"

"I don't think she sleeps," I said, slumping lazily over another broken chair. "Perhaps if she found what she was looking for she would do us all a favor and haud her wheest."

Kait crouched to pick up a hollowed container off the floor. "You want her to be quiet just for your convenience?" She gave me a biting glare. "Did it occur to you that she might be in pain?"

"Ye needn't worry. There are no injuries. The ol' welk is stronger than she looks." I flicked a fly off my arm and looked around for more flying predators.

"No wounds don't mean she isn't hurting," Kait said irritably. She clanked the container roughly on the bink then turned on me. "There is a pain that comes from the heart that is worse than being stabbed."

I felt my brow tighten in confusion. Kait was unaccountably upset, and I didn't like it. I struggled to understand. "What kind of pain would cause such madness?"

Her eyes moved slowly over my face as if she were confounded by my question or perhaps distracted by some other troubling thought. Her lips opened, but it was an eternity before any sound came out. "Pain your kind would know nothing about," she muttered. She turned away and subdued her thoughts into the crackling flames.

I crept cautiously behind her and slid my hands around her slender waist. Kait let out a soft breath and leaned into me. "It's ye that I wish to soothe, not the old felkyo," I said softly. "Dinnae be angry with me fer that."

Kait rotated under my arms and looked up at me with the same haunted expression that plagued her the night of the great fire. "Tipper's plight was right under my nose the whole time. Can ye not see that her pain is the same as mine? When ye leave me I feel the same pain. I am no different than her."

I shook my head confused. "I don't understand. You are nothing like the hag."

"We are the same," Kait insisted. "Tipper was enchanted by one of your own kind, and now she fruitlessly searches for the one who does not love her in return. If you leave for good, I will become like Tipper. The first signs of madness have already started."

"She is nothing like you," I growled, ruffled by Kait's persistence. "And you'll never be like her."

"Prove this to me," Kait challenged with a frightened look that twisted painfully inside my chest. More hooks! More snares! More nets! Losh, I didn't care!

My lips crushed down on hers as I gathered her face in my hands. I was the one in control this time and Kait the underling. I'd fully taste and savor what I'd had only glimpsed before. Behind Kait's rosy lips I explored more deeply with an impatient tongue that couldn't be satiated. The sweetness of Kait hinted that there was much more yet to taste. Kait, in return, pulled and tugged with heated breaths that only lured me in more deeply. A single tear rolled between us, and I startled to taste that a part of Kait was sea.

My face rolled alongside hers. "You're crying. Have I done something wrong?"

A sad smile touched her lips and cheeks now blushed deeply with my kiss. "It feels like a goodbye kiss. Oh, Eamon, tell me this isn't it."

I steadied her chin as a second tear trickled down her cheek. "This isn't the last time you'll see me. You've opened my eyes to kissin'. I'll be back after the sunrising." I kissed her cheek and picked up the stray tears with my lips. Salt melted pleasantly over my tongue.

Kait gave a tearful laugh and wiped her tears away with a fist. "You promise?"

"I can't be trusted, but I'll be back." I warmed inside to know that I had pleased her. Pleasing Kait felt like a safe venture I could do again and again.

A large, mischievous grin spread across Kait's face. "You've never kissed a woman before?"

I smiled down at her and bumped her ear gently with my nose. "Aye—once this very morn. I'm still reeling from the experience."

She shifted my hair pensively through her fingers. "Then ye have not killed any women either."

"Not yet. Would you be volunteering?"

Kait laughed and gave me a quick, delicious kiss. "You shouldn't make death so enticing."

"Kissing a human is not what the elders promised," I said with a steady gaze. "You are not succumbing to me but the other way around. Kait, you are fire, and I'm to be burned all over again."

"I'd never burn you. Why do you fear being together so much?"

I adjusted my skin between us. "Ye are a land louper, and I am a selkie. We are natural born enemies."

"You are not my enemy!" Kait protested. "You are not pure selkie, but a magnificent man. Look at how much we are alike!"

"Open your eyes and you will see that ye are the hunter, and I am your prey," I answered as I pulled away from her. "It has been so for thousands of years. You'd wear our coats on your backs as if they belong to you. The oil from innocent burds light up lamps all over the islands every night. How can we see the light and see the coats and not feel anger? Can ye not see that our skins are prized more than our spirits?"

"It's not the way of Shapinsay," she said defensively. "Fire lights up our nights and wool warms our bodies. I have always loved the selkies. Even my Da who sailed the high sea, only had interest in fish. Only a fool would not see that the eyes of the selkies too closely resemble our own."

"You see the world differently than most loupers," I murmured. I wanted to believe Kait, believe that she loved the selkie folk and honored selkie life. This *felt* profoundly important.

"I'd not ask you to love my brother or love Magnum," Kait spraffed anxiously. "I don't care if you hate them. It's me I wish your eyes to settle on. Can't you see that the spirit beneath your skin is what I long for? I value your skin only 'cos it is part of you."

My hand drew protectively to my coat. It felt less safe than it had a moment ago. Kait was more clever and enticing than I could predict. If she could lure me on land, could she also steal my coat with more of the same tricks?

"I wouldn't take it," Kait said. "If I tried to imprison you on land, it would only make you hate me, and that would be worse than you leaving."

"More wheedling words," I growled. How could Kait know the right words—know how much I wanted to stay with her? Like an orca, she would detect my weakness then ruthlessly attack over and over again. But my skin would never be hers. She had underestimated the strength of a selkie man.

"I only wish to touch it," Kait said decisively. "What harm can there be in that?"

I shifted my skin quickly away from her and held it around my throat. "Do ye think I'm a fool? There's nae need fer ye to touch it. It's mine."

"Aye," she said with a small smile. "I know it's yours, but I only want to feel it dry. It was wet before."

I narrowed my eyes suspiciously. "Why?"

"I'm curious. You are much stronger than me. If I try to run with it, you can pummel me to a bloody pulp."

"I no longer feel like pummeling you. You are nothing but a wee lassie—too small to offer me any contest."

"Then hand it o'er."

I glared down at Kait, wondering at the trick in her words. She *was* too small and too slow to cheat me of my skin. Where was the trap? Slowly I shrugged out of my skin. "If you run with it, I'll come after you with a vengeance. Maybe even kill you."

Kait smiled again, undeterred by my threat. I reluctantly watched her take my skin with surprising reverence. She looked up at me with a glimmer of a tease then ran her fingers down the tight yet supremely fine hairs of my coat, pausing at the thicket of hairs that crowded between my shoulder blades. "It's beautiful," she said dangling it over her legs to admire. "And not just any ordinary coat. It's a coat for a king—see the gold necklace you wear about your shoulders?"

"There's nae king worthy to wear my coat," I said gruffly.

She laughed and pulled it up over her shoulders, briefly nuzzling the smoky hairs against her nose and cheek.

I mused it was large enough for her to disappear under with room to spare. She began to turn my skin over. "Don't touch it there," I ordered, reaching for her hand, but she ignored me with only a flicker of glance. Every muscle in my body contracted as she gently glided her open palm along the smooth interior. The skin didn't respond to her but hung as inanimately as an ordinary blanket. This seemed strange to me.

Her eyes fluttered up in surprise. "It's as warm as your own flesh," she gasped.

"It's the living part of my skin," I said, relaxing only slightly. "The part that feels me and molds itself accordingly."

"It knows you," she said with a happy coo.

I nodded. "I'm useless without it, as it is without me."

She presented me back my skin. "I don't believe that's true. You are more like me than you care to admit."

"You are not a selkie, you couldn't understand. There is a connection between a man and his skin."

Kait looked up at me with a strange expression but held her tongue. I didn't have to read her mind to know what she was thinking. She wished I was human, endlessly bound to dry, rigid land. If I let her, she'd ignore that part of me that had flippers and a tail and would mold me into a ridiculous farmer or fire-maker. Losh, what was I doing here?

"You've had your feel. Are ye happy now?" I adjusted my skin around my shoulders. It clung and shifted, making its own comfortable adjustments.

"Am I the first human who has ever touched your skin?" she asked.

I stared at her a moment. "Ye are the first human I have ever spoken to." I suddenly felt like a traitor, a loathsome traitor who'd creep out of the sea and never look back.

She gently touched my skin again. "Eamon, ye can trust me."

"I can't do this," I muttered shaking my head. "The water calls me." I stumbled backwards for the door. I needed to think—clearly—when Kait wasn't watching with frightened blue eyes that rivaled even the deepest sea.

Kait seemed so certain of what she wanted, but was it really her? Eventually I would have to admit to myself that she was blinded by madness. I could not blame her for her weakness; selkie men had been punishing mortal women for thousands of years. But what of my weakness? Was it insanity that made me want to embrace my enemy as a lover? Was it insanity that made me want to completely trust her? Maybe Kait was the biggest lure of all and I was a fool.

Kait reached out to touch me then dropped her hand. "I—I'm sorry," she cried. "I was only trying to soften you to the idea—"

"What idea would that be?" I asked with a glare. "To dis-tract me into believing I'm safe? To touch my skin when it's loose and vulnerable?"

"You *are* safe," Kait cried with horror. "I was just trying to show you that."

"You show me only boldness and treachery." I lunged past her and into the blaring light. The smoke from the fire was slowing my senses and impairing my ability to think clearly. I stubbed my toe on a jagged stone then staggered towards the scent of the sea.

"Don't forget, you made me a promise," Kait wailed to my back. "You said you'd come back on the morra."

"I lied," I growled, but I didn't mean it. I was a fool who would always be lured back by Kait.

15

EAMON'S RESOLUTION

Would he come back? He promised he would, before promising he wouldn't. Which was the truth? The games tortured me, but wasn't that the mission of selkies—to make women miserable? Oh, dreich day, it was working!

Still, I was consumed with thoughts of him. I would play his games and think—think hard of him. Think of the curve of his jaw and the soft depth of his voice. I'd remember with crystal clarity, the hard slender of his body and the way he grinned so suddenly and mischievously. With every step towards home, I felt the space between us grow. Oh Odin, it was driving me mad!

He was more troubled than I knew and deeply suspicious of all humans. If I ever saw him again, I would work hard to dispel his fears about me, but I would never, ever force myself on his skin again. Stupid, stupid me. The awful fear that consumed his divine face when I touched his skin tormented me. Why had I pushed so hard?

The only thing that gave me hope was his kiss—not the one I had given him, but the one that he had taken so passionately without the smallest prompting. The warmth still lingered on my lips as I dizzily recalled it again and again. Eamon had enjoyed the kiss too and seemed decided to sample my lips again. If only I could know for certain that he would come, that he would forgive me.

By the time I pushed through our door, the earth had softened into a dusky shade of lavender, and I realized that I was exhausted. Had it really been two days since I'd slept?

Blair looked up expectantly from his driftwood chair. A sweet cloud of smoke swirled around his head. "How is Magnum?" he asked, regally lifting away his pipe and blowing out a stream of smoke. He had decided to grow out his beard again, but the result was a scratchy blonde halo that marred his youthful face.

His question stopped me in my tracks. I scratched a mosquito bite grating under my sleeve. "Oh, Magnum is fit like. Never better. He took me out on the loch in his wee dinghy. It was…um…nice."

A triumphant smirk twitched at the corner of his lip. "Did ye catch any trout?"

I ground my teeth together in restraint. "I only have interest in eating them, not catching them." I collected the food encrusted trenches lying on the table. "Would it hurt you to soak these?" I snapped, waving the remainder of Blair's lunch under his nose.

"I sold the sheep today," he said.

I drew in a sharp intake of breath. "They're gone?" My eyes swiveled to the window, blatantly green and empty of white woolly bodies. I'd been so distracted by Eamon that I hadn't noticed how quiet it'd been out on the moor.

"Even the new lamb born last night. But dinnae fash yourself, Ian Gillis was anxious to double the size o' his flock."

"You're really going to leave?" I asked slumping in a stiff backed chair across from him.

Blair blew out a long slow breath of smoke while I fanned the cloud aggressively with a couple of forced coughs. "Will ye miss me when I'm in the Mainland making the world's finest whiskey?" he asked.

"Ye dinnae have the first idea of how to make whiskey," I snipped. "It'll turn to poison and gag in the throats of dogs."

Blair looked amused. "Hmmmm, Mr. Yorston has a bit more faith in me. In fact, everyone does."

"What of our home?"

"You and Magnum can do with it as you wish. The Balfours will find another renter if you choose to live at his place. You won't miss the croft when you're keeping Magnum warm at nights."

"I'd not be leaving my home," I said. "Ma and Da wouldn't approve of both of us leaving."

Blair shrugged and took another drag on his pipe. "Suit yourself."

I chewed on my lip a moment, despaired by the fact that I'd have to find a way to double my increase. "Blair, the night of the bonfire, everyone seemed to know about the engagement but me. One moment I'm watching the gay festivities, and suddenly I'm dragged into the middle of a bachelor banging."

Blair tapped his pipe on the bink then looked up with a worried expression. "Would you have cooperated any other way?"

"It wasn't right what you did," I mumbled. "Arranging my marriage without my consent. It was... embarrassing. Such a cruel thing will come back and bite you in your arse."

Blair's voice turned authoritative, and I hated him for it. "I'm still the patriarch in this home, and I did what I thought best. You will marry Magnum; it's a good match—a necessary match, see?"

I bit back the urge to tell Blair that once again he would not have his way. That my betrothed was a bampot with a face like a gorilla's back. My brother needed to believe I was hopelessly in love with Magnum, else I'd never find time to steal with Eamon. "Magnum is a dream," I said instead. "A strapping man to be sure."

Blair smiled and bit down on the stem of his pipe. "I'd be visiting my own bride too. On the morra if ye'll be alright. Sloane wants to show me her dress and decide on a day. We'll be dropping a ring into Mr. Yorston's vat before the day's done."

I twisted a napkin through my fingers. "What, no bachelor banging?"

Blair laughed. "I suppose I'll be stripping down before I return. Her friends will insist upon a good show. If you wanted to come, I'm sure Sloane would let you sleep with her. It'll only be for three days."

Three days without any interference from Blair? I brightened considerably. "I'd not impose. Besides Magnum and I have our own chipper plans to make."

Eating my anger worked. The next day when Blair ferried off towards the Mainland, I took my anger out on Tipper's house instead, sweeping and scrubbing floors till my fingers were raw and wrinkly. After the floor was gleaming, I changed out the straw in the mattress and even rubbed the windows till an emerald green shone in from the moor once again.

When her house sparkled, I returned home for food. I was stocking a low shelf with the last of our wrinkled potatoes when I heard the door squeal on a hinge. "Eamon?" I cried, turning around. My heart leapt with pure happiness when I saw him standing beside a tin of blooming Sea Pinks I had collected that morn. My breaths quickened at his flagrant, in-your-face beauty. "Ye kept your promise."

He glowered at me through a streaming curtain of dark hair. "What are promises if not labels for meaningless chatter?"

I tried not to laugh from the overwhelming joy I felt. "You are feeling more selkie and less man today," I observed with a tight lipped smile.

"I always wake selkie and never man," Eamon grumbled. He was as bare as a newborn bairn with no skin in sight. Through every human interaction, Eamon remained durably ignorant to his own nakedness. His skin was most assuredly hidden in the most remote and clever of places—far, far out of my reach.

I removed my grimy apron and tossed it playfully on the butter churn. "Then maybe ye should not speak at all, but hit me in the head with a rock. I won't resist."

Eamon glared down at me. "I'm not opposed to speaking when there is something important to be said."

"There is something on your mind," I observed. "Is it important?"

"When did Magnum take you to the loch?" he growled.

"Loch?"

His black eyes moved aggressively over my face. "Are ye deaf?"

"Nae....what?" My brows wrinkled in confusion. "You heard what I said to Blair last eve?"

He crossed the room and inspected a pewter thimble before turning around. "If I'm near I hear everything."

"How near?"

"If I'm in the voe, I hear."

"You can hear me from the voe?" I cried.

"When did Magnum steal you?" he repeated with a growl.

"Magnum didn't take me anywhere," I said dazedly. "I lied to my brother so I could free my time for you. He'd never let me out from under his nose if I hadn't."

Eamon's eyes dropped to his tender white feet. "You told your brother that you enjoyed your time in his dingy. I thought I would have to kill him."

I stared at him a moment, stunned by his passion and jealousy. "You needn't worry about Magnum. I will set things straight with him soon enough." I took a few timid steps and boldly wrapped my arms around his hard, silky middle. "Did ye not know that ye are the one I love? By your own design, I could never love anyone else."

"Do ye wish to break free of me?"

"No, I like the way I feel, especially now when I'm allowed to hold you like this." My heart pounded vulnerably and garrulously between us. Did Eamon guess how truly pathetic I was without him? How brazen and shameless I was behaving? Blair would kill him right here and now to find me alone with a naked man.

Eamon buried his face in my hair. "I couldn't stay away," he groaned. "Nae matter how much I tried."

"You mourn your feelings for me?" I asked sadly.

"No, I mourn the sea."

"But, we are surrounded with water."

His silvery lips pressed against my forehead. "The sea is nae longer the same fer me," he murmured. "I spent the night thinking, and I've decided that I prefer land if that is where ye are."

I stared up at him—his heavenly words slow to condescend into my dull human brain. "Ye'll stay on Shapinsay?" I asked slowly. The words felt false on my tongue. Eamon's jealously for Magnum seemed suddenly strong enough to move mountains. I rejoiced at the brilliance of my own lie.

He gave a weak, uncertain smile. "Aye."

A selkie man stay voluntarily with no hostage or trap? Oh Odin, it couldn't be true. I'd wake tomorrow to be a hundred year old hag who forever searches. "Ye'll stay forever?"

"I can't make promises—tides can change."

Eamon must have made an excruciating arrangement with his skin, but it was good enough. Over time I'd convince Eamon that he wanted to stay forever. My brain began to buzz with happy plans. "Thankee, Eamon," I spluttered breathlessly. "I feel like I can breathe again."

Eamon gave a wide grin, and I threw my arms around his neck. "Keep saying that you favor me. It gives me strength and soothes my conscience."

"Heaven knows I need you," I whispered into his ear. "Odin may strike me dead if I'm lying. I need you—I need you—I need you."

Eamon gave a glorious smile before picking me up and swinging me around. "Then you shall have me here. The ol' welk's house is less repulsive than it was yesterday."

I stumbled away from him with a laugh. "I'll make it comfortable for you here. I even brought you something." I fumbled through an old feed sack to retrieve a pair of freshly laundered trousers and a crisp white leine. "To keep you warm," I said with a bright smile. "The wind can be brutal at night. I couldn't find Da's old cloak, but I'll start on some pampooties for your feet right away."

Eamon took the bundle from me and quietly fingered one of the tiny gathers. "My thanks, Kait. I hadn't thought to..."

"I know it's a big change," I said with a worried smile. "But, it's necessary to blend in."

Eamon turned the leine upside down and peered through the baggy armhole with a wince. "This upper covering has tethers. It's a flourish of some sort?"

"They're not tethers," I corrected. "They're ties to keep your leine in place." I slid the leine over his head. Eamon intently watched my fingers busy themselves first at his wrists and then below his throat.

Next, I showed him how to slip into his trousers. The slacks hung dangerously low on Eamon's very narrow hips. I stifled a giggle.

"I'm funny in your louper clothing?" Eamon asked with a glare.

"I'm sorry," I said with tight lips that wanted to break into loud claps of laughter. "You look a little out of place, like a mermaid wearing a bonnet."

"I feel out of place," Eamon said, trying out a couple of awkward steps and shaking his foot.

"Are you harboring bees in those trews?" I asked with another giggle.

Eamon glared at me then began to remove his trousers. "No—no!" I cried. "Leave them on. They'll be better once I steal some of Blair's panties and maybe a belt too." I brushed up to him and kissed the soft bluish skin of his neck with an encouraging smile.

"Panties?" Eamon asked with horror. "There are more clothes to put on?"

"Perhaps your trousers won't feel so coarse against your delicate skin with something soft inside. Ye'll like them." I stood back to appraise Eamon in his new clothes. He looked handsome, but far too exotic to be wearing the extraordinarily plain clothes of a peasant.

Eamon bunched the waist of his trousers into a fist. "When will you tell Magnum that you are not his to claim? This makes me impatient."

"I'm certain he's already guessed, but we'll speak in a day or two. I'm more fearful of what Blair will do when he finds out I'm not marrying Magnum."

"What will he do?" Eamon asked.

"He'll try to take me to the Mainland, but I won't go. He's counting on Magnum to take care of me—the eejit even sold our sheep. The wool was our primary source of income."

"Income?"

"Money, food, clothes," I explained.

"I'll get you more sheep," Eamon announced fiercely. "This island is full o' the hairy beasts."

"Ye can't steal sheep," I blurted. "They'll send you to Thieves' Holm to live with Tipper Gray. Besides I can't handle them all myself, and I'd be tanned by the ornery old men at selling time."

"What will you do?"

"Don't worry about me. I shall eat fat hens all the daylong if I must." I playfully pulled at the waist of his baggy trousers. Eamon gave a mischievous grin and staggered closer. "Tell me more about these keen ears of yours. I'm very interested."

Eamon's cool fingers glided and wove through my own. I shivered happily. "My ears are no different than any other selkie man or woman. We must hear well with our ears submerged underwater all the time."

"Have you been eavesdropping on me fer long?"

All humor left Eamon's face. "Since I've returned from the hunt, you're all I've thought about. Everywhere I go, I isolate your scent and hear your sing song voice. You're not the wan going mad."

"Yesterday ye mentioned your elders. Are they your parents?"

"Nae, my parents were snagged in fishermen's nets and drowned when I was still a young burd."

"I'm so sorry," I said. "My own parents died only a few years ago. The rattle slowly stole away their breath. It was painful to watch them suffer."

Eamon contemplated this deeply. "We are both orphans."

"Blair's all I have left."

"Do you miss your parents?"

"Aye, I miss my father for his adventuring heart, and my mither fer her companionship and soft words. You may have noticed that there are few women on the isle."

Eamon picked up a knife and inspected the point. "Why would I notice that?"

"I'm glad the other females don't spark your eye."

"You're the only wan I see," Eamon said gravely. "This is crime enough."

I gave a sad smile, but didn't pressure Eamon to explain his great offense. "Since the death of my parents, Blair and I have struggled to keep food on the table, but today I'm not worried. You make everything seem alright."

Eamon mused on this quietly a moment. "I'd take ye into the sea if I could. Beneath the waves, there is a safe and beautiful world full of delicious things to eat."

"Like raw fish?" I asked, scrunching my nose. "I'd rather swim and collect seashells in every color of the rainbow. Oh—and I want to see a manta ray fly."

"You sound like you've already been there," Eamon said with a laugh.

"I've a good imagination. Will you take me there?"

"Right after you grow a watertight coat and learn to hold your breath."

I gave a happy sigh and went to tend to the stew bubbling over the hearth.

Eamon wiggled his nose at the heavy aroma. "What are ye doing?"

I flipped my hair out of the steam. "I intend to feed you. You'll soon see that land is not something you just have to endure."

"Kait, I intend to still hunt."

"Right now you'll eat," I insisted. I ladled the creamy stew into two large bowls. "You don't want to leave, and I don't want you to leave. This makes us both happy. Now sit." I nodded towards a straw backed chair.

Eamon looked anything but happy, but obediently sat. I sat beside him and presented him with his own bowl of Cullen Skink. I took a nibble of potato, while nervously watching Eamon inspect a spoon. When he decided which end was most useful, he lifted a sample of smoked haddock to his lips. He slugglishly rotated the bite around inside his mouth. "Do you like it?" I asked eagerly.

His dark brows pinched together. "It's fish?" He peered at another cream sopped morsel on his spoon.

"Of course. I've thought this through—you eat fish. Do you not?"

Eamon smiled and the rest of the spoon's contents disappeared into his mouth and then a second more heaping spoonful right behind it. "It's already dead and not fighting," he happily mused as he shoveled in a fourth spoonful. At once, Eamon grimaced and gagged. Out of his mouth rolled a partially masticated chunk of potato.

"What is it?" I cried. "It's only a piece of mild potato."

Eamon continued to gag and carry on, clutching at his throat as if I had fed him poison not potato. "I'm so sorry," I cried frantically, patting his back. "I thought everyone liked potato."

"It's a vile root from under the ground," he gasped. With watering eyes he searched for drink. I rushed for a pitcher and poured Eamon a mug of freshly pumped well water. Eamon gulped at the water before violently wrenching and spraying the flagstones. He jumped out of his seat coughing and spluttering as his mug rolled to the floor and cracked. "What—is—it?" he rasped.

"It's only fresh water," I cried, confused. "I drew it this morn."

"Water?" his eyes grew outraged at the lie.

"I suppose it's not like the water that flows over your tongue when ye fish. The salt is missing. I drew it from a well out back."

"Well?" He narrowed his eyes suspiciously. "I never saw a well."

"It's behind the empty beehives. There's a small wall around it so the wee ones don't fall inside. It's quite deep."

Eamon's eyes grew large, and he became appalled all over again. "It's under the filthy *ground*?"

"Of course," I said irritably. "Did ye not know what a well is?"

"I can still smell and taste the soil on my lips." Eamon gave a hacking cough and made a show of violent shuddering.

"You're overreacting," I said, shoving my hands on my hips. "I don't taste or smell a thing!"

Eamon leaned on the bink as if he needed great support. "It's a sad disability I can do nothing about."

"Well your water would kill me!" I snapped. "A quart full would make me shrivel up and turn to sand. The salt is poisonous to humans."

This got Eamon's attention. "Then ye must not drink salt water," he said. "Also I must not eat and drink things from under the filthy ground."

"I'm sorry," I muttered reluctantly. "I didn't know how you felt about roots."

"It's forgiven," Eamon said. He slumped in a chair and watched me finish my own stew with his nose wrinkled in disgust.

After that, the low gray clouds rolled in, and it began to drizzle. We curled contentedly in front of the warm hearth while Eamon listened to me blather on about Blair. He was surprised to learn that he was more than just my sibling—he was my twin. He shared my outrage in Blair's attempts to rule over me and was quick to point out that I could have just as easily been birthed first.

Learning things about Eamon was difficult. He was robustly proud of the life he spent largely under the sea, but slow to share with me the mysteries of the selkie folk. He was still learning to trust me. With a great deal of prying, I discovered that he had two older sisters—pod members that he hadn't seen since he was a wee bairn.

When the tiny panes of glass turned a glimmering shade of pitch, Eamon closed his eyes and reclined sleepily on his side. "I'd be going now."

"No," I said, curling up beside him. "It's raining and cold. There's nothing out there for you."

"The selkie folk sleep in the water," he said with a yawn.

"The bed is not as bad as it looks."

Eamon looked blearily over his shoulder at the freshly stuffed mattress. "I'd not be sleeping on that."

"Why not?" I asked affronted. "I fixed it just for you. It's fresh and soft as a wave."

Eamon pulled me easily into his chest. "That bed belongs to a felkyo." He playfully nuzzled my neck before positioning his chin near my cheek. My lids set heavily over my eyes with one happy thought. Eamon and I were alone, and Blair would be gone for two more days.

16

TRANSFORMATION

My fingers sleepily explored the empty blanket beside me before my eyes sprang open. "Oh, dreich day!" I gasped when I realized Eamon was gone. Behind Tipper's broken loom was a stack of neatly bundled clothes. I scooped them up and indulged my nose into the very human scent Eamon had inadvertently left behind. My attention shot to the window as I clutched Eamon's lein to my chest. A cold, miserable drizzle was still soaking the ground. *He's only hunting*, I told myself. *Or exploring, or killing sheep.* Oh Odin! I resisted the impulse to flee to the beach in a maddening and futile search for him. He was coming back, wasn't he?

I paced Tipper's small room till I grew dizzy then stared hypnotically into the fire. When I could stand it no more, I fished out a hunk of burnt peat, carefully lifted my skirt, then peed over the lot of it. I'd punish myself no more and divine the color of my husband's hair. It was tradition for the women to know long before the men even asked. As the small urine soaked cake dried by the fire, I resumed my pacing. Eamon told me he intended to stay, but that was before he disappeared. What was the word of a selkie? *We're natural born enemies*—that was what Eamon had said. I couldn't stand not knowing and was desperate to know Eamon's heart. He seemed as elusive as the wind. Could he ever in a million years devote himself to a human woman? When the stink grew ripe, I cut open the peat and stared wondrously at the center of the cake. A black center with sable streaks gleamed miraculously back at me. I squealed with delight then threw the evidence back into the flames.

~Eamon~

Kait toppled into my chest when I stepped back into the felkyo's little house. "You're shivering!" she cried, frowning at the rivulets streaming out of my hair. "And without a stitch to keep you warm. I'll get you a blanket and some clothes."

She bolted away, but I snatched her arm. "I brought ye something."

"But, Eamon—"

I pressed into her hand the shell I had retrieved from the floor of the northern Sea. It was bumpy and white with a bright yellow opening that gleamed. "It was in a place ye couldn't go. I thought you'd like it."

Kait stared at the shell agape. "You brought me a gift?" She turned the shell carefully in her hands and held it to her ear.

"Nae, I brought ye a shell," I answered. "You were curious about them before."

Kait smiled up at me brightly and held the shell to her chest. "Thankee, Eamon. It's better than the queen's own jewels." Happy to have pleased her, I watched Kait place the shell in the center of the bink. She arranged it this way and that, before returning with a flirty skip.

There was something different about Kait, and it took me a moment to realize what it was. Her hair had been combed to a shine without a tangle or knot in sight. When she moved, voluminous yellow waves bounced gently over her shoulders and arms. I gaped at her strange human beauty, so clearly opposite from a selkie.

"I was afraid you weren't coming back," she said with ravenous blue eyes that floated down the length of me. Humans were always so interested in selkie spirits, even though they chose to swab their own bodies with coarse fabric. They could adhere to the vile customs all they wished. There was only one louper body that inflamed my curiosity.

"You mistake me fer a selkie who is strong," I murmured before gently kissing her. "I'm incapable of doing as I should." My time away had been too long, and I feared that I had missed much. Did Kait twist her hair like she does when she's nervous, or did she repeatedly cross and uncross her legs like she does when she's waiting? Did she search the voe for me or even think of me at all? I realized then that Tipper's house smelled of human food. Kait had been cooking over the fire again. It smelled intriguing.

Kait smiled roguishly up at me and twisted *my* hair around her finger. "Are we to be cooped up in Tipper's house forever?"

"That is my plan," I answered, pleased with her attention.

"What if I wanted to take you somewhere?" she asked.

"Do you wish to start a riot? Everyone can see what I am? I will be hunted by the men, and the women will trail me home."

Kait's eyes dropped with a not so coy smile. "Aye, it's true. When you flaunt yourself, it is plain you are a selkie, but would it be bad to try and fit in a little better? I don't want to always hide."

"How would I fit in?" I asked, following her as she swayed around me. She pressed her lips against the curve of my spine then gave my hair a playful little tug.

"We are more similar then you care to admit. Ye have ten fingers and ten toes, two eyes and a mouth, but your hair is not worn in the custom of our men. And ye cannot go streaking about the village. This will be quickly awarded by a trip to the Mainland jail."

"Ye wish me to hide beneath your father's clothes again," I responded dismally. I could already feel the itchy fibers rubbing against my flesh.

"It would be prudent when we go out," she said, musing over this and more. "Would you be opposed to a little help?"

"Help?"

"Mr. Lennie is like a friend. He's the village's trowlie doctor; the only one who knows you exist except my bampot brother."

"Take me to him if ye trust him." Kait would soon learn that there was nothing I wouldn't do for her. I had chosen a new loyalty and would mourn the sea.

I disguised myself like a human once again and allowed Kait to pull me across the boggy moor. The drizzle continued outside while a cold mist rose from off the ground, hiding the dirty yellow sheep that bleated in the distance. We were both soaked when we reached the hill where the doctor's modest domain was perched. It looked just like Kait's house except the roof was shingled with greenish slabs of stone.

A little man with red cheeks and a shock of white hair opened the door and smiled warmly at Kait. "Kait, fit like? Ye seem to still be living."

"I brought a friend," she said pleasantly.

The doctor turned and stared up at me. "Good heavens, Kait, what have ye done? I didn't think you'd actually go through with it."

What was *it*? I gave Kait a questioning look. The loupers were speaking in riddles.

"I haven't done anything," Kait said, flashing me a guilty look I'd not seen before.

"Is she supposed to do something with me?" I asked gruffly.

"Be a good laddie and let me take a look at you," the doctor said. He lifted his half-moon spectacles to peer up his nose at me. "He'd not be your betrothed I'd wager." He chuckled at an unknown joke.

"You know he isn't," Kait responded. "That's a debacle in itself. Magnum was promised me without my consent."

"There's nothing wrong with my ears," I said. "Why do you speak as if I'm not here?"

"Will you allow me to look inside your mouth?" the doctor asked eagerly.

I glared down at the land louper and held my silence. It didn't matter why he wanted to look in my mouth—his life was as thin and tenuous as spider's web.

"May we come in?" Kait asked. "We need your services."

"My heavens, where are my manners?" the wee man cried. "Come in and find yourself a chair."

We followed the doctor inside, and I immediately wrinkled my nose at the pungent smell of damp earth and weeds. The walls were covered with rough wooden shelves all holding bowls and bottles filled with powdery cures in sickly shades of green, grey, and yellow. There was a skull promptly displayed in the center of it all. I glared at it and wondered about the hidden dangers of the little man.

Mr. Lennie saw me looking at the skull and wrongly assumed I was afraid of him. "It's meant to be a warning to the pesky little faeries," he said gaily. "Dinnae fash yourself over it."

"Ye killed him?" I asked.

"Good heavens, no. I leave the killing to the queen's soldiers and of course your kind. You aren't in the mood for killing an old man, are you?" He lowered his spectacles and eyed me playfully.

"I'd not feel so confident if I were you," I warned. The louper was earthier than most with dirt under his nails and a moldy scent that made my skin crawl. I fantasized snapping his neck.

"Eamon wishes to stay with me," Kait interrupted. "Can you help me change his appearance?"

"Eamon is it?" Mr. Lennie asked.

"The name is fer Kait's use only," I growled.

"I'll be needing your silence," Kait told him. "Not a soul can know that he's been here."

Mr. Lennie adjusted his spectacles. "Aye, aye, but will he let me touch him?"

Kait eyed me nervously. "Of course."

172

Mr. Lennie scratched his scalp and peered up at me. "His hair gives him away. It's as long and carefree as a maid's."

"Ye'd cut my hair?" I asked Kait with surprise.

"I thought ye understood," Kait said with a pained look. "I'd not have ye angry with me."

I thought about the many advantages of being invisible. "I'd walk among the land loupers, and they'd not know the difference?"

"That would be the general idea," Mr. Lennie said. "Though I'm not certain it would work. The laddie's a wee too bonnie for his own good, and there's still the matter of his skin. It's too... pearly."

"Perhaps a hat would provide enough shade to mask it," Kait offered. "One with a very large brim."

"Kait?" I said. "My hair has *never* been cut."

Kait mournfully took a handful of my hair and stirred it in her fingers. "I don't wish to see it go, but you must decide. It will allow you to stay with me forever. We won't have to hide."

Mr. Lennie closely followed this conversation. "Is it the custom o' the selkie men to always wear long hair?" he asked. "And are they all so smooth?"

"Does this matter?" Kait snapped.

I glared at the eye sockets of the skull. "Cut it."

Mr. Lennie disappeared into another room and reappeared a moment later with a shiny tool equipped with pointy twin blades. I gruffly sat in a chair while Kait anxiously bit her lip.

"Ohhhhh," Kait cried, when the first massive lock spilled to the floor. She scooped the hair up and held it to her chest. "Oh, Eamon! How can ye ever forgive me? What have I done?"

"It will be alright," I soothed. "It doesn't hurt."

The little man continued to hack away the lot of my hair as if he were enjoying himself. As each streaming lock of hair fell away, Kait cried out before stooping to pick it up.

"It's only hair," Mr. Lennie observed with a sad shake of his head. "You're carrying on like a loon."

"It's Eamon's hair," she sobbed with a giant hairy heap held against her chest. "You'd never understand." She looked up at me with tears glistening in her eyes. "I'm so sorry, Eamon."

It was then I realized I loved Kait.

Mr. Lennie stood back to examine the results. "It's nearly convincing," he said with a grin. Kait froze with my hair clutched against her. Long brown shafts of hair folded over her arms and dangled over her knees. She was still sniffling and streaked with the most pitiful tears. I didn't understand Kait's torment, but it made my anger towards the little man grow. *He* was responsible for her pain.

"Nearly?" I asked. My fingers quickly cleared the short disheveled pieces lying over my ears.

"He looks plenty human. Can ye not see this?" Kait snapped at him. Her eyes were glued with horror to my scalp.

"There is still more I can do," Mr. Lennie said. "It's still too dark to look like an ordinary islander."

"What would ye do?" I asked.

"Isn't it obvious, laddie? I'd make it lighter." The old man chuckled and swept hair clippings off my shoulder.

"I can't bear anymore," Kait wailed. "Ye'll change him too much."

"Do it," I commanded. "I'd stealth among the loupers unnoticed."

The louper chuckled again and went among his bottles to inspect the labels. He picked up a wide necked bottle filled with a gritty orange paste, held it to his nose, grimaced, and then chuckled again. "Dungan sane—should do the trick."

"It's not necessary," Kait cried energetically. She dropped the hair and latched onto my arm as Mr. Lennie worked on dissolving the orangey paste into a bowl. "A hat will cover the lot of your hair," she breathed into my ear. "Ye'll see."

My finger stroked the curve of her jaw. Her golden freckles were no longer strange to me, but simply part of her—areas that had been kissed with rays of dappled sun. "I'd go where ye go," I said. Hair or no hair—what did it matter? I only wanted to be with Kait. She'd see the wisdom in my disguise later.

Kait wilted dejectedly against the wall while the louper dabbed the paste over the remaining spikes of my hair.

"We mustn't wait too long," Mr. Lennie said, "or he'll be as blonde as you." He gave Kait a wink then proceeded to rinse my hair with tainted water that smelled of earth.

Kait bit her nails while the louper dried my hair. When the cloth was pulled away, Kait didn't move but stared in bewilderment.

"Brilliant," Mr. Lennie beamed as he balled the stained rag in his little hands. "As long as no one studies him too hard, it should work."

He produced a looking glass, and I peered back at my own reflection only hazily seen before in deep pools of standing water. The concentrated blackness in my eyes didn't surprise me. All the selkie folk sported dark eyes, but my short tousled hair forced me to laugh loudly. It was scorched brown and perfectly ordinary.

"Kait?" I asked with a nervous grin. "Do ye still love me?"

She advanced slowly and lifted a small strand above my now cool ears. "Are you still in there?" she asked sadly.

I grabbed her waist and pulled her towards me. "Shall we go fer a swim and see?"

She squealed and made a play to get away. "No, I fear you would drown me."

"You should not tempt such a weak selkie," I said pressing my lips against her outstretched throat. "The enticement is almost too much to stand."

"Kait," Mr. Lennie warned with a frown. "Do I need to remind you of our conversation at Bay o' Linton. Your friend's influence is a dangerous one. You should be careful, or you'll end up like your friend whose name can no longer be spoken."

I stood and towered over the little man. "Do ye mean to frighten Kait? You're the only wan in danger here."

"He'd never hurt me," Kait said, wedging her small frame between us. "Mr. Lennie, tell me your fee, and we'll be on our way."

The louper didn't back away, but studied me with wild curiosity. "Ye wouldn't hurt her, would ye? She's got something you value."

"What would that be?" I asked.

"Don't speak of it," Kait warned him with a frightened expression. "The subject's not easily broached. Your fee, sir."

The louper licked his whiskery lips and looked up with a crazed expression that transformed his previously docile face. "Would ye be missin'... your *skin*?"

"What interest do ye have in my skin?" I growled with clenched fists. A fierce need to protect my skin swelled like a tidal wave inside me, and my thoughts turned black.

The man's eyes became shifty and deliberate, as if he were searching for my coat. "I only wish to try it on. Perhaps *I* could turn into a selkie."

My eyes grew with rage over the blatant plot to steal my skin. "Do ye wish to be permanently silenced?" I hissed.

"What's it like to be a beast one moment and a man the next?" he blindly persevered, ignorant to his own danger. "Can you transform at any time or does the stage of the moon bind your flippers?"

"Mr. Lennie!" Kait cried. "Eamon is very private!"

A firm lock and then a shift o' my weight right before the silencing twist—

"Tell me, laddie," the louper continued. "Why would you prefer to live as an animal?"

Kait was suddenly there, pressing her cool fingers against my inflamed cheeks. "It's alright," she soothed, forcing me to see her instead of the trowlie doctor. "Don't blame Mr. Lennie, your magick is maddening him—confusing his reason. He doesn't mean any harm."

I glowered back at the doctor, my heart still drumming with murder inside my chest. Why did he think Kait had my skin? Was it still safely hidden, or had my hiding place been discovered? The air was hot and rank with betrayal.

The louper's bushy white brows crushed together as he considered the possibility of being bewitched. He shook his head gently and looked foggily up at Kait. "There's no fee. I only wish to learn more of your selkie man. How did you capture him? I must know this at least."

"Why would you think I was captured?" I snarled. "Do I look like a prisoner?"

The doctor's probing eyes shot to Kait for answers. "Why, I only assumed..."

Kait pressed a copper into his palm while my head swam with onerous questions. "We'll come again when you're feeling better. Your questions are offending him."

He shook his head again as if realizing his madness. "Good heavens, be on your way but haste ye back."

17

THE LEGEND O' THE SELKIE FOLK

Eamon stalked out while I hurried behind him. Mr. Lennie had brought up his barmy plan to steal Eamon's skin, and I was stricken with the worst sort of fear. Eamon had promised he would stay, but like a beautiful buck, it still felt like he could be frightened off with the faintest breeze. The rain had stopped, but droplets of water sparkled on every blade of grass. "What's going on in your head?" I asked. "Are ye angry with me? Oh, please don't be angry."

"Do you have my skin?" he crowed, suddenly turning on me with fiery eyes. "Were ye spying on me when I hid it?"

"Nae," I gasped, shriveling under his burning gaze. "I'd never take it. Even now its location is a mystery."

"Then why did the louper believe you had my skin?" he growled, "Did you plan to steal it?"

"Mr. Trowlie suggested I try once, but I never even considered it. I would never hold you here against your will, but follow you under the surf and drown first."

Eamon's eyes grew wide with horror at the suggestion. "Ye would intentionally die to be with me?"

"Aye," I muttered, fingering a silken lock of hair inside my pocket. "I go where ye go."

He grasped me firmly by the shoulder and lowered his face near mine. "Would ye live fer me too?" His sweet breath whispered like an ocean breeze against my skin.

"Aye," I said more softly.

"Good, then do it." He dropped his hands with a rough thrust and turned away. "Do I seem young and helpless to you?"

"No," I cried outraged. "You are strong in body but in mind too. I know it's difficult for you to leave behind that what is precious—the sea and the part of you that lives in your skin. That takes great strength."

"You are wrong," he mumbled. "It takes strength to hunt and eat and swim." His eyes turned forcefully to my face as if he were trying to see every feature at once. "Because of you, it's hard to be a selkie, easy to be a man."

"I'm sorry, Eamon." It pained me to see him suffer, to see him give up his selkie ways, but I didn't have the strength to send him away. Every fiber in my body depended on him—craved him. If I had a life before him, I could barely remember it. Eamon was everything now. I wrapped my arms around his rigid body, mourning all the things he'd given up.

Eamon stood as stiff as a statue before folding himself into me with a tight hold. I felt a warm tingling as his silvery lips pressed into my hair. "I'm invisible," he mumbled. "Where would you take me?"

"I know it's not easy fer ye to go far inland," I said. "We can wait till you're ready. Maybe you'd like to go swimming."

"Ye would coddle me like a wean?" he asked with a hardened gaze.

"You're no child," I said with a small smile. I sifted my fingers through his short, messy hair. He no longer had the beautiful mane of a legendary selkie but the sun warmed locks of a fisherman. Still I mused, his beauty could not be tamed.

"There's a place on Shapinsay that is like no other," I said with a smile. "If you wish, I'd have you see the trees."

Hand in hand we crossed the moor, avoiding the gravelly roads that might encounter an expectant groom. Eamon's hand stayed in constant motion in mine, gently caressing and exploring with strong straight fingers. His touch was more sensuous than I had ever experienced, and it was a long time before I could muster the will to ask Eamon a question.

"What did you do to Mr. Lennie?" I asked with a dry swallow, forcing down the butterflies winging around in my throat. "I didn't know that your magick had an effect on men."

Eamon ran his hand across the back of his naked neck, uncomfortable with discussing this persuasive part of him. "I dinnae do anything," he murmured.

"He was out of control, obsessed even. I've known Mr. Lennie since I was a young lassie. I saw the madness in his face. Tell me, Eamon—please."

Eamon sighed and picked a small primrose. All at once he began to pluck the petals with a vengeance. "The selkie men have long been rivals to land loupers. Since the beginning we've held a draw—an advantage in some circumstances. The women are lured, but so are the men."

"Mr. Lennie is in love with you?" I asked, disgusted.

Eamon looked revolted at the suggestion. "No," he growled. "It seems that he's lured by the mystery o' the selkie folk. We've worked hard to be elusive—many are curious. For others, they may be lured by the enticement of battle. We bring out the worst sorts of aggression in some men, in others, nothing at all."

"And the women?" I asked, even though I already knew.

Eamon plucked the last silky petal and tossed the empty stem. "They are smitten."

"Eamon," I said tensely. "You must understand that my love for you is real—underneath the madness. I can feel it in my bones."

Eamon repositioned his leine with a heavy tug. He seemed suddenly uncomfortable, unable to hold my gaze. "You love me, that's all I care about."

Like Eamon, I didn't care how it was I came to love him— only that I did. Like the appearance of the sun after a long, dark winter, I never wanted it to go away.

When we scaled the final brae, Eamon tilted his head as if he were attentively listening. "There are voices ahead, mostly men."

"The Balfour's Castle is just ahead," I said with a smile. "You can really hear the workers inside?"

"And outside." He turned on his foot as he listened. "Are they a threat to us?"

"This is Shapinsay," I said with a smirk. "Other than venge-ful selkies, there is nothing to fear."

Before Eamon could protest, I pulled him up the summit of the hill. An unfinished turret appeared over the top of a glorious copse of trees. I held onto Eamon's arm and pointed below. "There they are," I said proudly. "The trees too mighty to be blown away."

Eamon's face lit with wonder at the hundreds of trees magically encircling the rear of the castle. Coarse, steepled evergreens intermingled among the tender, young green of newly blossomed leaves. In every direction, a lush, leafy canopy rolled. "These are not like the trees I've seen, but more...majestic."

I leaned dreamily into his arm. "They are majestic, aren't they?"

"My thanks, Kait, for showing me your trees."

"My trees? These all belongs to the Balfours," I said with a laugh. "Everything ye see is theirs."

"The sea can't be claimed as easily as your land," Eamon observed. "Men are too weak on water to conquer us."

"This may be true, but the forest doesn't have sharks!" I said, pulling excitedly on his arm. "C'mon, this isn't the best view."

We tumbled down the hill and became doused in shadow as soon as we entered the canopy. Brown leaves crackled under our feet while an unseen bird twittered from the green shadows above. "Listen," I said flirtatiously as I played with one of the ties dangling on his leine. "It's quiet here, and we've disappeared to the world."

Eamon turned distractedly to the south. "Not as quiet as ye believe. The men debate the proper cut for something called molding."

I tugged playfully on his leine. "I'd prefer you pay attention to me."

Eamon smiled down at me before kissing my lips ever so gently. My eyes fluttered dizzily open when he pulled unexpectedly away. It seemed that Eamon was not the hasty seducer of legends, but forbearingly patient. He was himself, and I loved everything about him.

"You're all I see," he said with a somber expression that moved slowly over my face. "Are there trees at all?"

I pressed my palms against his chest with a jaunty smile. "There are a few, and I'd have you see them properly. Now lie down."

"You wish me to lie in the soil?" His eyes broke quickly from my face to glare at the damp layer of last year's fallen leaves.

"The leaves are clean, but if you wish, pretend it's the beach or a sunny boulder." I smoothed my skirt then snuggled into the thick blanket of leaves. "Lie beside me," I ordered. Eamon was instantly at my side with his hand enveloped warmly around mine. I squeezed it and edged more closely to him. "Now look up. That's the best view."

Our foreheads gently touched as we gazed upwards. The canopy stretched like an extravagant lace above us, a million different shades of green elegantly overlapping below piercing shafts of yellow light. Eamon quietly took in the full view. "It's a singular sight," he murmured.

"The barrenness o' the island only makes it more beautiful," I said dreamily. "I long for a tree of my own. Every day I'd gaze up through the branches, so the sky would always be decorated."

Eamon was quiet as his dark eyes moved over the spectacular scenery. "Then I'll get you a tree. Do you want wan of those prickly kinds or the wans with the scalloped leaves?"

I laughed gaily. "There are none to be had that wouldn't strangle in the wind. These trees are a miracle—a gift from the gods. If you want to give me something, tell me more about the selkie folk."

"What do ye want to know?" His chest sank deeply, reluctant to speak of his people. I tapped another unwelcome topic. Why could my curiosity not be content just knowing what he was? Instead, I felt like an outsider that burned to explore every aspect of his private life.

I thought of a question that would not intimidate. "What do you like to eat best?"

Eamon gave a glinting smile, relieved. "Always herring, but squid and octopus are tasty too. Oh, and shrimp, even though they scratch my throat going down."

I rested my head on his chest and listened to the contented drumming deep within. "Would ye be opposed to trying something that grows above the ground, like a pea or a prune?"

Eamon shrugged and sank his hand beneath my hair. At once his fingers began to explore the nape of my neck. "If it doesn't smell like earth, I'll try it. This is all ye wish to know—what I eat?" His dark eyes floated down on me and rested on my lips.

I licked them nervously. "You would tell me more?"

Eamon shrugged and gazed back up at the leaves. "Depends on the question."

"Where do the selkie folk come from?"

He smirked down at me. "This is what troubles humans most. Do you question where the otters come from?"

"The otters don't have lithesome bodies that bewitch humans with a single glimpse," I said anxiously. Eamon's magick

185

seemed to be another unwelcome topic like his skin, and I feared him taking offense.

Eamon sighed and twirled a fallen leaf between his thumb and forefinger. "The selkies have always preferred the cooler water around the northern islands, but we have a history that is as old as the stars."

"I'd hear it if ye'll tell me."

He flicked the leaf away and turned to face me. "I'm not supposed to discuss it with humans."

"Why not?"

"We hold our history privately, sacredly. Besides, *we* choose to not forget."

I pulled a strand of hair out of my face. "Are you implying that my people have forgotten something?"

"I'm not implying. All Orcaidian memories have gone stone cold."

"It's a history we share then?"

"Aye."

"Please tell me, Eamon. That history belongs to me as much as you. If you tell, I'll swear to never forget—just like you. I too will hold it sacred."

"Ye won't share it?"

"Never. I'd have our history be the same."

"Fer ye, Kait, since I can't give ye a tree." Eamon gave a slow, deep sigh. "Our history begins long ago when there were less than a thousand humans on the earth. The gods above noticed that there were some people that preferred land and some people that preferred water. The latter would swim and dive while the land lovers huddled in groups and made fire."

"You were once human," I said with a small gasp. Somehow I had always known that we were too closely related. Only Eamon would push to emphasize our few differences and elevate that selkie part of him.

Eamon looked over at me to see if I would interrupt any more. I pressed my lips together, and Eamon continued with a squeeze of my hand. "The gods realized that the water lovers were ill equipped for the harshness of the sea, so they fashioned water tight skins so they'd never have to leave.

My people were delighted by the gift and grew strong in the water. Over time, we learned to hold our breath for a very long time and dive to great depths.

Those who stayed behind were jealous o' our newfound strength and sought every opportunity to undermine us. When we hauled onto rocks to bask, those doomed to land would sneak from behind and steal our skins. We thought this was the worst thing they could have done, but we were wrong. The contention worsened and eventually the loupers began to hunt and kill—cruelly crushing the skulls o' those once called brother or sister.

We were largely defenseless, and the injustice angered the gods, so they had mercy on our people once more. They gave us a subtle defense."

"Your lure," I interjected softly.

Eamon nodded. "Aye. It was barely noticed at first, but when the loupers saw the power that the selkie men had over their women, they became frightened, fearin' they would lose every last female to the waves."

"Ye drowned defenseless women," I muttered, thinking of Astrid.

"It was our only weapon," Eamon answered with a dark glance. "The women came in droves, cheerfully filling their lungs with sea water for men they couldn't resist. Eventually the loupers stopped provoking us."

I froze thinking on those foolish women. I too would gladly follow Eamon under the waves and fill my lungs, but I wasn't the same was I? I felt troubled, uncertain. "What about the lure you hold for men?"

"It's not so clear. But from some we attract aggression and the need to fight. For others, there is nothing but jealousy and the obsessive need for our skins. Still others wish us no harm and are immune to our lure. It's unpredictable as the wind."

"Mr. Lennie was curious about ye, fixated with learning all he could about the selkie folk. He didn't mean any harm."

"The louper points his nose where it does not belong."

"He was helping us. Ye should have tried turning it off."

Eamon sat up and folded his legs under his knees. "I can no sooner turn if off than become an otter. I may entice others to me, but I'm also a target. What ye call magick is also a curse."

"My brother, what will he do?"

"He may be blinded by his need to kill me."

"He'd have no chance of that," I said, deeply troubled. "I'd beat him to a pulp."

"I don't need protecting," Eamon growled. "I'm stronger than I look."

I sighed, frustrated by my error. "I just don't want anything bad to happen to you. Blair's soon to leave, and then you'll be all I have in the world."

Eamon hooked his forefinger around mine. "I'm not so fragile, ken?"

I gave a weak smile. "Aye." It didn't change the fact that I'd die jealously guarding my sea treasure. Eamon was everything now and couldn't be harmed. I'd tirelessly spend my life convincing him he loved the land and that he loved me.

"Ye remind me of someone," Eamon said softly.

My brow wrinkled. "Who?"

"Someone who was left behind—at the very beginning. Perhaps your ancestors were out swimming when the gods passed out skins. Ye do not fear the water, but swim as ferociously as your heart will allow."

I didn't understand, but sensed that Eamon was trying to tell me something very important. "Thankee, Eamon. You elevate me with the sweetest words."

"There is more you must know." I froze as he gathered my chin with soft pale fingers. His dark eyes moved over my face with a deep and tortured expression I hadn't seen before. "I love you, Kait, even despite myself."

My heart swelled with inexpressible joy. "Oh, Eamon, don't fight it. I've waited so long to hear those words—"

"—and I'd not be returning to the sea. Ever."

18

LOVERS

Eamon and I played a dangerous game. I felt this as an awful gnawing in the pit of my stomach. If Eamon's identity was discovered, there was no telling how the villagers would react. There was no precedent for a stubborn selkie who would audaciously claim a human in the plain light of day. The charges would be trumped up and severe—the villagers possibly even pinning the slaughtered lambs on him. He was guilty as those in Hel's realm, but I no longer cared. Eamon had a severe sense of justice and only killed the wee lambs to make restitution for the dead half-selkie bairn.

"The sound of your breath soothes me." Eamon's black eyes flickered up as his long toes wiggled by the fire. I was stretched out timidly beside him. Outside, the wind was howling like a banshee, but a sleepy amber glow warmed the small room like a cozy rabbit's burrow. "It's steady and constant like the sea. I can hardly hear the waves anymore."

I smiled warmly at what Eamon meant to be a compliment. "That's because the storm is muffling them." Maybe all my worrying was for naught. In the flickering light, with his new disguise, Eamon seemed very human in a royal, kingly sort of way. I shuddered to think what would happen if he were discovered. We were finally together—and in love. And I felt more vulnerable than ever. Like a mother bear on a murdering rampage, there was nothing I wouldn't do to protect him. To protect us.

"There's only one more day till Blair returns," I said, feeling utterly intoxicated by Eamon's close proximity. His beauty was so unfair and maiming my ability to think clearly. We weren't even touching, but I could feel the magick energy buzzing off him and pulsing like fire through me. I gave a hard swallow. "We'll have to test his reaction to you."

Eamon smirked and gathered his arms snugly around my waist. Our hips brushed dangerously against one another. "Let him meet me," he murmured into my neck with a warm tickle. "I'd not be afraid of any land louper, especially wan that orders you around like an elder."

Eamon's courage alarmed me. He was bold and reckless like an impulsive teenage boy. "He can't know you're a selkie," I warned. "You won't tell him, will you? There's nae telling what horrible thing he'd do."

"Who would I be?" Eamon asked. The corner of his lip tilted in an amused smile against my neck. "Do I form the bread in the village or build the boats that your people cling to?"

"You're none of those people," I worried. "The islanders have known each other their whole lives. You must be somebody new."

"A louper from another island," Eamon said scornfully. "A planter of the vile root."

"You can't say that anymore," I warned. "You're human— a very boring one who loves potatoes and fears swimming." I leaned against his chest and bit the inside of my lip. "You're from far away—a nephew of Tipper's. It only reasons since you're living in her house."

"What do I do?" Eamon asked. "Everyone seems to do something here. They all have *jobs.*"

"What do you want to do?" I asked as my fingers interlaced through his. We both pretended as if our bodies did not touch, but my mind flurried with distraction. When he lifted his finger, I felt the minute pressure shift away from my pinky. When he rotated his hips, my stomach clenched like a carpenter's vise inside. I felt the rise and fall of his chest and the vibration of his voice. "You'll be living here for a very long time," I said as his warm breath floated across my skin. "It should be something ye enjoy."

"I'd be a hunter o' fish," Eamon said fiercely.

I stifled a giggle. "Then I fear for the safety of all fish. They might as well all jump in your boat and surrender."

Eamon stiffened beside me. I had misspoken again, but I could only guess at my offense. "Until I can speak with Magnum, my brother may try and stop me from seeing you. He's got to believe you're human and the better match for me."

"He'd not interfere," Eamon threatened with a low, threatening growl. "I did not forsake the sea for nothing. I have my own plans."

"You can't hurt my brother. We *will* see each other, but we will have to be cleverer than he. He's a smoke blowing numpty who's easily distracted, but if you act aggressively towards him, he'll see you for what you are and spoil things for us."

Eamon gave a rough sigh and tightened his hold around my waist. My fingers slid contemplatively between his. "Eamon," I said cautiously. "My friend who died..."

"The wan who gave birth."

"Aye. Do ye know what happened to her?" Astrid's death continued to haunt me, even in my dreams. How could it not? Loving a selkie man was one last thing we would share—even to the grave.

His words stirred a few strands of hair at my cheek. "The burd's father may have enticed her to her death, or she could have drowned herself. The only thing I'm certain of is that *I* didn't harm your friend."

"Why would the father come back after so much time?"

"She didn't protect his son," Eamon answered gruffly. "It's a mother's duty to protect her young."

"She fought with all her might," I said, stirred by the unpleasant memory.

"Who did she fight?" Eamon asked with a growl, instantly piqued.

"I'd not be telling you that," I said emphatically. "It's over and done with." Eamon didn't hide that part of him that sought to hurt others, nor had I forgotten the warning from his elder: *He's not tame yet.* I was not certain what this meant, but I felt confident he'd hunt out Biorn and Astrid's ma and da for their part in the bairn's murder.

Eamon nestled his cheek against mine. "I'd never do that to you," he said.

"Fight me?" I asked, bewildered.

The cool tip of his nose stirred along my neck. "Nae, I'd never hump ye for pleasure then leave. I'm here to stay."

"You'd be the first of your kind," I said with a flirty grin. "It's your nature to wound unsuspecting women. Even now I fear you'll succumb to your instincts and drag me into the sea."

"Everything about you, Kait, goes against my nature as a selkie. Still I wish to show you." Moist lips folded over the tip of my ear at the same time his hot breath bore into me, wakening every fiber in my body with a shivering jolt.

I turned and gazed up at Eamon, catching my breath at the carnal hunger warring on his exotic face. Everything about Eamon warned of imminent danger, still, I could not move. My eyes moved over his imperfect nose, then his eyes too jet black to be human. Nervously, I reached up to finger through his ridiculously brown hair. Eamon tolerated this examination impatiently.

"Ye wish us to mate?" he asked with quiet uncertainty.

My heart raced like a bumblebee beneath my shift, and I struggled to speak. I was old enough to understand the intimate thing he'd asked. It's only Eamon. Why should I be nervous? I thought of that absurdity—it wasn't only Eamon, but the most ethereal of creatures—a selkie man from The Deep. His kind had been enticingly created by the gods for this very purpose. By simply walking away, he had the power to crush me. Oh Odin, was I to be his prey? Eamon's dark brows tightened when I didn't answer right away.

"Aye," I rasped. "I wish you to prove your love by staying, once our hunger has been satiated."

In need of no more encouragement, Eamon hurriedly rose and stripped off the clothing he secretly hated. "I'll prove to ye, Kait."

I stared up at his lithe form with renewed awe and reverence. He was painfully beautiful—opulent as a pearl, yet still sinewy and strong. Beside him I was abhorrently plain, and I battled not to remember the indulgent curves of the lovely selkie women that sprawled on the rocks that day.

He dropped to the wool blanket beside me and innocently fingered the neck of my dress like a bairn who thirsted for his mother's milk. His eyes fluttered up to mine as he silently asked for permission to explore what was beneath. I took a deep breath and nervously pushed my dress down to my hips. Eamon's eyes grew at the white skin and soft pink peaks that rose above the dark grey fabric. As my fear melted away, Eamon's iridescent lips opened, and I buried my face in his disheveled hair.

19

AN UNBREAKABLE VOW

When I woke, Kait was twined uncomfortably around me with her knees cutting into my ribs and her golden hair splashed across my chest. My eyes moved affectionately over her as she peacefully slept, pausing to admire the happy curve brightening her pink lips.

I had filled Kait and made her happy. She was my mate. Not Magnum's—mine. The truth of this made me want to run and roar, swim and fight, but most especially hump. Gone were the days when I cared if she was a selkie or not. Hadn't it been clear last night when we molded perfectly together as male and female that we were meant to be one?

My eyes greedily coursed down the willowy line of her smooth white back. Kait was more beautiful than she knew— the warm, joyous part of earth. My finger coursed down the delicate ridge while Kait purred and extended her bare arm across my stomach. Her slender fingers tucked themselves at the thinnest part of my waist. Had she realized she'd done it? Was she dreaming of me and the way we passionately explored each other till we were exhausted?

It had taken the whole of the night for the bonfire in my groin to be extinguished—only now was I cool—barely. My eyes had been opened to humping and the enticement of Kait under her coarse dress. She was more sweet and supple than I could have imagined, and I felt her power over me grow. I had no interest in fighting Kait anymore—I would let the power grow.

"Kait," I said, giving her a wee shoogle. "It's our last day till your brother returns. Shall we waste it sleeping?" I sat up and her head slid into my lap.

She gave a small moan then blearily peered up at me with a contented smile. "Eamon, you're still here."

"Are ye surprised?" I asked with a smirk as I traced along her collarbone. "If you wish, I can show you more assertion of my love if you aren't convinced."

Kait sat up and pulled a woolen blanket up over her bonnie diddies. The blanket was coarse and smelled of sheep. I didn't understand her attachment to it. "I thought maybe you'd have run off by now or be out hunting," she said silkily.

"Then you'd be worried, and I would be wishin' I was right here. If ye have food that dinnae grow under the filthy ground, I will try it."

"Really?" Kait exclaimed.

"A small taste."

I watched Kait lose her blanket in her excitement to get to the hearth, then scurry back for her two layers of clothing. Flashes of white tantalized and teased me. "You would still hide from me after I've seen your whole spirit?" I asked amusedly. "I already memorized it." The first layer was already over her head and unraveling to her knees.

Kait's shift gave her confidence, and she turned with a seductive wave of the hip. The shape of her slender form hinted beneath, and the fire in my belly alighted once again. "I was cold, like you should be," she said haughtily. She tossed her hair then dipped down to retrieve her dress that had been tossed carelessly in the onion basket. When I advanced upon her, her eyes grew in alarm.

"You'd not be getting dressed just yet," I said, capturing her by the waist.

Kait squealed with delight but didn't push me away. "Eamon, are ye planning on killing me slowly? Is that your devious plan?"

"Aye," I growled. "You've discovered me." My fingers scooped up under the thin white fabric at her pale thigh, and she became subdued beneath me. "I love you," I murmured into her ear.

It was midday when Kait finally finished preparing my meal. I was ravenous and prepared to eat just about anything. She placed two bowls before me to sample.

"What's it called?" I asked, poking the pasty white contents of the first bowl. It didn't look like food, but I *wanted* to like it and worried about hurting Kait's feelings.

Kait bit her lip nervously. "Porridge, made from meal."

I dipped the tip of my spoon into the mixture and cautiously licked it. The flavor of salt and something earthy melted pleasantly over my tongue. I smiled up at Kait and took a larger spoonful.

"You like it?" she asked.

"I like it," I admitted. I took a second and third heaping spoonful.

"I added extra salt," she said. "It was a hunch."

When my stomach no longer panged from emptiness, I turned my attention to the next bowl. It had an unfamiliar fish in it, mixed with tiny green pearls. "Spoots and split peas," she announced happily. "The wee rascals are dug up from under the sand not soil, and the peas grow far above the ground. It should be safe enough."

I tested a spoonful of the mixture and found it to be delicious. "Spoots and peas," I repeated. "It's my new favorite." I shoveled in another bite.

Kait clasped her hands together excitedly. "I know we can make this work. I'll feed you well, Eamon."

"This is your job?" I asked. "To feed me?"

"Of course, as you take care of me." Kait sat down beside me and stirred her porridge distractedly.

I swelled inside with the knowledge that I was to care for Kait. That would be my real job. I would be her protector as my name implied.

"We are now mated fer life?" Kait asked. She lifted her eyes nervously as she blew on her spoon.

"I'd not be going anywhere," I promised. "Ye'll be comforted to know that selkies mate for life like whales." I shoveled in another salty spoot then scoped out what was left of my porridge.

"Eamon," she said slowly. "I'm scared—the pull of the sea is great fer you. I'd have you make an oath."

I set down my spoon. "Oath? You're speaking to me in riddles."

"I'm speaking o' marriage," Kait said solemnly. "I've told you all about it. You make an oath to always love me and never leave me, and I vow the same. Would you do this for me?"

"We mated," I said, confused. "The meaning is the same."

"A vow at Odin's stone is unbreakable," Kait continued. "It is deeper than simply mating. I'd have you be my husband."

Becoming a husband was a louper ritual that meant nothing to me, but I could see that it was important to Kait. I returned to my spoots and peas. "If it would please you."

"Would it be the waxing or wane o' the moon?" she asked as she wrung her hands. "I've been so distracted, I can't remember."

I stared at Kait, wondering about her strangeness. "The moon still grows behind the clouds."

Kait dropped to her knees and kissed my hand. "Thankee, Eamon. It would be safe for us to get married this very day."

Later, we linked fingers and waded through shin deep grass. There was a thick grey mist clinging to the moor like a wet blanket, but this didn't stop Kait and me from celebrating our new union. I laughed as Kait danced gracefully around me with her damp skirt billowing about her ankles like a filled sail. "Won't Blair be surprised to find me married when he returns?" she asked breathlessly. She gave a dainty leap then spun around on her toes. It was unlike the brusque dance the women did at the bonfire, but the weightless and playful dance of an otter.

"What will he do?"

"There's nothing he can do," Kait said happily. "Oaths made through Odin's Stone can't be undone. He'll move to the Mainland, marry his Sloane and then we'll be free to do as we please. Come dance with me!" She bounced playfully around me and made a show of fluffing her tangled hair. I imitated her leap then captured her hand and pulled her to my chest with a peal of boisterous laughter from us both.

Getting rid of her brother pleased me as much as Kait. I'd have my private time with her and unravel her many mysteries. Her opinions seemed to be without end, as did her superstitious traditions. "Tell me about the waxing and waning of the moon," I ordered as my hands slid comfortably to the velvety bone at her hip. "You were worried before."

Kait's face turned grave. "I'd never enter into marriage at the wane of the moon. It's the worst of luck. All the hens would die, and then we would be cursed to never have children. Besides marrying you, this is my greatest wish. I'd hold a dozen of your sweet bairn to my breast."

"A dozen?" I laughed. "All at once?"

Her face paled. "Could that happen?"

"Ha, not unless you're a seahorse!" I clutched two handfuls of golden hair and promptly kissed her. Kait smiled radiantly up at me. She made me feel strong and virile, different from the truth.

"We'll go to the village soon and order a ring from the Mainland."

"What kind of ring?"

"A gold one for my finger," Kait said, wiggling her finger admirably under her nose. It's a symbol for all the men that I'm taken."

I snatched Kait up with a small growl and swung her around. "Who needs a symbol when you've got me?" Kait laughed wildly and lifted her toes into the wind.

By the time we reached the most northern neck of beach, Kait had a ring of delicate white flowers wreathed around her slender finger, and I had a flower tucked behind my ear—our gifts to each other.

Kait became more solemn when the Odin stone emerged nobly from behind a solid wall of rock. The stark black pillar was worn smooth from the wind and seemed older than the hollow cliffs. In the center of the massive stone was a polished hole large enough for a newborn burd to wiggle through.

"I've seen this rock," I said, running my fingers along the worn face. "It's rumored to have been thrown here by the giants."

"Close," Kait said. "Odin himself placed it here as a gift after he hung from the world tree. It has magical healing powers. Babies are passed through the center shortly after they're born to protect them from sickness."

"Aren't we a bit premature?" I asked with a grin.

Kait ran her fingers over the dark, rough stone contemplatively. "But that's not all. It also has the power to bind marriages and seal agreements. This is where one goes when they want to make a vow unbreakable. A broken vow is always followed by death."

I rubbed the back of my neck uncomfortably. "Death? Do you believe the stone's power is so great?"

"Aye," Kait said gravely. "Many years ago, Mr. Finnegan found his neighbor, Mr. Logie up under his wife's skirt in their own cow byre. He'd been secretly poking her between the stalls for months. Mrs. Finnegan tumbled right off the ferry the following year and sunk like a rock into the firth. Mr. Logie died silently in his sleep soon after. It's not natural to go at such a young age."

"Ye fear I'll stray."

"It's only a tradition," Kait blurted defensively. "Besides, I've seen the way you look longingly out to sea. The vow soothes my mind that ye'll return."

"My skin remains hidden. Is this why ye seek out a dangerous vow to bind me to you—wan that would kill me?"

"No!" Kait cried. "You misunderstand."

"Since you can't snare me wan way, you'll snare me another!" A deeply rooted rebellion bristled violently within me. I'd not be Kait's slave and conquest. I needed to be free and fly below the glassy blue surface with the speed of a porpoise. For so long I'd denied myself the pleasure—for what? An eternity of bondage! But it was my own fault. I had allowed Kait to dry me out and place me inside a *house*. An unpleasant and stifling word that made me want to buck in protest.

"I've not spoken of your skin," Kait said fiercely. "I'd have you as my husband by your own free will. I'd never force you."

"Losh, why must I be threatened!?" I pulled at the coarse fabric binding my neck. For the longest time I had forgotten the leine was there, but now it seemed like the harness for a beast.

"Stop tugging at your leine," Kait said with a strange and unaccountable calmness. "You'll get a rash." She glided her cool fingers behind my neck and forced me to see her. "The threat of death is designed for people like Mr. Logie and Mrs. Finnegan. We will always belong to each other whether we marry or not. Can't you feel this in your heart?"

Of course I felt it. Even now my heart drummed savagely for Kait. I *needed* her by my side as much as she needed me. "Aye," I mumbled in a failing voice. "I feel it."

"I'm not only asking for you to give something up, I'm asking ye to accept me. I'd always be yours—body, mind and soul. Take me as a gift, Eamon. Allow me to be your wife."

Kait would give herself to *me*. My eyes dropped to Kait's lips, enticingly full and pink like a venomous sea anemone. No longer caring if I got stung, I impulsively pressed my lips against hers then parted to relish her warm, sweet tongue. Kait kissed me exuberantly back with her fingers woven into my short louper hair.

"It's only one kiss of many," Kait whispered as our lips pulled apart. Her pale lashes fluttered up lethargically. "We could do that all day long if we wish after we marry. Nothing would stop us—not my bampot brother—not your elders. The oath cannot be undone. But we must marry first, or Blair will try to separate us." Kait's calm serenity melted into me like a sweet and enticing venom. Where had her surge of confidence suddenly come from? It was almost as if she'd seen the future and known I'd succumb to her will.

Why would I want the oath to be undone? Had I not already battled with my decision and chosen Kait? *She* was what I could not live without. Kait would not only be my mate but my wife. I was not entirely certain what this would entail, but it sounded like *more*. Comforted by her soothing words, I friskily bumped her cheek with my nose.

Kait smiled as she savored our kiss on her lower lip. "You really are a selkie, aren't you?"

"Did you mistake me fer a louper?" I asked with a playful growl. I bumped her again and nipped her chin with the edge of my teeth.

Kait skipped around Odin' Stone then peered up through the hole with hypnotic blue eyes. "Eamon, the choice is yours. If you don't wish to make the vow, I will have no choice but to always love you."

I tore my eyes from Kait and gazed out at the great expanse of blue sea. My home. Past the barrier of bony reef, there were no boundaries and endless adventure and beauty. Was I a traitor to my kind for wishing it would all disappear? A wave crashed over the rocks and sprayed into the air. The salt in the wind seasoned my tongue and beckoned me in, but I flexed my jaw and turned away. I would not see it. If I couldn't be strong in the sea, I would be strong on land.

Kait extended her hand through the hole. "Eamon, I'd have ye be my husband."

I crouched down in front of the hole and surrendered my hand into hers. "I'm not afraid."

20

BLAIR'S RETURN

There had been neither bachelor banging for Eamon nor foot washing for me, but still I was married. I regretted that Blair could not be there, but Odin, Heimdall, and even the seeress Etin were witnesses for what Eamon and I had done.

Eamon and I met at the other side of the stone where we exchanged secretive smiles. "It can't be undone," I promised. "No matter if Blair likes it or not."

"He never had a chance at keeping us apart," Eamon said serenely. His arms slipped around my waist as his nose disappeared into the base of my neck.

"Then you don't feel the chains of bondage weighing you down?" I teased.

"Nae, Kait," came the muffled response. "I feel like king of the world."

"Are you sniffing me?" I asked with a giggle. "All that steam is tickling me."

"Aye, your scent is new today. I'm trying to memorize the smell of a wife. I've never had wan before."

"I have a smell?" I asked horrorstruck. I began to paw him away.

Eamon grinned mischievously and held more tightly. He was stronger than he looked. "It's a lure to me and a mark for you." He laughed like a prankish teenage boy. "No selkie male would come within a hundred paces of you. You've been claimed."

"What does it smell like?" I asked, wrinkling my nose. I sniffed my arm, but couldn't smell anything but the salty wind.

"It smells like the musk of a selkie male," Eamon laughed. "What will ye do about it?"

I shot out of Eamon's arms, pulling my dress off over my head as I flew. "I'll wash it off!" I cried with a laugh. I splashed into the bubbly waves and dove under with a jolting shock of cold. After kicking a short distance, I resurfaced with a gasp. It was then I realized that Eamon wasn't pursuing me. He stood at the water's edge looking a wee bit wabbit in Da's wrinkly clothes.

"Are ye ill?" I called out.

Eamon stuck his toe in the foam clinging to each receding wave. "You could show me Ward Hill. You've been bragging about the view."

"But I'm already wet. Come in and show me how to swim properly." I gave a little shoogle and shook my hair with a laugh. Water rained all around me.

Eamon took a step then paused with a frown when water rushed over his white feet.

"I'm growing old out here," I teased. "Soon I'll have whiskers like Mrs. Treb."

Eamon looked up at me then began to loosen the ties at his neck. My eyes lit with wonder as his leine and then trousers dropped from his pearly skin. I was a fool to believe he would pass as a human.

"Ye really wish to swim better?" Eamon asked as he swept in beside me.

"I don't fear drowning when you're with me. We could go as far as Egilsay if you wanted." I took his hand and tried to tug him towards the deeper water, but Eamon stood as rigidly as a tree.

"I'll show you how to swim here in the voe," he said with a solemn gaze that frightened me. "It's safer for such a hazardous swimmer as yourself."

"The sea's pull is too great for you," I said as my stomach tightened. "You're afraid you won't want to come back, even now that we're married."

Eamon cast his dark eyes out over the water. "I'm not afraid of anything. The sea is not as strong as I am."

I followed his gaze, feeling grotesquely insecure about anything that pulled Eamon from me. "You could go fer a swim— stretch your muscles, frighten some fish, and then come back. You'll feel better, and I'll be waiting with a kiss when ye return."

Eamon's face darkened. "You believe I prefer the sea o'er you?"

"You don't have to choose," I said bewildered. "We're surrounded by sea—have us both. Just don't leave fer good."

"I'm staying here with you," he said. "We've only just mated, and I *have* chosen."

I felt a surge of relief and splashed Eamon playfully. I didn't understand him, but I heard the words I needed to hear. *I'm staying here with you.* "Then teach me how to swim."

Eamon's eyes lit with a challenge before he lifted me effortlessly and tossed me like a small child. I flailed into the deeper water with an unflattering splash.

There was a lot more to swimming than I knew. Eamon showed me how utilize my feet as flippers and then how to deflate my lungs before a dive. Eamon demonstrated graceful dips and turns then corrected endlessly when I scooped and struggled inside the currents. When my energy was spent, I floated on top of the waves with my arms stretched wide while Eamon disappeared under the surface for over ten minutes.

"You're showing off how long you can hold your breath," I said when his drenched head popped up next to mine.

He pushed the water out of his eyes with a laugh. "If I were showing off, you wouldn't have seen me for quite some time—maybe not till the summer dim."

"Ha!" I cried, splashing his sculpted chest. "Even I know that'd be a lie."

Eamon shrugged with a grin.

"How long *can* you hold your breath?" I asked, pretending not to be fascinated.

Eamon drew his brows together as he thought on this. "How long did it take to walk here?"

I stared at him in amazement. "About a quarter o' an hour."

"Then a quarter o' an hour, maybe more."

"What were ye doing down there?"

Eamon took my hand and led me back to the beach. "Thinking. What were ye doing up here?"

"I suppose the same thing. Were you thinking of me?"

"Always, Kait." Eamon lifted my dress from the warm stones and handed it to me. "Your lips are turning blue. We were out there too long."

I took my dress gratefully and dressed. Although pleasant when dry, the northern skuther assaulted relentlessly when wet. Eamon dressed begrudgingly but without complaint. He was missing the conformity and warmth of his skin, but would not say so.

Later, I stretched across Eamon's silky chest in front of the warm fire. "You're filled with surprises," I said as my fingers traced the soft hairs around his tight navel. "I'm just now learning that ye can hold your breath for an absurd length of time and smell ant jobbie from the other side of the island. It makes me realize that I know little about you."

"Kait, you're the mystery. Even if I spend my whole life at the bottom of the sea pondering, I'll never understand why you swim in your underclothes, and why you fear boiling water."

"I dinnae fear boiling water—just the curse that comes with nothing in it," I said with a scoff. "Adding a meat bone is easy enough, but I'm speaking of you. I don't know anything about the selkie folk, other than they like to eat fish." I repositioned my head in the velvety hollow beside his shoulder. Now that we were married, I felt somehow justified in asking Eamon more questions. "Tell me something I don't know. Do ye see especially far?"

Eamon wove his fingers absently through my hair. "No, not far, but I see well under the water where the sun does not descend."

"You can see in the dark?"

"It's easy. Selkies don't dread the dark winters like loupers do."

"This explains selkies' fondness for prowling around at night like cats."

"We prefer to be invisible," Eamon explained.

"What else?"

Eamon gave a deep sigh, sinking his chest beneath me. "You may not like the next one."

"What is it?" I asked, meeting his dark gaze.

"We live a lot longer than humans."

"Oh, that's nothing to get me riled. How much longer—five, ten years?"

Eamon shrugged. "If we are clever in avoiding the orcas and the hidden nets, we can live up to three hundred years."

"Three hundred years?" I bolted upright, stuporing over the impossible feat.

"Be happy," Eamon said. "You won't live another day of your life without me."

"I had no inkling selkies lived so long," I said numbly. "You've got so much time left."

"What I have is not bad, but another gift given to selkies long ago. The gods saw the injustice of the selkie being so easily slain, so they seasoned the waters and evened things between us. It's another passive weapon like enticing human women."

"But things aren't even at all!" I cried. "You do everything better—see, hear, smell. You're strong as a bull and too bonnie fer your own good. Where's the justice?"

"In the water we have nae weapons and little defense against those who would slay us. We gave everything up long ago 'cos we loved the sea more than land."

"But I could never keep up with you. What kind of mate will I make when I'm always ten steps behind—always struggling to see, struggling to swim?"

Eamon tucked his chin in near my ear and encircled my legs inside his. "You're the mate I've chosen without regret. There's no need for you to be jealous of my gifts."

"You think I'm jealous?" I asked incredulously. "I celebrate every inch of your wickedly alluring body. I'm sad because I'll never be good enough for you."

Eamon swept a bundle of hair aside and pressed his lips against my neck. "You already are. Stop worrying."

The next day, I woke feeling tired and newly disturbed. Eamon would continue to live long after I died and experience a whole other life apart from me. I shuddered with horror to think of the worthy new selkie mate he'd find once I was a rotting corpse in the ground. She'd be painfully beautiful with glossy black hair that swept over creamy white skin with no freckles in sight. Her eyes would be dark and luminous and would ceaselessly scorn the ugly.

I brightened a hair when I wondered if perhaps Eamon wouldn't prefer a plain human girl. He had in fact fallen in love with me, not bad by human standards but hideously reproachable for a selkie. When I calculated how many human wives he could fit in over his ridiculously long life, tears trickled from my eyes.

"I shouldn't have told you," Eamon growled. "You're falling apart."

"I'm rosey," I cried. "Don't keep important things from me." I roughly wiped my tears and noticed for the first time that Eamon was ruggedly pacing back and forth like a caged animal. Something was bothering him too. I rolled over on my stomach and peered up at him. "Why are ye up to a high doh, Eamon?"

"Your brother's back," he grumbled without slowing.

I clutched my pillow tightly. I had completely forgotten that Blair was to return today. "Not this day. I'm not ready to face him."

"He's cursing the empty hen house. He's discovered you're not anywhere on the croft."

"He's worried," I said. "We've nae choice but to show him I'm alive and well."

The croft house seemed strangely empty as we approached—an empty shell without life or spirit. Over the past several days I'd carried dozens of my possessions to Tipper's house, transferring the old house's life and energy.

"You're my future," I breathed. Beside me, Eamon still seemed too perfect—a radiant moonbeam that could vanish behind a cloud in an instant. He was my future wasn't he? I held onto his arm tighter.

Eamon pressed his nose into my hair. "It's going to be alright," he soothed.

"He's not alone, is he?"

"No, there's another deeper voice—the man Magnum. Your brother and he have been discussing you for some time."

When the door swung open, Blair and Magnum jumped to their feet then froze with bewilderment when they saw the glorious man protectively hovering beside me.

"Who in Hel's domain is this?" Blair blurted.

"Meet Eamon," I said politely, releasing my hold of his arm. "He's Tipper Gray's nephew. He's taken over her croft house." I suddenly realized I hadn't concocted a surname. Panicked, I gave him the only suitable name that could ever possibly be connected to him—mine. "Eamon Swanney."

Magnum gave a nervous chuckle. "You share Kait's surname? Are you sure you aren't Kait's brother or cousin?"

Eamon looked gravely down at me, unhappy with having yet a second name. "Aye, I'm very sure."

"The house has been stripped bare," Blair growled. "What's going on?"

"You've been gone for days," Magnum said with a deep crease branded across his forehead. "Every day I come searching for my bride and leave disappointed. I would have fetched Blair from the Mainland days ago, but someone's been collecting the eggs."

"I haven't been neglecting the hens," I said miserably. Magnum was dafter than I knew and hadn't understood my absence as a rejection at all. I immediately regretted not setting things straight days ago. "Magnum, we must talk alone."

Magnum gave Eamon an uneasy look. "Anything for you, Kait. Where shall we go?"

"This is not to be born," Blair cried outraged. "I want to know where you've been right now! Magnum informs me that he hasn't seen you since the night of the bachelor banging. You lied to me. Have you been with *him*?" He jerked his head unhappily towards Eamon.

Magnum's eyes darted rapidly between us. "Kait?"

"I'm sorry, Magnum," I said sorrowfully. "I should have told you sooner, but I didn't want to hurt you."

Magnum shot Eamon a dangerous look then advanced slowly, beseechingly. "But we're to be married in less than a week's time. Are you laughing at me?"

"No," I managed to rasp as I shrank away. "I like you for your good heart, but I never agreed to marry you."

"I agreed!" Blair raged. "We shook hands. Ye'll still marry Magnum. He's a good hardworking man who'll take good care of you."

"Kait stays with me," Eamon growled. Flaunting his advantage, his hand slipped into mine.

"Get your hands off my lassie," Magnum threatened with delirious eyes. He tramped a few steps closer. "You crawl out of the ground then attempt to despoil my bride when her brother is away?"

"Magnum, you misunderstand!" I cried.

"You think I come from under the filthy ground?" Eamon asked with a smirk.

Magnum's face flushed red while he hesitated in confusion.

"You don't have a say in matters of my sister," Blair fumed with his eyes set fiercely on Eamon. He had positioned himself between the two men. "What you do is not proper. Kait is my blood and my responsibility."

"I'd be her protector now," Eamon told him evenly. "Your presence only interferes."

I clung to Eamon's arm, fearful that one or the other would try and pull me away from him. "I know this seems very sudden—"

"You come from nowhere and seduce a young girl. This is not protecting her."

"Kait can make her own choices," Eamon told Blair flatly as he dropped his hand to squeeze my thigh. It was not an affectionate gesture. "Understand?" He cocked his head, meeting him with a fierce black gaze.

"*The act* has already been done?" Magnum cried with rage. His eyes shot to Blair as if he knew something he didn't. Magnum tramped closer and poked Eamon in the chest. "I said get off her!"

"Get out!" Blair ordered Eamon with wild eyes. "You don't belong here."

"No, Eamon's not going anywhere!" I cried emphatically. "You can't agree for me to marry anyone without my consent. We've been partners since Ma and Da died. I'm your sister not your daughter!"

"Go home, *neighbor!*" Blair repeated furiously, ignoring me.

"I'll take him home and clean the floor with him," Magnum growled as he shoved Eamon's shoulder. "Have ye been plotting on bedding Kait long?"

Eamon leveled his eyes with Magnum, not wanting to admit he was confused by the question. "Kait has made her choice. If ye were wise you'd not provoke me."

I positioned myself dangerously between the two men, leveling my palms against their chests. "I'm sorry Magnum, but just go. My pig-headed berk for a brother should never have promised me away."

"Nae," Blair raged. "It's my duty! Eamon must go—now!"

"Admit you've been poking Kait," Magnum hissed.

"Magnum!" I begged.

This time Eamon understood clearly. "Is this what ye fantasize about when you bob up and down in your wee boat?"

Blair rushed to the door and thrust it violently open. "Eamon, you're too late. Kait is to marry Magnum."

"You're wrong," I yelled, enraged by Blair's persistence. "It's you who's too late! Eamon and I are already married. We'll have the ring soon enough."

Blair's face paled with horror. "You went to Odin's Stone with *him?*"

Magnum knocked me to the floor in his urgency to get to Eamon. Pain seared through the corner of my temple when I realized I had severely struck the flagstones. A small scarlet rivulet trickled into my eye as I dazedly struggled to my knees.

My eyes grew when I blinked away the blood and saw two blurry images collide into one horrifying image of Magnum ruthlessly striking Eamon again and again. Eamon struck back, but Magnum was bulkier and fueled by a blind fury lured by Eamon himself. The pearly white skin on Eamon's cheek split open as he lunged for a chair.

"Stop it!" I screamed. "Stop it—stop it!" I swept up an iron pan the same time Blair lunged onto Magnum's back.

Magnum grunted and bucked like an angry bull, but Blair persisted in pinning his friend's arms. "Easy! Easy," he repeated until the fight was exhausted out of Magnum.

"Your new neighbor's going to jail," Magnum grunted, shaking Blair off his back. He cast Eamon a vicious glare and ran a fist across his bloody beard. His teeth and gums were stained red. "The engagement contract's been broken and my bride's been soiled."

Eamon glowered back. "There's nothing broken but your pride." He touched the spot below his trickling gash then rolled the blood between his fingers with surprise.

"Dinnae fash yourself," Blair grumbled to Magnum. "There's nothing anybody can do. Just go on now."

Magnum's eyes shifted painfully towards me, but my pity was spent on Eamon. "Go on now," I ordered. "But before you notify the constable, remember you attacked Eamon first."

He opened his mouth to say something but lumbered out the door instead.

I turned swiftly on my brother and pounded my fists against his chest. "This is your entire fault, ye dim minded headbanger. You're responsible for hurting Magnum and Eamon."

Blair wrapped two bear arms around me and restrained my arms against my chest. "Keep the head my lost sister," he said in a dark and troubled voice. "I'm not your enemy. I leave that role to your husband." Blair glared over my shoulder to Eamon awkwardly nursing his wound a few paces away.

"Ye know nothing about me," Eamon growled.

"I know what you are," Blair said in a coarse voice. "Magnum's been blinded by your flimsy cover, but I can see the animal in your eyes."

21

BATTLES NOT SEEN

I enjoyed fighting Magnum. If not for Blair's interference, I would have killed the hairy louper who lusted after Kait. As it was, his luck dangled heavily about his neck like an anchor. I lifted my nose to the distinctive smelling trail he left behind. It was a sweaty pitch-like aroma that offended my nostrils.

Blair looked dazedly towards the door, the place Magnum had disappeared. Kait was still restrained possessively in his arms. I debated the ease in snapping his sheepy fingers without harming a hair of Kait's. "I've never seen him like that. He was crazed in the head."

"He couldn't help himself," Kait said, pulling away from her brother with a scowl.

"It's me," I growled, meaning to shock Blair. "I bring out the worst in people." He may have sided with me in the fight, but the air was yet to be truly tested between us.

"Aye," Blair agreed. "I feel this in my bones." He picked up an overturned chair then kicked it into place with a loud grating sound. "What do you want with my sister, selkie?"

"Ye mean to rile me with your tone?" I asked. Fighting Blair would be fun. He was larger than the other louper, but less confounded by his anger. I suspected he wasn't as strong as he looked.

"What is the matter with you, Blair?" Kait asked as her cool fingers collected around my face. She shot Blair an irritated look before examining my cheek. "He got wounded in our home, and you can only think to interrogate him?"

"What do you mean by bringing him here," Blair questioned. "It's foolhardy."

Wounded? I touched the throbbing place on my face again. "It's hardly a wound at all—a mere scratch."

"Nonsense," Kait muttered as her lips gently brushed the corner of my mouth and then a safe place near the throbbing.

"You're the one who got hurt," I murmured, troubled by a small congealed gash above her eye. Magnum was as good as dead. The wound would scar into a reminder that I failed to protect her. My thumb glided over a spray of freckles.

"Never mind that," Kait said. "I'll pump some water for your cut."

"Nae, Kait. We'll both wash in the voe where the water heals."

With annoyance, I realized Blair was watching our private exchange. I brazenly met his gaze. "Do I interest you?"

Blair shoved his hands in his pockets, turning his attention over to his sister. "What happened while I was away, Kait? The selkie was gone and you seemed to be doing better."

Incredibly, another louper who'd speak as if I didn't exist. "Do I look gone?"

Kait looped her arm through mine as she obstinately met her twin's gaze. "I won't deny what you already know."

"Why did you have to get married?" Blair exclaimed with a wild expression. "Wasn't Magnum good enough? He's at least human!" He cut his eyes at me condescendingly.

"Eamon and I love each other," Kait answered sharply. "And getting married is the natural course of things."

"Ye think you are superior to me?" I asked her brother in a gruff voice. "Is it the grass in your hair or the earth under your nails that makes you better?"

"There are things he knows nothing about," Kait told me. "Be patient with him."

I couldn't see her. Blair's eyes were purposefully planted on Kait as if he considered stealing her away.

"He's a water dog—a selkie. He only wishes to capture your heart like a spoil of war. If you survive the night, he will only leave and hurt you as his nature dictates. He won't be able to help himself."

"Nae," Kait countered with a wince. "I'd be dead by now if Eamon wanted to hurt me. He didn't have to make Odin's oath, but he did."

"You're the only wan in danger here," I warned. "Kait belongs with me, and I weary of your excess company."

Blair gave a mocking laugh. "He's violent, see? He'd threaten me in my own home." I glared back at him. Kait made me promise not to hurt her brother, but he'd vilify me in her eyes. Killing him would be tricky without hurting Kait.

"You don't know anything," Kait retorted. "Eamon's given me less bruises than you."

"I don't wish to fight," Blair said with a groan. Earthy brown eyes settled unhappily on my face. I felt soiled by them. "Go play your games elsewhere, selkie. Let Kait live her life in peace."

"Don't even say it!" Kait ordered with large, frightened eyes. "He's staying with me. Always. He swore he would." Kait looped her arm through mine with the strength of an orca.

"She wants me to stay," I said with a smug smile. I felt needed, invincible, more certain than ever that I'd made the right choice. The entire ocean could sink into a giant black hole, and I'd hardly notice.

"He's doing something to you," Blair said with a look of alarm. "I'd not expect you to see it. You haven't been well since the water dog first stole into our house. But how many selkies do you see living among us? None! They can't resist the lure of the sea. They only creep up on the land for one purpose."

"Don't listen to him," I warned Kait under my breath. "He wants to control you."

"Eamon's different," Kait told her brother less confidently. "He's conquered that part of him."

"Look at him," Blair commanded. "Can you not see the wildness in his eyes? He's not one of us. He will most assuredly leave once he's had his fill of silly blonde lassie!" He ran a hand through his ridiculous curls in frustration.

"You know nothing about me, louper," I said. I pulled Kait protectively to my chest, but I couldn't protect her. Kait looked fearfully up at me to search for the wildness herself, while her brother continued to gouge salt into her deepest fear—losing me.

"When you leave," he continued, "will you drag my sister under the sea right away or first fill her belly with a deformed baby?"

Tears ran freely from Kait's eyes. "Eamon?"

"Don't listen to him," I warned in an unsteady voice. Her eyes were as dark as a selkie and uncertain once again. Her doubt wounded me. She did not fear the burd I would plant in her, only my leaving. That's what it always came back to. "I'd never do anything to hurt you. Why are ye swayed by your brother so easily when I've given you my oath?" I had underestimated Blair's power. Kait had disguised the strength of their bond.

"You're not the only one with instincts," Blair said. "Listen to them, Kait. Ask him to leave now. It will be much worse later. You and I can still go to the Mainland where there will be no reminders."

"Ye'll not try and take her from me," I warned, posturing to fight. "I dinnae wish to be your enemy, but you make me hate you."

"Damn ye to Helheim," Blair cried as he picked up an empty tankard and threw it.

"We are married, Blair!" Kait cried outraged. "And there will be no more bad tempered boys fighting. I can't stand it!" Her chest heaved up and down as she steadied herself on the bink. "I too have made an oath. Would ye have me walk away and break my oath? I'd not survive to the winter solstice. Odin would not be so charitable."

Her brother looked shilpit as he considered this. "What have ye done, Kait? It's suicide."

"He poisons your ears," I grumbled with tightly knotted fists. I felt frightened for Kait and frightened for us. Her brother would try and pry us apart. "I'd take you where ye can't hear."

"I've made a choice!" Kait cried, ignoring me. "I'll be with my husband as long as he'll have me." She took my hand and pulled me towards the open door. It was misting again and the cold pelted against us.

"Where's your choice, Kait?" Blair cried after us. "His magick has blinded you. You never had a choice!"

When we were huddled alone on the moor with nothing but green and wind all around, Kait buried her face against my chest and cried uncontrollably.

"I love you, Kait," I murmured into her ear over and over again. "I'd never leave you."

My words blew away unheeded while Kait trembled like a frail flower in my arms. I felt completely powerless to protect her.

"Where are the rest of your kind?" she asked in a wavering voice. She blinked away the raindrops that splashed on her lashes. "Why are you the only one?"

I smiled gently. "They are in the sea missing out on loving you."

"It's 'cos they hate the land," she sniffed, turning to hide her red swollen eyes. "No other selkie has chosen this life—not a single one."

I wound my hands into her web of damp hair and forced her to see me. "There's something ye don't understand," I said. "I need you more than I need the sea, understand?"

"Why should a king with a golden chain love a poor hen girl?"

"I don't know. I suppose 'cos he is compelled too, just as she is compelled to love him. Does the reason matter?"

Kait explored this thought with luminous eyes. "No, it doesn't matter."

"If anyone sought to take you from me, I'd snuff them out like a wet fire." My eyes moved over her sorrowful face before I caught her salty tears with my lips and tongue. She closed her eyes and leaned into me exhausted.

"Prove Blair wrong," she murmured. "Be there when I wake up on the morra."

"I'll prove him wrong every day," I promised with a gentle nudge.

The following day, Kait furiously whisked something over the fire while eyeing me nervously. "Ye slept like the dead last night." Lavender shadows bruised the tender skin under her eyes.

I kicked off the pungent sheep blanket that Kait insisted on draping over me. "Were ye afraid to close your eyes, Kait?"

She dropped her eyes embarrassed. "I may have slept fer a few minutes."

I thrust myself onto my elbows to admire the way her under-clothes draped over her slender hips and thighs. The vile clothes that Kait insisted on wearing weren't completely without merit. The sheer cloth seemed like a teasing trifle in a mating game.

"I kept my promise," I reminded her. "The honor of a selkie is everything."

Kait sampled something creamy from the edge of a spoon. "If ye wanted to hunt, I'd understand." Her words sounded confident, but her eyes were still occupied with the fear that I wouldn't return.

"I'd hunt today," I said with a devious grin. "It's not healthy for me to go so long."

"Oh." She dropped her eyes back into the pot and lethargically stirred. "That makes sense."

"Ye misunderstand," I said with a soft growl as I crawled to my knees. "Today I'd hunt you. Are you scared?"

A smile crept across her sun-warmed face, and I felt enormously happy. I made it better for Kait—even for a short time. "You can't hunt me," she said in a wobbly voice as she fumbled to rotate the pot off the flames. "You are *my* prey."

Later after we humped, Kait bit her lip and looked at me worriedly. "Are ye sure you are ready to be around so many land lovers?" She tucked my leine into my ridiculously baggy trousers then frowned. "I can always barter on the morra."

"It's the reason ye cut my hair," I reminded her, raking my fingers through the short, choppy pieces. "You can't hide me forever." Secretly I looked forward to an excuse to sneak among the loupers. I especially hoped Magnum would be there. He was a possessive and hairy numpty. Punching his chops only whetted my appetite for more fighting.

After my feet were grotesquely shod in another animal's skin, Kait collected a wagonful of eggs, and we followed the rolling dirt road towards the more occupied south side of the island.

"I'd not be welcome in certain circles," Kait murmured as we entered the first dusty street. Her eyes darted around nervously.

Loupers were milling about everywhere in multiple layers of foul bowfing clothing. The scores of men seemed especially fond of flat, cocked bonnets. They lumbered in and out of tall stony stops with an air of important business. Between the shops, alleys overflowed with broken crates, bottles, and other trash. I resisted the urge to skulk into the dark shadows and snag one of the men around the throat. There were so many it was hardly a sport at all.

"Circles?" I asked guardedly as my eyes drifted across a whirlwind of faces. I felt satisfied, even smug that my silky mantle was securely hidden from their covetous eyes.

As Kait strolled under a heavily runed sign dangling above the street, I peered into a shop displaying a rainbow of brightly colored bonnets. One of them was turbulently blue like the place where the North Sea meets Skagerrak. I debated the ease of taking it and improving my disguise.

"For what I did to Magnum," Kait continued with a grievous face. "I'll be thought of as a bint—a woman who kisses many lips and easily opens her legs."

"This is what Magnum will tell the other loupers?" I asked angrily.

Kait looked wounded. "They'll come to their own conclusions. Magnum is well loved with a loyal ring of friends. It looks bad that you are now my husband when yesterday he and I were to be wed."

"This means married?"

"Aye, can you imagine? He's old enough to be my father. He and Da shared a stall on the Mainland once. They couldn't sell the cod quickly enough."

I wrinkled my brow. I didn't want to imagine Kait with another man, neither did I understand selling. She removed a pail of eggs from her wagon and thrust her shoulders back before marching into a group of men and women arguing over the matter of ground roots, fish, and other unidentifiable foods that didn't seem fresh or even alive. "Finna, fit like?" she asked a grey haired woman with a peculiar cloth pinned to the crown of her head.

The woman named Finna lowered a small cask. Her nose was long and wrinkled and her eyes sharp like urchin spines. "Kait? Where have ye been? Magnum has been searching for you for days." She glanced up at me, before checking the coiled braids of her hair.

"Magnum points his nose where it doesn't belong," I told the woman from behind Kait. "Have ye seen him?"

An amused smile spread across her face. "You're wise to avoid him, laddie. The last time I saw Magnum, he was muddled with drink and ranting to whoever would listen about the evils of Tipper Gray's nephew."

"Is that all you heard?" Kait asked.

"Ha, of course that's not all I heard," the old woman shrieked. "My eyes are not so dim that I can't see the bonnie man standing behind you. You weaseled out of Magnum's musty bed in the nick of time."

"But you said Magnum was a good catch," Kait protested.

Finna tilted her head and winked. "Beets are tasty enough till you've sampled something as pure and sweet as sugar. I'd not blame you for what you've done. Tipper Gray's nephew, eh?"

"Thankee, Finna," Kait answered. "The whole thing is a repugnant misunderstanding caused by Blair." She looped her arm through mine. "This is Eamon, my husband, Tipper Gray's nephew."

Finna gasped with surprise. "Ye didn't say he was your husband."

"We mated," I told Finna.

"We wanted a quick marriage without all the spectacle," Kait said with flushed cheeks.

Finna narrowed her eyes and glanced at me. "Without even a foot washing ceremony? Did he plant a child?"

"Of course not," Kait said sourly. "It was done properly."

Silence filled the air as all sets of eyes turned towards us. It seemed everyone's business was suddenly done. I was uncertain of protocol, so I held my tongue and fiercely met their gazes.

"Did he say mated?" an elderly voice croaked from the crowd.

"Where you from, son?" a red face man asked.

"The sea," I responded. "Where there are nae boundaries or walls."

"He's from the Mainland," Kait said with a tight lipped smile. "But his heart belongs at sea. He's a fisherman."

A woman with bright green eyes and upswept hair gave me a flirtatious smile. She was pleasurable to the eye but reeked of another man. "Where do you live, Mr. Eamon?" She touched the apex of her abundant bosom to insinuate what was beneath. "I'd bring ye some o' my carrageen mould as a welcoming gift."

"We're staying at Tipper Gray's ol' place till Blair moves out," Kait interjected. "Thankee, Sarah, we'll look forward to that mould."

"Haven't we met before?" a burly man with a wiry blonde beard asked. He eyed me irritably and cracked his knuckles.

I bore my teeth with a smile, "Aye, the experience sours my memory."

"Eamon teases," Kait blurted with a panic stricken face. "Biorn, shouldn't you be working your magick inside the castle?"

I met Biorn's threatening gaze with my own warring face. His aggression was easily baited, and I hoped we might be able to spar. "I'd not be teasing."

"I'd have some ale first," he grunted as he glowered over the length of my body. "It'll help me remember where I've seen you,

Eamon." He lumbered down the street with his thumbs stuck in his belt.

"What are you doing?" Kait hissed. "You don't know him at all."

I shrugged. "Biorn enjoys the sport of fighting."

"Perhaps I should show Eamon around the village," Kait told the others fretfully. "He'll need to visit the cooper after he's caught a boatload of fish."

"I'd be delighted to show your new husband all the shops," Sarah simpered. "That way ye can stay and take care of unloading all those eggs." She squeezed my arm, squashing her rounded diddies into me. "My seamstress shop's at the end of the lane. We can start there."

"It's a cordial offer, but I'd stay with Kait."

Kait looked thunderstruck, like she didn't want me to stay with her at all.

"Welcome to Shapinsay, laddie," a friendly looking man said. "I'd hear all about my newest neighbor. The village is blathering with excitement."

"Mr. Dunlop, Eamon was just going to see our cooper," Kait said as she practically dragged me out of the crowd. "We'll be certain to visit the farmstead soon."

"I only wish to know his surname," Mr. Dunlop persisted after us. "All the dairy men want to know."

"It's Swanney, just like me," Kait blurted over her shoulder.

"What kind of man takes his wife's name," he asked in a not so friendly tone.

When we ducked behind the boot maker, Kait fell into my chest with an exasperated laugh. "I wish you could turn it off."

"I'd like to answer Mr. Dunlap's last questions," I said with the same polite tone Mr. Dunlap had used.

"Can't you see where that will lead?" Kait asked. "He asks a civil question, then ye try to goad him, then he tries to knock your lights out."

"I'm not afraid of him."

"It's a shame. You enjoy provoking the men—it's a game for you. But you've got to stop before you get hurt. It's bad enough that the mere sight of ye makes them want to pummel your brains in."

I sank my hands into her hair and gently bumped her forehead against mine. "It feels so good to be loved, but you shouldn't worry."

Her arms folded around my neck as her lip twitched into a reluctant smile. "I've got bartering to do without your evil influence. Do you think you'd like to explore a bit on your own?"

"Nae wan recognized me. It's fun to be invisible."

Kait released her hold and gave me an anxious expression. "Perhaps you'd like to visit the boatyard after you see the cooper. We'll need to repair the spongy underside of Da's dilapidated boat. You could get some ideas."

"I'll explore," I announced. I wouldn't tell Kait that the notion of bobbing inside a boat was preposterous. I'd left my home behind, not my pride. "And if ye wish, I'll sneak down to the boatyard later."

Kait smiled nervously as we separated. I watched her join the group of coarse men and women already arguing over their goods. Kait produced a pail of eggs and began to barter with a bearded man waving around stuffed tubes of meat. I marveled that she didn't seem to belong to the rest of the loupers—she was too... free.

I lifted my nose to the gentle breeze coming in off the voe. The scent of salt, gull, and pier filled my nostrils. The water was nearby. I imagined the waves splitting over barnacle encrusted pylons before cascading down my back and flipper. I quivered with excitement.

I loosened the ties at my neck and then the ones at my wrists. Wind filled my leine as I took first one tenuous step and then another. A woman with a small boy in tow, paused to watch with wide enamored eyes. When I met her gaze, she hastily jingled into the bakery with flushed cheeks. Pleased to have my audience gone, I shook my hair, expecting to feel it flutter and lift off my shoulders, but it was all gone. Losh! Had I been intending to dive? I became angry with myself for getting caught up in the rush and turned hastily back towards the center of the village.

After anonymously examining every storefront and alley, I made a quick pass through the vacant boatyard, kicking through pale curls of wood that had been planed from the side of a monstrous boat.

After fulfilling my obligation to Kait, I eagerly raced towards the castle, the place Kait expected Biorn to be. As my breaths slowed, I paced around the great structure, marveling at the jumble of complicated walls and windows singularly jutting towards the grey sky like the impressive cliffs of Hoy.

There were a few men lumbering around outside with boards straddled across their shoulders but no sign of Biorn. The deep rumble of voices told me that most of the workers were tooling away inside.

With disappointment, I kicked at a clump of weeds before spotting a shaggy yellow dog emerging from the unusual copse of trees. I had seen dogs before, barking senselessly at our kind and thrashing their tails at the water's edge. I strode forcefully towards the beast, never breaking my gaze from the large brown eyes that were deceptively friendly.

"You're a dog," I growled. "Ye wish to taste my blood?"

The beast trotted fearlessly closer, and I wrinkled my nose when the bowfing scent of its hide wafted near. I postured myself for battle, eyeing the pointed fangs and pink tongue grotesquely lopped over black wet lips. When he came within reach, I snatched him by his belly, hoisted him over my shoulder and then threw him victoriously into the grass. The dog yelped in surprise before scrambling to his feet with his filthy tail tucked between his legs. When he started to run, I heaved myself across the open field and dove on the dog's hind legs. This time the beast was prepared and sunk his wicked teeth into my shoulder. I cried out in pain before thrusting the beast across the field once more.

That was when I isolated Kait's voice from the rest of the noise and rumble. "Eamon!" The dog scurried away with the whole of his miserable life as I froze to listen. "Eamon! Oh Odin, not this day!" Kait was in trouble!

Furiously, I raced back to the crowded street with my heart swishing loudly in my ears. Who was the villain that would try to steal Kait from me—Mr. Dunlap, Biorn, Mr. Lennie? Dead—dead—dead, all of them! By the time I turned the corner of the first store, I was panting and blinded with rage.

"Where's Kait?" I roared.

The street had thinned considerably, but a beak nosed woman pointed her cane down the street. "She'd be crying her eyes out behind the butcher's. Would ye be her new husband?"

I threw myself down the road then collided into an alleyway where I found Kait folded up and sobbing. She shook and trembled with her knees pressed against her chest as if she fought to keep her lungs inside.

"Who did this to you?" I crowed, punching a stack of moldy boxes. The boxes splintered and rained all around. "I promise I'll get him."

Kait's red and swollen eyes shot up from under a mass of tangled hair. "Oh Eamon... you did."

22

THE NATURE O' SKIN

I failed to protect Kait. This awful thought resonated over and over again in my mind. "I'm here now," I whispered into her ear as I stirred her hair as my own source of comfort. I felt bewildered and lost by Kait's fear. It was my purpose to care for her, and now she suffered more than ever. I didn't understand Kait. I had become her husband as she asked. For her...I had become a louper.

"I looked everywhere for you," Kait said in a very frail and feminine voice. "I thought you'd be able to hear me if I called." Her eyes were full of pain and embarrassment and could not meet my own grappling gaze.

I moved damp strands of hair from her cheek and cradled her face in my hands. "If I'm listening, but I was caught up at the castle. How could ye panic so easily?"

"It's the madness. The real me is fierce and independent like our own fair queen but not when you're gone. Your weapons wound me and steal my breath." She held on to the front of my leine with a tight grip. "You were gone for so long, I assumed…"

"You assumed I went back to the sea," I grunted. Kait would never know about my temptation to dive and luxuriate in the water once more. I felt shame for causing her pain and for still loving the sea. I was failing as her protector.

Kait sighed deeply. "I'm sorry, but even though my brother is an eejit, his words ring true. You are not meant to live on land."

"Your brother *is* an eejit," I agreed. "You are getting nae better. Ye must try harder to trust me. We can't always be together."

*****

When I rose from our bed the next day, Kait moaned and felt around the warm space beside her. Her eyes fluttered fearfully but then settled on me with a comforted smile. I smiled back, pleased that I could reassure her so easily, but it wasn't enough. Kait was hiding the cruel and tender wounds gouged by the very selkie that loved her.

I hated what I was doing to her—I hated myself. Slowly an impenetrable wall lifted like a butterfly in my mind. There was more I could do to help her.

~Kait~

I didn't expect Eamon to stay attached to my apron strings forever. Truly, I wanted him to be strong and happy like he was in the sea. I wanted him to run and explore and release that part of him that was animal. When he told me he wanted to walk along the wall all alone, my heart strangled inside my chest. Alone? Why Eamon, why? Still, I didn't question him. I needed to trust him—*I needed to be happy.*

I wasn't happy. The wall wrapped the edges of the sea. The entire dreich island was encompassed with that wretched wall and in turn drenched in sea! There was no place for Eamon to escape his demons and everywhere for him to escape. What he would do was a surety—his need for sea coursed with fervor through his veins and defined who he was. Where did that leave me? Oh Odin—all alone with nothing but a handful of opulent hair to comfort me! I rushed to the crapping pot and turned my empty stomach inside out with several dry heaves.

Later, I paced with mad vehemence, wearing down the flagstones directly in front of the small recessed window. Again and again, I checked the horizon for his lithe form loping through the grass, but he never appeared. What was he doing that needed to be done alone? Perhaps my worrying was only stifling Eamon, and he needed fresh air. Perhaps he was craving the fresh herring he was so fond of. Would he return to me once his belly was filled with wiggling fish? He promised he would return—of course he would return. I twisted a strand of hair till it held its snarled shape then promptly decided I would visit Blair. Never mind that a northeast section of wall wrapped around our empty croft house. If I ran into Eamon, it would simply be a pleasant surprise—no it would be a miracle.

I felt disheartened when I found our bedroom bare and all of Blair's grass stained leins missing. He was finally gone for good and my home open once more. I should have yelped for joy, but instead I examined the layer of dust collecting in my absence and mourned the loss of my brother. There was no need for Blair to stay, neither need for him to come back. I was now married and no longer Blair's problem. He had a new life waiting for him on the Mainland and a sweet young bride who would serve as a new, more amiable companion. I decided I wouldn't feel jealous or sad at all. I collected a tin of Mountain Sorrel to brighten the dim room then rushed impatiently back to Tipper's house to check for Eamon's return.

As I thrust the door open, I held my breath, fearing that our last precious hour had been ignorantly and sorely wasted. When my eyes adjusted to the dim room, my heart leapt with joy. Eamon was waiting for me at the table with a handful of poisonous purple berries sprawled out in front of him. A broad and innocent smile spread across his beautiful face as he rolled the berries towards me. "They grow far above the ground. I'll eat wan if it would make you happy."

I laughed with relief. "I'd never forgive you if you ate one. Those are Foolsay Nitters. They'll make you wish ye were dead."

Eamon glared at the innocuous looking little berries before flicking them one by one onto the floor.

"Hey," I cried with another laugh as I scooped up the remainder into my hand. "They are clever little devils. Tell ye when someone's lying, they do."

Eamon gave a dubious smirk. "They strangle in the throats of the deceitful?"

"Of course not. It's obvious you should hide them under the bed of the accused. If a lie has been told, the scoundrel's teeth will turn purple the next day."

"That sounds like a handy tool for your brother."

I emptied the berries into the pocket of my apron, fully intending to use them on Eamon later. "Did you have a nice walk?"

"Did you think I had been leisuring about the filthy moor?"

"I—I thought ye said—" Suddenly I realized that Eamon wasn't wearing his leine, that his opulent skin was glowing too brightly for the shadowy room. My eyes roamed delightedly over his tight navel and sculpted belly, but then froze when I realized that he was wearing his mantle. "Your skin?" I asked dazedly.

"It's been in a safe place. Did you notice it was gone?" He reached for me, but I stumbled in my haste to distance myself from him.

"Do not touch me," I wheezed as my breath caught in my throat. I clutched a chair to steady myself. "There's nae honor in goodbye. You've made an oath!"

Eamon slid his skin solemnly from his shoulders. "Who's leaving?" He advanced towards me then gently placed his mantle around me. I gave a small gasp as his warmth enfolded like a summer day around me. "You're not leaving?" I choked out.

"I'd not be leaving today or ever. This is what I've been trying to get you to understand. I don't want you to hurt anymore, Kait. I'm giving you my skin."

"Eamon, you can't," I gasped. "It's part of you—the body for your soul."

He stroked my cheek with soft buttery fingers. "I'm whole when I'm with you. Tell me now if you are planning to go somewhere without me so I can tackle you and take it back."

"I—I'm your wife," I stuttered. "I would never leave."

"My home is here too, Kait. I need you to trust me—to feel secure. This is my job as yours is to feed me." His gaze returned dourly to his skin cradled limply around my shoulders. "There is a condition however."

"I already know. You need me to return your skin when you are ready to swim and hunt."

"Nae," Eamon said gruffly. "Promise ye'll hide it in a place I'll never find."

I stared at him with shock and horror. "I'd not keep you here against your will."

Eamon scooped me up in his arms, and I felt his mantle almost imperceptibly slide across my neck as it strained for its master. His lips floated warm, peaceable words into my ear. "I never want to fail you, Kait. Let me give you my heart without contest."

I held him back, listening to the rapid, troubled drumming inside his hard chest. Eamon almost convinced me that it was easy for him to give up his most priceless possession. My tears trickled with gratitude between us. "I couldn't keep such a great thing from you. The hardship would be too much."

"Hardship is separation from you," Eamon said gravely. "If I ask fer it, refuse me—even if I beg."

I turned from him, clutching the velvety skin like it was my own soul and not Eamon's skin. "I'll take it, but you'll never be my prisoner. It's yours the first time you ask for it."

I absently stroked the fine grey hairs, considering the horrible thing I would do. I would hide it and hide it well, but it would be for my own sanity. Never again would I believe that Eamon might disappear in the night while I ignorantly slept. He wouldn't survive long in the harsh sea climate without it. If he ever needed to leave, it would be on *my* conditions. My suffering would be short as I would most certainly follow him under the turquoise waves and be a selkie for a few exquisite moments.

"Hide it well," Eamon mumbled, rubbing the back of his neck.

"I'll sleep soundly tonight," I said with a joyful laugh. "Thankee, Eamon. I know that you'd rather give up your right arm."

Eamon wiggled the fingers on his right hand, wondering at such a sacrifice.

I looked back at Eamon's coat, mortified by the grotesque inequality between us. "Your gift makes me feel very, very small. I must think of something wonderful to give you."

Eamon looked up distractedly. "You are gift enough. I mean for you to understand my attachment to you."

I smiled bemusedly. I'd never understand Eamon.

"You will put it in a safe place? A place loupers won't accidentally stumble?"

"I'll treat it as if it were my own skin." I adjusted the smooth side around my shoulders and inhaled Eamon's windy scent.

"It suits you."

"It doesn't cling to me like it does you," I mused. I adjusted it over my shoulders to emphasize its looseness.

"That's 'cos it doesn't recognize you."

"Because I'm female."

"'Cos you're not me. My skin is part of me—body *and* spirit. That's who I am."

"That makes me feel awful and your skin feel stolen."

"Don't let it." Eamon slouched against the wall to scrutinize me inside his skin. His baggy trousers were slung over one hip like they would be dismissed any moment. Dressing Eamon was like dressing a lion and expecting it to become happily accustomed to wearing a jacket.

"Ye told me that long ago that land lovers stole the skins of selkies. I assumed they had used them to swim."

"Impossible. Our skins have memories of their owner's shape and smell. Every time I put my skin on, it memorizes me as I memorize it. As I change and grow, its memory adapts. If a thief had a desire to swim, the stolen skin would simply hang heavily about him like a wet blanket."

"Does it think?"

"Nae, it only remembers."

"Will it remember me?" I asked, pulling the skin more snugly around my shoulders.

Eamon looked amused. "Remember who?"

"Am I so forgettable?" I asked playfully.

"You're too clothed," he complained in a husky voice. Feral eyes moved hungrily along the length of my body, igniting a warm flame deep within my belly. He was paces away, but his thoughts caressed and tickled deep inside. "The fabric is too fluid. You're confusing it even now."

"This fabric?" I asked, unfurling the many folds in my skirt.

"It's in the way."

"Hmmmmm." I set Eamon's mantle aside and fixed him with a wide gaze. "It's a predicament."

"It's not a problem. I wish to see you in my skin."

"What a coincidence," I purred as I slipped out of one shoulder. "I would feel your skin against me." Eamon eyes were amorously glued to my subtle curves as I wiggled out of the remainder of my clothes. My dress fell in a heap, and I kicked it impatiently away. When I slid the smooth side of his skin over my shoulders, he gave a bark of approval.

"It holds your heat," I mused yet again. "I'd never be cold again with such a fine mantle."

"That's what I'm for," Eamon said. "I'd not compete with my skin but warm you myself."

"Thankee, Eamon," I said, fighting the emotion rising in my chest. "I know this is hard for you, but I'll take good care of it."

"It looks better on you anyway," he said, pulling me closer with smoldering eyes.

"Now you're the one who's mad," I murmured, embarrassed.

Eamon's flawless skin glided against me as he molded himself inside his mantle. He was bare once again. Hard skin and muscles taunted and teased, erupting a bonfire inside my belly. The magical skin inched around us until our bodies were completely cocooned like a warm glove. "It feels your presence," I gasped happily.

"Nae," Eamon breathed as his lips pulled and tugged gently on mine. "It feels yours and it's never been happier."

*****

It felt like I slept for days, but I was bound to waken eventually. When I pulled the charcoal skin from Eamon's shoulder, his eyes fluttered open anxiously. He immediately rolled over in bed and followed my every move with dark, brooding eyes. "Ye would hide it now?"

Soused with guilt, I tucked his skin against my chest. "I'll be back before ye miss me."

Eamon sat sullenly with an ordinary wool blanket bunched between his legs. He looked worried, even frightened. "I already miss you. Haste ye back."

He didn't say anymore, but I could feel his eyes silently boring into my back as I left with his most priceless possession—the companion to his spirit.

He gave it to me—he gave it to me, I repeated to myself over and over. *Oh Odin, I'm severing Eamon's body and damning my soul!* Pain squeezed like a coiling serpent in my chest, constricting one undeserving breath after another. Still I clutched the captured skin more tightly to my chest and stumbled into the glaring light with something that could never, ever in a hundred years belong to me. Hadn't I seen the velvety coat resurrect with life repeatedly for Eamon and only Eamon? I was no selkie but a wretched thief in need of a lair.

I took a few gulping breaths to calm the storm raging in my head. What did it matter who owned the skin and who belonged in the sea? I was helping my husband to love me.

I started towards home with my mind on the dark, shadowy places below the eaves when I stopped dead in my tracks. The croft would be the first place Eamon would look. I became sick considering it lingering above our heads day after day, just yards from Eamon's creamy white fingertips. Was I so certain he would look for it? I had to remind myself that Eamon was a deceiver—not only a man as my eyes would testify but a powerful and muscular beast with an instinct to swim. Of course he would look.

My heart pounded against my ribs as I kicked a rut in the soil. His coat needed to be hidden in a place that Eamon didn't know and would probably never go. It also had to be far enough from the village where it could never, ever become someone else's morbid cloak or hat.

My mind visually explored the various homes and structures on the island till I remembered Burroughstone Broch with an uneasy skip in my chest. It was an ancient, circular stone structure on the far side of the island, ignored by everyone except nesting Kittiwakes. It was the lair this thief needed. I changed direction and headed east towards the crumbling ruin.

A sleepy amber light swept across the moor like a silent wind as I neared the ancient remains. As I stepped into the long covert shadows, I felt cold and uneasy, for there was no faery protection here. The mysterious structure was no more than ten paces wide, but thick as a fortress with cool, dark walls that seemed as permanent as the sky. It would suffice as a hiding place and shrine for Eamon's mantle.

I crept down the rampart then handled and wiggled a hundred stones till I settled on one near the mossy floor that budged the width of a pea. I pried and twisted the stone back and forth until it slipped free, then worked on loosening the one behind it. My secret box slowly hollowed out until it was big enough to slip Eamon's skin inside unscathed.

With tremulous fingers, I fingered the yellow patches of fur one last time before tightly wrapping it inside an oiled skin and walling it inside. I felt immense shame as I stepped back to appraise the place where Eamon's skin had disappeared. The hiding place was too clever, too sinister, the stones too seamlessly wedged together like they had been that way for thousands of years. With a miserable ache inside my chest, I stumbled towards the bay to wash the evil deed from my hands.

I didn't wash, but guiltily gulped at the salty water instead. When my stomach cramped with pain and fullness, I wretched into the waves and burned my throat with vomit. My skirt was drenched with the scent of the sea, but I was too distraught to care. The water would serve as a small clue to Eamon and ease my pain. Burning with this thought, I waded in further then dove under the first rising wave. The sun blinked out behind the horizon as I feverously stroked into the comforting darkness.

23

EAMON'S BLIGHT

A small flicker of light glowed out from a window as I wearily made my way home. When I opened the door, I was not surprised to find him still naked, warming his ivory backside to the fire. He seemed very young and vulnerable without his skin to give him confidence.

"You've been gone a long time," he said with irritation as he scrutinized my still damp clothing and salt encrusted hair. "And you smell like sea and selkie."

I froze, realizing I had indeed swam in selkie colonized waters. "You know where I've been?" I asked with a thunderbolt of fear. A clue was very, very different from actually knowing.

"I'd not look fer my skin," Eamon said as he kicked up his feet in a chair. "Though I know it's somewhere near the eastern voe. The pure selkies frolic there."

"Do you miss it?" I asked mournfully, because I knew he not only missed it—he ached for it.

"I can feel it," Eamon said with an annoyed glance. "It's someplace cold." He thought about this a moment before his black eyes flickered back with a burning question. "Is it safe?"

"Aye, you'll never find it," I said miserably. "I pray to the gods that you'll never even try."

"And if I asked you to take me there—to the cold place by the eastern voe?"

"I'd drag my feet," I said queasily.

"That is the wrong answer," he barked as he shot out of his chair. He paced a short distance then snapped around. "Ye must die with your secret, understand?"

"But ye'll live much longer than me," I protested. "You only need to ask and I'd tell you—right now if you wanted. I can't stand keeping something so important from you."

"Tell your brother if ye trust him," Eamon relented. "If you die before I do, I'll go to his dwelling on the big island and punch it out of him, but ye must never, ever tell *me*."

"He wants nothing to do with us," I said. "And I can't keep it a secret. If you ask I'll tell. I'd not have you hate me but would rather die a leper—one body part falling off at a time." I slumped drearily into a chair and bunched my damp skirt sulkily between my knees.

"You think I could hate you?" Eamon asked as he circled around the bink. I froze as he lifted a strand of my hair to his silvery lips so he could inhale deeply and savor the salt. It pained me that Eamon would always reach for the ocean, even when he didn't realize he was doing it.

"You should hate me. I've made a grievous offense against you."

Eamon raised me with sturdy arms, squarely meeting my dodging gaze. "There's nothing to forgive. You're my mate, Kait. Did ye not know that selkie folk choose only wan?"

"Ye tell me lies to make me feel better."

"It's true," he murmured as his lips pressed into my hair. "The selkies are fiercely loyal."

"Even if ye live to be three hundred years old?"

"Even if I live to be a thousand."

I was a foolish wench, undeserving of Eamon's love. Had he not given up everything for me? Had he not proven his love by first giving me his vow and then his skin? I felt selfish for wanting more—for wanting an assurance that Eamon would never regret choosing me over the sea. It was an impossible wish. A part of him would always be looking away from me and towards the sea.

"A thousand years," I mused to myself. "Will ye always be so beautiful?" It occurred to me that I'd never seen a grey or wrinkled selkie.

"Ye think me beautiful?" he asked as his mouth twitched amusedly by my cheek.

"Too fine a man to be human," I answered honestly. Of course he would be. He was born to be painfully beautiful.

"My face is *your* skin," he said jovially. "Wan holds the other hostage. Do ye think I'd give it up and lose all I have?"

"Is that an answer?" I asked with a bunched brow.

Eamon gave a barking laugh but then swayed and caught himself against a shelf.

"Are you ill?" I gasped, snatching his arm protectively. "You're pale."

He gave a smaller, less certain laugh. "My skin is always white, but this alarms you now?" He shook off his arm, insulted by my rescue.

"Are you dizzy?" I persisted. "You were fine a moment ago."

Eamon stood to his full height. "My *wife* keeps me awake all night while she hazardously swims in the voe. She has nae right to worry."

All night? My eyes flickered to the window beginning to glow with a warm, peachy hue. "You're exhausted," I muttered.

Eamon playfully tugged on my skirt. "I'm finding I can't sleep without my naughty *wife*. You'd lie beside me now."

~Eamon~

I woke before Kait with no occupation. I listened to the sea wax and wane inside her vacant seashell then rapidly spun the hoop of Tipper's spinning wheel till it hummed and shook. When she continued to deeply sleep, I beamed peat bricks into the spitting fire then searched for the dried herring. Finally Kait woke up after I noisily explored the fittings of two heavy pots.

"You're still here," she said with a relaxed smile. As she propped herself up, a tangled mass of gold hair fell over her shoulders like a halo of light. Kait was bright and sunny—the antithesis of those that lurked in dark, watery shadows.

"This time you knew I'd be here," I said with muffled satisfaction as I swallowed a mouthful of fish head. The herring was lousily hidden in a deep kettle. "You have no more need to worry. I'm grounded as you are."

"Thankee, Eamon," she said solemnly. "The words are not enough, but I haven't slept like that since you first stole into the house."

I smiled and took another bite of fish. Every day that Kait was happy, I was happy too. She made my skin feel close at hand, and I wondered if it was as far away as I had first assumed.

"From the look o' this place, you've been bored," Kait said, sweeping a startled gaze across the cluttered room. "It looks like a toddler was set loose." She frowned at the roll of yarn I'd methodically and carefully unwound. It had taken me a very long time. "It's just as well; I'd move us home today."

"Your brother?"

"Never coming back," she answered solemnly. "He cleared out all his things. He may even be married now."

"I'd go where you go."

Kait gave a relaxed smile. "After moving all our things, we can take a look at Da's boat, and then on the morra, we can go into the village and barter for a net."

I stiffened at the suggestion. "I'd not get inside your father's boat. I swim speedily *through* water, not float on top like common spar. Did you confuse me for a land louper?"

Kait's sunny face wrinkled, and I immediately regretted the plainness of my words. "Oh—I—I misunderstood," she stuttered. "You said you would be a hunter of fish."

"I changed my mind. I'd *eat* fish instead."

Kait gave an unhappy laugh. "Aye, this I know; ye are a selkie. But how are the fish to find their way to the table? They don't swim through the air like birds, nor do they cooperate at holding very still when one intends to capture and eat them. Were you going to catch the fish from below with wrinkly white fingers?"

I blinked up at her, confused by the obvious. "We trade your eggs for fish. Let the clumsy loupers catch them with their nets."

"My eggs will not be enough," Kait said with eyes that were suddenly moist and bright. "Without Blair's sheep we'll be sorely vexed for food and supplies."

I reached for the disguise of my leine, frustrated and restive by Kait's unhappiness. "Dinnae worry, I'll return with Blair's sheep."

"They no longer belong to us," Kait cried, unaccountably anxious. "Ye just can't march onto Ian Gillis's pasture and steal his sheep. Shapinsay is not like the ocean where ye can take whatever ye see without consequence. Ian owns them now."

"Owns?"

"Aye," she cried, picking up a pot and waving it wildly around. "Like this pot is mine. If someone steals it, I'll be very angry and notify the constable."

"You're already angry," I observed, slipping an arm into a coarse sleeve.

"You're a master at catching fish," Kait groaned, dropping the pot with a loud clatter. "If you don't want to humiliate yourself by stepping aboard a boat, then net the fish underwater. You could catch hundreds at once if you hone your skills. You could eat all ye want, and we could sell the rest fer coppers."

I stared at her, wounded by her suggestion to succumb to the sea for even a little while. Could she not see that I would be less—a selkie without virtue, honor or strength?

"Aren't you going to say anything?" she cried.

"I'd not be going in the water anymore," I admitted.

Kait's eyes grew with disbelief. "What?"

"No more water." I folded myself into a chair and glared up at her. "I will not be weak. Would ye test me?"

"What are ye blathering on about? You went swimmin' with me the day we took our marriage oaths. You enjoyed blowing bubbles below the waves and pulling my toes. You were showing off."

"I was making sure you didn't drown. You forget, I've seen you swim."

"Why are ye doing this?" she wailed. "Are ye afraid ye might not come back?"

"I'd always come back."

"Then why? Are ye punishing yourself for something?" A small strangled sound escaped her throat as she leaned heavily against a chair. "Oh Odin, are ye punishing yourself for... loving me? Is it regrets you're having?"

"I've already explained to you," I said angrily. "I will not be weak!" I bounded out of my chair and darted through a flock of squawking white hens outside. Kait had no choice but to see through flawed louper eyes. She didn't understand at all!

When I got to the short wall, I stopped. There was no place for me to go. North, south, east, west—it didn't matter. Whichever direction I chose, I would collide with inviting waves and lots and lots of water. Losh! I picked up a smooth round stone and balanced it in my hand. It was warm and heavy—too heavy. Or was I just tired? I hurled it with a grunt towards the vast North Sea, satisfied by how far it sailed.

Kait ran up breathlessly behind me. Her warm fingers tenuously touched my shoulder then withdrew to her lap. "I would not complain if I understood," she persisted.

I whipped around and clutched two handfuls of windblown hair. "It's very simple," I breathed. The ground seemed to sway as I pulled her closer to me.

"Eamon," Kait squeaked with surprise.

"I have chosen you; therefore I cannot have the sea. Why do you test my honor?"

Kait trembled as her eyes moved slowly over my face. "I'd not have ye punish yourself. The waves call to you even now. I know ye can smell the salt and the fish. You ache to be weightless once again and feel the cool flow over your flippers—even I feel the longing to swim."

"Nae," I growled, giving her a wee shoogle. "I have forgotten those things. Ye are what lures me now. Over the filthy wall where your stone house dwells, that is where I want to be. I'd live there forever along with the grass, soil, and worms."

Kait withdrew from me with her eyes fixed wide on my face. "I know ye want to swim. I can see you're trying to hide it." She pulled her dress off and folded it neatly on the wall. "You'd swim with me—now."

My eyes floated down her fragile looking form—too weak to slice through the brutal currents racing past the rocks. "Don't do this," I warned.

But Kait smiled and clipped off towards the yellow grass swaying along the shoreline with her shift hiked high above her knees.

"Kait!" I crowed.

She turned with her hair storming about her face like a golden hurricane. "This will make things better, Eamon," she called, "for you and me. Guilt is twisting inside me."

"I can't go into the water," I choked. I took a feeble step and clutched my head. The ground viciously birled like Kait's spinning wheel. Further away, Kait pressed her advantage and slipped into a convoluted haze of spiraling green. Where was she? I blinked hard to clear my head.

"Then I'll swim in the firth alone! I do hope the currents aren't too powerful for me!"

I took another staggering step. "Nae, Kait, I'd be fair puggled." At once the spinning ground rose up to meet me, and everything went black.

When I opened my eyes again, Kait was hovering over me with a frightened expression. "Bloody, bloody, bloody," she gasped clasping my cheeks in her cool hands. I reached up to touch a throbbing place near my temple. "I'm a bloomin' bessie, but you could have at least given me a scoobie that you were feeling sick. I never saw anyone faint before."

The pungent aroma of damp earth filled my nostrils, and I scrambled to my feet. "I'm fine," I said irritably, brushing grass and dirt from my shoulder and cheek. The earth still wobbled, but I felt more certain of my ground. "I was only feeling puggled for a moment."

"You're sick—not tired," Kait pronounced with a wrinkled brow. "Are you too much man to admit it?"

"I'd be man enough to pick you up," I said as I scooped her up and threw her over my shoulder.

"Put me down," Kait shrieked with delight. She wiggled and kicked with no real intent to get away. "I should carry you!"

I snorted at the insult. "No chance of that. I'd show you how strong I am."

"You win!" Kait gasped. "You are as brawny as a giant and as stubborn as a mule!"

I shook the dizziness from my head and staggered on. "I win when your sandy little feet are planted safely back on the flagstones." Kait surrendered limply with a groan and allowed me to carry her back inside, away from the danger of water.

~Kait~

Over the next few weeks, I watched Eamon with the sharp eye of a mother osprey. It wasn't my imagination, he was becoming weaker. The day we moved all our belongings home, Eamon crawled into our bed early and didn't get out until the following evening. He was eating less and sleeping more, and I was beside myself with worry, especially when his ribs became more prominent under his translucent skin.

When I suggested to Eamon that we go visit Mr. Lennie, he angrily insisted there wasn't anything wrong with him. I tried to believe him, but my gut told me something was terribly wrong.

Eamon tried to distract me with gossip as he slowly shuffled back from the village one day. "Mrs. Neagar told me that your brother got married too. Made an oath amongst a lot o' hoopla. What's that?"

"It's a great celebration," I said bitterly. "He's still angry I snuck off to get married without his holy permission. And stay away from that Sarah Neagar. That bloody seamstress's got her beady little eyes set on you. Her hands will try to wander into forbidden places."

"Her eyes are green," Eamon said with childlike innocence. "And she can't help herself—my weapons lure her."

I ground my teeth together. "She will learn to control herself, or I'll skelp her bonnie face into the morra."

"Ye needn't be jealous," Eamon answered. "Her touch slithers and coils like a cold eel."

"She touched you?" I asked alarmed.

"She touches my hands before I occupy them in my pockets," Eamon said with a shrug. "I hadn't realized a use for them before..." Eamon's feet dragged behind him before he suddenly buckled into the ground.

"Eamon!" I cried, dropping beside him. Fear spasmed through me as my hand fluttered helplessly over his back. He lay motionless with his face in the powdery dirt while his breaths strained raggedly in and out. "Don't look at me," he growled.

I brushed away the dirt that was so repugnant from his ivory face while my heart trilled like a bird inside my chest. "I can help you. I'll empty the wagon and—"

"Turn away," he ordered. "I dinnae need your help!"

"Eamon," I wailed.

"Now!" He sounded dangerous though his strength had fizzled to that of a small child's. Dirt caught in his throat, and he gave a strangled sounding cough.

With angry tears I turned my back on him. "You need medicine. There are other physicians on the Mainland if ye are so opposed to Mr. Lennie. The faeries could have nixed you, or maybe your humors are off balance."

"I tripped on a rock," he said in coarse voice after a long period of silence. I turned and found him precariously balanced on two wobbly legs, his face scowling at my offer of help.

"We can rest awhile," I offered as tears blurred my vision. "I'm feeling so tired."

Eamon glared at me before stoically hobbling down the road.

24

TIPPER GRAY

Days later, Eamon strayed out onto the moor to collect a sea aster that had bloomed in the sanctuary of a rock. I was pinning out clothes when he returned to place the simple flower in my hair. "It's yellow and sunny like you," he said with a boyish grin.

I took his long hands and kissed the pale moons of his fingertips. "You walk so slowly these days. I can see you're not getting any better. Let me take ye to Mr. Lennie. He's gifted at pronouncing faery trouble. I wouldn't let him probe you with questions."

Eamon pulled away to pluck a sprig of clover. "No, Kait. I feel strong today." He didn't look strong, but like a waif teen whose body hadn't caught up with a rapid growth spurt. He spun the tiny green plant meditatively between his fingers.

"Then let us swim in the ayre. The salt water will stretch your muscles and cheer you."

"The ayre?" Eamon answered with a disgusted snort. "It's still sea, only a small part that's been captured by the envious arms of land. I'd not be tricked."

Tricked? Did my own husband view me to be some sort of foe—a scaly sea serpent who'd restrain him below the surface in tight coils? "It's not sea," I insisted. "It's no different than the familiar sea water I bring you to sponge off with. It wouldn't hurt to get a wee bit wet." I held out a hand to him. I couldn't explain my gargantuan, almost obsessive *need* to get Eamon to swim. "I'm no trickster but a wife who wishes her husband well."

Eamon frowned deeply, agonizing over this point a moment before flicking the sprig away. "No, Kait. There's no honor in swimming."

I huffed and shook my empty hand in frustration. It was obvious Eamon wanted to swim, but for some selkie masochistic notion, he was denying himself the pleasure. "No honor in swimming? What are you blathering on about? Might as well be speaking ancient Norse for the sense you're making."

Eamon's face hardened as he straightened beside me. "I wouldn't expect you to understand. The traditions of the selkie folk are not so soft as your own."

My mind swam wildly with questions. "What tradition binds you to land when your people can barely tolerate drying out?"

Eamon grumbled something incoherent while trudging over to neatly planted rows of bulging cabbages. His gait was steadier than it had been crossing the island, but it was slow and uncertain. The weariness was starting to show in his pale face too. No matter how much Eamon tried to reassure me; he wasn't getting better.

Blindly, I hung out shapeless, colorless articles of clothing while plagued with Eamon's symptoms. How long before he'd collapse all alone in some bland, nameless spot on the moor? Was it possible he could whittle away the last of his strength until...? Oh Odin, was it possible that I could lose him? The horrifying prospect could barely enter my mind without a violent shudder plunging down my spine and assaulting my stomach.

I worried that my new marriage to Eamon was the end of something too perfectly sweet to be real. Even as I watched him nibble the tip of a crisp cabbage leaf and wince, I knew that I didn't truly deserve him. He was too magically strange and alluring. He would always be a dweller of the sea, no matter how human he looked or how ordinary I dressed him. The fact was, I was ruining him—destroying a living breathing faery tale.

Is that what Tipper had done? My mind drudged unwillingly to that crazy old felkyo banished from civilization. In the old crone's eyes, I recognized the same haunting need to love and possess a man she should never have had. I never met her long dead husband, but I wondered how long they had lived together before Tipper suffered the unthinkable—the loss of her mate. Was her madness sudden, or did the insanity creep in more insidiously?

As I thought about Tipper, I realized that I knew almost nothing about her. A tiny spark of hope ignited in me as I wondered if she might have information that could help Eamon. Surely she had dealt with the bizarre behavior of the selkie males. My heart began to race as I realized that she was the one person who might be able to help Eamon—even more than Mr. Lennie.

"I'm going to the village," I called to Eamon as I wadded a damp dress over the line.

"I'll get my pampooties," he said, perking up from a crouched position. I marveled that there was a pile of pulled weeds in the soil beside him.

"You're not going," I said absolutely. "It's a long walk, and I'm fetching medicine for you."

"What kind o' medicine?" he asked, dusting his hands.

"Something to make ye strong again," I muttered. What if I'd given Eamon false hope and lied? Tipper had to have a morsel of important knowledge locked away somewhere in her crazy head.

Eamon was silent a moment. "You've discovered medicine that springs forth overnight like mushrooms? Something that wasn't there say...yesterday?"

"I just remembered something that's all."

Eamon mulled this information over with pulled brows. "Dinnae keep me waiting long," he ordered. "I'm not keen to the idea of staying here alone."

I sprang from the croft anxious to find Tipper. Boats didn't go out to Thieves' Holm unless they dropped off food or new exiles. Since the currents were most dangerous around the small island of criminals and outcasts, I had no choice but to resurrect Da's old fishing doree.

Away from Eamon's curious gaze, I circled around to our old beach before tugging the heavy wooden boat into the gently lapping waves. I smiled at my good fortune when I found the wind a soft whisper across my skin and the currents obediently in check.

I nervously approached the tiny island quicker than expected. As I passed the last lip of the Mainland, the violent currents in The String unexpectedly caught hold of my tiny boat and tugged me towards the Devil's Claw. With aching arms, I bore down on the oars and fought to break through the roosts to the more obedient waters. Sluggishly the bow rechanneled, and Da's boat slowly rolled south.

Panting and overcome with exhaustion, the bottom of the doree scraped over the pebbly beach onto Thieves' Holm. With a grunt, I hefted myself into the surf then staggered wearily onto the bank to appraise the flat, barren landscape. It was less green than seen from a distance, and more hopeless and dreary a place than I could have imagined. A few crumbly stone dwellings faced each other like warring siblings. Between the crude dwellings was a despondent little garden that grew little more than bug infested potatoes and shriveled beans. Nearby, a broken well pump dripped brown water over rust-stained ground.

"Tipper?" I called apprehensively. A lone tern squawked from overhead and floated over a rocky hill. I peered more closely into one of the shadowy windows as the rank scent of urine stung my nostrils. "Tipper? It's a neighbor come to call!"

From the dark shadows a dingy man crept. Tied about his waist was a filthy pair of fraying trousers. "What's this?" he cried, with delirious wonder. "You've brought me a boat?" Beneath a stringy beard, his skin was leathery and cracked like an ancient leather bag. I was uncertain of his age—fifty or one hundred? He crept a little further, squinting like a mole that preferred his dank hole to the brilliant sunlight.

I clutched one of the oars tightly against my chest. "Stay back, this boat's not fer the likes of a flea bitten thief such as yourself."

The man glanced at me then fixed his eyes eagerly back on the boat. "Oh, I think it is. It might even be sea worthy." With a gaping black grin, he crept closer and caressed the edge of my Da's boat while I watched with horror. "Aye, aye, it'll do," he exclaimed breathlessly. "It's not the luxury of Helga's Pride, but aye, it'll do."

"Back away from my boat!" I shrieked, raising one of the oars clumsily over my head. Aich! I couldn't surrender my boat. I'd be stranded for weeks, maybe even months till the next food shipment arrived. In my haste to find Tipper I hadn't thought things through. Of course there would be others—unsavory and grotty characters that would seek an escape. *Stupid, stupid me!* My heart pounded against my chest as my panic grew. I tightly re-gripped the worn paddle in moist hands.

The man turned to appraise my oar with a greasy sneer. "It's not a weapon, bint. Give it to me before I hurt you." He held out his dirt caked hand as if I would suddenly change my mind and surrender my oar to him.

"What did ye call me?" I asked outraged.

He laughed as he crept closer, his hand still outstretched. "Do ye not spread your legs fer coin? Perhaps you'll spread them fer me since I have nae coppers—just fer fun."

"Boil your head, maggot!" I cried swinging my makeshift club at the repulsive man. He was quicker than expected and ducked. As he did he scooped up my second oar from off the earth with a gleeful giggle. "One more to go," he sang. "Shouldn't be too hard. You're no stronger than a kitten—a wee pussy. That's what ye are, a mere pussy—all fluff no bite."

"I assure ye this kitty bites," I spat, circling my vile opponent angrily.

At once a ragged yet familiar old woman silently shot from the other structure with a narrow beam of driftwood balanced against her waist.

"Come here, pussy," the thief continued. "I'll judge your—"

I watched in sheer amazement as Tipper plowed the timber sharply and severely into the side of the man's head with the screech of a jungle leopard. The man crumpled into the dusty earth like an ugly rag doll.

I dropped my oar with a sigh of relief. "You'd be a fierce opponent in the New Year's ball game."

The old woman spat on the ground then tossed down her makeshift weapon. "I've always wanted to do that. Jerome's more evil than he looks." With an afterthought, she kicked him in the gut then smiled eerily when he twitched.

"Thankee," I spluttered. "He's old to be certain, but I wasn't entirely confident I could lamp him quite so well."

Tipper gave me an appraising nod. She seemed to have grown more ancient since I'd last seen her. She was a tall narrow woman with thin bones that seemed prone to frequent snapping. Over stooped shoulders, coarse silver hair trickled in yarn-like stringlets.

"Is there someplace we can go to talk?" I asked, backing away from the nefarious Jerome.

"Dinnae fash yourself," Tipper said, examining me once more. "If he wakes up, I'll pop him in the cheenies." She kicked him again as if to prove the point then snatched up one of Da's oars and held it to her chest. Did Tipper think I'd free her? I felt even less certain of my ability to bag the old crone. She proved to be feistier than she looked.

I scanned the deteriorating circle of dwellings. "Tipper," I said warily. "I must speak with you. Is there someplace we could go?"

Her sharp eyes moved slowly over my face. "I know you."

"Aye, I'm your neighbor—I use to be before…" It seemed too horrible to say. The whole island was too crapping horrible for even a goat.

"And we have business together?" Tipper asked, clutching my oar securely to her chest.

"Aye, urgent business." My gaze moved despondently over the oar.

"Then get me off Hel's forsaken island!" she cried. "I'm nae thief."

"Ye surely can't expect me—"

"I do expect!" Tipper shrieked. "It seems we have urgent business." Her sharp eyes shot over my shoulder towards the stony landscape.

"I'd get in trouble," I countered quickly, following her nervous gaze.

"You speak like a child," she said. "Have you a spine in that scrawny back of yours?"

"It's no small matter," I cried. "I'd be considered a menace to society and sentenced here too."

"You told the constable ye were coming?" she asked.

"Of course not," I said sharply. "I'd not be allowed on Thieves' Holm, would I?"

"Did you tell *anyone* ye were coming?"

"Well, ugh…no. I only decided."

Tipper threw down the oar with disgust and turned towards her collapsing house. "It seems you wish to meet the others. They'll be back any moment."

"There are others?" I asked marching after her.

"Of course," she said lazily. "A few other thieves and wan murderer. They're digging for spoots just o'er the hill." She gave a bizarre cackle. "Sigur loves pretty young lassies. They're tattooed all up and down his arms. He'll be most eager to meet your acquaintance." She thumbed over her shoulder, before screeching unexpectedly. "Keep it down ye snout faced headbangers!"

"Quiet!" I hissed. "We must talk. My husband's life may depend on it." I reached for her shoulder but thought better of it.

Tipper turned and leveled her gaze with me. Beneath sparse brows and wilted skin, the dark vivid eyes of a teenager stared back. "My tongue feels very stiff—this wretched island makes it feel so. Perhaps it would feel looser, say...on Shapinsay—in my own chair." She giggled to herself. "Oh...a chair. The soft luxury against my weary bones."

I writhed in indecision for only a moment, furiously searching for any connection between Tipper and me. I was her neighbor, but I couldn't be guilty of that, could I? Helping one wee lunatic escape from exile was such a small crime.

"Help me push out the boat," I ordered. "I'd not be trapped here forever."

The old woman cackled and swept towards the boat. Together we pushed the heavy boat back into the currents before climbing in with drenched, fishy skirts.

The thief on the shore began to rouse as we bobbed into the first currents of The String. He rubbed the back of his neck before scrambling to his feet when he found himself alone. "Tipper!" he screamed after searching the rippling water. "I'll kill you! I've not forgotten where you live!"

"I've bested you!" Tipper cried back happily. "Go bury your snout in defeat!"

"He knows where you live?" I asked with constricted breath.

Tipper looked at me then smirked. "I may have told him once, but the eejit doesn't swim. He'll die on that wretched island."

As the currents pushed us farther out, Jerome shrank to the size of a tiny ant furiously waving its antennas.

Tipper gave a girlish sigh while gazing towards the mossy hills of the Mainland. "Oh, michty me, I don't even care what you want. I'm grateful to you." She glanced at me then daintily wrung out a stream of water into the bowel of the boat. "She could be a friend," she said with an eerie smile.

"There's no one else here," I told Tipper uneasily, suddenly remembering why she made people so uncomfortable. Tipper often had conversations with no one in particular. Some said she whispered to the wee people, others said she communed with the dead. Either way, I felt itchy to be rid of her. With hard tugs I worked around the southwest arm of Shapinsay while crystal blue water splashed rhythmically against the frail boat.

Tipper looked over at me in surprise and then examined the vacant corners of the boat. "He was here a moment ago. He knows how to swim fer certain. Must have taken a dive when I wasn't lookin'." She giggled while fingering a button at her throat. "He'll be gone for a great while, he will."

"You're speaking of your husband?"

"We're hardly apart," Tipper said proudly as she searched the water.

"He's the reason I've come for you," I said. "I'm glad we find ourselves alone 'cos I'd have you tell me all about him."

Tipper gave a crinkly frown. "What interest do you have in a sun beaten old seaman?"

"It's all right," I coaxed gently. "I understand better than anyone what you're going through. I know what it is ye lost."

Tipper's knuckles turned white in her lap. "How could ye know," she hissed. "No living soul knows."

"I see the pain in your face. Please help me," I begged. "I've got my own selkie man who can barely walk. The townsfolk say you were married to your husband for a very long time. How did you do it, Tipper?"

"Selkie man?" Tipper quietly gasped. "That's impossible."

"We have more in common than you think. I'm not as young and ignorant as I seem. My finger is bare now but—"

"She lies to lure me to others," Tipper murmured with a hateful glance as she shifted her hips to the far end of the boat. I grappled to understand Tipper's sudden change.

"I'm not tricking you!" I cried. "I'm your neighbor not a constable wife. What I say is true—ye'll soon see. He's beautiful!"

"All selkie men are beautiful," Tipper spat. "This proves nothing. Tell me how someone as tiny as you could capture a proud and powerful selkie man, and I will judge the truth of your words."

I looked down at my sun pinkened toes with a guilty smile. Like a selkie, I hadn't worn pampooties in days. "There was no capture. We fell in love, and he surrendered himself to me."

"Your words drip with lies," Tipper said with a seething glare. "The selkie males are loyal to the sea and nothing else."

"Eamon gave me his skin of his own accord," I answered. "He wanted to. He's loyal to me as I'm loyal to him."

Tipper gave a bitter laugh. "This can't be. It's against the very nature of selkies to commit such a crime. There's nothing they value more than their skin."

I shook my head, confused. "Then tell me how ye came to marry a selkie. Did you capture your husband's skin when he was basking in the sun?"

Tipper's dark eyes bit back fiercely. "Nae," she answered in a quavering voice. "He captured mine. *I'm* a selkie."

25

AN UNEXPECTED BURD

Tipper Gray is a selkie, I told myself over and over again. I struggled with this impossible information, evidenced by the fact that she was not fair or beautiful and had been barred too easily with water. Water, the home of all selkies! My mind raced over this information, grappled, then retreated.

"Perhaps I should not believe *you*," I muttered. "I've seen selkie women and you…" My mouth snapped shut, unwilling to say that she was old and ugly. I suddenly couldn't wait to be rid of the fugitive I had foolhardily released. I winced to see my own beach rocking much too far away.

Tipper pompously tossed her hair. "Believe me or not—it does not matter. I have nothing more to lose."

"If you are a selkie then where is your skin?"

"If I had my skin I'd dive into these waters and never come back," Tipper promised. She gazed out over the water as her hair whipped and battered around her shoulders.

I studied her hard, taking new notice of the dark feral eyes that hid beneath brown wrinkled skin. I sank inside. "You've been searching for your skin," I concluded.

"Aye," Tipper said miserably. "Fer o'er a hundred years I've searched this wretched island. Hiding places are as numerable as the stars."

The pieces of the puzzle slowly came together in my mind. Tipper was a hostage to land—one of the poor selkie women caught and captured like the glorified legends of old. I could not say if there were others like her, or what happened to her beauty. She was the one with all the answers. "Who hid it?"

"My husband claimed he valued it as much as I did, so he took it from me and hid it. When he died in the Jack o' Bite rebellion, his secret died with him."

"I'm so sorry," I said. "You must have hated him."

"Aye, at first. I resentfully served him for o'er ten years before I noticed that his eyes were green like kelp. He was kind to me and never said a harsh word, so I learned to love him with time."

"What was his name?"

Tipper gave a reminiscent smile. "Bruce." In a lucid moment, her withered hands lifted to her face, no longer fair and opulent like a pearl, but brown and crumbly like a leaf. Her hands dropped in disgust as she looked out over the water. "Where did you put it, Bruce? Where did you put it?"

"He's not here," I reminded.

Tipper turned to look back at me. "I know. I'll always hate him for what he's done."

"Eamon is not my prisoner," I said quickly. "He gave me his skin by his own free will. I'd not ransom his love."

"He is a selkie?" Tipper asked with a strange new face that sparkled innocently.

"Aye," I said, troubled by her disturbing memory. "He is my husband—my mate. I know you can help him."

She clasped her withered hands together in delight. "A selkie husband! It's unheard of!"

"Cos of their loyalty to the sea," I surmised.

"Of course," Tipper said happily. "Yours is a strange creature who is turned upside down. Ha! Choosing to live on land—the notion is curious indeed! What I wouldn't give to see a selkie man again. Is he beautiful? Oh, what a silly question. Does the sky envy the ocean?" She leaned eagerly over a threadbare skirt. "Describe him to me. I'd have music float into my ears once more."

"You can meet him if you wish." I wondered about Eamon's enthusiasm to meet our most disturbing neighbor. Then again she was a selkie, would he not be eager to meet another of his kind?

"Oh, soon enough. Describe him quickly. It's been a hundred and twenty years since I've been in the company of a selkie."

"He may be a little different than you remember," I said. "His hair was cut and lightened so he'd better blend in."

Tipper looked horror struck. "Ye spoiled him."

"No," I cried. "He wanted it. Truly he's the most becoming a man I've ever seen." I readied for debate, but Tipper didn't challenge this very colossal fact.

"Go on, dear." She closed her eyes to visualize the picture I'd paint.

"Ummmmm, he's a few inches taller than I am with pearly white skin. His eyes are sleepy, even when he's wide awake and always contemplating something very serious. They're darker than your own." Tipper gave a slow sigh as she reminisced in her own memories. I continued with a smile. "He has an angular face and a tiny ridge at the end o' his nose." I gave a juvenile sounding giggle. "He likes to fight too, probably broke it in a scuffle."

"I had my own mate once," Tipper said dreamily. "He's as you describe except with gleaming black hair." She dropped her eyes to toy with a button on her dress. "He wouldn't recognize me. I too was once beautiful."

"Getting old is nothing to be ashamed of." Was it? Up until now I had taken a selkie's beauty for granted—assumed it was a gift given to all the selkie folk.

Her dark eyes shot up angrily. "Do ye mean to scorn me?"

"No," I blurted confused. "It's just that we all get old. How old are you exactly anyway?"

Tipper flexed her brow, instantly stupored in thought. "I—I'm not certain. I started counting when I got captured—a hundred and twenty years ago. I might have lived in the sea fer nearly the same amount of time. Selkies don't occupy themselves with human measurements of time."

"Selkies aren't supposed to get...*old*?" I tried to ascertain delicately.

"Of course not," she snapped, stung with the inadvertent insult. "This is what the land does to us." She ostentatiously flipped her hair like it was still lush and beautiful. "We are meant to live in the sea. It infuses us with youth and beauty. We are meant to entice until the day we die. It's your punishment."

Her words about the sea troubled me deeply, not because Eamon could grow old like me, but because he shouldn't—for him it wasn't natural. I couldn't help but feel that there were much greater implications for withholding himself from the sea other than simply growing old. He'd grown ill much too quickly.

"I'd sleep in a soft bed tonight," Tipper interrupted joyfully. "I'm tempted to dive right in and swim the last stretch."

"You no longer swim? Thieves' Holm is not so very far away for a selkie."

Tipper pressed her lips into a hard line. "Don't ye think I tried to escape? In truth, my frail body can't keep up with my heart. Always the nasty currents try to pull me to my death. I'd not be so desperate to get home that I would voluntarily drown myself in The String."

I rested the oars inside the boat a moment. "My Eamon wouldn't fare well in The String either. He's grown weak since our marriage. This is the reason I've come looking for you."

"He misses the sea," Tipper said. "Did you need to rescue a lone selkie woman to know this?" She was chastising me kindly, but it irritated me. Tipper hadn't even met Eamon yet. I missed golden brown plum tarts, but not having them didn't make me sick. Eamon's illness was greater than his need for rest or a dunk in the voe.

"I know he misses the sea even though he refuses to swim. I'm not so green a wife that I can't see this, but it's more than that. His strength wanes to that of a butterfly."

Tipper bunched her brow in astonishment. "Did you say he refuses to swim?"

My stomach twisted. "That's not normal selkie stubbornness, is it?"

Tipper gave a wry laugh. "Who's to say what's normal for a male who'd willingly subject himself into captivity. I've never heard such malarkey. Would a fisherman surrender to his fish?"

I picked up the oars and began to furiously row again. Talking of Eamon made me miss him terribly, plus I wanted to clout his ears for being so obstinate. "Ye must have some idea of what's going on in his daft head."

Tipper cackled at my frustration. "Selkie males are proud, complicated, and more loyal than you'll ever understand. I'd try asking him."

I snorted at the suggestion. "I tried. He says he can't go swimming if I'm to be his wife. But there's nothing chaining him to the land."

"What do ye believe, dear?"

I dropped my eyes to a soggy patch holding the bottom of the boat together. "He's afraid o' swimming 'cos he won't want to come back. I'll lose in comparison."

Tipper's hand curled over my own. Her fingers were splayed and swollen from a century of work. "He's not protecting you as you assume. If you understood selkies at all you'd know this."

Before she could explain, her ancient eyes shifted to the golden sun hovering above the hills. "He's a lot like me, Bruce. Remember how I subjected myself to your every whim? Oh, how it pleased you—but perplexed you, too! I wasn't like the other wives." She giggled as she reached out to her invisible companion. "I even learned to cook that terrible haggis you're so fond of." Her face clouded over as she drew a strand of wind-blown hair from her mouth. "I don't wish to upset you again, but I was wondering where you hid my skin. I'd only clean it before putting it back."

"What is it that I should understand about selkie males?" I asked impatiently. The kelp strewn beach was growing closer.

"What do you know about selkies?" Tipper asked as her dark eyes flashed to me. She seemed bewildered to find herself sitting in Da's doree with me.

"My husband, remember? He's a selkie."

"That's impossible."

"We're almost there," I said grumpily. "See for yourself."

"Truly?" Tipper squealed like a young lassie and clapped her bony hands together. "Oh, what I wouldn't give to see a selkie man again. They are truly a vision meant to torture us all. Will ye describe him to me?"

After dragging the boat ashore, I ached to skip ahead—sprint even, to see my groom, but Tipper ambled at a painful pace, content to admire the rocks and hills and comment on each and every species of flower. I mused at how human she'd become in a hundred and twenty years—learning to speak her mind quickly and hate the land slowly. At a glance, she could have been anyone's grandmother.

When I didn't spot Eamon outside nosing around the croft, my heart clenched tightly inside my chest. The sea had been calm and beautiful—a perfect day to break away. *His skin is hidden inside the walls of the broch,* I told myself over and over. *He has nowhere to go.*

"You're reeking of fear, dear. What frightens ye so?"

"I fear for Eamon's health," I grumbled, annoyed by the hag's bloodhound sense of smell.

I anxiously rushed through the open door while Tipper hung back at the threshold, wonder lighting up her face. Eamon was sitting at the bink with two thin legs propped over the arm of a chair. He was intently whittling a small piece of drift

279

wood with my paring knife. I drew in a quick breath when I saw the droplets of blood on the table and a maroon stained rag wrapped around his hand. He was so occupied in his project, he didn't even look up.

"After I took away the rough part and thinned this out, it began to look like the fin of a fish." He turned the miniature fish over in his fingers before glancing up.

"Eamon, you cut yourself," I said confiscating his wounded hand for a closer inspection. "Is it bad?"

"It's of nae consequence," Eamon answered as his eyes moved to the bent woman standing behind me.

I followed his gaze. "Um, er, this would be Tipper Gray, our neighbor."

"Is it true ye eat small children?"

"Would ye provoke a woman?" I said with a quick, nervous kiss on his cheek. Eamon gazed curiously up at her.

"It's alright," Tipper said with a puckered looking smile. She seemed to be withholding some tasty joke. "He's teasing me. I've been Shapinsay's felkyo for a long time. No one understands why I keep living and living. Hardly understand it myself."

"Was she not exiled on Thieves' Holm?" Eamon asked with a hard glance.

"Thieves' Holm?" Tipper repeated with a distant expression. "Oh, dreadful place. Bad men live there." She shuddered then fixed her gaze on me. "A golden lassie came to rescue me in her dilapidated boat. How unexpected she was."

"That was me, remember? Just a short while ago."

"Kait?" Eamon said urgently.

"We need her," I said with a nervous laugh. "I'm hoping she'll be your medicine."

"She's not a doctor," Eamon cried as he pushed out of his chair. "Where are her cures? Where are your medicines, felkyo?" he snarled.

Tipper cackled happily as she circled Eamon like a predatory bird—her eyes wondrously glued to the pale, pearly skin of his bare chest. "He's the bonniest thing I've seen in all these years. I could fill my weary eyes with him all the day long."

"Is there something funny?" I asked curtly.

"She'd make a jest o' me," Eamon said with a scowl. "She has nae cure to be seen."

Wild claps of laughter burst from Tipper before she wiped her eyes with a gasp and a hiccup. "Gaun yourself, dear. You've captured yourself a selkie pup."

My eyes flew to Eamon. "Don't hurt her, she's mad."

Eamon curled his lips up over his teeth.

Tipper thought this was funny and giggled again. "Oh, I'm not so far lost that I don't know a young burd when I see wan. Son, how old are you—nine months, maybe ten?"

I gave a small, nervous laugh, glancing at Eamon to share in the humor, but he stood frozen against the wall with a dark storm brewing on his beautiful face.

"Eamon?"

Eamon gave a panicked look between us. "What difference does my age make? I'm a man!"

My mind raced to remember. Had I ever learned Eamon's age? "Eamon," I sallied almost desperately. "How old *are* ye? Did ye not tell me you were twenty once?"

He glowered at Tipper before dropping his hands to the back of a chair for support. "I was born o'er ten moons ago. You only assumed I was older."

I gave a strangled sounding gasp as I slumped assaulted over my knees. "That can't be. I'm not married to an infant!"

"It's not as you think," Eamon growled with biting eyes. "Can ye not see that I'm fully grown? Selkie burds don't grow slowly like human children."

"We'd be picked off like tasty little shrimp if that were the case," Tipper added.

"What do you know of it?" Eamon growled, pushing aside his chair. "You've been in my home for only a few moments, and now you are an authority on selkies?"

Tipper flung her grizzled hair proudly over her shoulder. "Do ye not recognize your own sister of the sea? I too am a selkie."

"What are these lies?" Eamon cried outraged, his cheeks coloring in vertical pink splotches. "I'm not so young that I can be magicked with the words of a felkyo."

"It's not a trick," I said. "She's been living on land against her will for a hundred and twenty years. Her husband captured her skin long ago then died before he could release her. I know she doesn't resemble the selkie women ye know."

"The land is not kind to selkies," Tipper added in apology for her decrepit appearance.

Eamon stared at Tipper with horror. "If you are a selkie, then where do we congregate for the summer solstice?"

All humor left Tipper's crinkled face. "I'm sorry young wan, but Naraheem is a place of secret and will not be discussed."

Eamon's face contorted with confusion before he escaped into the glaring light outside, his chair clattering loudly behind him.

I rushed to comfort him, but Tipper caught my arm, surprising me once again with her strength. "Let him be," she hissed in my ear. "A woman's presence would only grind the salt in deeper."

"But he's confused and doesn't understand!" I protested. "He needs me!"

"Aye, of course he does," Tipper whispered. She held a bony finger to her lips. She glanced nervously towards the door. "But he must never know that. It's better you serve him without him realizing. I know that you can be more clever than he."

My head swam with excuses to be with Eamon. "He's too weak to be alone. What if he falls and hits his head on a rock?"

"It's better that he lies writhing in agony than for you to rescue him. Selkie males would rather die with honor than live with shame. Remember this, dear. It will go a long way in understanding your new burd."

I paced back and forth in frustration, biting my nails painfully past their cuticles while Tipper looked on with concern. "He didn't know that selkies could age," I muttered.

"He's young," Tipper pointed out for what felt to be the hundredth time. "Too young to be without his mither and father." She paused to consider this. "Truly he's barely old enough to mate. In land's name, how did ye find him?"

"Thanks be to Odin that he found me!" I said hysterically turning on the old woman. "That is not a bairn out there, but a well formed man, wonderfully functional in every way! He is clever and articulate with wisdom that exceeds my own! Don't speak down to him!"

Tipper shook her head sympathetically. "You are a land lover and slow to understand. That young wan is nothing but bait fer your kind."

"Watch it old woman," I growled. "You belittle the love we share."

"Don't get up to a high doh over me," she said sharply. "I'm not opposed to land-sea marriage. Bruce is the sweetest land lover you'd ever meet, but you must understand something about selkie men. What you feel is a mirage—a trick of sorts."

I crossed my arms brusquely under my breasts. "I already know about his magick, and I don't care a lick about it."

"You wouldn't would you? How many women have walked happily to their death for a handsome face, even thanked their executors with a kiss?"

Had Tipper read my heart? Of course I'd follow Eamon under the waves—there was no life without him, only a mundane existence devoid of all joy and meaning. I no longer wondered about Astrid's last moments. She had a blissful death.

"Beneath The Lure, I know how I feel," I mumbled. "There's no real mirage."

Tipper strolled around the firehouse inspecting my things, but she looked more lucid than I'd ever seen her. "Then do ye care about the aggression that courses through his veins?" Her dark eyes flashed back at me as she fingered my ashet. "He's not safe to be around for some time—another year maybe."

"He'd never hurt me." Of this I was confident. Tipper had underestimated the strength of Eamon's spirit, if not his age. I released a swath of my hair with a nervous yank. "How can you tell so much about him? If I hadn't known what he was, I would've assumed he was human."

"Ha!" Tipper cried, far too dramatically. "He's far too bonnie to ever look human, especially during his aggressive cycle. His skin is still too transparent—a rainbow of warning to all that he's not yet tame."

I slumped against the wall as Tipper held a bunch of fragrant rosemary to her nose. "His iridescence," I said glumly. "I thought all selkie men had it."

"No, dear. Where are his parents?"

"Eamon's an orphan," I muttered.

"Oh dear," she exclaimed, setting down a bottle of salt crystals. "I'll be certain to keep my nose and ears on him."

"He'll appreciate that," I said with a wince. I already felt Eamon's resentment towards his much, much older sister.

After that, I escorted Tipper back home. She giggled hysterically when she saw her home but didn't seem to realize she'd been away. Neither did she notice that her wee house was clean as a whistle from the days Eamon and I had stowed away there. "It's so nice to finally meet my neighbor," she said pleasantly, clapping her hands together.

"Long may your chimney smoke," I said with a tired smile. "Do you think Eamon will recover?"

Tippers eyes grew distant once more, as if she were trying to find her way through a soupy fog. "Eamon?"

"My selkie husband."

She smirked at her own private joke. "Oh, aye, the precocious young burd."

"I'm glad you remember him."

"Of course I remember him. I'll dream of his bonnie face tonight." She gave me a wink. "I'd not be alarmed. He's far too young for my taste, but oh, he is splendid to look at."

"He's sick, remember? How do I help him?"

Tipper looked troubled at this revelation. "He's sick? Heavens, we can't have this. Get him to the sea as soon as possible."

The sea was Tipper's answer to everything. Frustrated, I turned away. I'd visit Tipper again on the morra and every day thereafter till she thought of a cure.

Tipper touched my shoulder. "Kait, is it?"

I smiled wearily. "Aye."

"There's something I've lost. Do you mind if I visit you soon and have a look around?"

I enclosed her withered hand inside of mine, softened by her senility. Perhaps she needed me as much as I needed her. "You can visit me anytime you wish. Haste ye back."

26

A COSTLY CURE

What would it mean to have a young husband—a mate who was less than a year old? I reminded myself over and over again that he wasn't human, that it was natural for a sheep or a goat to be largely grown by their first year. But this didn't stop me from feeling disturbed. He was on the eve of adulthood—a reckless teen by human standards, no matter the lie his enticing and fully grown body told.

But wasn't I still a young human? Barely twenty, I was practically a teen myself and only slightly older than Eamon. At the rate he was maturing, he'd be older than me in less than a year. This thought soothed me, cheered me, and allowed me to breathe again.

Eamon was most definitely not ten months old, but more like seventeen or eighteen. I could hardly blame Tipper for viewing him as a helpless bairn. She was over two hundred years old, a walking, breathing fossil from the days of our Bonnie Prince Charlie.

I found Eamon slouched over a grassy dune staring across the sparkling blue waters of the voe. Where the water ended, the hills of Rousay and the Mainland rose like the humps of sparring green giants.

"Should I be troubled that you're here?" I asked, following his gaze. I still didn't understand his stubborn conviction to never swim again, but I felt his longing and mourned with him.

"Where's my fault?" Eamon asked with a dark glance. I looked hard at him, trying to see his true age. There were the thick dark brows and sculpted hollows aside his masculine jaw—the broadened shoulders and masterfully defined muscles. All traits of a fully developed man—no different than this morn.

"None found," I answered, curling up beside him. I slid my arm through his and rested my head against his hard shoulder, warm from baking in the sun. "It's your own silly rule to avoid the sea, not mine."

I *wanted* him to see the sea in all its beauty, to enjoy his life with me—I even wanted him to swim. I'd have him swim *with* me. I fantasized over the magickal places we'd visit—places full of pink coral and dancing forests with blue currents that rushed like city streets to secret locations like Naraheem. Such a place was not for my ears, but I wondered at its beauty. It was all in my head of course. I could never hold my breath and dive like Eamon… still we'd swim and be happy.

I'd visit Tipper on the morra. Perhaps she'd remember a cure and explain Eamon's refusal to swim. If I understood, I could help him reason through his irrational fears.

"Why did you have to bring her here?" he asked miserably. "She's sick."

"She's not sick, but very old. The land makes her old just like everyone else." *Everyone but selkies. They aren't supposed to age.* This thought worried me as it had earlier, but I fled from it, terrified of where it would lead.

"It's all wrong," he said gravely. "She's not supposed to be like that. The loss of her skin has made her go mad *and* grow old."

"Are you worried about getting a few grey hairs?"

"Aye, I fear losing my wits and my weapons against you. I don't want you to wake up and decide I'm of no worth."

I pressed my lips against the white fabric fluttering over his arm and breathed in his warm salty scent. "Can't you see that it's your heart that I love? If you wake up as ancient as Tipper tomorrow, I'd still love you. Even if you have warts, wrinkles, and not a lick of hair on the top of your shiny bald head."

"How can ye be so certain?" His eyes were drawn wide with insecurity, and I had to remind myself that I was all he had. For a split second he wasn't a confident seducer from The Deep but a frightened teenage boy without a mother or a father.

I pressed my hand over my nervously drumming heart. Even after all this time, I turned into a silly smitten girl whenever I sat beside him. "I feel the verity of my love here—in this deep place where it cannot lie. Besides I've made an oath haven't I? You shouldn't worry for your mind. Tipper keeps her husband alive in her mind so there will always be the hope of finding her skin."

"I can find nae fault with this," Eamon said as his pitch eyes swept contemplatively over me. "Ye would always be alive in my mind too; still I'd have you share your secret with someone. Land is a dangerous place to live."

"I'll tell my brother soon," I promised uncomfortably. What Eamon meant was that land was dangerous for *him*. Why could he not see that for the rest of us it was home? No matter how much I hoped he could acclimate, he would never see a home among four stone walls.

Eamon seemed satisfied with this and drooped into a tired huddle beside me.

"Why did you never tell me your age?" I asked.

"I'm no burd."

"You *are* very young," I said gently.

"I'm insignificant to the elders—too young to matter." Eamon snapped off a blade of grass and began to separate the ridges into curly green hairs. "The wan with laughter in his eyes says that I am a shark pup—a nuisance to the others. Ye never saw me that way, but strong and independent. Why should I tell the truth and change the way ye feel about me?"

"Joker is a bampot who tells hideous lies," I said angrily. "You should have told me the truth because you're my mate and can trust me. You're more important than anyone to me—even my Ma and Da—even my pig-headed brother. You matter the most!"

"Your Odin's oath consoles me," he admitted.

I gave a feeble sounding laugh. "I'm not going anywhere, are you?"

Eamon's dark brows pushed moodily together. "I gave you my skin. Do you need more oath than that?"

"No, sorry, you've given up too much already."

Eamon was quiet a moment as he appraised the aquamarine waves thinning across the sloped beach. "There's something I want to try."

"What?" I asked following his somber gaze.

"I want to try humping there." He nodded towards the surf. "I wonder about the rhythm of the waves and the slant of a sandy bed."

"Eamon," I laughed. "It won't be fully dark tonight. Someone might see."

He looked strangely at me as he sorted out the dilemma in this. "There's nae wan here but us." He stood and removed his trousers before confidently discarding them like a chewed up bone.

I laughed before glancing at a tiny ship in the distance. "But you're so weak," I protested, "and young." *Seventeen, definitely not ten months. Seventeen not ten, seventeen not ten, seventeen. . .*

"Test me," he growled, dropping into the grass beside me. "I'm neither." With the same self-assurance he finagled off my dress and tossed it into the wind. His lips were at mine before I could complain, tenderly pulling and tugging with the restrained patience and expertise of a fully grown man. His rigid belly teased me with its tender silk, while his foot gently locked around mine. When I blissfully subdued under his proficient touch, Eamon rose with a boyish grin and offered up his hand. Was he learning too quickly the weapons of his species, or was loving my body ingrained into him? I surrendered my hand with a worried smile before Eamon led me joyfully into the warm surf.

That night I slept as soundly as the dead. As the sun spread its amber rays across the dewy moor, Eamon stirred restlessly beside me. He peered out from under the dark lashes of a single, sleepy eye. "She's coming," he complained.

"The North Wind?" I moaned, nuzzling deeper into my pillow.

"Nae, your felkyo-selkyo. Whoever Bruce is, I'd like to kill him. She's been complaining to him since she opened her mouth near a tide ago."

I smiled as I stroked his velvety ribs, already planning the double portions of porridge I'd feed him for breakfast. "You're too late; he's her late husband. 'Sides, I'm certain she's not nearly as loud as you think. You just hear annoyingly well."

"You like my keen ears," he reminded. "I warn you of guest's approach and boiled over stew."

"That almost never happens," I said with an injured sniff. "You should talk more softly, you're not the only selkie inhabiting the island."

Eamon grunted in disagreement. "She's too ancient to hear us. Already one foot is being eaten by bottom dwellers—the rest will soon follow." Eamon didn't hide his disdain for Tipper. I wondered if she reminded him of his own mortality, or if it was her insanity that sat ill with him. Eamon was young and not yet seasoned to such disturbing things.

Anxious to interrogate Tipper once more, I crawled over Eamon to retrieve my salt laden shift crumpled over a basket of spools. As I raked a comb through my hair, the door rattled with a gentle tapping. Eamon glared silently at the door while I rushed to answer it. Tipper stood looking bashful in an ancient dress, adorned with a chunky white clam necklace. Wisps of wiry pewter blew wildly into her creased face. She looked like the witch she was accused of being. "Fit like, Kait?"

"Tipper," I said with a relieved grin. "You remembered my name."

"Certainly," she said. "You promised I could have a look around fer...er—a lost item."

I took her by the elbow and led her inside. "I know you are lookin' for your skin. You don't have to keep that a secret from us."

Tipper became engrossed when she saw Eamon adjusting his trousers with a little hop and a jiggle. "Ohhhhh," she gasped. "A male—a young wan too."

Eamon glowered at her, his hands still awkwardly secured about his baggy waistband. "I'm fully grown—twice the size as ye."

"And still untamed," she observed with a wee chuckle. "Does he bite?"

Eamon gave a broad teeth baring smile that looked more aggressive than friendly. "Eamon," I warned. "I'd not have you pick a fight."

Tipper tossed her hair haughtily. "Your young pup's milky white teeth don't frighten *me*." After that she began an exhaustive search of the house, beginning with a slimy barrel of potato peelings. She tapped the barrel at various depths before diving in with both hands. After the barrel, she moved like an irritated moth, fluttering from rafters to floor as she searched every conceivable nook and corner. Only when I placed a bowl of food before Eamon did her nose pop up from the basket of rags she was inspecting.

"I'll eat later," Eamon murmured with a deep frown, pushing the bowl away. "I still feel full from before."

"Yesterday?" I practically shrieked. "Can't you see that you are growing too thin?"

"The weakest of us will get swallowed whole by orca," Tipper chastised as she fluttered towards the bink. "Do ye wish to die?" She shoved his bowl back under Eamon's chin before staring him down with small black eyes.

Eamon glared up at her, but then amazingly lifted a spoonful of porridge to his mouth without protest.

"Go on then," Tipper urged with long claws planted across her bony hips. "That would only feed a wee minnow." Eamon gave an annoyed sniff, but lifted the spoon to his lips again and again. When he set his spoon down for the last time, I stared assaulted at the vast amount of food still in his bowl.

"I could sweeten the porridge with some herring," I coaxed.

Eamon glared at his food bowl. "I'm full."

"Only five more bites," I pleaded.

Eamon shook his head defiantly and pushed off from the bink. Stoically he moved back towards our bedroom. As he crossed under the doorway, he wobbled unsteadily. I moved to check on him, but Tipper held her finger to her lips, slowly shaking her head against it. I silently sat back down, my eyes hypnotically glued to the dark adjoining room.

Tipper seemed to want to say something, but then her eyes dimmed. "Bruce, did ye hear that? Mr. Drever is giving that bowfing beast another sound lashing. Next he'll be wanting it to give him favors."

After breakfast, I impatiently watched Tipper search below the hearth stones, dig to the bottom of a barrel of barley, and then scour through my trunk of clothes. When she was satisfied that her skin was not inside, I escorted her through the morning mist to the byre. "He's ill; did you notice?" I whispered as the plank doors clattered behind us. The cool, dense walls insulated our voices.

"Aye," Tipper said distractedly. "He needs the sea, dear." She pushed aside braids of garlic to peer at the rusty tools behind them.

"He's too stubborn to get in the sea, remember?"

Tipper looked both surprised and bothered by this. "Your burd won't swim?"

"Not even in the ayre. He won't allow himself the pleasure. Why is he doing this to himself? Is the pull that great, or does he fear breakin' the oath he's made?"

"He's chosen land o'er sea?" Tipper repeated, her face fogging over in confusion.

"Neither—he's chosen *me*," I corrected briskly. "We love each other."

"Hmmmm, he's not like any other selkie man I've known," she said, shaking her head decidedly. She nosed around the inside of a rusty metal drum a moment. "The sea has choices aplenty o' selkie women—women so beautiful they make mortal women weep. His young age makes him ridiculously rash."

There was no fault in Tipper's crass argument, so I continued with my feelings bruised. "But why does he do it? You said before that it was obvious."

"Did I?" she asked, straightening with two fistfuls of gardening twine. "Hmmmm, I suppose it's 'cos he's betrayed the sea—a grave offense."

I felt the confusion in my brow. "How can he betray the sea? The sea does not live and can't be offended."

"I wouldn't expect you to understand," she said with a condescending sniff. "But I will correct you this one time. The sea is more alive than you and me. Every droplet breathes with life. It is the opposite of the air that is so dead."

I stared at her a moment, baffled. Was her madness speaking, or was she referring to the countless fish and plankton that penetrated every corner of the ocean?

"Think for a moment what that betrayal means to a selkie," she continued as if I understood. "Is your burd a lowly traitor with the worth of a barnacle?"

"No," I cried outraged. "There's no one as precious as Eamon."

"Haud your wheest," she hissed, glancing towards the door and dropping her voice. "Selkie men must have loyalties to define their worth. So your burd will not be without honor, he's given you his heart—a transfer of loyalties ye could say. In doing so, he's preserving his dignity and his pride."

My mind teemed with this bizarre information. "So in Eamon's mind, going for a swim would mean he is worthless—a traitor with no honor?"

"That sounds right, dear." She studied me sadly a moment. "You don't know your blessing. Bruce wants us to have our own wee burd."

I stared at Tipper, processing the grotesque misunderstanding. She had forgotten the sacred oath we'd made as husband and wife and thought Eamon to be my son. "Ye don't have any children?"

"Heavens, no. Bruce has been trying to fill my belly, but his seed won't plant. His heart is set on a strapping son with black hair like mine." She laughed boisterously then looked guiltily captured. "Don't tell him I told you. He'll be angry at having our laundry hung out fer others to nose."

"I won't tell," I said with a sad smile. "You would have made a good mither."

The old selkie smiled pleased. "I haven't given up yet. I'd have my own shimmering rainbow to hold against my breast. How wonderful the wee ones smell."

"Tipper, how is it that the selkies live so long?"

"In the name o' the wee man," she giggled. "Only a land lover would ask such a question. Is it not obvious that the sea keeps us young and beautiful?"

I looked over her face, crinkly and brown like a worn out potato sack. "Do selkies get sick often?"

"No," she said proudly. "Sickness is reason to haul out—a sluggish selkie would not survive long in the deep waters."

"So this is what Eamon needs to get better?" I asked hopefully. "Rest?" It seemed so perfectly simple. My mind retraced all the days Eamon worked beside me, helping with my chores. It kept him from getting bored, but now fear debilitated me that I'd personally made him worse.

Tipper's brow creviced deeply. "We're talking of the young burd—the wan who won't swim?"

"Aye, aye, my husband. He's sick."

Tipper tossed the twine back into the barrel with a deep frown. "Kait," she said with a clear firmness that let me know she was back in the present. "He's too young to live on land; you must return his skin to him now."

I winced at the very suggestion. "He wants me to have his skin. It's mine now. If you think very hard, you will remember something that will help him. Maybe something made from kelp or blue algae."

"Those things won't help," Tipper said severely. "The time we can survive on land is proportional to the time we've spent under the surf. It can be stretched out only if the selkie spends a lot of time in the water, but he can't give it up completely without punishment."

"Eamon's spent a year in the sea," I murmured aghast. "Are ye saying he has one year to live?"

Tipper dropped her voice even further so that I had to strain to hear. "Less, 'cos he refuses to swim. Your burd will soon die if you don't set him free."

"Oh Odin, we're married! I can't bear to hear this!" I crumbled into the damp dirt floor with my hands clenched tightly over my ears. "Say nae more. It's too cruel."

Tipper was as mad as she was ancient, but I knew in my heart that what she said was true—Eamon couldn't survive long without the sea. Hadn't I known this all along—known that I had stolen Eamon from the very habitat in which he so naturally belonged? Hadn't I always known that Eamon was too good to be true, that I would never be good enough to love him? My heart twisted in anguish inside my chest. I was a fool—an ugly land louper with an eye for the beautiful blue sea.

Tipper crouched beside me. "His magick has hooked you, dear. Do ye want to always live in bondage?"

"Aye!" I cried. "I'd rather rip out my heart than not feel the sweetness in my chest."

"Haud your wheest! He's listening," the old woman rasped sternly. "O'er time ye would forget—the sweetness would dull. The sooner you set him free the better."

I realized I was cold and trembling even though a large warm sun was melting away the damp fog outside. Tipper had no heart—only a small stony place that chilled the space around her. I clenched my arms against my chest and fought to speak through clattering teeth. "Do *you* wish to forget Bruce? To close your eyes and have all memory of him gone?"

Tipper's eyes grew large and frightened. "He has my skin," she whispered.

I stared back at her finally understanding. The love Tipper felt for her husband was a small droplet of water compared to the oceanic feelings she had for the sea.

"Do you wish to forget *your skin*?"

Tipper was quiet a moment as her dark eyes ruminated clearly over my face. "Listen carefully," she whispered coarsely. "This isn't about your pain. If you don't want to bury that young burd, you must release him back into the sea."

27

TIPPER'S SEARCH

Why did Kait have to follow the old woman outside? I was agitated at her sudden intrusion into our lives and frustrated by Kait's interest in her. There was tragedy in the old felkyo's story, but she had nothing to do with us.

I strained to hear their words as I moved around the bink collecting dirty bowls. With irritation I realized they were discussing me and the nature of the sea—two things Tipper knew nothing about. It had been a lifetime since she lived in the sea. She was more louper than selkie now. As I tipped the bowls into a wash basin, Kait burst through the door like an unleashed tempest. "Drop that bowl!" she shrieked. "You won't work and weaken yourself any further. We must go for a swim, now!" She tugged frantically on my arm. "Please, Eamon!"

"The old felkyo's got you upset," I said with an amused chuckle. "Is it the beautiful selkie women that are making you weep? It's nothing but rubbish. Tipper's an eejit—too blind to see your own beauty that's so completely different from the sea women."

"Is that all ye heard?" Kait asked tearfully as she collapsed against me.

I shrugged and snuck two spoons and a knife into the soapy water. "I stopped listening after that. The ol' selkyo's too mad to have anything worthwhile to say."

"No, she's not," Kait protested. "She's been around a long time and knows vital things about your kind."

I smirked at the notion as I held Kait tightly. "Losh, her mind is gone."

"You wouldn't say that if ye got to know her," Kait said fretfully. "She says you'll get much worse if you don't get into the sea. It's the sea that keeps you young and strong. The longer you soak in the sea, the longer you can stay with me. Please, Eamon. Come with me to the water. We'll take it as slow as ye wish. Today we'll wade in up to our knees, and then on the morra, we can go in up to our waists."

"Why do you listen to the rantings of a maddened woman?" I asked. Kait's large blue eyes were pleading with me, tugging me towards the water, but the allure did nothing but freeze me inside. "There is nothing wrong with me that sleep can't cure. I'm not used to sleeping in a bed, that's all. Is the felkyo's word of more value than mine?"

"But you are young," Kait cried. "There are things you have not yet learned, things your mither and father would have taught you had they lived."

"The land is good enough fer *her*," I spat with a resentful nod towards the door. I could hear the old felkyo rummaging around in the byre, nosing where she didn't belong. "She is as strong as a whale. For a hundred years she has complained o' suffering, but I don't suffer. *I* am happy."

A tear rolled out of Kait's eye. "You haven't been fortified by the sea long enough to live a hundred years. You will die much sooner."

I took Kait's sunny face in my hands and kissed each moist eye. Her salt melted deliciously over my tongue. "Dinnae fash yourself over such grave matters. The thought of dying together cheers me. Do you think I wish to live hundreds of years after you are gone?"

I was grieved to see more tears spill down her sun speckled cheeks. I wasn't able to cheer her this time, and the innocuous little drops wounded me. Kait had been strong and happy before the old welk's intrusion into our lives. The felkyo was robbing me of my power to protect Kait, and I hated her for it.

"You still don't understand. You are much too young. If you don't return to the sea, you will die before you've begun living."

Too young? I clenched my fists together. Why did Kait insist on treating me as a helpless burd that bellies about the sand? I was a fully grown selkie man with nae authority over me! "There is nothing wrong with me, and I won't be tricked into the sea by *her*. I am strong!"

"Aye," Kait agreed with a broken sob. She rubbed her tears on her sleeve, her fingers still clenching a handful of my leine. Foolishly she thought she could still lose me. "You are too strong, but only on the inside."

For days Kait pestered me mercilessly about surrendering to the sea. She continued to amaze me. Her schemes were as endless as the sunrisings—each new one more cunning than the next.

I woke one morn to find Kait anxiously nudging me. "The live herring that school in the cool deep water are the tastiest, are they not?"

I peered sleepily at her, brushing the sole of her foot with my toes. Sleeping without Kait was impossible, and it soothed me to feel her so close. "It's a sorry revelation. You got that from me."

She propped herself on her elbows and tickled my neck with her dangling hair. "Well I've never tried one live before. How should I know how delicious it is?"

I chuckled at the image of Kait downing a live fish. She didn't have the teeth nor the gumption for such a delicious thing. "I don't know, Kait. How should you know?"

She brushed her lips against my cheek with a smile. "I'd have you eat your fill then bring me back a sample. Mmmmmmmmm, think how good they'll taste when they're still fighting to get out of your stomach."

"I'm no longer hungry for live fish," I told her flatly. "You could make me spoots and peas."

"You'd have me slave o'er the hearth for you?" she shrieked. "Breakfast is only a wee swim away. I could go out in Da's boat and help you collect your victims."

I rolled away from her, feeling suddenly fatigued. "Never ye mind. Fresh nor aged, I'd not be hungry anymore."

"I'm sorry, Eamon," Kait spluttered. "You—you *are* hungry." She scrambled over my shoulder and cried profusely in the next room. Later I was woken by Kait. She nestled a bowlful of spoots and peas large enough to feed an entire pod. Out of guilt, I hefted myself up in bed and ate a few bites, but it sat like a boulder in my stomach.

A day or two after that, Kait lured me to the beach by making me chase her own nude spirit. One moment we were discussing a trip to the big island, and the next, Kait was grinning from ear to ear and pulling her dress off over her head. She vanished out the door with a giggle and a tantalizing flash of white. I had no options but to chase her down. When we got to the flat packed sand, Kait breathlessly swayed around me, moving her hips in a seductive, serpentine way. I grinned broadly with my chest heaving between us, curious as to my next treat. As she orbited me, her pouty red lips paused to kiss strategic places on my body—spine, elbow, nipple. I stared bewildered at my mate, pleased by her brilliant new game.

"I'd try lying with you in a different spot," she cooed as she tugged on my hand. Losh, it was a trap—a decidedly transparent one. Only paces away, the water enticingly splashed and reached.

"I dinnae understand." Kait would try to force her will on me again, but all the orcas in the world didn't have the power to drive me into the voe. I would not be weak.

A strange expression flashed over her face before she quickly corrected it into a seductive smile. "In the water—here. I'd sample your gift again." She tossed her hair over her bare shoulder and tugged on my arm with an eye-popping jiggle.

"Gift? Ye only honey your words to entice me into the water." My eyes moved down her lissome body eagerly. It had been too long—days since I'd subjected my will over Kait. "There's nothing wrong with this spot."

Kait's eyes grew with indignation. "In the itchy grass? I'd feel the cool flow of water over my body!"

"Overrated. We'll do it here and be satisfied."

"Nae," she cried. "I'd have us couple over there." She thrust her finger rigidly towards a mounting wave—blue and buoyant and wickedly tempting.

I laughed at her cuteness, and Kait immediately started to tug on my arm.

"Stop—being—stubborn!" she grunted between tugs.

"Kait," I chortled. "You have the charisma of a hammerhead shark."

That bought me a stinging skelp in the face. Kait stared at me a moment before diving into my chest with the most heart wrenching sobs.

As much as I wanted to please her, I knew it was more important to stay strong for her—to stay whole. I didn't expect Kait to understand. She knew nothing about being a man and even less about being a selkie. After the full moon was eaten by night once more, her pressure began to wear on me, and I began to feel genuinely tired.

~Kait~

"He didn't get out of bed again," I complained to Tipper as she hoed around the base of a crisp new head of cabbage. In the few weeks she had been back, she had already planted neat little rows of turnips, potatoes, cabbages, and climbing beans. At the head of her little garden were the brittle brown remains of a once magnificent fig tree—a monument to Shapinsay's fierce winds. "He barely opened his eyes before I left."

She wiped her brow as she surveyed her work. "Don't ye worry, dear. Have a little faith in this old selkie. The time draws near when he won't have a choice." She smiled wearily as she leaned on her hoe. "Oh, truly I envy him. If I had my skin again, I'd never take it off. At the first sounds of those lusty fishermen, I'd race and dive. It was my vanity that captured me. Did you know that?"

"What happened?" I asked politely, having heard the story reiterated a half dozen times.

"You might be surprised to know that I *wanted* them to get a peek o' me." She gave a vixenous smile and stroked her stringy grey hair. "I wanted to hear their gasps of admiration and feel their hungry denial—just to punish them." She gave a hysterical laugh. "Oh, I was wicked back then. Just as the cutter broke the edge of the peninsula, I thrust out my pale bosom and pointed my toes as if I were completely oblivious to their gawking. When they spotted me, they dropped their sails and started shoutin' excitedly. I was young and ignorant and didn't know that they were hiding the rumpus of the one that had slipped into the water. By the time I got nervous, it was too late. A man with strong, calloused hands popped out of the water wielding the nastiest net you could imagine. He threw it over me before thrusting me back under. I thrashed for my life, but the net was too strong. When I feared drowning, I became placid. That was when I was rewarded with breath and my skin violently cut from my body."

"The man was Bruce," I added sadly.

"I had no choice but to marry him," Tipper said with a shameful glance. "He made me promises." She dropped her head and began to turn the rocky soil with a vengeance. "I wonder where my skin is. There are so many places still to look."

"Tipper," I asked. "How do you know that Bruce didn't destroy your skin?"

"Bruce never lied to me," she said with a frown. "It's in a safe place." She nodded her head vigorously as if to convince herself of this very vital fact. "Aye, it's in a very safe place. Bruce always promised he'd set me free before…" Her eyes grew wide and distant, locking up at the precise moment Bruce died.

"I've searched there," she snapped over her shoulder. I followed Tipper's gaze to the crumbling limbs of the fig tree. "Why do you tease me like this?"

"Where does he tell you to look?"

Her eyes slowly focused on me. "What?"

"Where does he tell you to look?"

"Fool o' a man," she growled. "He tells me to search the caves along The Foot although I've searched there many times. They hide nothing but fish skeletons and broken clam shells."

"Those caves fill with water at high tide," I remembered aloud. "Would the salt water not spoil your skin?"

"I've not spoiled yet, have I?" she asked gaily. "My skin and I are one. It won't decompose until I do." She cackled with laughter. "I hope that I won't be worm food for a long time yet."

My interest piqued with this new intriguing link between selkies and their skins. "Does Bruce know that your skin lives as you do?"

She shrugged her wiry shoulders. "I suppose he knows by now. He's had a hundred years to become accustomed to the idea."

I brushed a fly away. "But then... when he hid it—did he know?"

Her dark eyes strained as she reviewed over a century of memory. "No, I don't believe so. Is this important?"

"Aye, he wouldn't have put in the caves if he thought it would hurt your skin. I was very careful in choosing a safe place for Eamon's skin."

"Where did ye put it, dear?" she asked innocently. "It might give me an idea of places to search."

I couldn't ignore the yearning in Tipper's eyes. If I confessed the location of Eamon's skin, Tipper would be driven to retrieve it, wrap it around her stooped shoulders, and then what? Would she try to mold herself into it and disappear into the sea? She wouldn't be successful, but I shuddered at the unnecessary risk. Blair was the only one I trusted with my secret.

Weeks ago I visited him and Sloan in her father's attic apartment. The reunion was stiff and awkward, but I fulfilled my promise to Eamon. Should I drown in the sea or become trampled by Mr. Drever's horse, I wasn't the only living soul who knew where Eamon's skin was hidden.

"You know I can't tell you," I told her. "The location would burden your mind."

She sighed as she stabbed at the soil. "I suppose you're right, but perhaps you have more ideas in your head that could help me—a fresh perspective for a desperate woman. You've already saved me a day's walk to The Foot."

"Maybe you could tell me more about your husband."

"Kait wants to hear about you," Tipper clucked happily to herself. "Go on down the way, dear. We'd be having some girl talk." Tipper stalled for a few moments before she started gushing about her husband. "The first thing you should know is that he's a gentle man with never a harsh word. He loves my hair loose and would feast on roasted grouse every night if I allowed it."

"What did he say when you asked to be released?"

Tipper's face darkened as she thrust her hoe violently into the soil. "He told me that he loved me too much, then embraced me with the suffocating arms of an octopus."

"You felt suffocated by him?"

"Even though he has my skin, he doesn't let me far out of his sight. He's a possessive man, always worried that another will steal me away." She flipped her hair ostentatiously before looking down her sparse lashes at me. "Never am I allowed into the village without him. The men are too lured by my beauty."

"But he allows you in the voe without fear of you swimming away?"

"Did he wake up last night when I snuck out? Nae, I tell you. I'm having an affair with the sea!" She gave a girlish shriek. "The waves rocked me like a lover till dawn. Bruce was still sleeping when I returned."

"You swim every day?"

Tipper gave a mischievous smile. "Most days. His eyes are growing dim so he doesn't notice my wet locks."

"For how long?"

"You're a curious soul," Tipper said brightly.

"You've lived a long time," I reminded her. "I'd have Eamon for just as long."

Tipper twisted the hoe's handle back and forth with a happy sigh. "An hour, if I can steal away that long, but dinnae tell Bruce. It'll only worry him."

"I wouldn't tell," I said, perusing her small plot of land. There were few suitable places to hide a velvety coat. Except for the garden, most everything else was stubbled with rocks and moss. Still there were possibilities. "Your skin could be *here* on your own croft."

Tipper's gaze snapped hungrily back to my face. "Here? Why would you say that?"

I immediately scolded myself for stirring hope in the old woman. Who could understand the desperate mind of a man who would steal himself a wife? Oh, bloody, not an eejit like me. Tipper would never find the peace she deserved until she let all memories of her skin go. "Was there any time when ye were content living here with Bruce? A time when you were truly happy?"

"I'm only truly content in the sea," she answered as her eyes swiveled towards open sea like the needle of a compass. "I'll always hate Bruce for what he's done."

Her answer was not the one I'd been hoping for. If only I'd waited a few minutes more—she'd love her husband once again, and see that she could be happy living on land. "Perhaps you should stop searching," I suggested gently. "Eamon would never find his skin—no matter how hard he looks. I'm certain Bruce hid your skin in an equally hard place."

"You'd have me give up? Become a land lover who enjoys sticking their hands in the grime?" She threw down the hoe in a show of disgust. "I have dirt under my nails!" she shrieked. "Always there is dirt, no matter how much I scrub and clean!"

"I don't want you to hurt anymore. As long as you search, you'll never be content. You're a pruny ol' woman, as squirrely as they come, but you're a friend, and I want you to be happy."

Tipper's eyes grew in shock and outrage before she crowed with laughter. "A heartfelt insult from a freckled burd thief!"

I smirked, uncomfortably. "I didn't know he was so young."

Tipper dried her eyes with the bottom of her soiled apron. "In the name o' the wee man, you speak your mind. Though, I wouldn't want it any other way. Only debauchers and thieves always speak honey."

"I'm sorry, Tipper. I was only going to remind you that your husband was a possessive man. He would've kept your skin close under his nose—just like he did you."

"You really think my skin is somewhere on the croft?"

"You know your husband better than me. Do you think he'd keep it in the house?"

Tipper shook her head vigorously. "No, I've scoured every corner many times. Where else would I look without disassembling each stone?"

I took Tipper's arm and drew her away from the garden. "Perhaps in a place the wee people would oppose," I whispered.

"You'd have me dig in the faeries own realm?" Tipper asked with horror and repulsion.

"Perhaps not so deep," I said with a smile tugging at my lips. "Your husband would have known how disgusted you are by the soil. One look at your face would have decided the matter for him. I do believe it's the one place ye don't *want* to look."

"But where?" she asked with a crinkly scowl, her dark eyes shifting distastefully over the mossy ground. "Where would *you* have put it? It seems your devious mind equals my husband's."

"I don't know, but he would have marked the place if it wasn't obvious to him." I gazed at the short wall dividing the two properties and remembered Eamon lying weakly in bed. "I really must go. Eamon must eat a few bites to keep his strength."

"You're only prolonging the inevitable," Tipper said with a snort. "A missed meal or two won't hurt him."

"I'd not have him suffer," I snapped. Every minute I worried that Tipper's plan would backfire, that we wouldn't save Eamon in time. It was a stupid plan—a dangerous one, but it was all I had.

"Kait," she called as I turned to leave. "Think hard."

"I'll put some thought into it," I promised. "But you must not get your hopes up too much."

As I turned home, Tipper lifted her skirt and raced to the byre to retrieve a spade.

28

BETRAYAL

When I blearily peered out, I found Kait smiling worriedly over me with a cup of steaming broth. I wiggled my nose to separate the strands of scent—celery, pepper, and chicken—probably the ornery rooster. "I'd have you take a few sips," she ordered. "It will strengthen your marrow and build you up from the inside."

"Do I have a choice?" I rasped. I struggled to keep my eyes open in order to see Kait fully. Her cheeks were flushed pink from a hot summer wind, but her bright blue eyes reflected the coolness of the ocean. She was too lovely to have been conceived on land.

She put the cup to my lips and drained in a few spoonfuls. I coughed then collapsed back into my pillow exhausted.

"I tested it on my wrist first," Kait said looking frightened. "Was it too hot?"

I sluggishly cleared my throat. "I'll have no more."

"But I melted all the tasty fat—"

"No more."

Kait stirred over me a moment then clattered the cup down on the table beside me. I listened to her breathe stiffly in and out a few times before I realized that my eyes were closed. "Something's blooming out on the moor," I observed softly. The rich voluptuous scent of an unfamiliar flower wafted over me. I inhaled deeply, wondering at the bloom's shape and color.

"I've gone to all the trouble to make the broth." My eyes fluttered back open to see Kait's brows pinched angrily together.

"I've upset you."

"No more sleep till you've eaten your share," she ordered in a gruff voice. "Good or bad, there's still an empty hole to fill."

"Is there any point in countering you? Ye get brawnier every day." My head swam bleakly as I struggled to sit. Kait seemed to relax as she tipped some of the hot liquid into me. The broth tasted less than it smelled and scorched my tongue.

"It's not me who's getting stronger," Kait murmured. "You're getting weaker. For how long will you deny yourself a cure when the sea is only paces away?" She stirred her fingers roughly through my hair then tested the heat of my forehead.

"There's nothing wrong with me that your presence can't cure. Sing me that lullaby about the fat-bellied puffin."

Kait hung her head. She seemed more exhausted than I'd ever seen her. "I know what you're doing, and I won't allow it."

My fingers found their way to her tense hand. "What am I doing?"

Her eyes blasted icily on me. "You're trying to kill yourself."

"There are easier ways to kill oneself," I said amusedly. "Take an orca fer example. They have a row of tiny white teeth that smile right before they shred you to bits."

"Do not make jokes, Eamon," Kait cried as tears streamed down her face. "Is that what you want—an honorable death for a stubborn selkie? Damn to Hel's domain your bloody eejit pride!" She crumpled under my chin and trembled violently. Muffled sobs escaped from under a mound of tangled hair, paining my heart and my ears. Her body that had once seemed so slight, stifled my breath heavily.

"Dinnae cry," I whispered. I wasn't daft; I knew that I was dying, but neither was I afraid. It was only Kait's sorrow that wounded me. As my strength waned, my power to protect her—even comfort her, slipped away. Now I had to pretend to be strong.

"You'd cheat me," she gasped as a warm tear rolled down between us. "You are not meant to be mine, but I'd have you for more than just a little while."

"I've chosen you," I said tenderly, wishing my strength and meaning into her. "I'd rather die than be a half selkie forever. I'd be a full man fer ye, Kait—even if just for a short time." Losh, I loved her. Never would I regret abandoning a lifetime of sea for the moments we laughed and cuddled, talked and kissed. I pressed my lips into her hair, pausing to smell the unfamiliar flower.

Kait tore away and stared at me through horror filled eyes. She hadn't understood the depth of my love at all, nor had she understood what I was giving her. I only validated what she already suspected—that I was dying. "How could ye be so heartless and cruel? You're selfish Eamon Swanney, and I hate you!" She fled from her wee house with more tears streaking down her cheeks. My ears strained to follow the angry oaths, to *see* where she was going—north…no west, definitely west. Kait was going to the sea.

"Kait!" I crowed. "Stay in the shallow waters!" I tried to roll to my feet to pursue her, but my knees melted like jellyfish, and my hip slammed painfully to the cold stone. A panic rose in me as I imagined Kait finding me degraded on the floor in the ridiculous louper panties. My heart pounded as I scrambled to get up, to compose myself before Kait's return. I clutched the bed and slowly dragged my torso into it. My legs followed more quickly. My hip throbbed painfully against a lump as I gulped at the warm, damp air. Never had I been so little—less a man and more a burd. Losh, I was utterly helpless.

When my eyes fluttered open again, a strange amber light was slanting diagonally through the bedroom. A new day had started. "Oh, Eamon," Kait moaned when she saw me awake. She dropped the leine she was repairing into her lap. "I'm so sorry. I could never hate you."

"I never thought you did," I rasped in a weak voice, comforted to see her unharmed. "Are you whole?"

"Did you think I would drown?"

"Aye, there was that very real possibility." I reached out to still the hand nervously smoothing my cover. "How about sharks? Did any take a bite out of you?" I inspected her slender fingers. "They all seem to be there—one—two—three—four—five. Aye, that about sums it up." I kissed her smallest finger, pausing to taste the salt with the tip of my tongue.

She gave a morose smile. "I suppose the sharks prefer the taste of obstinate selkie."

She crawled in beside me and folded herself under my chin. Her hair was still damp underneath and smelled of salt and kelp. I gently nudged her cheek with my nose. "Were ye away long?"

"It was a short swim," she murmured. "I've been memorizing your face while you sleep."

"You waste time," I complained sleepily. "I'd have you beside me." My fingers curled around her peedie waist, determined to hold her in place.

She was quiet for a long time, and I troubled at her thoughts. "Eamon?"

"Hmmm?"

"Would you have me fetch your skin so it can mold to you?"

"Nae," I murmured. "I'd have you stay here and mold to me instead." I stirred uncomfortably, suddenly realizing that my skin felt closer than before.

"You do know that I'd never hurt you on purpose?"

"Aye, Kait," I mumbled too sleepy to consider her words. "Ye made a vow."

~Kait~

My legs grabbled and burned to reach Tipper in time. By the time I hurdled the wall separating us, I was too breathless to speak—and astounded. Everywhere I looked there were holes— dozens and dozens of sloppy holes randomly scattered across the rocky soil. As Tipper turned from the hole she'd been digging, her dark eyes grew harried with alarm. "Michty me, what's got ye puffed and prickled, lassie?" Her face was smudged with dirt and vacant of all recognition.

I gulped hungrily at the air and pulled on her sleeve. "It's no time for you to be forgetting who I am," I gasped. "It's Eamon, he—he won't wake up. We've got to move him—now!"

Tipper winced as she withdrew from me. "Eamon?"

I resisted the urge to skelp the old woman. Some days she couldn't stop blathering about the ailing selkie man who lived next door. "Would ye like to see a selkie man?" I baited breathlessly. "He's right over yon, and he needs your help."

Tipper's dark eyes moved suspiciously over my face. "What's happened to him?"

"The land is making him sick. You must help me throw him back in."

She blinked at me a few more times before the lights seemed to come on. "Eamon?"

I brushed a tear of relief away. "Aye, it's time to save him!"

Tipper dropped her shovel and followed me with an excruciatingly slow pace that made me want to cry. "It's going to be alright," she wheezed behind me. "Selkie young are stronger than they look."

My chest constricted with pain as I approached the croft. It seemed like an eternity since I first set out for help, and I feared what I would find inside. Inside the dim room, I drew in a sharp breath. Lying limply in our bed was a gaunt angel tarnished with a sickly yellow hue. I dropped with terror to his side and curled my hand over his cool chest, wincing at the ribs tightly articulated under his pale skin. His chest slowly rose and fell a miniscule amount.

"Oh, Eamon, forgive me," I groaned, kissing his silvery lips. I ran my fingers mournfully through his hair, terrified that he still would not stir. "I'll be here waiting for you."

Tipper bounded in a moment later. "Oh, michty me!" she exclaimed when she saw the frail form sleeping in the bed. "He wrestles with the grim reaper even now!"

"Oh, bloody, bloody," I cried fretfully. I rushed to retrieve Eamon's skin from my chest, my shaky fingers struggling to match the key with the wobbly hole. After an eternity, the lid creaked open, and the expensive scent of cedar wafted out.

"My skin!" Tipper joyfully gasped when she saw the velvety coat fall open above the hinged lid. She rushed towards me, clutching two fistfuls of Eamon's silky coat.

"No," I said firmly, holding the precious mantle tightly to my chest. Incredibly it still held Eamon's heat and his scent. "It's *his* skin."

Her eyes flew to Eamon helplessly sleeping as she continued to caress the mantle. "You're wrong," she cried shaking her head in vigorous denial. "It's grey like mine." Her bony fingers roamed covetously over the velvety folds before she pulled them to her chest. "I've searched for this skin for o'er a hundred years."

"The marks," I said urgently. "See them? They are unlike any other coat." I smoothed out the area that encircled Eamon's neck. "Just as your own coat must be very special."

"A golden chain," Tipper said sadly.

"Aye, a golden chain for my prince. Do ye feel how it quivers for him?"

The skin not only quivered but strained for the master it sensed so near. Tipper slowly released her grip and peered over at Eamon miserably. "Hasten, your young burd is ill."

I gingerly placed the skin over Eamon's shoulders then stepped back to watch the edges of the skin curl contentedly around his shoulders as if it had a life and a heartbeat of its own.

"Bruce, where did you put my skin? I'd try it on again if you don't mind." Tipper gazed off towards the window, fingering her bulky clamshell necklace. The loss of her skin was much too great to endure yet a second time. For just a little while, she'd be young and beautiful with a husband who knew where her skin was hidden.

"Tipper, take his feet," I ordered. "This young burd needs the water now!"

"You're freeing him?" she asked bewildered.

"Aye," I answered angrily. "This was your plan—release him when he's too weak to fight. Can't you see that we have little time?"

Tipper's eyes grew to understanding even though she was not yet remembering. "Poor little thing—so young too." She flustered a moment before securing his feet and helping me hoist his frail body out of the bed. Eamon moaned softly and turned his head. "He's heavier than he looks," Tipper gasped as we hobbled outside where a steamy, overcast sky drooped.

"Don't you dare drop him," I shrieked when she adjusted her grip. "Haste ye now."

Eamon continued to involuntarily sleep as we struggled with his body down to the deserted beach. When we reached the lapping waves, I froze ankle deep, staring out at the abundance of turquoise water. "He'll definitely drown," I muttered dazedly.

Tipper gave a tired cackle. "He'll hold his breath instinctively, dear. It's where he craves to be."

What choice did I have—death or possible life? It would always be life. Together we plunged in up to our waists before unfurling Eamon's limp body into the water. Eyes foggy with confusion fluttered open as the cool brine plunged over his head. My heart flooded with relief and joy at how easily he revived.

"I'd not have you kill yourself," I shouted over the water. "Dying is not a gift!"

My eyes searched the waves before I caught a glimpse of Eamon's white shoulder as he instinctively rolled to orient himself. A moment later his head broke the surface. "You've ruined everythin'," he rasped as he staggered to stay upright, his face wincing with pain and betrayal. Like a fragile statue made of glass, he seemed likely to fracture with each new wave that toppled over his shoulders. "Is this really what ye want me to choose?"

"You are still loyal to me," I wailed. "I am the one that returned you to the water. *You* had no choice!"

"I have a choice now," Eamon growled as he cut forward through the water. He stumbled and fell as a wee wave uncoiled at his waist.

I rushed to block his path as he struggled back to his feet. The land would only sap away the last of his strength and prolong the inevitable. "The choice is still mine," I boomed, willing myself to sound strong and certain. "I will return you again and again to the sea until you are fattened. You don't have the strength to fight us both!"

"Haste ye, your freedom awaits," Tipper called wistfully.

Eamon surveyed me with a miserable expression before choking on his words. "My magick is gone for you?"

"You are a goat-eyed headbanger if ye believe that," I cried, my vision blurring with tears. "I love you more than that first night when ye cast your spell, but I cannot kiss myself or cuddle a grave. If you love me, go away and come back when you are whole."

"I was whole before ye cast me back," he choked. "But now I am no good for you, nae better than the leathery animal that slithers like rope atop the soil."

"You're a fool not a snake," Tipper barked as her sparse grey hair blew like smoke into her leathery face. "I have two lovers— my captor and the sea. Are you more selkie than me? Take your skin and go." I looked curiously at Tipper as she fiercely met Eamon's loathful gaze with her hands abreast her hips. There was cognizance stirring in her eyes once more.

"I wouldn't expect you to understand, selkyo," Eamon snarled as he shrugged his skin higher onto his shoulders. "You're older than the hollow cliffs and have forgotten what it means to be wan of us."

"I've forgotten?" Tipper shrieked hysterically. "This is what you think?" She picked up a hefty rock and hurled it at Eamon. It plunked into the water just shy of his chest. "Naraheem burns painfully in my memory!"

"Go back to your garden of snails," Eamon growled. "Ye have nothing to do with me and Kait."

"Listen to her!" I wailed. "She knows about healing your kind."

"You feel the water healing you, don't you?" Tipper cried. "Does the feeling frighten you? It should! You can't sever yourself from the sea completely—only an arrogant little burd would even try!"

Eamon's black gaze shifted dangerously towards me. "I'll never see you the same, land louper. You've spoiled everything that was good."

"I wouldn't have you die when your cure is so close!" I cried alarmed. Eamon was meant to see reason. He was meant to forgive me.

"I am half a man!" he raged. "Look at me!" He held emaciated arms wide under layers of mantle that seemed likely to topple him.

"See *me* and try to understand," I sobbed. "I did it for us!"

Eamon glared loathingly before securing his skin over his head and posturing to dive.

"Nae!" I screamed, sloshing in after him. "It's my fault, not yours. You're guiltless! Stay and talk to me. We could plan a secret tryst at Dronsday Island!"

"I'd rather die," he groaned before lunging into the water. I reflexively plunged into the place he disappeared, but when I broke through the surface once more, two little grey flippers sliced through the water a great distance away.

"Oh Odin, not this day!" I cried as water streamed in my face. "He's not ever coming back!"

"Was he ever really yours?" Tipper asked as she threw another rock.

I wailed before taking a big gulp of air and diving beneath a wave. Silty grey water churned and tugged all around me as I furiously kicked after Eamon in an uncertain direction. The sea was fighting me and protecting him—sea against land. Eamon would fly like graceful osprey, while I crawled like a slug.

I surfaced with a blinding gasp and spun to orient myself. The green arm of the The Galt hovered nearby while I frantically scanned millions of glaring ripples all potentially hiding Eamon. Bloody, bloody! Water stretched for miles in every direction. Surrounding the Mainland, hundreds of islands and even more skerries carved out endless waterways that branched out like a complex system of veins in every direction. Eamon could have gone in any direction: Scapa Flow, the North Sea, even Naraheem.

"Eamon, come back on the morra!" I screamed. My voice resonated weakly out over the vast water. After a few moments, the only movement out over the water was a swooping tern. Eamon was intentionally closing his ears. Devastated, I turned and swam back. Tipper was watching with a frown as I stumbled back onto the beach. "Your swim is poor, but your heart is great," she observed gravely.

"He's gone," I cried, clutching my chest. "I can feel it here! Every moment the distance between us grows!"

"Celebrate his freedom," Tipper said softly. "Setting him free was the right thing to do. He's too young to know what's good for him."

"But will he ever come back?"

Tipper took her time gazing across the firth as she considered my young and reckless husband. "He's torn once again and searching for his place. If he's smart he'll stay put."

"His place is by my side," I snapped.

"He's wiser than he was before," Tipper reminded, "And so are you. The life ye both imagined will never happen. By the time your burd is mature enough to sustain life permanently on land, ye'll be an old woman with a kertch pinned in her hair and saggy diddies."

"But he made a vow to love me! He can come as his strength allows, or I can go to him! We don't have to always be apart!"

Tipper shook her head sympathetically. "That little burd has an attachment to you, for certain, but after today all he'll remember is that you discarded him like garbage."

29

TORMENT

That night I clutched Eamon's quilt miserably to my chest, wallowing in the only hint I had left of him—his windy scent. Nothing had gone as planned. Eamon still lived but rejected every notion of reuniting with me, and the pain of that loss ate chasms in my heart. I could not understand my great offense in saving Eamon's life. Was he so unhappy on land that he was eager to die? This didn't seem right, but neither did Tipper's claim that Eamon was reinforcing his loyalty to me by denying himself the sea. Why must loving me be hard for Eamon to feel whole inside? I was desperate to talk to him, to convince him of his irrational ways.

In the morn, I mounted the rocky tip of Galt Ness and stared longingly towards Gairsay. To my dismay, the waters were filled with bulky sea craft, but no hide nor hair of selkie. I wiped a tear, mourning the loss of the husband I'd never have—a husband who'd return every evening with a fresh haul of halibut or flounder. He would eventually return wouldn't he—even now and then? Oh Odin! Not even Tipper could predict what Eamon would do. I clutched my head and dropped it between my knees. I was ill—terribly ill. Eamon's absence—my betrayal, it was all too much to bear.

I decided to visit Tipper later and found her digging under an ancient animal's trough. "Have ye seen him?" I asked anxiously. My heart pounded with anticipation as my eyes darted around the corners of her tiny house.

Tipper wedged her spade into a tuft of lavender. "Bruce just got back, dear. You'll find him stacking peat in the shed."

"To high heaven, how long must ye forget?" I cried impatiently. "I'd be lookin' fer my burd—remember?"

Tipper frowned as she wiped her shiny brow. "Aye, I remember... the mean wan that went into the sea. You're looking peaky. Are ye fit like?"

"What difference does *my* health make?" I practically shrieked. "*He's* the one that suffers. Has he been here?"

Tipper shrugged her shoulders dismissively. "Who's to say?"

"You're the only other selkie I know," I growled. "*You're* to say."

Tipper sighed and leaned against her spade. "Aye, he's been here. I'd like to wring his untamed neck and feed him to the fish." She pointed to a pair of footprints randomly cutting through her neglected garden. "A wee token the nuisance left behind."

I rushed to inspect the muddy prints. Clearly displayed between the first and second toe was Eamon's gap. "He must be much better," I said excitedly. "He's walked farther than he has in weeks."

"Oh michty me, he won't be prowling about for long. A short spell in the sea will only buy him a short spell on land."

"He was so close and didn't come to me," I complained.

The old woman pressed her lips together as if she were concealing a horrible secret.

My eyes grew harrowedly. "What did he say about me? I can see you're hiding something. Is he coming back?"

"He didn't *say* anything," Tipper said dourly. "*He* stole my clothes from off the line and then scattered them in the voe. He left Bruce's things undisturbed. Took me half the morn to collect my personals and rewash them all."

"What does it mean?" I asked, my brow furrowing in confusion. "He's angry that you helped me?"

Tipper stroked her hair as if she were suddenly unbothered. "Nae, dear. He's sending me a message. I'm selkie and selkie belong in the sea. He didn't have the courage to toss *me* in himself, but he might as well have called me a land louper to my face."

"But why would he do that? It's cruel to remind you of your loss and what's been hidden."

Tipper sniffed uncomfortably. "Remind me? My memory is not as short as ye think. What you should be concerned with is that your little burd is showing loyalty to the sea once again."

~Eamon~

The soft grey light would serve as night for several more moons, but this didn't stop most villagers from sleeping. I slunk into the dimly lit alley then froze at the sound of voices.

"Your lovely round hip fits nicely here, see?"

I glared up at the second floor apartment where a deep-voiced male skillfully primed his female with compliments. The ritual was invented by selkie males to trick fair loupers into lying with them, but today the act only disgusted me. The female giggled her appreciation, then heavy breathing followed an agonizing span of silence. I struck out at a barrel then split my knuckle open. I glared at the raw place before angrily shaking my hand. The blood would serve as salve for my pain.

I adjusted my skin while Kait's image burned angrily in my mind. Why could she not accept the great gift of my life? To no one else would I have offered such a hard thing, but she rejected me—land completely and utterly rejected me. The injustice was cruel for I'd chosen them both. Stumbling against a wall, I steadied myself. I was exhausted and craved the deep slumber of sleep, but justice couldn't wait.

I stole into the tavern then wrinkled my nose at the musty stench of human sweat and spilled spirits. Crude tables and driftwood chairs entangled around the filthy flagstones with no other furnishings or ornamentation to imply the importance of the place. I searched under the cracked tables and chairs before wandering into the crowded back room where I found a stack of casks and rows of tankards lying on end. I gave one of the casks a wee shoogle and found that it sloshed with the loupers' beloved treasure.

Forcefully I stabbed one of the offensive bellies, then watched with satisfaction as a muddy brown stream shot rapidly out of the narrow slit. Curiously I stuck my mouth under the stream of coveted drink before coughing and gagging as the poison burned its way down my throat. Losh! The pungent ale was as inhospitable as the land that produced it. I angrily kicked the bottom cask before stabbing the remaining bellies. All around me the liquid emptied onto the floor in great lochs of poison. Ill from the suffocating scent, I buried my face in my elbow and staggered outside.

The cool harbor air soothed my spinning head, and I steadied myself against the tavern's wall. I was alone and disappointed that no soul was about to discover the horrible thing I'd done.

I wondered about Kait then loathed myself for failing her so completely. I could never give her what she and I both wanted—a life together. Why did she have to spurn the last and only thing I *could* give her? Now I'd be doomed to see her rosy lips every time I closed my eyes as she was doomed to die of madness. I was deeply resentful towards her for making me lose everything.

With resentment, I realized that the old selkie had been right. Land was a hostile place that scarred the places it touched. Hadn't I always known this? I had been in denial when I first saw the disturbing old woman—raggedly scarred by a land that she hated. I would have recognized the penetrating eyes of a selkie from half an ocean away. She should have known more than anyone what it meant for me to return to the water, how obligated I would be to love it once more. But even with her knowledge, too much time had unraveled behind her. She was too much land and only a wee portion of sea.

My legs began to tremble beneath me as I realized I had been dry too long. With little strength left in me, I staggered along the pier then closed my nostrils before diving deep beneath a harbored ship. The cool water rushed pleasantly over me, shrouding my ears and lungs in a comforting weight. In a single twist, I rolled myself into my skin then shivered with satisfaction when the edges closed seamlessly around me. At once I felt completely wild, dangerous and strong. My mind began to buzz with fantastic ideas of what to do next.

~Kait~

"It's been a week and he's still here," I told Tipper after returning from town. A misty rain had been dampening the earth for days and my hair was already soaked. Running for cover seemed pointless.

Tipper looked up from the barrel where she was perched, seemingly contemplating the bizarre mounds of earth that were spread from moor to garden wall. "Hmmmmm?"

"The whole village is abuzz with rumors o' a rogue selkie," I said anxiously. "Mr. Shopshire said that someone doused the fire in his kiln. He was spittin' mad and throwing his tools."

"Don't look at me," Tipper answered defensively. "I've not been into town."

"It's Eamon!" I cried. "Remember my very bad husband? Someone also burned down the abandoned mill and strangled six o' the Anderson's geese."

"The Andersons will eat well for days if they don't share. Besides, it was a small crime compared to what was done at the Marwick's farmstead."

"I dread to know," I groaned.

"He stole their wee Eliza from her cradle and deposited her in the cow byre. She was found in a basket filled with onions and tiny creepie-crawlies. The poor dear was wailing to the high heavens and bit from head to toe. Even the cow was shaken and stopped giving milk."

"Oh, Tipper, when will he stop and come home? I can't bear to sleep, and I can't bear to wake. What if another sun slides across the horizon without him?"

"Ye'll survive, as you have the other nights," Tipper said, surveying her vast number of holes one last time. "Come now, I'll ladle you some fish stew." She rose from her barrel and led me into her firehouse.

"He will come back won't he?" I asked following after her. I could think of no other alternative without feeling the first creepings of madness set in. The nightmares had already started. Night after night I turned into a lonely old crone who searched for Eamon at the bottom of muddy holes.

Tipper didn't answer, but swept to the hearth, silently over-investigating the contents of a steaming pot.

My insides turned cold as I peered into her face. "He *will* eventually tire of these shenanigans and come back, won't he?"

Tipper dropped the ladle back inside the pot with an unhappy snort. "Stop? He'll stop when he feels justice has been served."

"And then he'll come back?"

Tipper's black eyes shot up. "He's chosen his side."

"He also chose me," I said uncertainly. "We both made Odin's oath. He's only getting his anger out of his system."

Tipper shook her head, ladling two heaping bowls of stew. "What is Odin's oath to us? This is what happens when ye couple with a young burd who is not yet tame. You've filled his head with all kinds of naughty ideas." She clattered the bowls onto the bink and sucked gravy off the edge of her finger. "He's a menace and needs a mither still."

"Blaming me doesn't help," I said grouchily. "He's *nearly* mature and full of alluring magick."

"His skin warns against coupling," Tipper scolded with a spoon paused halfway to her mouth.

"His opaline skin is very enticing," I mumbled, lifting a spoonful of Tipper's stew to my lips. It was surprisingly creamy and delicious.

Tipper wrinkled her nose in disgust. "It's improper."

"Why is Eamon seeking revenge against people who haven't done anything to him?"

"It's you he's angry at," Tipper said pointing her spoon at me. "You should never have taken his skin."

"He gave it to me willingly. Ye can't compare me to Bruce."

"Hushhhhhhhhhhh!" she hissed. "Ye'll not speak badly of Bruce. He's the kindest, gentlest land lover there is." She brooded over a potato a moment. "He promised he'd give it back if I don't find it first."

"What made you dig in half those places?" I asked grumpily. "There is no logic in most of those holes but the random workings of a maniacal old woman."

"Dinnae take your misery out on me," Tipper warned with an eerie smile that exposed her upper teeth. "You'd better become accustomed to living alone 'cos your burd is never coming back."

"How can ye be so certain?" I cried angrily, pushing my bowl away. "Eamon clings to Shapinsay 'cos *I'm* here. He's still angry, aye! But he'll soon reason that I had nae choice but to save him!"

Tipper gave a mocking laugh. "This is your understanding of selkie males? How easily ye forget that he is not human, but a complicated creature of The Deep. All the signs point to his new loyalty—a loyalty that he'd die to protect. A loyalty that's been deeply ingrained into him for thousands o' years. It's obvious he needs the sea more than he needs you."

The truth of her words stabbed painfully into me. Of course he needed the sea more than me. Had I not seen his precious life restored in those salty currents? He gleaned strength from the sea, like a suckling gleans strength from his mother's milk. He was a fool to ever have chosen me, but this did not change the fact that every particle in me ached for him. *I—needed—him.*

I struggled to speak. "I—I've never asked him to choose between us. He can come back the days he is strong—even a minute here and there. This I could endure."

"You still don't understand," Tipper challenged with dark selkie eyes. "Our males define themselves by their loyalties. It's against their nature to love a little here and love a little there. Only the weakest and most despised selkie would indulge himself so much. Since he is attached to you, he will fight harder to deny himself of your companionship."

"You've known this all along?" I felt my face wrinkle into an ugly grimace. "Known that he'd never, ever come back?"

Tipper slumped, no longer satisfied with her victory. "You had no choice but to return him, dear. Now understand that he has no choice but to live a life of dignity. He'll never be divided as you'd have him. Now is the time to forget."

I blindly rose from the bink and stumbled towards the open door, but Tipper appeared and caught hold of my arm. "Ye said something a moment ago—about the holes I've dug. Where, Kait? Where should I dig?"

I struggled to understand the meaning behind her words. Her skin—the old loon was still searching for it. "Your husband must have marked the location," I muttered. "Otherwise he wouldn't have been able to find it again as he intended." I pushed past her and into the drizzly grey hagger. "Dig some-place you're certain it could not be."

He'll never be divided as you'd have him. Tipper's words assaulted me over and over again. Eamon and I could never be together, not even for a little while. Now that I'd rejected the death he'd been so happy to proffer me, he'd surrender himself fully to the sea. Where was his choice to be happy? Where was mine?

My sanity swung like a pendulum on a tiny thread. Should I search for Eamon among the kelp forests or visit Blair? I felt my resolve to breathe weaken. I turned determinedly towards the scent of sea, straining to hear the sound of waves breaking across a sugar-packed beach. Somewhere among all the blue currents was Eamon.

"Eamon!" I cried, breaking into a run. "Are ye there?" The wind twisted and hummed in my ears as I tore through the brittle shore grass. "Eamon!" I struggled with my dress and tossed it recklessly to the wind as the misting rain sprayed and beaded on my bare skin. "Eamon, take me with you!"

I dashed frantically into a cresting wave, but then froze when I saw a small cutter bobbing just off the coast. One familiar seaman was securing rigging around the boom while another bearded man leered from under a black hood. "Do you swim, lassie?" he shouted as he leaned eagerly over the edge of the boat. "Owen, you'd better have a look..." His voice trailed off as he turned towards his brother.

With utter humiliation, I realized I was naked. Did Owen and Chick Brown recognize me through the foggy mist? Oh, bloody, bloody I was yards away from my own cursed house.

"Swim to us, lassie. Show us what ye can do." Chick gave a jubilant laugh as he unclipped his rain jacket. "I have some grapes waiting for that lonely thistle."

Did they think I was a selkie? At once I turned and fled while Chick hollered more crude invitations.

That night I dreamt Eamon came into my bedroom and crouched silently over my bed. Streaming black locks of salt scented hair dropped between us and shadowed his face.

"At last," I sighed happily, wiggling deeper into the mattress. "It's been an eternity since you left. I was beginning to worry."

"What do ye want from me?" he growled.

"You're my husband," I cried, reaching for the tender white skin of his abdomen. "I want you to lie beside me."

"I know nothing of husbands, louper," he snarled recoiling from my touch. His hands closed tightly around my throat, and he began to squeeze.

I bolted upright and gasped at the air. The eerie grey light of a summer night was still beaming through the small window. Oh Odin, I was alone—I'd always be alone. My eyes dragged miserably to the cool, empty place beside me.

Outside a metallic clatter caught my breath. I froze, listening. The hens gobbled their annoyance at being disturbed, and then there was only the steady pitter patter of rain. "Eamon," I cried as my feet hit the cool flagstones. I flung open the door and rushed outside to where a stack of overturned pails wobbled in front of the byre. I quickly scanned the moor before spotting his bare form lithely fleeing through the mist like a beautiful white stag. He was too thin, but strong once again!

I wanted to cry with joy for he had come back! I pulled him back once again! "It's alright," I croaked as I stumbled after him. "Take me with you, please. I'd not be afraid of the sea anymore." My voice grew in strength as I found my legs. "Please, Eamon, I'd die in your arms."

But he didn't come back, and by the time I reached the sea, he had already folded himself into his skin and disappeared beneath the waves.

30

FORGOTTEN

I hesitated going back there, but I told myself there was no harm in looking. After all, she didn't hear the wind rush in as the door swung open, neither did she hear me quietly pad to her bed. I was simply passing through—filling my eyes with indulgences as other selkie men had done before me.

When I saw her peacefully lying in the bed we once shared, my throat tightened, and I began to feel weak. I began to turn, but guiltily I peered back. Oh, losh, even asleep she was beautiful. Pink flushed her cheeks while tangles of gold fanned chaotically around her slender shoulders. She moaned softly then with short chewed nails reached for the empty space beside her—my place.

Painfully, I reminisced in the way her pink lips closed against my chest when she felt cold or frisky and how malleable, even limp she became in my hands when I planted my scent on her. She never even knew the power my scent had over her. What would it mean to lie for a moment beside her again? To feel her heart beat gently against my bare skin and hold her protectively in my arms? What was a moment if nothing?

A moment was everything—the difference between strength and weakness—the difference between being a man and being a traitor! I squeezed my fists together and escaped towards the door. *Keep the head! Keep the head!* I couldn't be weak and entertain thoughts of her anymore. As the door closed behind me, I heard sounds of Kait shuffling inside. As I turned, I clumsily knocked over a bucket and stumbled to my knees. The clatter rang painfully in my ears and alerted Kait. At once, I scrambled to my feet and fled towards the open water.

"Please, Eamon, I'd die in your arms!"

Nae! Nae! Nae! Kait must live! I kicked at a stone and expected it to roll, but it was deeply buried in the ground, and my toe tore open, spilling my blood in the soil. I hated the land—it was loathsome and hostile—but not Kait. I'd always love her.

~Kait~

Days later, I was exhausted from waiting up nights and deeply depressed. *He loves me,* I convinced myself over and over again. Eamon heard my plea to die that night and now was preserving my life on land as I had preserved his in water. This thought didn't cheer me. He was gone, probably forever, and I'd never been more lonely and miserable.

On the third day of waiting, I scrubbed my face clean and dragged myself to Tipper's. I was straddling the wall between us when I caught my breath in astonishment. Hundreds of holes and piles of dirt were lumped together in an enormous brown peat bog. I mused that the old crone had the ability to perform such a disastrous feat. I lifted the hem of my skirt and carefully traipsed through the mud.

"Tipper?" I cried, rapping loudly on her door. "Have ye completely lost your head?" I hoped she was home and not out searching the Balfour Castle as she'd suggested. It was a barmy idea that would only get her hauled off to Thieves' Holm again. I eyed the place where the garden had once been, then cursed softly under my breath. The crazy old woman had torn all her onions and potatoes out.

"Tipper?" I pushed open the door and peered into the darkness. Tipper was lying in her corner bed with her hands folded neatly across her chest.

"What took you so long?" she asked sleepily. "You left ages ago. Have ye been dilly dallying among the primroses?"

I drew closer with a frown. "Are you feeling under the weather?"

"It's worse than sick." Her eyes shone up at me like two black beetles. "I'm dying—at least I hope so."

My eyes drew curiously to Tipper's furry blanket. As my eyes became fully accustomed to the dimness, I realized that she was nestled under a cloak...no, a skin!

"Tipper," I cried happily. "Is that your skin?"

Tipper peered down her chest at the beautiful milky grey coat minutely shuddering across her belly. A tear slowly leaked from her eye. "It's just as I remembered it." Her wiry hand sifted through the fine hairs as a small sob caught in her throat. "Only it has forgotten me."

My knees folded weakly beside her. "I don't understand."

She mounded the skin onto her chest as she looked shamefully up. "I've tried for days to get it to stick, but it just flops to the floor when I stand. I even went swimming with it in the voe, hoping the magick would wake it up." She gave a miserable sounding laugh. "My skin doesn't have an inkling of who I am. Perhaps I've changed a bit more than I thought in a hundred and twenty years."

"I'm so sorry," I whispered, placing my hand gently over hers. My heart sunk for my friend. It was so unfair. There would be no happiness for those of us who had married outside of our kind, only endless misery. "Where did your husband put it?"

"It was right where you said it would be," Tipper said with a grim smile. "In a place no selkie or Orcadian would dare to look."

"Someplace unexpected," I prompted impatiently.

"Aye, Bruce planted my precious skin under a tree."

"What tree?" I asked confused. "There are no trees for miles."

"You've forgotten my fig tree—my gift from Bruce. It seemed like sacrilege to uproot it, but I took your dare, Kait. I dug someplace I was certain it could not be. He took great care to protect it inside a waxed box."

I gave a slow sad sigh. "What will ye do?"

Tipper shrugged sleepily and arched her brow. "Die. If that does not work, I suppose I'll plant a garden. I got a wee bit carried away out back."

"I noticed," I said with a grim smile. "I'll lend a hand if you promise not to be a bessie."

Tipper gasped as her skin shuddered over her belly. "Oh, michty me. What's got my skin all aquiver? I can feel it straining." She lifted it to study the warm, silky interior.

"It must remember your voice."

Tipper brooded stiffly a moment. "Wrong yet again." Her black eyes flickered resentfully to my face. "My skin is straining fer *you*. You bewitched it."

"What?" I cried bewildered. "I know no magick. Why—why would I do such a thing?"

She thrust her skin over to me with a grimace. "Just take it. It's been crawling for you since you first walked in the door."

I backed into a table the same time the corner of Tipper's skin floated up and fluttered out like a tiny bird's wing. "I'm no selkie," I gasped, unable to tear my eyes from the quivering mass of fur.

Tipper shoved her coat at me again. This time her eyes glistened with tears. "Let my skin judge whether you are a selkie or not," she croaked. I stared at the skin as my mind retraced Eamon's own spoken thoughts. Were there water lovers left behind that fateful day, thousands of years ago? Was there enough sea in my blood to be mistaken for a seal woman?

The enticement was too much to bear. Slowly, I lifted the velvety folds from her hands and ran my fingers appreciatively over the tiny flecks of black. At once the skin inched along my arm and folded contentedly around my wrist like a tight glove.

"Go on," Tipper urged tearfully. She propped herself on her elbows, enraptured by the activity of her skin. "All the way. I'd not have my skin idle any longer."

Cautiously I slipped Tipper's cloak around my shoulders. The skin immediately rearranged itself and clung to my exposed arms and ankles. When it was settled, the quivering stopped.

"I've never seen a skin so impatient before," Tipper said with longing. "I suppose I was once shaped a bit like you."

"It thinks I'm you," I mumbled numbly. I stroked the silky hairs and thought what it would mean to be a selkie. There would be endless swimming and adventure with perpetual youth and beauty. I might even chomp on a raw fish! It was too incredibly wonderful to be true. Shamefully I fantasized shedding my dress and feeling the warm extension of Tipper's skin mold to every part of me. Could Tipper's skin be part of me—really part of me?

"Aye, it is memorizing your shape just as it once memorized mine. Its memory is very hazy, but I suppose your form fits more clearly than mine."

"But the bond between you," I protested.

"Heaven bless me, it's broken. The skin now belongs to you." She wiped a tear with the back of her bony hand as her lip trembled. "Perhaps you'll let me visit it now and then."

"Visit? We see one another nearly every day."

"Were you intending on ruining another burd, or were you planning on going after your mate?" She shook her head in disgust and wiggled to the edge of the bed where she peered around for her pampooties.

Go after Eamon? I stared at her as this wonderful thought settled like a warm cup of tea in my brain. I had been so fixated with Eamon rescuing *me* that the idea had not occurred that I could go after him. My mind raced with fear and excitement. Could Tippers's skin really be the miracle that would bring us back together again? Eamon needed me to be a selkie so he could embrace the sea and live. I only needed Eamon. For me it had always been about him and nothing else.

It was then my heart sank like a cannonball into my gut. "I'd swim like a fish to be certain, but I can't hold my breath for more than a minute. I'd drown in the deeper waters."

Tipper sighed before shuffling to retrieve her dress from the back of a chair. "You've a lot to learn, dear. You've always had the spirit, now you have the body." She slid fluidly inside her dress and adjusted her long hair. "Everything ye need to live as a selkie is inside that skin. If you're gonna doubt it, give it back. It will still keep me plenty warm at night."

"But you can hear halfway across Shapinsay and smell things that don't exist to anyone else."

Tipper crawled sluggishly back inside her bed, physically spent from digging so many holes. "The selkie folk have had thousands of years head start o'er your kind. Dinnae be greedy."

"But how can I be a selkie? Does it not matter that I have blonde hair and blue eyes and an eejit brother named Blair? And...oh—oh, I adore potatoes. This is a detestable crime to Eamon."

"It's not for me to judge," Tipper said with a morose shrug. "It's true that the sea is not kind to those that do not belong."

"It's for the sea to judge where I belong?" I asked.

"You've already been judged, dear. Are ye daft? You wear the sea's finest ambassador about your shoulders."

I snugged Tipper's skin securely around my shoulders. It wiggled over my shoulder blades as if it were looking for a place to cling to. It *was* accepting me. Like Eamon's own fine mantle, it felt silky, warm and alive. When I looked up again, it was through a blurry haze of tears. "Do you understand what this skin means to me?" The word *gratitude* came to mind, but it seemed too pathetic and weak a word.

Tipper was proving once again the strength of her kind. She didn't want to give up her skin—she'd rather die, but the love in her heart was great. The capacity of a selkie to love another was greater than anybody knew.

Tipper gave a grievous smile. "Of course I know what it means to *you*. You get to be with your infant mate, though the sea hasn't won you over as it has me."

"Thankee," I mumbled feebly. "This changes everything." I was deeply aware that I didn't love the sea as much as Tipper. It would always be Eamon that drew me more than anything else. What was shapeless blue water compared to the beauty and allure of my own naughty husband?

Tears trickled out of Tipper's eyes as she squeezed them shut. "I have not forgotten that you saved me from Thieves' Holm. Neither have I forgotten that your cunningness led to the recovery of my skin. Thanks to you, I'll no longer search. I'm tired. Perhaps we're even now."

She was being gracious. We'd never in a million years be even. The gift—the sacrifice—like Eamon's own sacrifice, was far too great. I was eternally indebted. I stroked the tight grey hairs pensively. "Will he still have me?"

"He's still wreaking havoc on the island," she murmured sleepily. "I'd say this is a good sign."

"How do I do it?" I asked timidly.

"Do what?"

"Ummm... get in the water. Put it on."

"Ye don't put it on, dear. *It* wears you."

I ran to Veantro Bay, elated at my good fortune. When the surf rushed over my feet, I froze too terrified to go any further.

"Eamon!" I cried. "I can't journey out on my own!" A pair of terns laughed at me from overhead and criss-crossed paths. "I know that you hear me! We don't have to be apart anymore!"

I settled on a boulder and impatiently fingered the fine fringe on my miraculous new skin. Eamon would never expect me to possess my own selkie skin. He would never expect me to become a sea lover. Why would he come? I wanted to laugh and cry at the same time. What if he was away hunting, or worse, what if he moved to a new nook in the sea? How difficult would it be to find a single selkie in an ocean filled with activity and life?

I fingered the mantle's fringe thoughtfully before dropping it to the rock beside me. At once it began to shiver as if immediately traumatized from the brief separation. I looked down at the gray coat, trying to *feel* a connection to it like Eamon described, but there was nothing, only sympathy for whatever void it felt. Why should I feel connected to Tipper's skin? The bond and the burden would always be hers to claim. I had no right to my luck and happiness.

"Patience," I ordered my new quivering skin as if it were a dog that might listen. I lifted off my dress and allowed it to flutter out of my fingertips into the jagged rocks behind me. I laughed loudly then spun exultantly in the sand. My hair whipped around and celebrated like streamers in the wind.

Taking a deep breath, I lifted my new coat and laughed gleefully at the two tiny wings that swept towards me. Securing the skin over my shoulders, I gasped with exhilaration as it pressed and molded like a wave down the length of my body.

I took a step in deeper and felt the mantle twitch as it suddenly seeped up inches of sea. "I don't know if I have the courage," I whispered as I gazed towards the green tip of Egilsay.

"Oh Odin, give me strength." I felt like an eejit standing on the edge of a high cliff with the outlandish promise that I could fly. *I'm human,* I told myself over and over again. *Not selkie.*

If you're gonna doubt it, give it back.

I didn't want to ever give it back, but be with Eamon always. I felt selfish and cruel for taking the skin from Tipper. Why must her grief be my joy? It was all wrong. I was too human and Eamon was not here to guide me. I slowly withdrew, still unable to break my gaze with the water. When my foot brushed up against toasted kelp, a fishing doree broke the tip of the Galt Ness peninsula, and the weathered men inside stared wildly.

Bound by the spell of the water, I watched them. My sun bleached hair whipped ferally around my partially nude body. "It's a lone selkie!"

Selkie—me? The men were fools. Did they not know that selkie women were pale and beautiful with hair like midnight? The harsh summer sun left my skin brown and freckly and so very unlike a selkie.

The men began to paddle furiously towards the shore as if they meant to capture me. I hesitated for only a hair before plunging into the surf, gripping my new skin around my neck as if it could possibly float away from its possessive grip.

As soon as my head ducked under the foam, Tipper's skin developed a life of its own and twined itself completely around my body. I writhed in surprise at the sensation of being completely shrouded. It took me only a moment to realize I had a powerful tail and two fore flippers that thrashed wildly in the surf.

Blinded by the silt, I panicked with no sense of sky or floor. *Keep the head, keep the head.* I'd be captured and forced to wed a stranger if I could not calm myself and sort out an escape. I thrust my tail up and down and found myself swiftly moving beneath the belly of the boat. Oh, bloody, bloody! An inconspicuous net was waiting for me to be clumsily captured. I thrust my head sharply towards the darker water and instinctively dove.

After what felt to be a wee distance, the cold blast of a roost spilled over my body. I was already in the firth, and I hadn't taken a single breath! A school of shiny grey pollock divided and fluttered across my body as if I were as inconsequential as the kelp they nipped at.

As I moved upwards, the water became clearer, and I realized that I had been traveling along the basin. My eyes feasted on the swaying meadows and rainbow gardens of rock and coral. Everywhere I looked there was color and light, mysterious shapes and shadows. The tail of an eel slipped into the dark crevice of a rock and disappeared. I shuddered in disgust and searched for someone to share it with, but glimpsed only a lone manta disappearing into the blue haze.

When my chest ached for air, I pointed my nose towards the surface and within seconds filled my nostrils with warm, welcoming air. Bobbing just above the water, I anxiously scrutinized my unfamiliar surroundings. It took me a moment to realize that it was Shapinsay that stretched unexpectedly to my south like a skinny green arm. It had taken me only minutes to swim halfway around the island! I tried to laugh, but only a ridiculous growl burped out.

Where are ye, Eamon? After that, I searched the coastline for my mate, deliberating for a very long time at the Bay o' Linton where scores of selkie bodies with human eyes warmed themselves on the rocks. My mind began to play tricks on me when I saw his grey skin wiggle through the crowd here and there.

With great effort, I shook my head and forced myself to turn away—the selkie folk didn't mingle with the pure selkie.

Exhausted and disappointed, I returned to my own familiar beach as the sun slid behind the hills of Rousay and the Mainland. With a hop and a series of uncoordinated wiggles, I hauled out, wondering how I was supposed to undress my skin. As if it had been commanded to do so, my damp coat loosened and fell away, revealing my own dry, pale legs and sun freckled arms.

Tipper was still in bed when I returned, looking more shilpit than ever. Overnight her energy and fire had extinguished, her eyes faded to catch up with the rest of her aged and decrepit body. "Are you truly sick?" I asked worriedly.

"Aye, my dear. I'm still trying my hand at dying." She sluggishly reached for her coat still heartily clinging to my skin. Obediently I slid it from my shoulders and handed it over. Tipper nuzzled the silky side to her cheek while I self-consciously snatched a dirty apron off the floor to drape around my middle.

"Have you found that young rascal of yours?" she murmured.

"Nae," I answered as I secured a bow across my chest. "I've searched all along Shapinsay's coasts. I think he hears me but hides. What should I do?"

"His curiosity will not allow him to be away for long. It's a fault the young burds have—that and their impulsiveness. Let him see ye as a selkie, anything else will frighten him away." She stroked her coat a moment. "Did you swim?"

The happy memory exploded in me and a smile forced its way across my face. "Aye, I swam better than a mermaid. Inside your skin, I can hold my breath almost as long as Eamon."

Tipper was bored with this fact. "But what did ye see? Any other selkie folk?"

"No, they are as elusive as Eamon. I was the only selkie maid on the shores this day, though I gave a rusty pair of seamen quite a start."

"Tell me what happened, quickly," Tipper ordered. "I am an old woman with little time left."

I went on to tell her all about my awkward new start and my near capture in the fishermen's net. Tipper was fascinated with the story and made me retell it a half a dozen times. After the topic was wrung out to dry, we changed sails and talk about all the adventures I'd have beyond the bony reef. Tipper made clear that she would spend her remaining days living vicariously through me.

"You'll find my sister," she insisted. "She thinks I'm dead, she does."

"But how will I know her without a name?" I asked bewildered.

Tipper held her skin to her cheek with a poignant smile. "She'll be the beautiful wan with a ring. Only five days was she prisoner. Found her skin inside the very mattress she was forced to lie on."

"She was captured," I muttered sadly.

"Aye, she always wore the ring as a reminder. Ye'll not find her near any inhabited islands to be certain. But I'd see her again—michty me, how I miss her."

I marveled that Tipper didn't seem the least bit resentful of her sister's good fortune. "She's as good as at your threshold," I said determinedly. "Even if I have to drag the wench back, kicking and screaming up the beach."

Tipper extracted the promise from my eyes then smiled. "There's someone else I'd have you find."

"It's a lot to expect your ma and da to still be ali—"

"You misunderstand. There's another one who holds my heart ransom—one I've not forgotten about."

"Your mate."

"A strapping male with death in his eyes—he'll be mourning my absence."

"That was a bloody long time ago," I blurted before I could bite my tongue. Eamon's mellow voice echoed like sweet music in my mind. *Ye'll be comforted to know that selkies mate fer life like whales.*

Tipper stroked her hair with a vixenous smile. "Are ye jealous that my mate is not as fickle as yours?"

"Of course not," I began cautiously. "Only do you think it wise? It's possible...well, he may not recognize you."

"It's no matter," Tipper said with an insulted sniff. "If I'm lucky, he'll mistake me for a land lover and grant me a most titillating death."

"You'd have him muscle you like a brute and drag you under the water?" I asked horrified.

"A beautiful way to go."

"Ye'll only hold your breath," I protested. "It won't work."

Her dark eyes flickered towards me mischievously. "Aye, don't ruin my lovely dream, dear."

After coaching me of the many dangers in the water, Tipper fell asleep. I stood over her bed admiring the sweetness in her deep lines and the jaunty joke at her iced winter lips. My eyes moved over the downy lashes, and the powdery-like texture of her extensive hair. I had been so blind before. Underneath it all, Tipper *was* beautiful.

Guiltily I removed my new skin bundled securely under her arm, and returned eagerly to the water's edge to wait for Eamon.

Through the night, I struggled to keep my eyes open for the roguish selkie I hoped would still be lurking about. A thousand times I watched the waves tirelessly wax and wane across the ocean door, but still he did not come. My vigil involuntarily wound down as the birds took to the yellow morning sky.

"I'd not keep you from burning if that's your intent."

A tickle deep in my mind tried to register the soft, raspy voice. Could it be? My eyes flew open to find Eamon glaring down at me only paces away. An intense summer sun was burning high in the sky, scorching my bare arms and legs. I struggled to sit, gazing eagerly up at the beautiful seal man. It seemed impossible that he could be my husband.

Eamon's skin was stretched recklessly over the stony beach like he'd been trailing it carelessly behind. His white skin opulently shone and shimmered in the bright light like a hint of rainbow. A warning—my arse. "You've been hard to pin down."

Eamon shrugged his dark hair behind his ear. It was growing fast and showing pitch colored roots. "Ye wish to pin me?"

I collected my skin around my shoulders and rose beside him. I tried to look seductive, but I only felt burnt. "Aye, as your mate, that is my right."

Eamon's eyes dropped to shadowy areas inside my skin before he kicked vigorously at the sand with a wince. His toe was badly bruised and encrusted with dried blood. "Why did you do it, Kait? You made things worse."

"But you're alive," I blurted. "Can't you see there's no reason for us to be apart anymore?"

"Things have changed, Kait," he said angrily. "The life that you and I planned...it's gone with yesterday's tide. It would be better if I were dead."

"You don't have to choose between me and the sea any longer," I insisted. I reached for him, but Eamon recoiled as soon as my fingertips brushed the coarse hairs behind his neck.

"I chose you and you rejected me!" Eamon raged. He punched at the air and swung away.

"Your death is not a gift but the cruelest of curses!" I fumed. "Do you not notice *anything* different about me?"

Eamon's black eyes toppled to the velvety grey mantle folded contentedly around my shoulders like a great sleeping cat. At first he seemed confused, then his face hardened into a baleful glare. "Selkie," he hissed as he snatched the coat from my body. "You'd wear this like an everyday cloak?"

"No," I cried stung by the abhorrent misunderstanding. "I'd never hurt a selkie!"

The skin began to shudder in Eamon's hands, and his eyes grew wide with revulsion. "The owner lives?" he gasped. His fingers fell limply open. "Where—did—ye—steal—this?"

I took back my skin and slid it quietly around my shoulders. Eamon watched with a dazed expression as the mollified skin curled and molded itself to my body. "The skin was given to me," I answered curtly. "Tipper finally found her skin, but it does not know her."

Eamon scratched his head dazedly. "It's impossible. Only a selkie—"

"I am selkie enough for this skin. Yesterday I swam as a fish and held my breath like a selkie. The sea accepts me without prejudice."

"The skin mistakes you fer Tipper?"

"Aye, its memory has grown dim." I stroked the tightly woven hairs coiled over my shoulder. "And as you can see, it's anxious to have someone to cling to. I suppose Tipper's shape once closely resembled my own. She too is a malinky longlegs."

Eamon laughed boisterously before scooping me up in his arms. "I thought I would never hold you again. The gods are still smiling on the selkies!"

I melted into his shoulder with quiet sobs. His warm, magickal energy immediately began to vibrate through my skin and heal my wounded heart. How easy it had been for Eamon to give me up. I didn't understand him, but what did it matter? Eamon was free to love me again! I didn't need to have pride; *he* had enough for us both. He could leave me a million times, and a million times I would unconditionally take him back. "Oh, Eamon, I've missed you so much it hurts."

"You are not the only one who suffers," he admitted. "I haven't had the strength to go beyond the firth. With each new sunrising, I think of you and grate my ears. Always I fail at leaving."

"Damn your strength," I cried joyously. "You're too strong for your own good."

"Tipper's skin senses the part of you that is sea," Eamon said happily. "I always knew ye were out of place."

"A little bit of your selkie has rubbed off on me."

"Nae," Eamon said solemnly. "There are a hundred young loupers on the islands that are the same height and size as me. Not a one could successfully wear my skin. Your skin's memory may be as ancient as Tipper, but it must sense salt in your blood for you to have accomplished so great a thing."

"What do you sense?" I asked, as my chest constricted with fear. "Am I enough sea for you to love?"

An odd expression formed on his lovely face. "Did you think that just because you live in this barren place, and I live in The Deep, that I don't love you anymore? You will always be my mate." His lips pressed against my neck then floated across my skin till he found my mouth. We kissed until more tears beaded in my eyes, and Eamon bent to pick them up with his lips.

"Dinnae cry," he ordered tenderly. "Everything's as it should be." His hands slid underneath Tipper's coat and delicately stroked the small bone at my hip.

"Don't ever leave me again," I said in a wavering voice. It drove me mad that he was still untamed and masochistic, a complicated adolescent with a penchant for aggression. Still... he was the most beautiful part of the sea, and I needed him more than I needed breath in my lungs. "I will always pursue you," I promised, as I gazed into his dark languid eyes. "Your magick pulls more powerfully than that very first day."

"That's impossible," he said with a boyish grin. He held out an ivory hand to me. It was covered with tiny cuts and a peculiar semi-lunar injury that looked like a dog bite. Eamon had learned to coexist between land and sea but not peaceably. He enjoyed his war against land. Timidly I surrendered my hand into his as he pulled me into a crashing wave. "Come Kait, I'd show ye anything and everything."

Made in the USA
Charleston, SC
10 June 2012